A Boy Named Rindy

Olivia Talbott

DEDICATION

When a book takes this long, there are a lot of people responsible.

To my husband, Steven. Thank you for not allowing me to quit, even when I wanted to and when it would have been much more convenient for you if I had.

To my mom, Jill Knoll. Thank you for praying me through. I owe much to your love and sacrifice.

To Rindy, thank you for entrusting your story to me. I pray I have done it justice.

FORWARD

By Rindy Nong

Life is unpredictable. There are things in life that shape and mold us even though we don't want them or choose them. We do not choose our parents, we do not choose the country we're born in, and we do not choose the year we're born. However, we are tasked with doing the best we can with the life we are given. It is the human condition throughout history. People oftentimes wonder why they were born in this condition or why we are not self-determined, although some might think that they are. Whatever we feel about our condition, there are things or events that are not under our control.

One of my American friends told me my story is the story of Cambodia, and another said that my story follows the same pattern as Cambodia's story, but I think that is a mirror image. I don't think Cambodia's story is isolated or that mine is isolated, as it has happened throughout human history. The Cambodian Genocide did not happen in a vacuum.

The world dove into the Cold War after World War II and struggled between powers: the United States, the Soviet Union, and China. The small countries around the globe became the battlefield. Indochina, which includes Cambodia, Loa, and Vietnam, played a major part in that struggle. Due to the United States's desire to counter the rise of communism, France dragged her into the Vietnam War. The United States did not plan to go to Cambodia or be involved in Cambodian politics, but she became involved with the regional politics, and invaded Cambodia although she denied it ever happened. She dropped more bombs on Cambodia than she dropped in all of World War II. Meanwhile, the USSR supported Vietnam, and the Chinese Communist supported the Khmer Rouge. Because of these actions by major powers, the Cambodians suffered and many lost their lives. Cambodians had no control over these things, especially common people like my family.

My life story is set in this context. I was born into poverty and grew up in poverty and war. We struggled in our personal lives in the midst of a world in conflict filled with tragedy ...but then we found redemption.

CONTENT WARNING

This book is based on a true story.

By the end of the Cambodian Genocide, between 1. and 3 million people were killed at the hands of the Khmer Rouge communist political party. This is a story of one of its survivors.

In an earnest effort to provide an accurate representation of the time period and the story told to me, this book contains sequences that may be disturbing to some readers. This includes sequences of childhood neglect and abuse, starvation, violence, murder, and the mention of rape. While I have endeavored to handle these events with delicacy and much consideration, I have sought to be true to both history and Rindy's story.

Each chapter opens with a quote from transcripted interviews I've had with Rindy.

At the end of the book, I've included key historical excerpts that coincide with certain chapters for the enhancement of historical context and depth of understanding. It has been my utmost aim to provide a well-researched and accurate description of Cambodia during this time period. If there are errors in execution, content or voice, they are entirely my own and are no reflection upon anyone mentioned within these pages.

MAP OF CAMBODIA

1

THE STILT HUT

"I don't know the date I was born.
My mteay doesn't remember." — Rindy

JANUARY 1968 BATTAMBANG PROVINCE

I reached for the frayed rope, but the last knot slipped through my fingers. Too late. I leaned over the brown edge of our hut, gazing downwards, only to find the ground devoured by the starving darkness. The basin that held our rainwater rippled in the moonlight, laughing at me in my carelessness. Despite my thirst, the rope and water jug had vanished from sight.

Looking at my mother—*Mteay*—I pleaded silently. Her form was barely distinguishable through the falling light and the mosquito net. My younger brother Vuthy, lay asleep at her feet. Even without seeing them, I sensed the icy darkness in her eyes, even as the world melted into the throbbing heat. Her waist-length hair cascaded around her shoulders like midnight water, a sight only seen when she slept or washed it in the stream. She was singing softly, a song from her childhood. Mteay had sung at the terrors of the night for as long as I could recall, wrapping herself in melody as darkness fell.

"Sleep well, my precious child. The night is growing late; Mteay is lulling you to sleep..." The melody rippled through the air and reminded me of a mournful bird's song. She didn't sing this song to anyone but herself, although I always pretended she was singing it to me.

"I didn't drop it." Her words sliced through the song, like a machete. "You go get it."

Quickly, I glanced to my other brother Kiry, four years older than me, who was also sleeping, exhausted from the day's work in the heat. Faint snores came from where he lay on his mat, his pointed hat perched on his face to ward off the mosquitoes.

I needed to stiffen my resolve. Looking up, the night sky was sprinkled with stars like discarded grains of rice. The moon hung above the palm treetops that lined the small valley where we lived, flicking shadows across the ground. I had lived here for as long as I could remember, far from others and even farther from the nearest village. My *aupouk*—my father —farmed the land around our hut, clearing more of the lower vegetation and sparse trees to plant various food crops that he sold at the market. He had planted the banana's first, but now they were towering. Their purple flowers sagged their limbs to the earth. After the bananas, he'd cleared land and planted papaya, agave, cassava, sugar cane and sesame plants. Now, all around us rustled with the promise of food. It appeared safe.

"Rindy, get the jug!"

I didn't risk another glance at Mteay, I just obeyed. My palms wet on the rung, I made my descent. Through the gaps in the ladder, past the belly of our hut, I witnessed the hue of night dissolve into the deeper blackness of the jungle. But in the jungle, it was always night. Its voice sounded like the eerie chanting I heard monks whispering above the rustling of their cloaks. I heard it only once, while visiting the market with Aupouk. We had passed by the pagoda, and that single occasion indelibly scorched the sound into my memory. I didn't know what every word meant, but I knew its thrum, like the croaking of tree frogs and the screeching of monkeys. It was the dance of life; it was the dance of death.

"Quickly!" Mteay's voice slipped through the gaps in the floor. A surge of courage propelled me to wrench my eyes away from the jungle, over-powering the fear that threatened to consume me. I picked up my pace and skipped the final rung; my bare feet landing in the dirt.

There is no tiger. *There is no tiger.*

Lowering myself onto my knees, I began searching for the rope near the water basin. Feeling my way over the hard ground, my hands sifted through the dirt.

Nothing.

I had to stretch up on my knees to reach the bumpy edge of the water basin. Where was it? Would I have to fish it out of the dark water? I shuddered and glanced into the jungle again. Something glinted from its heart. Were those yellow eyes? I scrambled back up the ladder, my limbs quaking. I wasn't thirsty anymore. There was a noise behind me and a scream escaped my throat as arms enveloped my waist.

"Rindy! Why aren't you in the hut?"

My aupouk's voice. Relief pounded in my chest at the heat of his breath on my ear. My body spun to face him, but no words came. I swallowed hard against the dryness. His dark form blotted out the moon.

"I was thirsty, and the water jug—I dropped it." My words croaked.

He spun me back around and gave me a shove up the ladder. Behind me, I heard his hand plunge into the water as he retrieved the lost jug and rope in one fluid motion.

"I've told you,"—he was close behind me again—"of what happens in the darkness. Especially to five-year-old boys."

"I've never seen a tiger, though!" I wondered if all the stories were true.

"Just because you haven't seen one doesn't mean it can't see you." His words were hot on my cheek again. "Besides, you're always asleep when tigers venture out of the jungle. They always come at night." That thought chased me the remainder of the way up the ladder.

I arrived at the top and crawled deeper into the shadowy hut. Our hut stood ten feet off the ground to make it harder for any predators to get in while we slept. "Harder, but not impossible," Aupouk had said. Hearing him say that was one of my earliest memories.

Moonlight spilled through the open door after me. Aupouk had made our walls out of palm leaves woven between bamboo poles. He'd used the same material for the roof, but it was woven more tightly together. The hut had three windows, one at the back and one on each side. To prevent monkeys, pythons, or tigers from climbing through them, Aupouk had interlaced each window with bamboo poles.

The hut groaned as Aupouk climbed up after me; his outline emerging from the abyss. In silence, he pulled it up after him and slid it against the thatched wall before closing and securing the door with a thick rope looped around a peg. I felt the water jug slide into my hands, and I drank, droplets spilling down my bare chest. I smiled at him, although he couldn't see it.

Aupouk pulled back the mosquito net and lowered himself beside Mteay, but I heard her shift away from him. No song was coming from her now. There was never much talking inside the hut; it just didn't feel natural somehow. But there wasn't much talking outside of it either.

I crawled from the plank boards and lay on my stomach on the cooler part of the floor, with larger gaps made of bamboo poles. The gaps were perfect for spitting through. I spit and watched as the glinting drop disappeared into the night. Was the tiger out there, watching me? With closed eyelids, I heard the jungle's night time chorus, trapped in the web of sticky humidity. All the sounds were at war with one another. My eyelids grew heavy and the song faded.

2

THE EYES

"But I remember my childhood in the jungle. We were always afraid of the danger." — Rindy

LATER THAT NIGHT

The darkness loomed near, suffocating me. What had awakened me? Uneasiness clung to me like dew. The floor where I lay wasn't safe. I had fallen asleep on the bamboo poles rather than my mat, which lay on the more solid boards. Something had its eyes on me. I could feel it. I peeled my ribs from the floor and rubbed them. A faint rustling sounded beneath me. I froze and scanned the darkness below me. Two yellow eyes stared into mine. They reflected the moonlight, then vanished in the hut's shadows, reemerging a few steps away.

The tiger.

I knew it could lunge higher than the floor of my bamboo cage. I'd heard stories of tigers lunging twenty feet in the air. Had it smelled me? If I moved, would it tear through the floor and pull me down, making a feast of me beneath the moon?

"Aupouk," I squeaked, my voice slicing through the silence before disappearing into the expanse. Could he even hear me? Aupouk's hand landed across my shoulder blades, heavy and warm.

"Be still." His words were a low growl. "It will leave soon." I felt his presence beside me, he had moved without a sound. I lay still, panic surging through my veins as the tiger paced below. Its deep, rhythmic breathing pounded in my ears until my heartbeat reverberated with the same cadence. Its purring swelled, growing louder and louder until it blocked out the roar of the jungle. When I blinked into blackness, I could still see its eyes taunting me. I couldn't escape.

I had once seen a picture of a tiger at the market. It was printed on a small card with intricate gold trim. It had massive paws and protruding claws that sliced through the air. Bared teeth emerged from pink folds in its mouth. Black stripes ran over its orange body that glowed like the blaze of a fire. The photo haunted me.

The tiger screeched. I clutched my ears as the sound ricocheted in my skull, a rock in a cavern. The sound threatened a chilling and gruesome death in the clamp of powerful jaws.

"Hey, hey, hey!" Aupouk hit Mteay's pot with a wooden spoon. "Get going!"

The tiger lunged back into the jungle, breaking the spell. Trembling, I released a breath and rolled to my back. After several moments, the jungle's roar filled my ears once again. My heartbeat pounded in my temples and echoed in my curled toes. I unsteadily pushed myself up, crawled to my mat, and waited for sleep to save me. Aupouk returned to Mteay's side.

But the rescue wouldn't come. I stared at the ceiling, unable to close my eyes. They remained wide, fixed on the darkness, searching every corner for a distraction. I twisted and turned, but I felt like I was lying on a million tiny rocks. Would the tiger come back? Would it kill me one day? The thoughts kept sleep away until at last, they drifted into the grayness of the early morning sky.

"Get up, Rindy. Come watch Vuthy!"

I jerked awake. The sunlight's slender fingers reached through the holes in the floor as if to entice me from my place of safety. No one else was inside the hut. I rubbed the tender spots where the mat had eaten into my cheek and crawled to the edge of the open door to peek out.

No more tiger.

Slowly, I descended the ladder, knees wobbling all the way.

"I'm taking them to the river," Mteay called over her shoulder. "Watch Vuthy." She tugged three water buffalo by the rings in their noses. Where was the fourth, the calf?

Vuthy sat in the dirt, patting and smearing the edge of the water basin with mud. I went to the nearest banana tree, pulled the end of a low-hanging leaf off, and walked to the pot sitting atop three rocks, blackened with ash. The embers of last evening's fire had long gone cold, but there was some rice left. Using a wooden spoon, I gathered some and placed it onto the banana leaf before squatting just above the dirt to eat. I popped a cluster in my mouth but couldn't swallow it, so I chased it with a gulp of water.

Vuthy walked over, his hands outstretched.

"Have some?"

I set the leaf on the ground in front of him. As he scooped the puffy kernels into his mouth, I smiled. I was glad someone had an appetite.

A loud thud sounded behind me. Springing from my crouched position, I spun around to see Aupouk dropping chunks of wood onto the ground beneath our hut.

"Doubt all the tiger stories now?" his eyes creased in a smile.

I shook my head. He walked to me, and I handed him the water jug at my feet. As he drank, I watched a drop slide down the hollow of his neck and onto his bare chest, turning the brownness of his skin a shade deeper in its path.

"What happened to the water buffalo calf?" I asked.

"The tiger got it last night. I found its half-eaten carcass buried on the edge of the jungle this morning."

I stared at the jungle, and it stared back at me as if it didn't conceal a secret.

"Did you have a hard time sleeping last night?"

I nodded.

"Scary things sometimes come in the darkness. Sometimes you must be bigger and scarier than they are, but other times you need to know when to lie still because you're no match. Knowing the difference is important. Do you understand?"

I nodded, staring at the slow path the water was making down his stomach.

"Both ways require bravery, but enduring the darkness while keeping calm is the hardest. It's an important thing to know how to look death in the eyes and yet live."

3

THE STRANGER

"That is when everything broke loose in my family."
— Rindy

JANUARY- FEBRUARY 1968

When the jungle roared at night, Aupouk would build a raging fire, and his eyes would gleam in the burning glow.

He would lean into Mteay's ear and whisper, "Why live like fish caught in a rain-filled rut, when we can be free to swim in the expanse of all this?" Then, smiling, he would throw his arms wide motioning to me and my brothers.

Mteay never replied to this, only lowered her head, face shadowed, and muttered to herself, bristling in her private thoughts. This silence burned and bubbled, like lava hidden deep in the earth, not visible but still exuding a powerful presence I did not want to accidentally upset. But one night, this silence exploded, hitting us with unexpected force.

"You never said we would stay here this long!" her voice hissed and popped. "You lied to my mteay when you said you'd make a good life for me and took me to live like an impoverished peasant where my children can get eaten by tigers and live like wild animals!"

I was stunned, but Aupouk didn't seem to be.

"I thought you would adjust to this place." His words were carefully chosen, soothing. "See that it's better than the crowded villages."

"I don't want to! Why should I be content to live in the past instead of living in a more prosperous future—a future that the city offers with electricity, roads and schools?"

Aupouk rose, the heat of her words poking him between the ribs.

"This is the future! Don't you see? Cambodia has never been more prosperous, but that is because of those willing to work the land to produce crops to sell and export. It's the golden age! Prince Norodom Sihanouk is giving land away to those willing to farm it. He's asking people to move from the city to cultivate the land—like we have done. The sugar cane factory is beginning to expand and hire more workers and people are coming from the cities—"

"The world is at war!" she interrupted. "Vietnam is torn in two, fighting the communists and the United States. Before that, we fought French oppression for nearly a hundred years. The Khmer are not meant for peace. This dream you have of a peaceful life, living as a simple farmer near the jungle, is a childish one."

Aupouk clenched his fists, slumping back down on the log. I glanced at Kiry and opened my mouth to speak, but he shook his head, telling me to remain silent.

"It's not childish to seek peace and stay as far away from the conflict as I can." He looked up, his eyes searching Mteay's face. "For my family."

"If you were thinking about your family, you wouldn't have taken us here! My parents gave me a much better life than this, and my aupouk has rich land—he could still help us! I want a better life for myself and for this baby..."

She let the words hang in the air, mingling with the smoke burning our eyes.

"What baby?"

"This one." She pounded on her stomach "Don't pretend you haven't noticed my growing stomach. I've been showing for months. There will only be a few more until I give birth." She turned and lunged for the stilt hut, nearly running over Vuthy who dozed by the log.

Aupouk raked the black hair out of his eyes and stood with his back to us, peering into the formless jungle. After a long time, he spoke. "Kiry, take Vuthy and Rindy and go to bed. The harvest is coming and there is a lot of work to do."

When I turned, I noticed the joy shining in his eyes, glowing like the rising sun. He was happy about another baby.

I don't know how long he stayed by the fire, but I watched its light dance through the gaps in the floor until sleep took me.

One afternoon, as I returned from the canal, where Mteay had sent me to wash filth from Vuthy's shorts, a stranger approached.

"It's been many years my friend. I hardly recognize you." Aupouk threw his arms wide and invited the man to eat with us. Mteay handed him a banana leaf filled with rice topped with bits of stewed fish. "You've come a long way from the scrawny temple boy who was always snatching my food."

The stranger was smaller than *Aupouk* and had paler skin than most Khmer men I'd known, but something about him seemed darker. I learned his name was Khan and like the meaning of his name, he seemed to carry a sword. He had shadows about him, and he was captivating. He never noticed me much despite his shifting eyes. But he didn't overlook Mteay. His gaze flicking across her.

"*Arkoun*," Khan thanked her, their eyes meeting briefly as he took the banana leaf from her hands. "Same reason as you, I'm sure—the King Aupouks incentives."

I smiled to myself. I liked the idea that Prince Norodom Sihanouk was an Aupouk to us, watching over our needs and supplying us with a better future. I had been hearing of his greatness since I could recall and I always asked to hear more. He was the one who helped make Cambodia free from the French, without even shooting one bullet.

"You won't miss the city?" Aupouk asked, his eyes locked on the stranger's, but the question was for Mteay. Her eyes remained on the rice she was dishing.

"I might, but I feel obligated to humor King Aupouk and his ideals to see Cambodia's uncultivated areas become rich and prosperous with crops. More and more people are coming from Phnom Penh daily to work in the sugar cane fields. I hope to gain a good position there."

"Yes, I've noticed all the new people." Aupouk smiled around his mouthful of rice.

Khan's eyes shifted as if searching to see if someone were spying on him from the jungle. "Do you think Sihanouk will make China stop its communist propaganda? It's like a mosquito trying to bite anyone it can."

Aupouks's expression changed, the light in his eyes darkening.

"We are fighting many wars, even in rural Cambodia. Battambang has been struggling through land reforms and a flood of native Khmer are returning from Vietnam because of the war, which has also added a strain. Battambang has been one of the major places for resettlement. The wealthy Chinese landowners are getting the best land and the high taxes on rice exports have aggravated the situation further. Everyone is angry. The locals don't feel they've been treated fairly by the Sihanouk government, and many sympathize with the communists and their ideologies. So it seems that communist mosquitoes are finding many willing targets, especially in this area. Have you heard what happened in Samalaut? It's not very far from here."

"Talk of the uprising in Samlaut was all over Phnom Penh last year." Khan tossed his hands around like his words. "Did the local farmers really arm themselves with axes, clubs and pitchforks and attack government buildings and soldiers collecting rice? Rumors say they even stole guns and are arming for a revolution."

"Many have fled into the jungle, and more are joining every day as discontentment with the government grows. Last I heard, nearly ten thousand have fled into the trees to join the rebels, but I'm sure it is more now. Lon Nol, the Minister of Defense, and Norodom Sihanouk have been cracking down on counterattacks, saying the rebellion will not be tolerated."

"Will you join them?" Khan leaned in, his eyes hungry.

Aupouk shook his head, staring at the dirt. "I don't want any part of it. I just want to be able to farm in peace."

"When I asked for directions to your place, everyone in the village knew about you. Why do they know you when you live out here?"

"There is much talk at the market, and sometimes I participate." Aupouk shrugged. I knew this to be true, as the villagers often came and talked to Aupouk and asked his opinions on all kinds of topics.

"Will you work in the sugar cane harvest?"

Aupouk nodded. "Just this year. Next year I will have my own crops to harvest if rainfall is good."

Mteay called me to bed, so I went, but I listened to them talk late into the night through the gaps in the floor. I heard them say ugly words about China's communist propaganda and how the "Aupouk King" wanted it stopped. They also talked of the tug-of-war that places called "United States" and "China" were playing with Cambodia, and how the Red Khmer and Green Khmer were like two squabbling monkeys from different trees. Their words sounded strange to my ears, but they etched their way into my memory, like a beetle into a log. It seemed that the world around me was fighting. Little did I know that their words cast a shadow, like a grim prophecy.

When it was time to harvest, Aupouk, Kiry, and I walked five miles to the nearest village. There, the cleared land ate into the trees to make room for the rice paddies and sugar cane fields that stretched as far as I could see. We walked on the red dirt road, beside the Sangke River, which flowed with less water than usual because it wasn't yet the rainy season.

"Do you know how sugar cane is grown?" Aupouk didn't slow his stride for the question.

We both nodded, as we had been with him when he planted sugarcane around our own hut the year before.

"Tell me then."

We both were silent, hoping the other would talk.

"Rindy you tell me, I know Kiry knows."

I swallowed, trying to remember all I'd seen him do.

"First you plant them in good soil before the rains come in May or June."

"What is good soil?" Aupouk interrupted.

"No rocks or underbrush, to let water flow."

"What do you plant?"

"Chopped up sugar cane stalks, so the new plants pop through the soil towards the sun."

He nodded, clasping his hands behind his back and listening intently. I was glad he liked my answer, so I talked faster.

"When it grows tall, over my head, you must keep the bugs off and make sure the plant is healthy by giving it chicken poop and other gross things. You also burn old, lower leaves off before harvest time to make them easier to cut." I imitated my hand slicing through an imaginary stalk.

"Does sugar cane like water?"

I grinned. "It slurps it right up but gets sick with too much."

"Just like you." Aupouk bumped into my shoulder. "How long does it like to grow before being chopped down?"

"A long time?" I shrugged.

"Almost a year," Kiry said, impatient with my lack of experience. "Will we grow more of our own next year, Aupouk?"

"I think I will grow more sesame plants next year; there's more money in it."

The farther we walked, the more I smelled smoke. A thick blackness veiled the clouds that stretched across the sky like a giant fishing net. Soon we approached the harvesters burning the leaves off the stalks to make them easier to chop and handle.

When we reached the cleared portion of the field, Aupouk and Khan cut the stalks. Kiry and I bundled and loaded them into tall stacks on water buffalo carts. It was much easier for Kiry than it was for me. The poles were three times my height and heavy for me to drag, so Kiry helped by taking the heavier end. The sun beat down on our bare backs, and we wore floppy hats to cover our faces. Mine kept getting in my eyes and the soot from the stalks coated my skin like a black rain. I watched the others, thinking it was like an exhausting dance, their movements calculated and in perfect rhythm as they moved over the charred earth in an endless repetition, shrouded in smoke. I learned all about sugar cane and how much hard work went into making it. Aupouk always said it took fire and sweat to extract the sweetness out of life.

Four weeks passed in the sugar cane dance. The harvest was nearly complete when angry voices came from where Aupouk and Khan were working. Kiry and I approached with an emptied cart and looked at each other with a shrug. Were they fighting?

Aupouk stood clutching the sickle, his shoulders erect. He looked more massive than usual. Khan stood planted, with dark, glaring eyes. He didn't seem afraid of my massive aupouk. Instead, he was puffed up and sneering. He reminded me of a chicken vulture circling just beyond the reach of a snapping dog, right after it steals his food. He must have done something terrible to cause that reaction in Aupouk, for I had never seen him so angry.

"I'm not blind!" Aupouk thundered. "I see the way you look at her when you visit and always shift the conversation to her."

"It's not my fault your wife finds me amusing and easy to talk to." Khan smirked and turned his back to walk away, making a mock effort to resume work. "She's wonderful and has a head full of ideas!"

"Don't play dumb with me! I can't believe you'd come to my home and try to take advantage of me after all we went through as temple boys!" Aupouk's frame loomed even larger, smoke curling around him. "I thought you'd risen above your itch to steal what isn't yours."

"You're taking this all far too personally my friend. I have not overstepped any bounds with your young wife."

"I don't want to see your face around my fire again!" Aupouk's finger was an inch from Khan's face.

"Understood, my friend." Khan bent down to retrieve the felled sugar cane, breaking the glare. "I understand. But know"—his words oozed, and he let each one drop from his tongue like bitter molasses—"that you may not be able to keep her." They resumed work, but a deafening silence swelled between them with each sickle stroke. Their words sat like a rock in my stomach. I began fearing Khan's darkness, which he cast like a shadow over my family, and I wished he had never come.

4

ARRESTED

"It's one of those things that's a wound." — Rindy

MAY 1968

I felt the stilt hut shift, stirring me from sleep, and I rolled from the wall toward the door. Aupouk undid the latch and creaked open the door, pausing before descending the ladder. The sun burned through the sky, smearing it in orange and red flames. Then the door closed, and I was left in darkness. But the memory of the sky still stung my eyes, and it chased the rest of sleep away. I pursued Aupouk and the blazing sky.

Slipping down the ladder, I jumped past the last few rungs and my feet landed softly in the dirt below. I wove my way through the rows of growing sesame plants, which were about as tall as me. Their pods, which once held pink, tube-like flowers, were growing crispy, and I knew we'd be breaking them open to remove their tiny seeds soon.

In the light of early dawn, the land surrounding our hut, growing with various plants, wasn't a place I feared. I imagined that every plant knew me and the leaves and branches reaching out to touch me as I passed were giving me their blessing. I noticed Aupouk ahead, pulling the water buffalo toward the Sangke River that snaked along the dirt road a few hundred yards from our stilt hut. Not wanting to follow him and the lumbering beasts, I busied myself trying to get a banana.

I spied a large cluster, just turning yellow, and reached as high as I could. But I wasn't tall enough, so I searched for something to stand on. Spying a stack of logs beneath the hut, I carried several over and stacked them, before trying again. Climbing onto my precarious platform, I reached as far as I could when a commotion sounded through the trees. Curious, I followed the sound. The water buffalo had made a small path through the underbrush with their coming and going to the river. I followed it and lowered myself to my stomach, inching closer to the road bank.

"I'm not going anywhere!"

It was Aupouk's voice, cracking in frustration.

"I don't know what I've been accused of, but I live back there with my family, I'm not a part of the rebel forces."

Being careful to stay hidden, I saw several men wearing green uniforms surrounding a group of men who looked to be their prisoners. I crouched closer to the earth. They held black machine guns, pointed at my aupouk.

"That's a likely story for a communist gorilla," a man growled around his cigarette butt. "I heard in the village that these parts are crawling with you." He spat motioning to his comrades.

Aupouk stood like a tree in the road, gripping the ring of one the largest water buffalo, the muscles on his arms bulging.

"At least let me return my livestock to my home."

"No! Fall in line. I have no problem shooting revolutionaries and their sympathizers. Or their families." The man poked his gun into my aupouk's chest. "Get moving!"

I burrowed my face in my arms. What should I do? Would they let him go if they saw me so they knew he was telling the truth?

Aupouk's words played through my memory. *"...other times you need to know when to lie still because you're no match."*

Crack! Crack! Crack!

I curled my arms over my ears, my whole-body trembling at the sound. Did they shoot Aupouk?

Soon the ringing in my ears gave way to the crunching of boots on dirt. Lifting my head, I watched as they marched my aupouk away. The three water buffalo were shot, dead on the road. Their blood mingled with the red dirt.

Backing into the underbrush, I fled.

I reached the clearing where the stilt hut lived, but something was different in the air. It no longer felt like the comforting place it had always been, for it was deserted except for a few chickens pecking the ground. I ran. Is anyone here? Mteay? Kiry? Vuthy? Climbing up the ladder I peered into the dark room. No one. I curled up on my mat and cried myself to sleep.

I sat up, rubbing the sleep from my eyes. Voices drifted up from below. The door stood open to the midday sun, and I crept toward it.

"I've asked around. He's being held in Battambang."

I knew the voice—Khan. I crawled to the place on the floor where I could see through the bamboo.

Mteay stood below, hanging wet clothes on a string hung from the leg of the stilt hut to a banana tree. Ly, her newborn baby, was tied to her chest, her black hair barely peeking from the folds of dull fabric. Vuthy chased the chickens. I pressed my face against the bamboo, trying to see farther.

"I don't understand." Mteay's voice shook.

"Apparently, he is being held for questioning. He's been accused of being a communist leader."

Khan's bare chest and sandaled feet came into view. He stopped just behind Mteay. I squirmed. I had never seen them alone before. I remembered the taunting look on Khan's face and the anger in Aupouk's voice as they talked about Mteay. My stomach lurched with the feeling of a million flies swarming.

"I don't know all the details." Khan's voice crackled with an eagerness I didn't understand. "I learned that the police believe he contributed to the communist ideology that's being spread through Cambodia."

"Why? How could they think that?"

"You know how he always parades about as if he has authority? It comes from his time in the temple." Khan chuckled. "The people in the village know him and his ideas. He's always spreading ideas and new ways of doing things; it's no surprise they believe he contributed to the unrest in the village."

"How long will he be kept there?"

Was it fear I heard in Mteay's voice or something else? It didn't tremble anymore, but she talked as if she were snatching each moment before it passed. Khan closed the distance between them, placing his hands around my mteay's waist, hiding her from my view.

"This is our best chance." Khan's voice was in her ear.

Confusion buzzed around my thoughts. Why did Mteay allow the stranger to be close to her when she almost always seemed to avoid Aupouk's touch? I wanted to shout, startle them from their closeness, but my throat was tight and my mind fuzzy. I said nothing but slunk back to my mat as they continued to murmur below.

"Why don't you let Aupouk touch your face?" I blurted out later that evening when we were alone. It felt good to get the burning words off my tongue. She sat nursing Ly by the evening fire. "Is it because of his rough hands?"

"I never wanted to marry him." She didn't look up, her words coming easily. "Years ago, my mteay made me marry him. Your aupouk used to be a monk and is well educated in both the Bali and Sanskrit languages."

"My mteay loved that he was a religious man." She smirked. "He was fifteen years older than me. I was just a girl and didn't want to get married. My mteay dragged me to the temple, but I screamed the whole way." She paused, her voice disappearing like smoke into the night air. "I do not love him." She stared absently into the fire. "I never have."

Satisfied with her answer, I continued to eat my rice. Although her words sunk like burning embers into my stomach, they were not surprising. It felt both good and bad to have them hang in the air between us.

"Love is not a necessary part of marriage in Cambodia." She looked up through the fire, her eyes black, tearless. "It's like salt, you can dump it in or leave it out—without ruining the texture."

During the day, I didn't fear the jungle—I found refuge there. To escape the absence of Aupouk, I spent the next few days exploring, careful not to venture too far into its heart so I could still find my way home. I made a fort of large banana leaves on the edge of the bushes and smaller trees at its border. I shaped it like an egg and only had enough room for me. I crawled in, shutting the flap, and it cast a green hue over me.

The rumble of thunder rolled across the sky. The rain was about to come. Would my shelter keep me dry? I decided to find out. Crawling in and pulling the flap shut behind me, I waited out the storm. The angry sky poured. I lay there listening to the voice of the rain rippling on my leaf roof. At first it was hard and loud, but became lighter and quieter, eventually satisfied with its wrath. I watched a drip sneak across a banana leaf and follow its center downward before dripping onto the earth, pulling the colors of my green world with it. I did get a little wet, but I was still proud of my creation. It stood secure, despite the darts sent down from the sky. I watched the drips until they made my eyes heavy with sleep.

When I woke, the air was cooler and clean. I needed to return home and get some food. The landscape looked bright and new from my green cave, and the earth made sense to me then. The sky poured out its rage when the earth was tired and hot, to cool it down and make new life rise through the rough spots. I appreciated the sky. Even the water on the leaves reached out and clung to me as I walked past. They must have known I needed to be washed clean too. Everything was quiet, except the sound of my own feet. My stomach rumbled. Would Mteay be making rice yet?

When I reached home, I called out, hoping I hadn't missed the evening meal. Searching the familiar scene, I spied two legs swinging from the edge of the stilt hut as I approached.

"Rindy!" Vuthy sang as I climbed the ladder and sat beside him.

"Where are ma and Kiry?" I asked, looking into the darkening room.

"Mteay l-l-left, took Kiry. Said stay here." I investigated his three-year old face, seeing the innocence and lack of fear. "Said wait for you."

I looked around the stilt hut while an acid sensation ate at my stomach. The spot on the bamboo where Mteay usually slept was bare, and her few belongings were gone. Instead, a pot sat alone in the shadows. I opened it and found three heaping scoops of rice. I picked up the pot and stared at its contents in my hands. Is this all we have left in the world?

I pulled up the ladder and latched the door, laying down on the bamboo slats, pulling Vuthy close. I tried not to let Vuthy see my tears, because I had to be strong now. The world that had just been bright and clean, had turned gray, dripping onto the edge of the window. Vuthy was asleep on my arm. The sky was crying again, so I did too.

5

THE OLD WOMAN

"I don't remember how long I was left." — Rindy

MAY 1968

The next morning, we ate some of the rice with our fingers, saving some in case it was hard to find food. After another day, it was gone. I gathered bananas and papayas, but most weren't fully ripe, so our stomachs hurt after eating them. When the sun was high in the sky two days later, I knew I had to ensure our survival. I needed a plan. We needed rice.

"Vuthy, it's best if you stay here because it's a long way to the village."

Vuthy nodded, his eyelids sagging. I waited until he was asleep, then crept down the ladder and found Aupouk's machete beneath the stilt hut. Going to a banana tree, I cut down a bunch of bananas which were just beginning to turn yellow. I hoped they would be good enough to warrant a trade. When we worked in the sugar cane fields, we had passed a hut where Aupouk had traded sesame seed for rice. I would start there. The trail was narrow, surrounded by jungle, but even amidst the trees, I knew where I was.

Staring hard at the road ahead of me, I thought about my problems. Looking over my shoulder, I imagined Vuthy sitting alone in the stilt hut, spitting through the slats like I used to. It felt good just to leave him there, for now, so I could think. I had to figure out what to do with him. Maybe Mteay should have taken him too? Why did she take Kiry? I felt very old for the first time, but not old enough as I pulled at my baggy shorts, which had been Kiry's a few seasons before. The bananas were getting heavier.

I passed a group of men sitting beside a radio, the familiar voice of Norodom Sihanouk—the "Father King" crackling from the speakers.

"When I went to France and pleaded for Cambodia's independence, I did so without guns and without force backing me. I had ideas and a desire for freedom for my people. And without a single shot fired, we won the war against the French!"

His voice swelled loudly through the sputtering speakers, and I imagined his arms moving dramatically to the rhythm of his words. Aupouk had said Sihanouk was a good actor and loved the theater and plays. He even directed many of his own movies. It sounded like he was acting in his own show again. I was captivated by his words.

"We became an independent nation; we became an island of peace, and that peace will grow and grow. But there is danger lurking around us, like a tiger waiting to pounce. We must protect ourselves from this danger. This danger is not only the war in Vietnam, as the United States and China wish to pull us into their game. No, this threat also comes from the rebels calling themselves the Communist Party of Kampuchea, but I will call them the Khmer Rouge. They are selling their communist propaganda to those in the rural areas and the villages, trying to trick unsuspecting people into joining their rebel cause. But they want to destroy Cambodia. Cambodia is an island of peace!"

The men smiled, puffing on their cigarettes as a beautiful Khmer melody followed the speech.

"We're lucky he's the father of Cambodia," one man said, reclining in his hammock, which he had tied between two trees. "He's not abusive like my father was." He chuckled.

"Yes, but not all would agree, especially in the rural villages. There they fear him because of the bombs."

"What bombs?"

"Haven't you heard? Sihanouk has been bombing the Khmer Rouge hiding places in the jungle. I've heard they've moved to the mountains near Naga's Tail to get away from the bombing. They'll be wiped out soon. Some of the bombs destroyed farms and paddies and even caused deaths in the village. People are joining the Khmer Rouge because they feel they can no longer trust the King Aupouk. His bombs are adding to their number."

I continued on my way pondering their words. What was a bomb? Soon I came to a hut that sat on the ground. A woman was hanging clothes in the trees for them to dry, and I watched as faded browns and pinks flapped in the breeze. Why would anyone want to live on the ground? I grimaced, missing my hut in the trees. I wanted to run back, but I also wanted food, so I kept walking. I began to run, but the hardness of the ground hurt my feet, so I slowed to a walk before long. Looking down, I could tell the path had seen many feet, for it was firm and pressed together.

Soon I came upon another hut, and then another. Then I saw many huts scattered between the coconut trees. I searched for something familiar. Seeing a hut I recognized, I stopped to make sure it was the same one before approaching. Faded prayer flags flapped in the wind, beckoning me forward. One large water pot sat beneath its eaves, carpeted with moss. A ragged blanket was tacked to the roof, which fell out over a bamboo frame. A wooden platform made of slats sat out front, and I knew the old people would often sit there and watch the world go by as they spat red juice out of their jigsaw mouths. Approaching the hut, I poked my head inside the doorless frame.

"*Sousday,*" came the abrupt greeting from inside, making my heart thud.

"*Sousday Bong,*" I squeaked, remembering to be respectful.

"My name is Rindy." I didn't know how else to begin the conversation. "Can I trade some bananas for rice?"

"Hmmm," a body emerged. The old woman looked much older now, her eyes shining with a cloudy, eerie light. Looking at them made my hair stand up, so I shied away. Her back was bent at her waist, like an old tree that had been battered by the wind so much it had stuck crooked.

She grabbed my shoulder for support as she walked toward a resting place. Her skin felt like fish scales against mine, and I tried not to stare at the wrinkles covering her. She had four fingernails on one hand and three on the other. Was she born like that? Or did they fall off with time? I stole a glance at my own hands. I hoped mine wouldn't look like that one day. She had long toenails though. They looked like yellow rocks, not having a smooth place at all. Looking back to her face, I saw some redness peeking out behind her lips.

Smack!

She spat hard, hitting the water pot at the base. I smiled in admiration because I couldn't spit that far or that fast. She smiled back and her mouth was like a cave, with a few black stubs poking through the top of her gums. I ran my tongue over my teeth and sat down beside to her.

"I lost my family." I felt like we knew each other well enough to get straight to the matter.

"Have you?" she asked absently, as if she didn't hear me the first time.

"Yes, I have." I tried not to get agitated with her lack of concern.

We sat in silence for some time, and I watched the tail of the water buffalo across the street flick at the flies trying to eat its hide.

"You must be hungry." Her voice startled me.

"Yes." I smiled wide.

Scooting off the platform, she placed her feet on the ground shakily, and her hunched back hunched even further as she disappeared into her hut. She clanged around and muttered to herself, before returning with a piece of dried fish.

I took it gratefully from her outstretched hand, but it was tough, and it balled up in my mouth, making it difficult to swallow. It tasted salty but good, and my stomach thanked me as it gurgled its approval.

"My aupouk got taken by the police." The words spilled out, between chews. It felt good to tell her. "Mteay left with Khan too, two days ago."

The old woman nodded at me, her dull eyes stared but showed no emotion. Was it any use to expect an answer? We didn't seem to be making any progress. I had one last idea.

"My little brother was left alone in my stilt hut too."

The little weak spots next to her eye sockets beat rapidly. I'd hit a nerve. I was glad to see she was hearing me, but she still didn't reply.

"Do you live alone, too?" Maybe she'd like to talk about herself, since she didn't seem interested in me. She turned her head slowly and looked into my eyes. She looked surprised and hurt. I dropped my gaze. Shouldn't have asked that.

"Yes..." She took another bite of her red root and spit.

Thwap!

I gave up trying to talk to her, as I swallowed the last of my fish. We sat there a long time, staring at the water buffalo's tail. The flies irritated me, and I had the urge to march across the dirt path and swat them myself. No matter how many times the buffalo would swat, they kept coming back to the same spot.

Vuthy! I had almost forgotten about him. I needed to get going.

"I have a little brother at home..." I let my words trail off into silence, hoping the old woman would catch my drift. She heaved herself up again and disappeared into the house, emerging out of the darkness and giving me a small sack of rice before heaving herself back down. I smiled and put my hand on hers, her skin warming under my touch. She smiled back, her eyes disappearing into the folds of skin. We understood each other.

"Is this enough to trade?" I hefted the cluster of bananas. I was doubtful, but I didn't have anything else to offer.

She took them in her knobby hands and inspected them carefully, before nodding and taking them inside.

I visited the old woman every day as constant as the sun, sometimes with Vuthy and sometimes alone. We would sit and talk and watch the world go by. It made me feel less alone and as if someone in the world knew we existed. Each time we visited, I brought some fruit or casava root, and we returned with food.

6

AUPOUK

"His world fell apart." — Rindy

TWO WEEKS LATER

In the darkness one night, I felt the stilt hut swaying familiarly. I jerked awake, searching for Vuthy with my left hand. I found him and tried to recoil it so I didn't wake him. I lifted my head to look around the small room. Tingling with fright, I realized I had left the ladder down the night before, falling asleep before drawing it up. How could I have been so foolish?

Searching in the darkness, my fingers groped for a weapon and landed upon the pot, Mteay had left rice in, two weeks before. I gripped it and crouched on my curled toes, staring hard at the doorway. It was dark, except a few stars shining through the treetops. I imagined the yellow eyes of a tiger, peaking over the ledge, and I closed my eyes to erase the thought. Heavy breathing rippled up from below. Holding my breath, I waited, gripping the handle in my shaking hands.

A tall shadow emerged into view. It was familiar. It belonged.

"Aupouk!" I lunged forward, catching my toe on an uneven place in the bamboo floor, making me fall hard. Aupouk grabbed my shoulders as he gently set me back on my feet. It was reassuring, and it felt right. Then he froze, staring into the corner where Mteay had always slept. Letting go of my shoulders, he took a step closer to the dark, vacant space. I retreated into the darkness, so I didn't have to see his face.

"She—they left soon after you did." I choked. My throat felt like it was clenching dry rice.

He said nothing, just stood and stared. I crawled back to the wall and sat with my knees pulled in close watching *Aupouk's* back. I could faintly see him breathing, because his shoulders rose and fell against the backdrop of the sky. To the sound of his low, murmured breath, my back against the wall, I drifted into sleep once again.

Startling awake, I lifted my head from my chest, my ears smarting with an unusual sound. I looked around. The night had grown deeper. I heard the sound again, cutting through the thick air, throaty and mournful. Blinking my eyes, I looked for Aupouk, hoping he hadn't been a dream. He wasn't anywhere.

The sound repeated. More of a yell than a wail—a man's yell. I covered my ears. It came from the darkness and echoed through the air like thunder. Then I heard the crack of wood against wood with a force like the wind. I knew it was Aupouk then, because I had seen the strength of his arms many times while I watched him work. To escape the sad sound, I curled up and hummed myself back to sleep.

The next morning the smell of rice porridge enticed me down the ladder. Peering out of the stilt hut, I saw Aupouk and Vuthy, sitting by a small fire. The sight was like eating warm soup, familiar and inviting. I paused to look once more, before climbing down to join them.

"I'm so glad you're home, Aupouk!" Ignoring the last few rungs of the ladder, I jumped down.

"Me too."

But there was no smile on his face or in his eyes. Instead, his eyes were filled with clouds, surrounded by deep, puffy lines. I stared at my toes to avoid them. Vuthy was prattling on about his broken sandal. Would he just shut up? I held the words in because Aupouk didn't like when I yelled at him. Aupouk handed me a bowl, as he continued to eat his own porridge, chewing slowly, as if he didn't like the taste of it. His jaw worked in and out, in and out, with each bite, before he swallowed.

"When is Ma coming home?"

Pain streaked across Aupouk's face. I reached over and pinched Vuthy's leg to discourage him from saying anything else stupid. Vuthy wailed, I reached out to pinch him again because I knew it didn't hurt that bad. Aupouk grabbed my hand before I could. He held it for a minute and squeezed before letting it go. The gentle squeeze made me want to cry. It hurt worse than a slap across the face. I felt his pain, like the deep burn I got last summer after embers from the fire had landed on my leg. They'd sizzled on my skin for a few seconds before I could get them off. That's how this pain was, but deeper.

A week after Aupouk returned, yelling came from the stilt hut. Sprinting through the underbrush, I made my way home through the banana grove. I recognized the sound of Mteay's and Khan's voices, mixed with baby Ly's wails. Sneaking up close to hear, I lay with my back in the dirt beneath the stilt hut, careful not to be seen.

"I have no need for them!" Aupouk's voice was deeper than the rest, cutting through the chatter.

"Neither do I!" Mteay was rocking Ly, her weight moving from side to side above my head.

"You are their Mteay! You must take them. I have to work."

My breath jammed in my throat, but hot tears threatened to break through.

"Rindy will grow big and strong one day." Her words made my eyes burn. "He will be useful to you then."

"I told you; I don't want him! I can't take care of him!" Aupouk thundered. "You aren't just going to take who you want and leave me with who you don't!"

"I'm taking Ly and Kiry!" she yelled back even louder than he did. "Our divorce will be official, and you'll never have to see me again."

The voices from above didn't sound like my parents, but then again, I'd rarely heard them speak to one another. Did I still belong to them? Was I no one's? The thought snuck up on me, like dusk settling over the jungle treetops.

"It's final then," Khan's voice oozed mockery. I cringed at the sound. "There appears to be nothing else to discuss."

"Get out!" Aupouk erupted. "Or I will throw you out!" I could see the bamboo move as he sprang to his feet towards Khan. Ly started crying louder and Mteay screamed at them both.

Peeling myself from the dirt, I ran into the jungle. I didn't know where I was going, and I didn't care, but I went a bit farther than I'd ever dared before. I stopped by a stream that gurgled over mossy rocks, where the world seemed trapped in vines and muted light. The palm trees stood still, and the air was alive with the sound of distant birds and bugs. I knew I couldn't stay long, but I couldn't help but linger for a moment. I sunk to the ground, smoothing the grassy plants by the water's edge.

The words played over in my head, stinging repeatedly like a swarm of bees.

I don't want him.

I don't need him.

Someday he will be useful.

Had I ever been wanted? I must not have been. My life felt like the burned rice clinging to the bottom of a pot; I was meant to be discarded.

Dropping my head between my knees, I rubbed a piece of grass between my fingers. The words buzzed in my head until they made my eyes swim. The grass cut my finger and a prick of blood oozed from my skin, but the pain came from deep within my chest.

A rustling sounded from the jungle canopy overhead, and I scrubbed my eyes free of tears. A gibbon and her baby emerged, swinging from the trees above my head. The mteay was light grey, with tuffs of white surrounding the black eyes and nose on her face. One long leg dangled from the tree aimlessly, while the other clutched her baby tenderly. Her feet and hands looked like mine. She studied me and made a "whoop, whoop, whoop" sound as if to ask, "are you my kind?"

"I wish I were," I whispered. "You seem to want your babies." Soon the cry of more gibbons could be heard through the treetops telling me, "go back to your people."

So, I did, just in time to see Mteay walk east with her new family and new husband. Ly was asleep on her chest and Kiry walked behind her, but he looked over his shoulder and waved, his face an apology. Aupouk wasn't anywhere to be found, but Vuthy sat with his back to me, his body still shuddering from the suppressed sobs. My chest constricted. I went to him and wrapped my arms around his bare shoulders.

"I'm sorry you're unwanted, with me. It's just you and me again."

He pressed in closer to me and his sobs lessened.

7

THE RECRUITERS

"Now, he tried to raise me." — Rindy

JUNE 1968

When Aupouk was upset, he worked. He hadn't stopped working since he had been released by the police and Mteay had left. I hurt for him. Not only because he was left with us without a choice in the matter, but also because his wife had left him. He was also unwanted.

A man approached the stilt hut one morning.

"This is your *Pou* Kim, my little brother," Aupouk announced to Vuthy and I, clapping the man on the shoulder. He looked like Aupouk. "I'm glad to have your help, little brother, I've cleared more land for us to plant sesame."

Aupouk handed him a banana leaf of cold rice. I nibbled mine in silence, happy to see the hollows under Aupouk's eyes lessen.

"While you build your hut, you must stay in mine. There's plenty of room."

"Thank you, but I don't want to intrude on your family."

"No intrusion." A cloud passed over Aupouk's face.

"No, I'll find somewhere to camp out, I'll be fine."

"I insist. A tiger killed one of my water buffalo calves, and it's not safe on the ground."

"Ma left." Vuthy put his hand on Pou's knee.

"What, little man? Your ma left?"

Aupouk pulled Vuthy away by his wrist. "We have much to catch up on."

Pou searched my aupouk's face, as deep lines etched into his brown forehead, reaching his shaggy black hair.

"With Khan Nong."

"Khan? Not Khan from the temple when we were boys?"

Aupouk nodded but said nothing.

Pou Kim muttered a curse under his breath.

"I knew he was sly, but I didn't think he'd stoop as low as that. After everything we've been through together too, as temple boys—"

"Let's get to work while it's not raining." Aupouk cut off his words.

He left the words hanging in the air, like a foul-smelling odor. I had never heard my Aupouk talk about his memories as a temple boy. Every time the subject was brought up, Aupouk quickly changed it, or an uncomfortable silence remained. Why wouldn't Aupouk talk about his memories from his time at the temple? Why did his face grow old every time it was mentioned?

To pass time as Aupouk and Pou Kim worked, Vuthy and I spent our days at the edge of the jungle. My job was to watch Vuthy because Aupouk said he just got in the way and I was too small to help. After building one leaf hut, we built another, then another, until there was a small group of huts scattered across the jungle floor. We'd hide there for hours when the rain poured. The jungle canopy helped keep much of it out, but sometimes we got wet if we were near enough to the edge of the thick trees. When it rained, Vuthy cried for Mteay, but I held him and told him everything would be all right. Being unwanted had stopped stinging on the surface of my skin, as it sunk deeper into a dull throb somewhere in my chest. It became a part of me somehow. It was becoming a part of Vuthy too.

If we weren't building, we were exploring every log, boulder and tree. I knew each turn of the jungle by heart, up to three miles in, as I was always pushing the boundaries of what we called home. When darkness approached, we'd retreat to the stilt hut, sometimes to find rice, sometimes not. If not, we would raid the fruit trees for anything ripe enough to eat.

Aupouk tried to do the best he could, but sometimes it wasn't enough. Each morning he and Pou got up before dawn and worked until after dark. He didn't seem to know what to do with us. One night he made soup instead of the usual rice with fish paste, but it tasted terrible. Vuthy made a face and let it dribble out of his mouth. Aupouk ate a bite and gagged, then stood up and dumped it over the log. After that, Aupouk just stuck with rice with fish paste and fruit. With partially full stomachs and sticky fingers, we fell asleep whenever we wanted, sprawled over the bamboo floor.

One evening, two men approached as we sat around the evening fire. Aupouk stood up, curious, as their black clad frames snaked through the underbrush toward us. They wore odd grins, with their eyes narrowed on us.

"*Sousdey*." Their voices leaped over the distance between us.

"*Sousdey*," Aupouk growled.

Curious, I searched his face. His jaw muscle worked.

"We greet you as members of Democratic Kampuchea. The free Cambodians." They approached and sat on one of the logs around our fire.

"Are you the communists Sihanouk has been searching for? Those called the Khmer Rouge?"

The men looked sideways at each other.

"Where have you all been hiding?" Aupouk asked. "The police are scouring the country looking for you, and they arrested me a few weeks ago instead of you." He swore, spitting into the fire, making it pop and sputter.

"We don't disclose the information of our whereabouts."

"What do you disclose then? Why are you here?"

"Because of the injustices happening in Cambodia," the loud one raised his voice. "Have you heard of the U.S. special forces that have been sneaking into Cambodia dressed as Viet Cong soldiers?

Aupouk's eyes narrowed, but he didn't reply.

"They are called the 'Green Beret'," the quieter one interjected.

"Yeah, yeah, whatever they're called, they're killing innocent Cambodians with their land mines. They blew up a bus loaded with women and children and nearly everyone was massacred. Sihanouk is doing nothing to curb these invasions—"

"He's too busy making friends with the ones bombing us." The other one leaned forward.

"I've heard of the bombs." Aupouk poked the fire. "What does that have to do with us?" He glanced at Pou Kim who remained silent.

"Norodom Sihanouk is killing his own people and doing nothing about the United States trespassing on Cambodian soil to do the same," the more vocal one shouted, rising to his feet, eyes dancing in the firelight, cheeks hollow shadows.

"Join our numbers. We have 100,000 villagers who have joined us in the jungles," the quiet one continued, his voice swelling like the smoke. "So our homes and families aren't targeted next."

No one spoke. Pou Kim looked at Aupouk and Aupouk stared into the fire. The men squirmed in the silence.

"I'm not a revolutionary man." Aupouk sighed at last. His voice sounded like cool water, pouring on their words full of fire.

"Every good Cambodian is a revolutionary if he wants to preserve his homeland," the louder man fired back, his tone sharp.

"We don't want to be a part of your war." Aupouk rose to his feet, standing a few inches taller than the other Khmer men. "I suggest you leave now."

"Don't be a fool," the loud one shouted, rising to his feet too.

"You can't come to my home and call me a fool. Leave."

"We'll be back," the loud one called over his shoulder. "You'll see we're right in the end." But soon their black clothes melted into the darkening horizon.

Over the next months, just as they had threatened, they returned, but I never again stayed for one of their conversations. Instead, I took Vuthy into the stilt hut to watch and listen from a safe distance. The conversations always ended in shouting, with their arms thrown wide and their eyes glinting at one another. Whenever they left, Aupouk and Pou Kim sat in a squat, with their buttocks resting just above the ground as they smoked cigarettes. Their faces aglow in firelight and words of war.

Aupouk changed after Mteay left. He reminded me of hard, cracked ground, the kind without water — the kind you couldn't drive a stake into.

8

THE RIVER

"I saw yellow and green, before I passed out." — Rindy

SEPTEMBER 1969

When the rainy season came, the Sangke River was swollen with rainwater and fish; even the red dirt road was waterlogged and soggy under our bare feet as we approached it. I handed Vuthy a piece of my sugar cane. I had peeled the hard bamboo-like shell away with Aupouk's machete before we left home, to get at the cream-colored sweetness found in the center. I knew he'd like the treat.

"Why it rain so much?" Vuthy sucked on his sugar cane. His brown eyes looked in wonder at the landscape that had changed overnight, after hours of relentless rainfall. I realized he was too young to remember last year's rainy season.

"The sun shines on the ground so hard for months that it takes a lot of water to get down to the bones of Cambodia." I jumped into a puddle. "Rice, sugar cane and even the trees need it to drink or else they'll all burn up in the hot sun. We'd burn up too, without water."

Even when it wasn't raining, the air was wet, and it clogged in my lungs and nose as we approached the river's muddy edge. The river was almost filled to the brim and was wider than I could throw a rock across, its brown water flowing in a gentle current.

"Look, Rindy."

Vuthy pointed at a cylinder fish trap bobbing in the river, floating near the edge of the bank.

"Think of all the fish we could catch with that. Do you think it's broken?"

The water was so high that it was almost level with the ground I stood on. Getting on my stomach, I reached as far as I could, trying to grasp its bamboo framework. I couldn't quite reach, so I slid a little further. I was frustrated by my short, six-year-old arms that just couldn't reach far enough. Almost there. Straining, I was so close when the bank under me began to shift.

I heard Vuthy cry my name, as a lukewarm sensation engulfed me, filling my mouth and clouding my eyes. I plunged head first into the water with the crumbling bank. Mud and water filled my mouth, and I kicked hard trying to resurface, fighting through the sludge spilling into the water behind me. Once I resurfaced, I found I was out of reach of the bank. The water was so much deeper than I had expected. I struggled to stay afloat, as the current carried me along.

"Get—" I screamed to Vuthy who stood crying on the bank, but muddy water filled my mouth and washed away my words. I went under again. Kicking hard, I resurfaced, but I found I was getting farther from the bank.

I kicked and grappled for something to hold on to—anything to grasp. But the groping arms of the water that had seemed so innocent while on the bank, pulled me under again, deeper into its grip. My lungs were filled with fire and it was getting hotter. Kicking my legs hard, I came back to the top, gasping for a breath to put out the burning in my chest, but I took in another mouthful of water instead. Sinking beneath the surface, I bumped against something hard, and my mind whirled in panic. A foreign idea, one I had never stopped to ponder before, sounded in my brain, like a thunderclap. Fear filled my nostrils like smoke from my lungs, in a suffocating realization. *I was going to drown.*

I kicked harder and screamed, taking in another mouthful of water. I couldn't reach the surface; I didn't even know where it was anymore. An unusual cold and stiff feeling oozed through my body, snuffing out the fire-like one. My brain grew foggier with each passing second of immersion. Strange and beautiful colors paraded across my senses, like a liquid mirage, swirling in vibrant yellows and greens. They drew me in with their trance. Content to gaze at them forever, I succumbed to their power and stopped kicking. I drifted, rocked back and forth in the river's warm embrace. I tried to think, to remember how to breathe air, but the river's deadly lullaby hummed in my ears. The once vibrant colors turned dark and grew darker still, until darkness was all I knew.

All at once, I saw light. It swelled before me. Pressure pounded in my head and water ran from the depths of my stomach. I choked on a surge of liquid coming from somewhere deep inside of me. As if through a fog, trees grew out of the sky. My arms and legs were lifeless. I couldn't breathe. My throat felt like mud.

I must be dead.

A sudden rush of pain wracked my body. The pressure in my chest worsened, relented then repeated.

"Breathe, Rindy." My mind struggled to comprehend the command and recognize the voice.

I forced my eyes open, and my head felt as if it would explode from pressure. I couldn't tell if I was suspended in the air or lying on the ground. A familiar face appeared through the haze. Shaggy black hair and broad shoulders blocked the sunlight spilling across the sky.

"Pou Kim?" I wheezed.

Why hadn't he let me drown? It hurt so much worse to be alive. My body released the water it had so greedily eaten. I retched, and it poured from my mouth and nose.

"Just breathe Rindy...deep breaths.... deep breaths."

I sputtered and coughed. He grabbed my ankles and raised me high in the air, and the trees were rooted in the clouds again.

I tried to swallow, but my throat was sandpaper. I tried to open my eyes, but they hurt.

"I'm taking you to the hospital. You aren't breathing right." I felt my body become weightless as he picked me up and held me against his chest. "Hold on, it'll take a bit—it's ten miles away. Vuthy, stop crying and go find your aupouk in the sesame field."

I didn't try to open my eyes again, but I felt the rhythm of his body as he held me tightly, and the pounding of his feet lulled me into darkness.

9

THE HOSPITAL

"I have no idea how he found me in time." — Rindy

THE NEXT DAY

I woke up naked, lying on a small, wooden bed with a thin, white sheet draped over me. I was in a room with pale walls and hard, unfriendly floors. A woman came over to me with a glass of water. She touched my forehead, but her fingers were hard and cold. I didn't want to swallow any more water, so I shook my head. She tipped my head back, shoved a pill between my lips and poured water into my mouth anyways.

"Swallow."

I did, but my throat felt raw.

"What's wrong with me?" My throat wrung out the words like a soggy blanket, and I couldn't manage a deep breath.

"You have a high fever, aspiration pneumonia and you're being monitored for a blood illness called lactic acidosis due to all the water you swallowed."

Setting the drink on a small table by my bed, she turned and walked away. I didn't know what her words meant, but I didn't feel like calling after her to find out.

I don't remember much from the first day I spent in the hospital, lying on the hard bed. The nurse brought me a bowl of watery soup with small bits of pork in it and pills to drink. My body contorted with long bouts of coughing, and sometimes blood showed in my hands afterward. My chest felt like it was on fire.

There were beds to my right and a cement wall to my left. There was one little window in the wall, but it was too high for me to see out, so I spent most of my time staring at that wall. It had many little cracks in its gray face, and they reminded me of the river, with many little streams flowing from a bigger one. I couldn't stop thinking about the river and how it had held me in its watery grip. How had Pou Kim heard my scream with the river's fist in my mouth? How had I survived?

I knew what it felt like to drown, and that feeling haunted my dreams. When I closed my eyes, I felt the water's anger beating against my body. The water would rush in, curling me in an endless game of somersault, as I pictured myself like a leaf being crushed in its midst. It had almost eaten me without a second thought. It was black and cold, and each night I was there, trapped in its depths again, unable to breath. I woke up gasping, and it was difficult to take a breath, even when I escaped the nightmare. Lying on my back was all I could do, thinking hard about breathing and nothing else until it grew easier. I stared at the cracks in the wall until the darkness faded into light.

The next day, I woke up to a boy crying in the bed beside me. I tried to ask him what was wrong, but he just cried and held his bandaged arm. Soon a nurse came in to take the bandage off because she said the air was good for it. Flies came, and the boy cried harder. They kept landing on it, sucking out the blackness of his skin. He tried to chase them away at first, but there were too many. Tears rolled down the side of his face, making streaks in his brown skin. I inched over to him, sitting beside him on the bed and tried to swat them away. He smiled slightly, but soon fell asleep. I retreated back to my bed, exhausted from even that small effort.

When I woke, Pou Kim was standing over me with a handful of lychees.

"Want some?"

I shook my head, but he dropped them into my lap one by one, as if to call forth my appetite. Picking one up, I tore through the furry exterior to get to the soft, transparent meat with my teeth. It tasted good, and my stomach gurgled its approval. Pou laughed at the sound, and so did I. I had difficulty breathing, so we sat in silence while I ate. I wanted to ask him how he had heard me scream from the river, but it was all I could do to take a bite and swallow. But the question sat between us on the mat.

"Good?" His eyes smiled at me, the corners wrinkling.

I nodded, swallowing the last bite.

"Are you feeling any better?"

I nodded again, coughing uncontrollably.

"You'll have to stay here a few more days." He measured his words before letting them spill out. "Your lungs are infected by all of the water you swallowed."

I wanted to cry.

"It's only for a few more days." He patted my leg. "You'll be back, playing with Vuthy before you know it. Someone will come in a few more days."

Through blurry eyes, I watched him leave. Once again, I was alone. The crying boy was still there, but he made me feel more alone than ever. I watched as the sun rose and sank, casting a pink glow across the cracks on the wall. I thought of Aupouk and the way he used to be before Mteay left. His strong arms, his kind eyes, but most of all, the way I felt when I was with him. It was the same feeling I got when I'd lain in my banana leaf hut, wrapped in safety and peace. Focusing on that feeling, I tried to sleep another day away.

Hearing familiar steps in the hall, I jerked up, resting on my cocked elbow. I felt the urge to cough, but I sucked it back into my chest so I could listen. Straining, I waited to see who the steps belonged to. At last, the familiar face rounded the corner.

"Aupouk." I sprang from my bed, my feet padding on the concrete floor. I could still feel the rasp in my chest and the room spun, but I didn't care, because he had come.

"Sousday, Rindy." His greeting was dull, as he looked around the room. There wasn't much to look at besides the handful of other children occupying the beds. Soon his dark eyes were resting on me again.

I sat back down on the rickety bed and studied him, as he studied me. His face looked so much older than when I had last seen him, and his sunken eyes had red snakes running all over the white parts. His broad shoulders were bent, his hands clenching.

"I told you to never play near the river." His gaze skirted my eyes as he stared at the tips of my disheveled hair. "Do you understand? You could have drowned?" His gaze dropped to mine.

I nodded mutely, dropping my eyes to.

"I was getting a fish trap." The words were barely a whisper.

"I can't hear you."

"I was trying to reach a fish trap floating in the river." I swallowed. "So, I could catch fish for supper."

His face crumbled, and he lowered his head.

"I can't watch you all the time. I can't always keep you safe."

I nodded, but he seemed to be muttering the words to himself. We continued to sit in silence, and I sat in shame.

"How did Pou Kim hear me scream?"

"That's just it Rindy. He just happened to be walking by to get supplies in the village. There's no way we could have heard you scream from the field. You could have died."

Silence settled over us again.

"What happens when you die?"

Aupouk's face relaxed and he looked into my eyes again.

"You are reborn into another form, depending on how much karma you have."

"What is karma?"

"The good thoughts and actions that you have will determine what form you will be reborn into."

"What do you mean by form?"

"Well, there are a few different ones: gods, demi-gods, humans, animals, hungry ghosts or hellish creatures. How good you are decides what you will become in your next life."

"I would come back a frog or even a"—I took a wheezing breath—"wicked ghost?"

"Perhaps."

I didn't like that thought at all.

"So, I would just keep dying and being reborn, forever?"

"Well, yes, until you have so much good karma that the cycle can stop."

I thought about his words, trying to understand them.

"Does that make sense?"

I nodded, but it was a lie.

"That's why you must try to be very good in life, so you have a better next one."

I knew lying was wrong, and I hung my head.

"Vuthy's been getting into all kinds of trouble while you've been away."

I looked up grinning, shaking off the scary thoughts, hoping to draw one out of him too.

"He tried to climb a cut bamboo pole, and it poked a hole in his shorts." His eyes softened as he remembered the spectacle. "He hung there screaming like a monkey."

A glint of a smile flickered across his face, but it disappeared even faster than it had appeared. Had he smiled at all or had he just thought about it? A smile wasn't something he wore much anymore.

I laughed, hoping he would too, as I pictured Vuthy hanging from a bamboo pole by his shorts, but Aupouk's hinted smile didn't return. We sat in silence.

"You'll be released in a few more days. They say your blood infection is not good quite yet."

"But I want to go with you." I shoved my fists in my eyes to stop the tears.

With a pat on my arm, he turned to go. He stood for a moment, his hands hanging limply at his sides. I didn't stop him or call out to him because I knew he couldn't stay, and I couldn't go. Tears blurred my vision, and I did nothing to conceal their fall.

I awoke to a nurse I hadn't seen before, bending over me. Her hands were gentle as she touched my forehead and sat me up to take my pill.

"You've had a rough time of it, haven't you?" Her eyes and lips smiled. "I'm sure nearly drowning was a very scary thing for you." A black strand of hair slipped from her bun and brushed the gentle slant of her eye. She shouldn't have been beautiful, with her sun baked skin, round face, small lips and thin features. Yet she was.

Suddenly, the questions I had been pondering spilled out of me, as if some unseen force drug them up from the pit of my stomach.

"Why didn't I die? My aupouk says my Pou Kim should not have been by the river when he was, to rescue me."

She looked up from taking my pulse, her eyes shining.

"It was a miracle, because God has a plan for you."

"What is a miracle?"

"Something only God can do to show you his power and his love for you. He sent your Pou Kim before it was too late."

She sat patiently, as I coughed.

"My aupouk taught me that death just leads to rebirth." I coughed "I could have come back as another person, animal or"—I stammered—"a bad creature."

"I think God needed you to live. To continue to be Rindy—that's your name, isn't it?"

I nodded.

"God wanted you to be Rindy for a while longer. God loves you and wants you to know that he created you for a reason and with a purpose on this earth."

There was a bustle in the hallway, as a bed wheeled past carrying a person covered in blood.

"I have to go, but maybe we can talk more later?" She stood and hurried away, but turned one last time. "God has a purpose for you, I know it."

I thought about her words before drifting into sleep again, no longer haunted by winged bat creatures and creeping frogs.

—⟫⟫⟩ ⟨⟨⟨—

The days passed in rose-colored sunsets and my endless study of the crack on the wall. Another woman came in to give me medicine and food.

"How many days have I been here?" my voice squeaked reluctantly.

"Two weeks."

Her voice, like her attire, was free of frills and color. She placed a pill in my palm and waited for me to swallow it. Time was cruel. I held the chalky sensation in my mouth, feeling like I might gag. My lifetime seemed to fly by before, but these two weeks were like a gapping, black hole, where time inched by, almost stopping completely.

"You're leaving today."

"When?" I blurted, forgetting the pill on my tongue.

"Right now. We need your bed and you've improved enough to walk home. Take the rest of your antibiotics, twice a day until they are gone." She shoved a small paper bag into my hand. "Now, get going."

I smiled gratefully, rolled off the bed and slowly walked toward the door of the room, strength returning to my trembling legs. I walked past the boy with the re-bandaged arm, down a hallway pocked with rooms and out the front door. No one stopped me. No one even seemed to notice me. I had to stop several times to catch my breath, but I was determined to make it the whole way.

My bare feet felt good in the dirt, and I closed my eyes, feeling the sun on my face. I opened my arms wide, hugging the world. Unable to hold back, I ran. It was hard to breathe, and my side hurt, so I stopped after only a few paces. It felt like I still had water trapped inside of me, left over from when I had almost drowned. It was a long walk home, but I didn't mind, because the sun was shining on me again and all was right with the world.

10
GOODBYES

"I loved my Aupouk, even though he said he did not want me."
— Rindy

OCTOBER 1969

"**A**upouk! I'm back from the hospital."

The stilt hut was watchful, as if it had forgotten me in my absence.

"Vuthy!" My echo didn't even return to me.

"Pou Kim?" I inspected the vacated premises. My foolishness for expecting anyone to be home burned on my face. Of course, they were working in the fruit field and wouldn't be home until later. Worn out from the walk, I crept into the stilt hut to take a nap before finding them.

With the rainy season almost over, it was time for the second mango harvest. Aupouk had planted the first mango trees the same year he had built our home and continued to plant them every year. There were so many trees I could get lost in them, with their beautiful bushy tops and lush leaves. He used to laugh and say he planted the trees before he built the slit hut, because he knew what was most important. "A house can be built, and you can live in it, but a mango tree needs years to grow in order to produce fruit." He had said, "first plant food then build a hut." I spotted him on the far side of the mango grove, pulling the almost ripened fruit from the leaves and placing them gently into crates.

"Sousday." I stopped behind a tree trunk. An odd feeling of shyness crept up my neck.

"Sousday, Rindy." Surprise was evident in his voice. He stood staring at me, shielding his eyes from the brutal afternoon sun.

"They let me out of the hospital this morning." I dropped my eyes, not knowing what to do next.

Aupouk nodded, staring at the fruit in his hand. He clutched it tighter, absently, before realizing what he was doing and placed it gently in the crate. I stood staring for a moment, disappointment snaking down my spine like sweat.

"Can I help?"

He nodded.

Climbing higher on the ladder, he plucked the fruit from the tree and handed it to me. I placed it gently into the crate.

"Where are Vuthy and Pou Kim?" I stared up, trying to see Aupouk's face, but it was concealed by green leaves.

"Pou Kim is with Vuthy working on the other side of the grove. Vuthy is likely asleep in the shade or getting into trouble."

There was no humor in his voice. He continued to hand me mangos, but each one got heavier until it felt as if he were handing me boulders.

Time seemed trapped in the sticky air, like a bug in a web. Sweat evaporated from my body, and the sun began to dip its head behind the treetops.

"Are you hungry?" He spoke for the first time in what felt like hours. My mind had grown fuzzy.

"Rindy you don't look good. Go sit down before you fall over."

I stumbled over to the biggest tree to sit in its shade, leaning my back against its trunk. Aupouk climbed down the ladder and handed me a jug of water. I felt his hand on my forehead.

"You're warm and not ready to be working out in the heat after being so sick." He looked up at the sun, the lines in his forehead plowing deeper. "You need to be in the hut, resting."

"No, I can—stay." I struggled, taking another sip of water.

Aupouk brought me a mango. I bit into it through the skin and enjoyed the sweet flavor that trickled down my throat, reviving me. Looking up with a mouthful, I met Aupouk's gaze. The look in his eyes mirrored sadness, and it made me squirm. He stood and turned as if to resume work, but he didn't move. I stopped eating my mango and nervously tried to get the strings out of my teeth with my tongue.

"I have to send you away. I just can't take care of you anymore." The words were barely loud enough for me to hear. He stood as if planted. I didn't move; I didn't even breathe, hoping I had just imagined what he said. He went back to work and left me with the words, sitting in my lap with the half-eaten mango.

Did he mean it? I stared at the mango in my hand. Had he really said it? Not wanting to rouse the words again, I let them lie, buried in denial.

Pushing myself to my feet, I swayed, my head still feeling dizzy. I needed to be useful and show him that I didn't need to be taken care of. I needed him to be glad that Mteay had left me behind.

"I can help. I'm fine now."

"No, Rindy, just rest." His words barked, and I knew he meant them. I obeyed. A fly came and landed on my half-eaten mango, but I didn't even swat it because I wasn't hungry anymore.

I stared at Aupouk even harder, tracing the outline of his frame with my eyes. I wanted to stay with him. Looking at my small hands and my short legs, I compared myself to him. I wanted to be him one day—just like him.

How would I know how to be if he sent me away? And where would I go? The thoughts plagued me like the flies eating my mango. I wanted to cry, but I wouldn't allow the tears to escape my eyelids. I pinched them closed for a few minuets before opening them again. I continued to watch him, holding my breath, until the sun had all but disappeared behind the jungle's dark face. Aupouk climbed down the ladder. I scurried to my feet, hoping he would remember I was there.

Walking to where I stood, he extended one hand toward me. I just stared at it, unsure what to do. He had never done that before. He flicked the ends of his fingers back, as if he wanted me to grab his hand. I did. As my hand slid into his, I melted into his sweat, and we walked back toward the stilt hut.

I looked up at him, but he didn't look back. My hand being in his was like swaying in my hammock during a rainstorm. It was the feeling of home I had never experienced before. I didn't need his help back because I knew the way, and it was hard matching his long strides, but I didn't want to let go of his hand. I walked faster and tried not to stumble. He slowed his pace.

The words I thought he had said earlier, about sending me away, must have been imagined by my foggy mind. Even if he did say them, he surely didn't mean them anymore. My hand in his made them impossible. The bitter taste of nausea and dread melted like the sunlight.

When we got back to the stilt hut, Pou Kim and Vuthy were already there. Vuthy ran to hug me, and I squeezed and lifted him up, making him laugh.

"Good to see you're feeling better, Rindy!" Pou Kim patted my shoulder as if I might slip through his fingers, his eyes lacking the lightness of his words.

Aupouk placed rainwater and rice over the flame. He plucked a few limes and red chilis. We sat in a squat, our bottoms just off the ground, waiting for the water to boil. Placing the limes on a stone, he cut them up into jagged chunks before tossing them into the bubbling water. Last, he added *prahok*—fermented fish paste. Hunger returned with a full force, and I couldn't wait for it to be ready as Aupouk ladled the rice mixture onto our outstretched banana leaves.

We sat in silence, except for the occasional slurping sound. I looked around at the trees, watching the way they danced at their tops, their limbs alive with the song of gibbons, birds and insects.

"I'll take them to their *Chidaun*, near Phnom Sampov in the morning," Aupouk said the words to his rice.

"How far is it?" Pou looked up, seeming to expect the news.

"30 miles or so, I'll get a ride on an oxen cart or a taxi."

Pou Kim nodded but said nothing more, as he avoided my gaze.

My throat tightened, making it hard to swallow the last of my soup.

"The food was good, Aupouk." I panicked, trying to find some way to get him to not send me away. Standing up quickly, I balanced on the log. I stretched as tall as I could and puffed out my chest, hoping he would notice how much I had grown. Aupouk didn't respond but continued to eat his rice without looking up. I tried not to cry in front of them, so Aupouk would see that I wasn't a baby, but when I crawled onto my mat later that night, I cried myself to sleep.

The next morning, Aupouk woke Vuthy and me. We walked to the road and hitched a ride on a passing ox cart until we reached a bigger village and then rode in a cramped bus. He didn't hold my hand again, but I craved it. I fought back tears and stumbled a few times because they made it hard to see as I climbed onboard. Vuthy had no idea what was happening but was just excited by the bus. At last, I worked up the courage to ask the question burning on my tongue.

"Where are you taking us?"

"I'm taking you to your *Chidaun* and *Chi Ta* — your Mteays' mother and father, your grandparents. She's agreed to keep you and Vuthy," he said at last. I didn't respond because it felt like I had a dirt clod jammed in my throat. "They are wealthy and your Chi Ta owns many rice patties and has many workers. You will eat well. You will likely also see your mother some."

He was silent for what felt like hours, until he said, "I just can't take care of you anymore, Rindy. What happened in the river..." His voice trailed off into silence.

Tears poured down my cheeks in silent streams.

"I will come back for you in a couple of months. I promise I will."

I looked up at him, wiping my eyes. Swallowing hard, I tried to dissolve the dirt lump to make it easier to breathe. I could endure a couple of months if it meant he would come back for me. Why hadn't he told me before?

We walked into the village and toward one of the biggest huts I had ever seen. It had a porch hemmed with a wooden railing. It stood a few feet off the ground, on thick posts, with smooth wooden sides and a red metal roof. Shutters adorned the windows, blocking out the blistering sun, and a small set of stairs led to a closed door. Aupouk hesitated, as if he didn't want to approach.

An old woman came onto the porch and shielded her eyes, beckoning to Vuthy and me. Aupouk waved, his mouth a thin line.

"I have to go back to work now." Aupouk put Vuthy's hand in mine.

"Don't want to stay here," I cried, throwing Vuthy's hand away from mine. Pressure was building inside of me like rushing water.

"I will return for you Rindy." He took my shoulders in his big hands, his eyes large and dark. "I promise."

Tears blurred my vision, and I couldn't see his eyes any longer. I stumbled forward until my head rested on his stomach. The tears ran from my eyes and dripped onto his ragged shirt, which he wore for the occasion as he rarely wore a shirt at all. He stood, slumped over, like an old water buffalo stuck in the mud. I cried harder, unable to stifle the sobs.

"Please, want me. How do I make you want me?" I sobbed into his shirt.

The old woman, who I knew must be my Chidaun, was beside me now, leading Vuthy away by the hand.

"Come, child. Enough of this." A bony hand gripped my arm.

Slowly, Aupouk peeled himself way from me and turned to go. I stumbled to the steps and sat down, I watched him walk away, my body shaking with sobs. I wanted to run after him, but I knew it wouldn't do any good.

Look back. Please look back.

But he never did.

11
EAVESDROPPING

"Somehow, she convinced Mteay." — Rindy

JANUARY 1970

Chidaun and Chi Ta were kind to me, but didn't talk to me much. I counted the days, waiting for Aupouk to return. I looked for him every day with the sunrise and every evening with its setting, but months passed without any word from him. Mteay and Khan—my new stepfather—lived in a different part of the house, but I was no longer her responsibility, so I didn't see them often. Mteay had a new family to take care of. In addition to Kiry and Ly a new baby named Sotha had been added to their family. I had given up on Mteay ever wanting me, but I hadn't given up waiting on Aupouk because of his promise.

Until one day, several months later, the waiting came to an end.

"Have you heard about the man?" Chidaun asked Chi Ta, her tongue clicking. "The man" was the phrase she used to refer to Aupouk, so I stopped playing with the rocks I had collected to listen, peeking through the gap in the wall. Chi Ta shook his head slowly, his eyes transfixed on the sandal he was mending. I glanced at Chidaun, hoping she wouldn't probe the subject further, but confident she would. She always had.

Chidaun was sometimes a harsh woman, bickering with everyone around her like a crow. Chi Ta would sit and watch her, taking slow puffs of his cigarette with squinted eyes. Sometimes he laughed at her in one big "Ha," before resuming his smoke. She would stop jabbering, look up from her hands and the little movements they had been making, whether it was grinding a mortar and pestle or weaving beautiful fabric on her loom. After holding a hard scowl for a few seconds, her face would relax, and a tiny smile would peek out from behind the corners of her mouth. I looked hard to see that smile at other times, and I could never find it. Perhaps it was hiding, just behind the folds of skin.

"It's disgraceful is what it is," she continued, more to herself than to Chi Ta. He didn't respond, so she poked him with her boney finger.

"If you weren't such a worthless ox, you might have intervened in the unnecessary divorce." She kept her voice low so Mteay wouldn't hear, although she was a few rooms away.

"You are the one who arranged the marriage in the first place," he responded, looking up from his hands at last, her words prodding him out of his lethargy.

"That's because he was the best fit for her," she prattled. "At the time." Her straggly hair, snuck out around her face as if it was flustered too. "He used to be a monk and was well educated in Buddhist theology and the ancient Bali and Sanskrit languages, in case you forgot."

"But he was nearly two decades older than her." Chi Ta breathed, his voice sounding as tired as his face looked. Chi Ta spent a lot of time overseeing his workers in the rice paddies and I didn't often see him at home, lately he had been gone almost every day.

I knew happiness was not the important thing to Chidaun, religion was. She was a strict Buddhist and would go to the temple many times a week and put fruits and flowers in the house shrine sitting inside her front door. It stood a few feet off the ground on a pedestal and was shaped like a miniature temple, intricately painted in bright red and yellow colors. A small statue of a chubby Buddha sat nestled between all the gifts, surrounded by smoking incense, the smell of which wafted through the entire house. Chi Ta was not religious, but seemed happy that it took her away from him, to give him peace.

"Well, none of it matters now, old man." Her voice hummed to a subdued lull.

"The news. I almost forgot," she said sharply, sitting up straight again. "The man has gotten married again."

Her words lodged in my ears, sticking there like a lump of wax, just out of reach. They blocked out Chidaun's continued chatter. I sat there, unable to take a deep breath and leaned my head against the wooden slats. I wanted to tell her it wasn't so and that Aupouk was coming back for me because he had promised.

But I knew the promise burned my hands like a rope I needed to release but wanted to hold onto as long as I could. I pictured Aupouk with his new wife, who would soon bear him children. Children he would want. Children to replace the ones he didn't. I glanced at Vuthy, who was rolling rocks into a cup outside on the porch. I wished I could be as young as he was, so the reality of being unwanted would sting less. I sniffed, wiping my nose. I would be what he needed.

When I was the loneliest for my Aupouk after gathering firewood for Chidaun, Vuthy and I would go to the jungle and search for snails in the trees surrounding the mountain. Phnom Sampov was named for the mountain that stood at its heart, with its great boulders, tree-cloaked mountainside and the grand pagoda that sat on the top. It was said that there was a cave in the side of the mountain, but evil spirits lived there, so Vuthy and I avoided the place. I tried to talk to the trees, but they looked so still and fierce that sometimes they scared me, especially when the sun was slipping away for the night. I hummed the song I had heard Mteay sing while she lived at the stilt hut, finding comfort in the familiar sound.

"Do you remember this song, Vuthy?"

He continued to flip over rocks and logs, hunting for snails.

I sang softly, my cheeks pressed against my knees, as I sat on a log and poked around for snails in the mud between my bare feet.

"Little lovebird, where did you go?
Your lovebird is waiting for you beneath the shimmering moon.
Don't fly too far and don't fly too high,
Your lovebird is waiting for you beneath the shimmering moon."

Hearing voices through the trees, I stopped singing to listen. They sounded like Chidaun and Mteay, so we followed them.

We snuck up to a small clearing where the water ran clean and the light was soft. The leaves reflected the sunlight, and the whole jungle was illuminated in its glow. I could see Chidaun and Mteay bent at their waists with their colorful skirts pulled between their legs, washing clothes in the shimmering stream. The scene was peaceful, and I crept closer and closer, careful to stay concealed by the leaves. Their conversation took a turn and piqued my curiosity. I stopped to listen.

"With their father gone, it's time for them to go,' Chidaun said, her voice barely audible over the trickling of the stream. "They need to be disciplined and made into good young men."

Mteay said nothing.

"Your former husband was much too soft on them, and they need a strong hand to guide them." She was undeterred by her daughter's silence. "I thought he would have enrolled the boys in the temple years ago, considering his background and how knowledgeable he became as a monk."

Mteay remained silent, working as if she hadn't heard.

"What a shame. Such a waste." Chidaun looked sideways at Mteay but must have decided against speaking further on the subject.

"Kiry is almost too old, but I will see if they will accept him for a time as he hasn't received an education. But Rindy and Vuthy are just the right age. What is Rindy, about seven and Vuthy five?"

Vuthy poked his head up and opened his mouth to speak, but I pulled him back down next to me. Mteay paused, appearing to ponder our age, before nodding absently.

"An education in Buddhism will be very good for them." Chidaun slapped a blanket against a tree. "They have a Pou—an uncle, your brother—who is a monk in Battambang."

There was a pause, and I could tell Mteay was thinking hard as she scrubbed her blouse. Even from a distance, I could see the deep lines in her forehead. I held my breath, wondering what it meant and wondering if I would be sent away again. I wanted to jump out from my hiding place and tell them I didn't want to go, but it would only reinforce Chidaun's argument that I needed more discipline.

"How long do we need to hide, Rindy?"

"Shh," I hissed, pushing him back down.

"Their father refused to send them to the temple and said he would never permit his sons to go there," Mteay said. She remained bent, her elbows on her knees and the blouse dripping from her hands as if she were searching the water for answers. "It never made sense to me given his religious background, but he never talked about his time while at the temple. Come to think of it, Khan doesn't talk of it either. They both were at the same temple as boys."

"There aren't any other good options for them to acquire a good Buddhist education," Chidaun huffed impatiently. "It's tradition that they go."

"I'm not sure I can spare Kiry though; his income will be missed."

"He'll bring far more money with a little education than he would otherwise," Chidaun reasoned. "It will bring good karma to you, if you make this sacrifice. You need much good karma, daughter, after—" Chidaun let her words go unsaid.

I knew she wanted to say because of Mteay's divorce, but didn't.

A faint cry sounded from the leaves. It must be Sotha, Mteay's newborn baby who had awoken from wherever she had been nestled to nap.

Mteay stood erect and waded toward the crying infant, all indecision erased from her features. "Kiry can go for a brief time. Do whatever you want with Rindy and Vuthy. Their father left them with you. They are yours to do with what you will."

"It's settled then," Chidaun chirped. "I'll take them to Battambang the beginning of next week—just in time for them to begin the new school year."

12

THE TEMPLE

"Living in the temple influenced my life a lot." — Rindy

JANUARY 1970

It was a long way to Battambang. My backside hurt from bumping up and down on the seat, so I sat on my knees to buffer the blows. We rode in a *tuk-tuk*, a motorized bike trailed by a passenger carriage. The driver sped along the rough and uneven road in a hurry to end his errand. Kiry glowered at the world, slumped low in his seat. Vuthy sat on the bench opposite me, smiling at the passersby's, and I sat beside Chidaun. I glanced up at her and she looked down at me. Little smile lines cracked the corners around her eyes. I smiled. I had grown to love her and my Chi Te. When Aupouk left Vuthy and me at their home, they had taken us in when no one else wanted us, feeding us and keeping us safe. Clutching the side of the cart, I tried to sit tall. Despite Chidaun's sometimes rough exterior, I would miss her. I would especially miss Chi Te's kind eyes and playful manner.

At last, the tuk-tuk jostled to a halt. I jumped down from the cart after Chidaun, but my legs felt like they were immersed in a sack of rice. I steadied myself against the side of the cart until feeling returned to them. I was glad we had arrived because I needed to use the bathroom.

"Come, Rindy," Chidaun called. She and my brothers had already begun walking down the road, her bow-legged stride showing through her skirt.

"Arkoun," I called my thanks over my shoulder to the tuk-tuk driver who had stopped in the shade of a tree to nap.

A tall cement wall with elaborate gold flower engravings ran along the road beside me. I ran my fingertips over its bumpy surface. The wall seemed endless in both directions. Craning my neck to the sky, I tried to see what was on the other side. A red rooftop, adorned with golden, fire-like spikes, rose into view.

"Rindy," Chidaun called again, and I started running after them.

I caught up at the temple's entrance, cut from the wall. Together, we stepped into a courtyard filled with trees and pagodas of various sizes. At the center was the most impressive building I had ever seen. Its cream-colored walls were trimmed in green, red and gold, surrounded by a low blue wall. It stood in layers with a triangle piece at the top, which seemed too heavy for the rest of the structure. Pillars surrounded it and glinted in the sunlight and looked as if they had been splashed with melting gold. Leering creatures attached to the tops of the pillars kept watch around its perimeter. Two lions guarded the front steps, their manes curled in gold and their mouths laughing in red.

"That's the great Samrong Knong temple," Chidaun exclaimed, her voice leaking out between her scanty teeth.

My hands trembled, but I tried to stop them, so my fear didn't show. Men wearing mustard yellow, blood red and orange robes walked about, their shadows trailing them in submission. They had shaved heads and serious faces. I wondered if they had forgotten how to smile. Not wanting to anger them, I didn't stare long. My eyes searched everything around me, trying to take it in. Several other buildings were scattered around the temple, smaller, less extravagant versions of the big building. I wondered where I could relieve myself.

A man wearing a yellow robe strode toward us, his face showing no emotion and his shoulders perfectly erect. Chidaun's rickety bones creaked with excitement as the monk approached us. She waved a hand, and her wrinkled face tightened into a smile. She pushed her opened hands together at her chest and bowed her head low, making her shrunken frame shrink even further. The monk's face didn't change. With a flick of his long, slender fingers he indicated for us to follow him.

"That's your Pou Ponlok—your mothers' brother," Chidaun whispered, pushing us up behind him. I walked on his shadow, trying not to step on the edge of his dirt-hemmed robe. He led us up a small set of steps at the side of the temple and onto the main floor. The stone was oddly cool on my feet. Opening a small, red door, splashed in golden curls and figures, Pou Ponlok led us into the temple.

As my eyes adjusted to the dim light, I could make out gold shimmering ahead of us, peeking through layers of darkness. As we approached, I realized it was a life-size version of the golden man Chidaun kept in her shrine. He was sitting cross-legged atop a golden box. Smaller images sat around his base, with the same strange, pointed hat and huge sagging ears. Their eyes were black circles and their lips, which seemed too large for their faces, were bright red.

Upon approaching the figurines, Pou Ponlok knelt to the ground and began to bow in low and exaggerated movements. His hands were clasped to his forehead and the heels of his bare feet poked out of his robe, behind him. Chidaun grabbed me by the arm and pulled me down with her, indicating for Kiry and Vuthy to do the same.

"*Araham samma-sambuddho bhagava Buddham bhagavantam abhivademi,*" Pou Ponlok murmured, his voice rising and falling eerily. My mind replayed his words, only understanding bits and pieces: "The noble one, the fully enlightened one, the exalted one, I bow low before the exalted Buddha."

The words were mournful and sad, full of shadows and snuffed out candles. They filled my head, crowding out the sound of the birds singing in the fruit trees outside. Looking up briefly, I stole a glance at the golden man's face, before dropping my eyes quickly to the stone. Even with my eyes closed, those gaping eyes stared at me through the blackness of my eyelids. I glanced at the walls to the right and left, but everywhere I looked, the man was there, staring back. His lips were curved, not in a friendly smile or even a scowl, but in something else entirely. It was like he was laughing at me in a deep, rumbling way, like faraway thunder ever coming closer. It didn't make me want to laugh too, but to shrink in terror. Vuthy looked at me, his eyes wide and black, his cheek nearly touching the cold, stone floor. I grabbed his hand and squeezed.

At last, Pou Ponlok's voice ceased, and he pushed himself to his feet. I reveled in the silence for a moment, but I could still hear his chant, whispering to me from the shadows. Pou Ponlok led us to the door and pulled it open, letting a flood of sunlight in. I lunged for it to escape the temple, but Chidaun grabbed my arm tightly, pulling me back in line with Vuthy and Kiry. Kiry looked indignant, his brow furrowed and his eyes piercing, but Vuthy looked almost too petrified to move.

"He's a good boy, and I'm sure he will serve you well." Chidaun smiled at Pou Ponlok while gripping my arm. We followed him down the stone steps.

"We discipline all the temple boys for any sign of disrespect," Pou warned, his voice dry and emotionless. His feet appeared to be floating on air as he descended the steps. He didn't turn his head to look at me, but I could feel his eyes.

"I'm sure you do an excellent job at guiding the unruly youth." Chidaun glared at me. She looked each of us over with glimmering eyes. "You will learn to be good, Buddhist Cambodians here. Make your family proud."

Kiry wore the same expression of indignation, but Vuthy's eyes welled with tears. She turned back to Pou Ponlok.

"*Joom reab lea.*" She bowed her goodbye. We watched in silent dread as she hurried across the courtyard, her errand completed. My throat twisted into a knot as I watched her leave. The shadow of the temple spilled out over the ground, as if to eat us where we stood. I could feel Pou Ponlok standing behind me, his eyes boring into the back of my skull.

"You each have an assigned age group," Pou Ponlok began, as two other monks appeared at each elbow.

"How old are you?" Pou asked, standing in front of Kiry.

"Ten," he answered before Pou got the question fully out, standing as tall as he could.

He took a step forward to stand in front of me. He glowered down from his enormous height, expecting me to answer, but not asking a question.

"Six." My voice squeaked.

"You?" he asked loudly, peering at Vuthy who was hiding behind me. He hid further.

"He's four," I answered, finding my voice quickly.

"I want to stay with Rindy," Vuthy pleaded. I put my arm around him.

"That's not possible." Pou Ponlok yanked me away from him. "You must go with the other boys who are your age. It's the rule."

"It'll be all right," I whispered into Vuthy's ear, but I couldn't swallow the tremor in my own voice. Vuthy cried harder, but one of the monks grabbed him and led him toward one of the smaller buildings. The other led Kiry. Each monk cast a long shadow and pulled along their trailing robe.

"Come." Pou Ponlok flicked his long fingers.

"Um, I need to use the—bathroom," I stuttered. But he made no indication of hearing me, so I held my tongue.

I followed him toward one of the larger, rectangular buildings, propped up by peeling pillars. Unlike the temple, this building sat level with the ground, its exterior cracked in a smeared hue of yellowed paint, with faded and chipped blue doors. Creaking one of the doors open, Pou Ponlok led the way inside. A wave of self-consciousness enveloped me as I came face to face with a few dozen boys, lined in rows, staring with unblinking eyes and sullen expressions. Their unflinching faces frightened me, and I hid behind Pou a little. He grabbed my arm and jerked me into the line, pulling me so hard that my leg smashed into the knee-high tables stretched across the brick floor. Every eye turned to me. Heat rose to my face from somewhere near my belly button. I studied my toes, my eyes locked on their dirt-rimmed nails.

An orange-cloaked monk entered and began another droning prayer. The room erupted in a chorus of murmurs, as they recited words I didn't fully understand. The sound throbbed in the air. I closed my eyes and envisioned a swarm of bees swelling in the sky as they buzzed near then retreated, always humming relentlessly. The boy standing to my right, nudged me to start chanting. I didn't know the words, but I pretended I did. My mouth moved, without any sound escaping. The few words I knew tasted bad and stung my tongue. I spit them out into the air, mixing with the smell of rotten breath exhaling all around me.

As suddenly as it began, the hum ceased. In a sullen line, we inched toward the door, shuffling our bare feet. We walked in silence toward another rectangular building, similar in appearance, but with peeling, blue shutters closed against the setting sun. The room was filled with thin mats, scattered all over the cool floor. The door shut behind us, concealing the last of the dying sun.

Sitting down, I glanced at the boy who had nudged me earlier, but he appeared to be already asleep. This type of darkness felt different than the darkness of the jungle. It wasn't a friendly darkness. It was cold and damp and made no sound or movement. Somehow, a tiger felt less scary than this place. I tried to sleep, but the darkness crept up around me as if to smother me. I rustled on my mat, to make it retreat. It seemed to feast on quietness and fear. I closed my eyes to escape it, but it was just as black. I needed to urinate so badly, my eyes watered. I stood up groping through the darkness for the door, walking in the direction I assumed it was.

"Ouch," a voice yelled as I felt an arm beneath my foot.

"*Somtos*," I apologized. "I'm trying to find the door...I...I need to go pee."

He rustled to his feet before he grabbed my arm and thrust me to the corner of the room. Stumbling, I collided into something that splashed onto my feet. It was warm, and the stench was strong. I grimaced and added to the overflowing pail, trying to hold my breath. I crept back, shaking the liquid off my foot while avoiding stepping on anyone else.

"I'm sorry you're a temple boy," whispered a voice next to me, coming from the boy I thought was already asleep.

"Shhh," a chorus of boyish voices sounded.

I wanted to tell him I wasn't a temple boy, but I said nothing.

I was Rindy from the jungle, and this place was not my home.

13

TEMPLE BOY

"People in America have a wrong idea about Buddhism."
— Rindy

THE NEXT DAY

Jerking awake, I looked into the eyes of the boy who lay next to me, blinking curiosity written across his features. He looked away when we made eye contact and pretended he hadn't been staring, but I knew better.

"Where is my little brother, Vuthy, kept?"

"How old is he?"

"Four." I swallowed.

"He's kept in the next building. They don't want siblings to be together."

I had to find him somehow—check on how he was.

"Maybe you can see him at school."

"They let us go to school?"

"Yeah, they have to, or else parents wouldn't want to send us here. The monks don't teach mathematics and stuff."

"What's going to happen today? Will we go to school?"

"School starts in a few days." He picked at a scab on his arm. "Hopefully, we eat."

Hunger rattled in my stomach.

"Then we clean the temple, run errands for the monks, prostrate and say chants."

"Do you have a jungle close by?"

"No, no." The boy looked nervous. "You just do the things they tell you, got it? You can't go exploring."

I nodded but didn't understand.

"Hey, do you come from a family with money?"

I shrugged.

"You just do everything they tell you."

"Up." An orange robed monk called inside the stuffy room. Then he walked away. The sleepy little room erupted at the single word into a frenzy of bare arms, disheveled hair and the stench of morning breath.

"My name's Sov."

"Rindy."

I followed the crowd toward the temple and the golden man. With a sinking stomach, I realized I would have to face him every day. Like the other boys, I bowed down on the cold floor. With our thumbs bent in and our fingertips touching, we prostrated and chanted the melodic prayer. I understood little of what I was saying, but I followed along the best I could. I stared at the long crack in the floor, only daring to look at the enormous face once before my eyes darted back down.

"Do you like him?" I asked a boy next to me as we rose to our feet to file outside again. He looked startled, and shook his head, putting his fingers to his lips. I swallowed my other questions. As we descended the stairs, a single, silent row of monks stared back at us from the bottom. Each one wore a large pot attached with a strap to make the pot easier to tote. I laughed into my hands because they looked like a row of pregnant women with their pots held tightly at their cloaked stomachs. An older boy caught my eye and shook his head hard, his eyes sharp and stern.

I stopped smiling but too late.

"You," a voice called. "Come." I looked through the crowd and saw Pou Ponlok staring at me, with eyes like fire.

I wove my way through the silent boys on the stairs, the laughter dissolving in my throat. As the others stepped aside, I read fear on their faces. My bare feet landed in the dirt, and I stood before Pou Ponlok.

"Your brother ran away last night."

It must be Kiry. Vuthy was too young to figure out a way to escape.

"Since he disdained tradition and authority, you will take his punishment."

My pulse quickened and I licked my lips, unsure what that meant.

"*Aon Choh*— bow down," he barked into my face, his body rigid. "Aon Choh!" Redness crept up his skinny neck.

Cupping my hands, I touched my palms to my forehead, over my mouth and to my chest in a respectful bow. Another monk handed Pou Ponlok a long, black whip. I had seen farmers use these on oxen and water buffalo.

My eyes found their way to the dirt, my heart thudding, and my mind fuzzy with confusion.

"Aon Choh," he yelled, his body riveting in agitation. I got on my knees and lowered my nose to the ground, my buttocks in the air, trying another prostration I had seen performed. I felt a sharp sting on my back, and my head spun in disbelief and pain, but the dreaded command sounded again.

"Aon Choh!"

I gathered my thoughts to try again, hoping the first blow was just a cruel joke and the onlookers were on the verge of bursting into laughter. Glancing up into the horizon of faces, I saw them all staring back at me, but there was no laughter in their eyes. I quickly reverted to a different position to try again. Putting my legs out straight and my toes curled inward. I lowered my head to the dirt with my hands overhead as I had seen a monk in Chidaun's village bow.

The whip licked at my side, slicing through my flesh. It hurt worse than the first. My face smashed into the dirt as I sputtered in tears and confusion.

"Aon Choh!"

I got back on my knees to try a new position, a different way to bow. I looked to the other boys for a hint, any clue how to take part in the monk's mind game, but their faces only read sympathy. I prostrated myself again, my arms starting above my head and lowering to my nose, before dropping all the way to the dirt. In the shadow on the ground, I saw Pou's arm rise into the air.

Another lash struck right between my shoulder blades. Unable to resist, I glanced into Pou's face questioningly, my eyes straining into the glaring sun.

"Aon Choh," he thundered again, answering my pleading glance with another blow. I prostrated in quick repetitions, hoping it was speed he wanted.

I felt another strike hitting my lower back.

"AON! AON! AON!" The commands continued, and so did the lashings. Tears veiled my eyes, and I quivered beneath the whip. The sunshine searched my open flesh, and the boys eyes burned holes into my bleeding back. The whipping continued.

In desperation, I collapsed, sobbing. My face planted into the salty puddle I had made in the dirt. My bladder released, soaking my brown shorts. The pain in my back throbbed, but the confusion was worse. No matter what position of prostration I tried, they all were fruitless.

Pou Ponlok administered one last blow. Then he was done. I winced in relief as I lay with my hand on my arm, to muffle my crying.

"Get up."

I pushed myself from the ground and to my knees, head lowered, my body trembling from pent up sobs. I didn't want to look at him or anyone else.

"If you attempt to escape, your little brother will get double what you just did."

The words slammed like a slap against my ears. Vuthy was still here, and I couldn't let this happen to him. No matter how bad life got.

"Fall into lines."

My knees were weak and my back felt as if a million blades of grass had serrated my skin. How much blood was there? Without hesitation, he walked between the row of the colored robes to my left and the bare feet to my right. Hot adrenaline pounded through my veins, and I staggered after him. I willed myself forward, hoping he wouldn't turn around to administer another blow. Chanting, he paraded out of the temple courtyard and onto the street. I didn't even try to understand his words because my head swarmed with confusion.

The street was alive with people as the monks walked with their pots in a parade of color. Chanting filled the air, enveloping all other sounds in a rhythmic drone. The usual bustle of the village subsided as the street cleared a path for the monks and their boys, lining up with their gifts on either side. A row of women squatted, holding bags and pots of food to their wrinkled foreheads. As we walked past, they dropped their offerings into the pots, bowing their heads in respect, keeping their eyes on the ground.

We paraded through the street and Pou Ponlok's pot was filled to the brim with food offerings. The villagers began handing me their offerings to carry. The pain in my back gave way to disbelief. The spell of the monks held the whole village captive. I witnessed the great extent of their power and how incapable I was in its destructive wake. Fear, like a python, tightened around my neck.

The smell of freshly baked bread rose to my nose, agitating my hungry stomach. Nausea from the beating had temporarily chased the hunger away, but smelling the bread brought it back with a vengeance. My arms were bursting with food and my back hurt as salty sweat slithered into my open wounds. Stumbling, I wondered if we would ever return to the temple courtyard.

"Don't drag your feet." Pou Ponlok's black pupils jutted to the corners of his eyes as he cast me a disapproving look over his draped shoulder. It didn't help to ease the quivering in my legs.

At last, the trail of somber, chanting monks retreated to the temple, towing a string of food-laden boys behind them. I gripped the various items that weighed me down, afraid I might drop one of them. The pain in my back ached, but I could only focus on one thing at a time. I held mangoes, lychees, a bag of noodles, and a bowl of rice porridge. It was a feast by anyone's standards. Will I get to taste any of it? Saliva danced on my lips, but I tried to swallow it back down. I hadn't eaten since the day before, and I didn't know if I could take the gnawing of my stomach much longer.

We followed the monks back into the temple's domain and into the building filled with low tables. The tables sat just far enough off the ground to sit beneath them cross-legged. I gave up my burden, setting it on the floor at Pou's feet, before filing out of the room with the other boys. Huddling outside beside the pillars, we listened as they ate. I looked around, my eyes begging for answers.

"It's the rule," one boy said, leaning against the wall, his foot propped up. "It's disrespectful to eat with them."

"Or before them," another boy added.

"You better get used to being hungry." The first scoffed at my inexperience.

I sat down, the pain in my back consuming my thoughts. I was careful not to lean against the stone. I wanted to cry, but I didn't want the other boys to see, so I sat with my head lowered between my legs, trying to stare my stomach into silence.

"How many times do we eat in a day?" I dared another question as Sov made his way over to me.

"They eat twice a day." He sat down next to me. "So, we eat twice a day. Once after sunrise and sometimes right before noon, but they will not eat later than that."

He peeked at my back.

"Why did he hit me?" I grimaced at his touch.

"They do it to all of us." His answer wasn't lacking sympathy—he was just telling the truth. "The punishment just depends on what you did or what they think you did."

"Yours really wasn't that bad." He shrugged.

"I don't know how to prostrate how they want!" My voice squeaked.

"They don't tell any of us how to prostrate. It's like a game of mind reading. There are over a dozen ways to prostrate according to their tradition, and they never say which one they require. They don't hit you as much if you have a rich family member who pays them. You get more food that way too."

"Shut up," the others hissed as the door creaked open.

The monks exited the dining hall in a long, solitary line, their hands resting on their stomachs beneath their robes. They walked out of sight down the long corridor. The boys rushed through the doorway to pounce on whatever food remained. Being one of the smallest, I was lost in the chaos of groping hands and mouths. The older boys swept through the hall, shoving their mouths full, leaving almost nothing behind. I searched the room, peeking into every black pot, but there was nothing left. I panicked, afraid another day would pass without a bite of food. Seeing a half-eaten baguette on the floor, I grabbed it and stuffed it into my mouth. It was dry and hard, nearly impossible to chew, but I made myself savor each bite. Seeing a bucket of water in the corner, I ladled a cup into my mouth to chase down the scratch of the bread. The room lulled into silence. Not a silence of satisfaction or full stomachs, but a silence of acceptance. We checked each pot one more time before exiting the hall, my stomach clamoring for more.

"Now we get our work assignment," Sov whispered close to my ear as we entered the next hallway. The walls dripped with dismal chants and chipped paint. We stood with our backs against the wall. A monk went down the line, assigning each boy a job. Mine for the day was to scrub the mosaic floor in the dining room with a brush and a bucket of soapy water.

As I lowered myself to my knees, the cuts in my back separated, making me freeze in pain. Flies crawled all over me, sampling on my torn flesh. Swatting them only hurt worse, so I gave up trying. In desperation, I lifted the brush and let the murky water trickle over my back to dull the pain. It helped little.

The corridor was big and dark and scrubbing took me most of the day, since I couldn't scrub quickly. With no one around to see, I cried into the murky water. I cried because of the pain on my back and because I hated scrubbing the floor. I cried because any doubt about who I was had dissolved into the soapy water, strewn in puddles across the colorful floor. I was now a temple boy.

14

WATER BOY

"That is all I could afford." — Rindy

JANUARY-JUNE 1969

If we woke up early before school started, we were permitted to use that time to try making some money, before we'd accompany the monks to collect food and perform our other duties. I was hungry most days from the meager scraps, but not all the monks were like my Pou Ponlok. Some hid food for me and the other smaller boys. Yet my hunger egged me on to be able to buy food for myself and Vuthy, if I could sneak him some. There were many jobs a temple boy could get, like collecting firewood, digging snails, fishing or picking through other people's garbage to find items to sell. Sov and I decided to sell water because we heard it brought the most money. I had seen a few of the other temple boys toting water from the river, which flowed through the heart of Battambang.

We found a broken, two wheeled cart in a trash heap, which we repaired with some wire and rope. We then got two empty yellow jugs from a noodle shop, which had once held oil. I tied one end of the rope to the loop of one of the jugs. I filled it by tossing it into the river and dragging it out by the other end of the rope. I repeated this until both jugs were filled to the top.

Each held a few gallons of water and to make transporting them easier, I loaded them onto the cart. One of the wheels was cracked and wobbled, but it held the two plastic jugs of water perfectly. Sov and I took turns pulling the cart behind us as the other held it together, until I reached the outskirts of Battambang. At first, we stopped at every home, but soon we discovered there was much more demand several miles from the river. I'd sell to noodle shops, to women who did laundry and to the elderly who couldn't carry the jugs for themselves.

"I've got water," I called breathlessly as I approached a hut. Rapping my knuckles on her door, I hoped my effort wouldn't return empty. The monks would be beginning their rounds for alms soon. An old woman emerged, her eyes cloudy. She held her container out and felt around for the water. She reminded me of the old woman who had helped me when Vuthy and I had been abandoned.

"Here, let me."

I set her canister on the ground and carefully poured the last of my jug into it.

"Arkoun, boy," she said, staring, but not seeing. She pulled two rumpled *riel* out of her pocket and extended them in my direction, but another four riel fluttered to the ground as well. I could barely make out the image of a temple framed in faint blue scrolls, but I knew for sure what it was. I hesitated. Should I steal it or give it back? I looked down. My pants were so worn that I was afraid even the wisps of paper might be too heavy for the pockets. My knees too had eaten through the fabric, creating two large holes. I had worn the pair for months and the elastic was so stretched out around my waist that if I wasn't careful, I would lose them around my ankles. I would need something else to wear soon. In an instant, I bent down and snatched the riel from the ground and walked away. I handed Sov his share, but stuffed the stolen ones into my pocket.

"She must have been very bad in her past life to be blind in this one. That's even worse than being a snail or a frog." Sov nodded toward the old lady. "Seems kind of sad, doesn't it?" She was already boiling the water over the little fire in front of her house. Her hands moved cautiously over the flame. I swallowed, wanting to change the subject, fingering the riel in my pocket.

"Should we make another trip?"

Sov didn't reply. He was already headed for the noodle stand.

"Sov, should we make another trip?"

"No, I'm sure the other boys have finished selling their water for the day. Probably would be a waste of time." He received his bag and began eating hungrily.

My stomach curled at the thought of food, but I continued past the tantalizing aroma of lemongrass and coconut milk.

"Ok, I'll catch up with you later."

"Don't be late for going into the village with the monks," Sov called, around a mouthful. "Or you'll catch the whip."

I deposited our cart in an overgrown bush to hide them for tomorrow's deliveries and continued into Battambang. I tried to convince my stomach that it was a sacrifice it must make for the present. For the previous few days, I had given into the temptation of the noodle shop, spending every riel I had on a steaming bag of noodles, which I had slurped down before even reaching the road again. My mouth watered and the rage of my stomach was relentless, but I continued down the street, bustling with ladies bartering and old men calling out their best prices of the day. The shopkeepers eyed me like a thief, so I was careful to walk in the middle of the road, only searching the merchandise with my eyes. Seeing a pair of pants that looked to be about my size, I approached the shop.

"30 riel." The shopkeeper came and stood beside the pants. I traced the fine seam of the deep, blue fabric.

"And no less." His glare narrowed.

I had an urge to reach into my pocket to count the riel one more time, in hopes that perhaps another had sprouted, but I didn't. I knew it hadn't. I had the pathetic sum of eight riel, even with those I had stolen from the blind woman. The price the shopkeeper demanded was outrageous, but he held true to his word and wouldn't budge despite my efforts to barter. Perhaps he didn't want beggar boys wearing his goods or perhaps they were an extra fine pair. Regardless of the reason, I was forced to continue my search at the next shop, then the next, then the next. By the time I had exhausted every shop selling clothes, I was desperate. The closest I had come was twenty riel. Not enough. I continued back toward the temple. It was growing late. Rolling over the elastic of my pants one more time, I hoped they would hold up for the walk back. My stomach grumbled again. My mind wandered over the desperation of the state of my pants.

Then I got an idea.

Hurrying back toward the temple, I skirted the entrance and followed the perimeter of the fence to where the garbage was dumped. There wasn't much food in the scattered piles, as the temple boys had taken care of that, but there were piles of excrement. I walked warily, being careful to steer clear of the areas swarming with flies. The stench was stale and smarting, hanging in the air with a putrid haze. I would have vomited, but my stomach had nothing to offer, so I kept my arm over my nose and continued my search. Desperation sank further into the pit of my hungry stomach. Then a yellow bundle caught my eye. I pounced on it, untangling it from a smashed wooden crate. Pulling it into full view, a trailing robe paraded across the rubbish in a mock show of extravagance. It had a charred hem and a big hole in the middle, but other than that, it was perfectly intact. I scooped up my prize and toted it proudly, surprised that my unlikely plan had paid off. I began to make quick work of the robe, cutting it down to my size. I draped one end over my shoulder and tied the other end around my waist. The knot bulged. I had tied it a little too tightly, but I wore it proudly, knowing I had clothes and still had riel to buy food with.

I walked back toward the market, this time holding my riel. I purchased a bag of noodles, being careful to make them last longer than I had the day before. I had barely begun my walk back to the temple, with a few slurps of noodles left, when I began to feel a stinging and itching sensation around my waist. Loosening the knot a little, I continued walking, but the itching continued to worsen. The itching became so intense that it overpowered my preoccupation with my last bite of noodles. The other boys were lining up to walk with the monks to the village to take alms, so I hid in the back and peaked beneath my clothes. Hot, red, itchy bumps covered the middle section of my body and crawled between my legs. Dropping my cloak back in place, I fell into line and grabbed a pot to collect alms for the monks. I tried not to itch.

"Where'd you find the robe?" Sov surveyed me. "You look like a little monk boy."

"I found it in the trash behind the temple." I scratched my leg, gritting my teeth.

"What's wrong?" He laughed.

"It's made my skin become hot and covered in itchy bumps." I scratched again, shifting the pot to one arm. "Maybe something got spilled on it that my skin doesn't like. I'll buy some soap and take it to the river and scrub it."

"I think you have bad merit."

"What's merit?" I was afraid I'd itch myself raw, but I couldn't get naked on the busy road following the somber procession of monks. The whipping I'd get from that would be horrible.

"You know—that thing the monks keep talking about?"

I shrugged, itching my stomach.

"It's the good force you build up over time with the good things you do, the good thoughts and by making sacrifices. But you get bad merit from doing bad things—getting bad karma. Did you do anything bad?"

I squirmed.

"Stealing the water cart?"

Sov shook his head. "That was in a trash pile. That was good karma for us."

I didn't have to think farther. I knew. The money I'd stolen from the old, blind lady was bad karma.

"You'll have to try to earn lots of good karma to gain good merit again." Sov shrugged, holding his pot out to receive the first offering.

15
SCHOOL

"I still have a scar." — Rindy

JANUARY-JUNE 1969

"How far is it?" I looked at Sov, enjoying the way the warm dirt padded under my feet. Birds sang from the trees. The early sun cast long, palm-tree shadows across my path. It reminded me of my home near the jungle.

"Not far, about two miles."

"Can you earn good karma from trying hard in school?"

"Yep, that's probably a part of *Bhavana*—developing your mind." Sov plunked on my forehead. "The monks say *Bhavana* is a good way to earn karma, but the best way is through meditation and chanting."

My shoulders relaxed. I'd work hard in school then.

I looked down the snaking path, filled with temple boys, and I felt my confidence swell. I had always been curious about school. We approached a cement building that looked like it had grown out of the ground, being eaten by vines and branches. It was a faded yellow, with peeling blue trim. The Cambodian flag was tacked over the door and dozens of kids congregated nearby, some already playing a game of soccer beneath the sprawling trees.

"Rindy!" I spun around, seeing Vuthy running down the path toward me. We collided, and I hugged him tightly.

"Are you okay? Are they treating you all right?"

"I hate the temple, Rindy. It's dark and full of ghosts and the monks are mean." His dark eyes widened. "When can we go home?"

"We can't go home Vuthy." I took his shoulders, making him look at me instead of the soccer game taking place behind us. "Do you understand me? We must stay at the temple until Chidaun comes and gets us. If we do escape and make it back to Phnom Sampov, she'll just bring us back here. It would be very bad merit for her if she didn't."

Vuthy nodded, but a tear slid down his cheek.

A bell began to clang from the schoolhouse, and we all flooded inside.

Over the next semester, school became my escape from the temple. Each day I tried to learn one more character, but there were thirty-three in all, making it a difficult task. Vuthy was with the young kids. I was in first grade, but I was the smallest in the class and seemed far behind everyone else. The teachers didn't call on me often, for which I was thankful, because I dreaded the idea of not being able to read what they had written on the smudged green board tacked to the back wall. I wanted to be ready when I was called on. Sometimes I stayed in from the soccer game to practice. I practiced writing my characters on a single page, then erased it so I could start again. My paper soon became so worn and full of holes that I could lift it to the sky and see sunlight through it.

"You're wearing out your paper." I looked up to find my teacher, Mr. Thach standing beside my desk.

I nodded, looking up at him, wondering if I would be punished. His eyes were kind, and he smiled. I smiled back and I curled my stiff toes from under the bench.

"Here." He retrieved a small writing pad from behind his back.

"Akroun, Mr. Thach," I stuttered my surprised thanks. As I ran my fingers over its smooth cover, I could tell it hadn't seen many other hands. I opened the cover. It had lines and everything.

"I—I don't have any money for it," I stammered, handing it back to him.

He shook his head quickly. "I'm glad to see you working so hard on your characters. I see you making great progress."

I kept my head bowed, but his kindness was difficult to swallow, and it stuck in my throat like the piece of hard candy that I had picked off the street one day.

"You better go outside now. They've already started the soccer game without you."

I only nodded and smiled, not knowing what to say. Taking the gift, I shuffled out of the schoolroom.

I rarely played soccer with the other boys, as I was usually the last boy to be picked for any team because I was small. But I didn't mind. As I walked outside under the shade of the sprawling trees, my eyes devouring my new writing pad, I was surprised to hear a voice calling my name.

"Hey, Rindy. Want to join?"

I shielded my face from the sun and tried to see who had called to me and was surprised to find one of the older boys, his hair wild and drenched in sweat, staring in my direction.

"Sure," I squeaked, trying to ignore the sudden dryness in my mouth. I had never been good at soccer or any sport really, but I knew I would be foolish to pass up the rare opportunity of being accepted into the older boys' game. Every head wagged in my direction as they waited for me to cross the small, dirt field. I could feel sweat sticking to the hairs around my neck. I wanted to run and hide, to pour over my characters, but my six-year-old pride wouldn't let me, so I walked toward the boys. Vuthy clapped his hands from where he sat on the tree roots.

"Go, Rindy." He beamed at me.

"Come over here, by me," one of the biggest boys shouted, and I picked up my pace, breaking into a jog.

The game started in a frenzy of bare feet and a cloud of dust. The boys shouted and shoved, their bodies contorting with their quick reflexes. I had enjoyed watching, but it was even better to be right there in the middle, in the dance of the game, tasting the dust and feeling the adrenaline. I caught glimpses of the uneven silhouette of the ball lumbering between their feet as a seam in the leather had long come undone. It cut through the air like a jagged knife. I tried to keep my eye on it, but it was going fast.

Feeling a jab on my shoulder, I rocketed face first into the finely sifted dirt. Through the dust stinging my eyes, I could see the boys draw away from me. It was rhythmic; it was too deliberate, but I couldn't get up fast enough. A foot launched the ball, catapulting it toward my face. I braced for the shock, my eyes pinching closed, my hands hugging the back of my head, but it was too late. It hit me, hard and true. All went black.

I awoke to someone shaking my shoulder and calling my name. I blinked my eyes, trying to chase away the white dots that filled them. Mr. Thach bent, looking into my face. My back was leaning against the schoolhouse wall. I searched my face with shaking fingers, trying to locate my numb features. The grime tasted metalic on my teeth, but the point of my nose and the indentation of my eyes felt normal. But something strange and hot oozed around my left eyebrow, and a wet thickness licked at my fingers when I touched it. Tracing its path, I felt a gash across my forehead, my flesh split and open. My head felt strangely weightless, yet surprisingly large.

"You ok, Rindy? You got cut." Vuthy crouched beside me too, his hand on my shoulder. Sov stood bent over with his hands on his knee as he inspected me.

The bigger boy, who had invited me to play, stood just past them. His face was smeared with the grime of satisfaction and triumph, but there was also a crack in his expression, which looked a little like regret. I wondered which would win the tug-of-war inside him. If I had been bigger, I would have punched him in the nose to help him decide.

"Bad karma will get you for this," I called out. "I bet you'll be born with a missing leg in the next life."

The bigger boys laughed but turned aside.

Mr. Thach brought something in a little bottle.

"This may sting a little." He poured dark liquid over my forehead and mopped up the excess with a rag, then cut a piece of white tape and cloth and stuck it over the wound. "I don't think you'll need stitches."

I rubbed my forehead and smiled up at him.

"I know it's hard when the bigger boys pick on you, but don't hate them, Rindy. Don't allow *kum* to grow in your heart."

"What is kum?"

"It's like a sickness that gets into your heart. As it grows, it takes over a person with plans to destroy the person who caused them pain. Revenge. Hatred. Bitterness. Kum hurts you worse though. It'll eat away at you until you become sick with it. It's a sickness that runs rampant through the streets of Cambodia, like it's a part of her soul—" Mr. Thach's voice trailed off, as if he were no longer thinking about the boys who had kicked the ball at my face. Shaking his head, he looked me in the eyes again.

"Want to know how to get rid of kum?"

I nodded.

"Loving even when you don't want to. It's like this iodine; it washes away the yuck so you don't get sick."

I nodded, but not fully understanding.

"We'd better get back inside and to our studies."

With unsteady legs, I retrieved my new writing pad from beneath the tree before the bigger boys could steal it.

A few weeks later, I pulled my cart behind me on the way to sell water to the noodle shops. Both jugs were filled to the brim, and I struggled against the weight, pausing to take a break. Sov was already up ahead, trying to gain customers for the day.

"Hi."

I looked up. A boy walked toward me, leaving a small group of boys in their early teens, who were congregated near the noodle shop I was hoping to sell water to. I recognized them from school but hadn't ever talked to them before. They usually studied or talked to Mr. Thach while the rest of us played soccer. Distrust twisted in my stomach, my fingers going to the scar on my forehead.

"Your name is Rindy, isn't it?"

I nodded.

"Yeah, I remember you from school. Mr. Thach told a group of us who meet with him on Sundays that we should pray for you and your heart."

Pray for me? Mr. Thach?

"He often prays for all his students."

I was puzzled.

"Except he doesn't pray to Buddha." The boy leaned closer. His brown eyes grew wide. "He prays to a God—named Jesus. He's told us all about him."

What did this mean? I had only heard of Buddha and the way to enlightenment, and I didn't know people could possibly worship someone else. Was there another path?

"Jesus is alive, Rindy. He's alive!"

The boy's eyes glowed with passion, and he acted like he had just let me in on the biggest secret. I didn't understand who this Jesus was because I had never seen him like I had seen Buddha, sitting tall and frightful in the temple.

"I've never seen or heard of Jesus from the monks." I turned again to face him, balancing my cart handles against my waist.

"Here, Mr. Thach gave me this."

He shuffled through his pocket and handed me a tiny pamphlet picturing a man descending from the sky, wearing a white robe surrounded by clouds. Sunlight shone around him, and he was smiling with his arms extended outwards. As if he were extending his arms to me. It was a pleasant picture to look at. It didn't look like any of the gods I had seen at the temple. Taking the pamphlet from the boy's outstretched hand, I scrunched it in my hand against the wooden handle of my cart and continued to the next noodle shop.

16

THE COUP

**"The CIA was trying to counter the communist party;
a tug of war." — Rindy**

MARCH 1970

"What's going on?" I looked at Sov, but he looked as confused as I felt. There was a commotion on the streets. Men and boys shouted and yelled. This was unlike anything I'd ever seen, where stray dogs lingered and old women sat chewing *betel*—an addictive red root—in the afternoon shade. As we approached a group congregating in the middle of the road, one boy threw a piece of red cloth with a yellow star in the middle onto the ground. The flag of North Vietnam.

"They're going to burn it," Sov said, leaning close to my ear. The group began shouting, "Vietnamese, stay out of Cambodia" and "down with the Vietnamese" until the air rang with the cry and the flag curled in flames.

I had always heard people making fun of the Vietnamese and making crude jokes, but I'd never seen anything like this. Sov looked confused too. His head swiveled from side to side, taking it all in. Then he grabbed my arm and said, "let's join in."

I followed him and a group of the older boys into the center of the mob.

"Why does everyone hate the Vietnamese?"

"What?"

I leaned closer to Sov's ear and shouted, "why does everyone hate the Vietnamese?"

"Many reasons. Have you ever heard the stories of the cooking stones?"

I shook my head.

"Vietnamese soldiers took three Cambodians captive many years ago. You see, Cambodia and Vietnam have fought many wars over the years. Anyway, these soldiers took the Cambodians and buried them alive up to their necks with just their heads sticking out of the ground. Then the Vietnamese built a fire between their heads and set a pot on top, to use them as cooking stones."

I stood dumbfounded. Could this be true? The idea of being burned alive as the Vietnamese ate their dinner on my head was horrifying. I shuddered and began to chant with the crowd.

A few days later, while Mr. Thach was teaching calculations on the blackboard, an older boy ran up to the open window, shouting all the way from the road, "There is an important announcement on the radio. Down with the Vietnamese! Stay out of Cambodia!"

We crowded onto the porch of the school next to the principal's open window and listened to the crackling of the radio, until the news broadcast from Phnom Penh became clear.

"The National Assembly has passed a vote of no confidence against Norodom Sihanouk, while he was away in France. They have closed the borders and all means of travel."

The radio crackled; everyone drew a breath.

"Prime Minister Lon Nol has assumed emergency powers, in his efforts to remove North Vietnamese troops from Cambodia. Queen Kossamak is now being forced to leave the royal palace by the new government under Lon Nol and will remain at her villa under house arrest. I repeat, Lon

Nol is the new head of state and has overthrown the longstanding rule of Norodom Sihanouk."

The radio clicked off. No one breathed. A fly buzzed through the air, then landed. I looked around, searching each face. Mr. Thach slumped against a wall, no smile softening his features. He looked ten years older than he had moments ago. He removed his glasses and rubbed his eyes. The principal sat in his chair at his desk, his back to us.

One of the senior boys began to speak, his words coming halting and unclear. "How could this be? Sihanouk was the good Aupouk King of Cambodia. The one who fought so hard for her independence from the French. He is responsible for the island of peace Cambodia has become. How could they do this to him?"

The principal turned in his chair, coming to stand before the open window.

"I've been hearing talk. Lon Nol probably had help from the CIA. Norodom Sihanouk has been neutral in the war, not siding with the United States, and there are Viet Cong soldiers on the border of Cambodia. I think the CIA helped Lon Nol take power because Sihanouk is so loved by the people—" his voice broke, and he stared out into the blue, cloudless sky.

Mr. Thach put his glasses back on. "Let's all go back to class, children."

As the weeks progressed, the streets rattled with endless chatter about Lon Nol and what he would do for Cambodia. Radios and televisions played on overturned crates, and people gathered around, listening to the voice of Lon Nol—a new voice— as he accused Sihanouk of turning a blind eye to corruption in his own government and letting incompetent people run Cambodia. He said Sihanouk cared more about "play acting" and traveling the world than protecting Cambodia. People shouted and fights erupted, as some said Lon Nol was spreading propaganda and others said it was the truth.

Lon Nol was the opposite of Sihanouk, the radio claimed. He was a dark-skinned man who was proud of his pure Khmer heritage and who had a military background, unlike Sihanouk's theatrical one. He'd risen in power, becoming the Minister of Defense, before being elected as the Prime Minister of Cambodia twice. He was known as "Black Papa" by his followers. Yet, his hatred for the Vietnamese was the bridge he climbed across to connect with the people. He promised to rid Cambodia of the Vietnamese communists, and the Viet Cong soldiers who had retreated into Cambodia.

Soon after, things began changing for us at school in the grip of this new government. When arriving one day, I saw Mr. Thach's face sad, with deep shadows beneath his eyes. Some of the kids didn't seem to notice as they laughed and joked, pulling the small wooden chairs from beneath the person sitting down beside them.

"Quiet down, children," Mr. Thach raised his hands as he stood. The classroom fell silent, surprised to hear Mr. Thach raise his voice. Every eye turned to the school teacher we all dearly loved.

"I've been instructed to give you a brief," he swallowed, "talk on behalf of our new leader." That's when I noticed the principle standing in the doorway as he walked over and handed Mr Thach a piece of paper.

Mr. Thach sat down again, shaking his head, looking to a piece of paper in front of him.

"Many of you have loved Sihanouk as do your parents, but much of what you have heard is not true. He's been a traitor since the beginning, looking out for his own interests and not the good of all. He has not been the good 'aupouk king' that we all thought him to be. We expect you children—who are bright and young— to receive this news more easily than your parents." Mr. Thach swallowed. "Your parents may be more resistant to this change, but please enlighten them that Sihanouk is in his rightful place—out of Cambodia."

I looked from side to side; confusion was written on everyone's face. What did this mean? I wished I could talk it over with Aupouk, who I hadn't seen in over a year. He had always respected Norodom Sihanouk. What would he say to believe now?

Over the next week, when walking to class, I noticed several of the older boys limping in pain and some even had long welts across their backs. They weren't temple boys, so I wondered about their beatings.

"What happened to you?" I asked one boy, as we shuffled into the classroom.

"My aupouk beat me."

I asked two more and received the same response.

I shrugged. It was common for boys to be beaten by their aupouks, but I didn't understand why so many were beaten at once.

"What did you do?"

"I told my parents what we talked about at school, as we were told to by Mr. Thach. Everyone is talking about it. How we are supposed to spit on the name of Norodom Sihanouk and call him a traitor. My aupouk beat me and told me he would teach me respect."

Another boy leaned in, "Mine said the children of this generation are being taught to disrespect their elders and forget their place. To spit on the name of Sihanouk who has been our 'Aupouk King,' is spitting in the face of the authority of my own father. It's about saving face."

I sat down in my chair and looked ahead, understanding the price of Mr. Thach's words. Saving face was very important to Cambodians, as their dignity and good name depended on their public appearance and how they were respected. Lon Nol—with all his insults and accusations—had broken the Sihanouk's good name, like punching him in the nose. I knew the boys had been punished because they had trampled on the tradition of saving face in Cambodia, especially for one so loved as the Aupouk King.

Mr. Thach knew what his words had cost too. But what choice had he had with the principle making sure he supported the new Lon Nol government? Mr Thach stood slowly from his chair and looked over his class, sadness staring from his eyes as he looked at the battered boys. Slowly he lowered himself back down to his chair. He looked worse than any of my classmates, but I suspected his welts couldn't be seen on the surface of his skin.

17
THE GLASSES

"There are certain things in life that you never forget."
— Rindy

JANUARY-DECEMBER 1971

I watched the specks of trapped dust whirl inside a slice of sunlight. I had just completed cleaning the abbot's house—the largest of the monks' quarters, as he was the chief of the temple. Glancing around, I mentally checked off all the things I had cleaned. I had beaten the rug, scrubbed the floor and dusted the spacious, yet simply adorned, room. I had even taken down the cobwebs that clung to the corners with a stick for good measure. Feeling accomplished, I allowed myself time to admire the flying dust lingering in the air, captivated by the warm sun invading the dungeon of a room.

"Boy."

I jerked into reality, having no idea how long I had been standing transfixed.

"Boy."

The abbot emerged into view, filling the doorway, wrapped in a yellow robe. I spun to face him, head bowed slightly as a sign of respect and submission.

"You should have been done here hours ago." He stalked across the room and grabbed me by the ear, thrusting me out of the door and into the sunlight. My ear throbbed, but the abbot had a reputation of brutality. I had gotten off easy.

Hearing a commotion from the street, I stole through the courtyard, happy to be leaving. Several radios were cranked up, tuned to the same station. A familiar voice spilled from the speakers. *Norodom Sihanouk.* How could it be? His voice swelled with passion and rage.

"How's Lon Nol allowing this?" a lady asked, approaching where I stood.

"He's broadcasting from a radio station in Peking, China."

Sihanouk's voice was shrill. "Lon Nol and Sirik Matak have shown their gratitude by insulting and humiliating me, overthrowing and condemning me as a man who has sold out his country. Such accusations by these ungrateful, ambitious, power-hungry, money-hungry cowards who didn't hesitate to stab me in the back, are unimportant." His voice pulsed with rage. "My personal indignation cannot be compared with the magnitude of my concern for the sad fate of our country. These traitors have thrown the country, which had a good reputation as an island of peace, into the furnace of the Americans' war."

People pressed in around me.

"I am setting up a government-in-exile. I call on all my children, both military and civilian, who cannot stand to remain under the traitors' power and who are courageous and determined to liberate the fatherland, to fight our enemy. If the children already have weapons, I will bring the ammunition and new weapons to strengthen them. I will take measures to help them leave for the military school, deep in the jungle, to avoid enemy detection. Long live Cambodia!" His voice crackled to a stop.

"He's joining forces with the Khmer Rouge—the communists? The ones he's been hunting through the jungle and killing for years?" one man asked, staring dumbfounded at those on the street.

"Yes, but he really has no other options," another man spoke up. "He can't become allies with the United States because they are backing Lon Nol, his enemy. He can only ally with China and Russia. Their Marxist and Leninist ideas are what Khmer Rouge are built upon—they are his only option."

People mumbled their agreement or stared dumbly in disbelief.

"He's just saving face," the knowledgeable man continued. Everyone nodded.

"But this means war, doesn't it?" A woman asked, her voice shaking and uncertain.

"This means war. The island of peace is no more."

"Rindy! Hello, Rindy." I turned and saw Sov running toward me from the temple. "You need to hurry; a monk asked me where you are."

I swallowed, dryness creeping into my mouth. I ran. The monks would not tolerate any sign of reported tardiness or lack of concern for being summoned. I picked up my pace, catching up to Sov.

"What's the matter?"

He wouldn't look me in the eyes.

Sov, what is it?"

"I don't know, Rindy. Something bad though."

As I entered the temple courtyard, the eyes of the boys who congregated beneath the trees were on me. Monks stared sternly, narrowing their gaze at me. Their superiority burrowed into my soul, making me feel even more insignificant, more targeted and more afraid. Unease crept from the shadows of the temple and crawled up my legs. Something was terribly wrong and each quick glance added another tooth to my fear.

"Come." A monk approached, as if he had been waiting for me. "You are wanted by the abbot." This face was an odd mixture of pity and reserved obedience, like a pond swirled by a stick. Not every monk was cruel. Here cruelty grew like mold on the ornate ceilings and wafted like incense, infecting some but not others.

My dread mounted.

Seeing the abbot twice in one day could not be good luck. I knew the way well, as I had cleaned his house many times, but I followed the monk obediently with my head bowed. The monk who had summoned me walked carefully on each step, to not squish an innocent bug that happened to be crawling across his path. I replayed the words I had heard the monks say in my mind, to distract myself: "insects are of great value in Buddhism, as Buddha professed respect for all life on the earth. You may reincarnate as a bug, so give them respect as you would want respect." The idea seemed so strange after receiving my first beating. Apparently, bugs held a higher importance than boys did.

We arrived at the abbot's home. The monk opened the door with a creak, as if he were expected. I kept my head bowed low, tracing the dirt filled gaps of the stone floor. The fear eating my gut bit harder. I shuddered.

"Come," The abbot barked.

I trembled with each step, and my mind whirled, trying to piece together any possible mishaps from my time cleaning his home. Had I forgotten to empty the chamber pot or missed dirt somewhere? I dared a quick glance into the abbot's face. He stood before me, hands clasped behind his back. Anger peeked from the shadows draping his face. I stopped a few feet away from him and bowed lower than normal to signify my respect. Nothing changed in his expression, so I lowered myself to the ground, bowing low.

Two monks shuffled through the door behind me. *Thud.* My heart responded with the same sound *thud, thud, thud.*

"So, you know all about this then?" He didn't seem to want an answer. "Look up."

A glinting object in the monk's hand reflected an eerie light on the stone wall, which danced as the abbot rotated it in his fingers. The reflection looked like water caught in space. My head pounded as I recognized what the disfigured object had been. Cracks spider webbed over the transparent glass in a million places.

The abbot's reading glasses.

He smiled. A coolness creeped over my skin, and my knees shook. Denying his accusation would only make my situation worse. What should I do? He looked at me as if no response confirmed my guilt.

"Of course, you did it," he bellowed, his voice echoing off the barren walls. "You've been the only one in here today."

He was having an invisible conversation in his head, one that could not tolerate even a whisper of my innocence. I tried shaking my head, but my neck wouldn't move. I tried to swallow, but even my saliva had deserted me.

"Do you have any idea how much these eyeglasses cost?" the abbot screeched, his voice mounting in volume as he spat each syllable into the air. Again, I was unable to respond, unable to move, and my mind spun. I pinched my eyes closed. An image I had never been able to forget flashed into my memory. A tiger, pacing below me, taunting me. This time, I was alone with nowhere to hide.

"Bare him."

My eyes flashed open.

The two monks who had entered behind me jumped into action. One of them was Pou Ponlok. They jerked at my makeshift robe, yanking my bottom free, before retreating into the shadow of the doorway. The room felt small. I couldn't catch a breath. My body trembled, and I couldn't swallow the sob.

"It wasn't me." I didn't know if the sound had made it out of my throat.

He took the whip from the Pou Ponlock. I had seen them many times before as farmers used them to get their water buffalo to move. It was about the length of a man's arm made of a flexible white wood, which started out fat, then tapered off at the end. The shadow of the abbot's arm raising over his head reflected on the wall. His movements were slow, exaggerated, ticking with rage.

The abbot began to count, his voice swelling.

I braced my spine and clasped my palms until my knuckles turned white. The first whip came with force, slicing through the air. The second snapped even harder. I shuddered from the pain, a sharp moan escaping my lips.

Terrified by the idea of prolonging the misery, I focused on the light shining through the window and onto the floor, licking the hem of the abbot's robe. His bare feet emerged then retreated into the recesses of their yellow shroud. The particles in the air whirled as his arm rose then fell, rose then fell, the whip stinging my bared flesh.

"You should cry."

An invisible force held in my sobs, as if the waves of pain crashing against my insides, my every bone, were walled in, preventing them from spilling out of my mouth. His bare feet pounded closer to my head with each crack of the whip. Jerking my head up, I writhed in pain, delirious and light-headed. A foot pushed my skull to the ground, and I collapsed beneath it. The same foot that was so careful not to tread on an insect, crushed my ear to the ground. The foot that made a great show of sacrifice as it walked bare, pressed into my brain. The foot that proclaimed a path of peace, crushed me beneath it.

I lay like a crumpled piece of rubbish on the floor, the flesh on my back and bottom raged. I didn't try to move.

I didn't want to breathe, and I didn't want to exist in this misery any longer. Closing my eyes, I became lost in the darkness that pulled me into its depths.

18

MTEAY

"Even though I had a bad experience at the temple, I still wanted to be able to learn. But it was a family decision, and I was old enough to work." — Rindy

MARCH 1972

I swept the courtyard as the silver morning light crept over the cool ground. The chanting of the monks filled the air, thrumming from the temple. The sound had become as common as birds singing, leaking from the temple to the courtyard surrounding it. I pushed the broom blindly, barely noticing the pile of leaves and trash littering the courtyard.

As the weeks passed, the aching of my beaten flesh had lessened. My skin was rough and wasn't as tender to the touch. My flesh had built a million, tiny webs across my back to pull my body back together like magic. My hand made its way to the familiar scar snaking across my lower back, tracing its jagged line. I was mending—at least physically—but a pressure somewhere deeper inside my chest didn't relent. It felt like pain but hotter as it bubbled up inside me whenever I encountered the abbot or saw the sweep of a yellow robe out of the corner of my eye. It tasted like ash and smelled like death. Despite Mr. Thach's warning against the evils of kum,

I suspected the infection ran through me. I did nothing to quell its rage inside my bones. In its wake something else had dried up in me. Since being beaten by the abbot, I found I never cried anymore. I shrugged this realization off. I was growing up and becoming a man.

I had lived at the temple for the better part of two years, but somehow it felt like I had always been there and would never leave. My longing for Chidaun to return or even for Aupouk, was only a distant memory. Did my aupouk ever think of me? I understood him now and his silence about his time at the temple. His memories were too dark, too painful to remember. He must have been beaten too.

Vuthy had eventually been moved to my room and often at night we whispered about running away as Kiry and many of the older boys had, but we had never settled on a plan because we had nowhere to go. Chidaun would likely return us back to the temple if we ran to her, to save not only herself from bad merit but to save us as well. This was also my only way to gain an education, and I loved school.

I glanced up at the courtyard. There was still much to sweep. When Vuthy had completed whatever chore he had been assigned, he was supposed to meet me by the noodle shop so we could sell water together. Sov had saved up enough riel for a water cart of his own, so Vuthy and I could use the other one. I always breathed easier knowing where Vuthy was, especially when he was safe with me. The brutality of the monks was a constant threat. As I swept, I kept my back to the abbot's house, so I wouldn't see its door.

We were a few weeks away from school ending for the summer months, and I was nearly done with the second grade. I didn't want it to end though, as I loved to learn, and Mr. Thach made life better. He taught us not only to love learning but also to love life. What had begun as a desire to gain good karma had become my favorite way to escape the reality of the temple.

"Rindy." A familiar voice echoed around me. I blinked, chasing away my thoughts. I searched the surrounding courtyard, littered with temple boys, to find the owner of the voice. A woman walked toward me. She looked uncertain, lost almost. Even her *sarong*—the common Cambodian wrap-skirt— clung to her legs timidly.

"Rindy," she called, her eyes sparking to life.

It was Mteay. She looked so much older than I remembered her being, the places under her eyes more sunken with wrinkles creasing her skin. She wore sadness and clung to it like a blanket draped around her shoulders.

"Soonsday." I walked hesitantly toward her. Why was she here? What did this mean?

"What a big boy you have grown to be." She smiled, turning me around. "You must be nine now."

I shrugged, not knowing.

"Temple life has been good to you." Her eyes were gleaming. "You look like a monk in your little robe—exactly like your father."

I nodded again, not knowing how else to respond. Should I let her see the scars? I understood why aupouk had never spoken about his time at the temple. Why share pain, when it didn't change anything? Boys were sent to the temple and monks were mean; that was just life. I swallowed my memories of the shadows, the fear and the beatings, into the pit of my stomach. I would be silent as my aupouk had been. It was the Cambodian way.

"Where's Vuthy?"

"I was supposed to meet him at the noodle shop." I motioned toward it.

"Go get him I'll talk to a monk to let them know you both are leaving."

I obeyed, finding Vuthy near the noodle shop, waiting to begin our morning water deliveries.

"What's wrong, Rindy?"

"Mteay, is here."

His eyes widened.

"What about Chidaun?"

"I don't know, just Mteay came. She said we're going home."

"Going back home to Chidaun's house? Or to live with Mteay?"

I shrugged, motioning for him to follow. Vuthy ran to the courtyard, stopping just behind Mteay, who stood with her back to us as she talked with Pou Ponlok. Vuthy stood shyly as if he didn't know how to approach her. When she was finished, she turned and saw him. Pou Ponlok strode away without giving us a glance.

"Why, Vuthy, you've grown even more than your brother has. You must be seven now."

As he talked to her, uneasiness clenched inside me. Why did she want us now? What had changed?

I spied Sov leaving the courtyard to begin his own water deliveries. I ran after him, saddened that I was leaving our friendship behind too.

"Wait, Sov."

I caught up to him, his smile curling as it always did.

"We're leaving, Sov."

His smile faded, but he nodded as if he understood. We'd seen many temple boys come and go, but it had never been one of us. Until now.

I motioned toward Mteay. "That's my mteay over there. She's come to take us back with her."

I saw my sadness mirrored in his eyes.

"Come, Rindy. We need to go." Mteay was already walking toward the gate with Vuthy beside her.

Sov and I embraced, both of us wiping snot from our noses with the backs of our hands.

"I'll miss you, Rindy."

"I hope I see you again one day, Sov."

I started to run toward Mteay but remembered my water cart.

"My cart is hidden in a big bush near the trash pile behind the temple. Maybe you can sell it." He nodded, arm raised high. Would I ever see him again?

"Rindy, hurry." Mteay's voice was sharp, cutting off my goodbye.

I turned and ran out of the temple courtyard, over the carefully swept stones. My pulse quickened in disbelief. My time of being a temple boy had come to an abrupt end. The shadows and beatings were over. I ran even faster past the abbot's house as if he would storm out at any minute and drag me back inside. But nothing happened, so I continued running until I reached Mteay at the gate. She told us we'd walk the five hours home to avoid paying for a taxi.

When we walked past the road leading to the schoolhouse, a whole new sadness lodged in my throat and stung my eyes. I imagined seeing the papers waving gently to me through the open window and its friendly blue door. I imagined Mr. Thach staring out the open window at me, waving, a kind smile stretching wide across his face. I could almost hear him say he would pray for me. Pray to his God named Jesus.

"Can we go to school when we get back to Phomn Sampov, Mteay?" The question was hard to ask around the lump in my throat. I looked up at her face, her profile a dark silhouette against the rising sun. Mteay had always been distant and drawn, but now she reminded me of a piece of worn cloth, wrung into a tight rope and left in the hot sun. She remained stiff and coiled.

"No, there is no school there. You and Vuthy will both go to work."

I glanced sideways at Vuthy, his eyes downcast and lips in a tight line.

"Kahn—your stepfather—has joined the Lon Nol army, and they are fighting against both the Viet Cong and the Khmer Rouge armies. The fighting is bad, and I'm afraid it will only get worse." She paused, and we walked in silence.

"Why did he join the Lon Nol army?" I was timid. I didn't want to sound disrespectful and risk a slap in the face, but I also wanted to know why he would join the side fighting against Norodom Sihanouk.

"He wanted to rid Cambodia of the Vietnamese—the scum, as he calls them. He believed Norodom Sihanouk did nothing to stop them from setting up sanctuaries in Cambodia, so he's joined in a bad marriage with the United States, the country fighting in Vietnam. But so far, Lon Nol has only made empty promises. He's an incompetent fool." Mteay's voice popped and seared, but she wasn't talking to me. She just needed to talk. "Kahn said he barely trained his troops before sending them out against the Vietnamese army. He just gave them Buddhist charms and sent them out to fight—to fight against the most brutal army in the world. Lon Nol truly is a fool."

After that, we continued a long while in silence.

"Life will not be so easy for both of you anymore." Her words sparked, landing hard against my chest. "It was your Chidaun's decision to put you in the temple, and now you've both gotten a little education—far more than I was able to get." Her words indented my skin like the sharp rocks beneath my feet.

"Where will we go? Can—"

"You'll both be hired out as farm laborers." Her words came quickly. "I've already got places arranged for you with some distant relatives. Kiry's been working ever since he ran away from the temple—I should have never let him go in the first place. Your little sister Ly and stepsister Sotha are still at home and are all working to contribute to the family. Now you will too."

I paused, my unanswered question burning on my tongue.

"Will Vuthy and I go together?" My words were quiet. Had she heard them?

"No."

I grabbed Vuthy's hand, giving it a tiny squeeze. He looked at me through tear swallowed eyes, and I smiled at him.

"It'll be ok." I mouthed the words.

When we made it home at last, Chidaun made a delicious *Amok*—a fragrant and spicy coconut fish curry, steamed in banana leaves. But as I looked around the room while eating it, the friendly and warm presence of Chi Ta—my grandfather—was missing. Even his tools and sandals were nowhere to be seen.

"Where is Chi Ta?" I dared to ask during an interruption in the conversation.

Chidaun's lips tightened into a line. "He passed into the next life while you were at temple."

My throat constricted as I tried to swallow. For the short time I had known him, I had loved him. I swallowed down my sadness with the savory yellow broth. I looked around. An odd feeling of warmness filled my chest as I watched Ly, who was four, and Sotha, who was three, giggle and eat while Chidaun clucked about. Mteay even looked content, the lines around her eyes dipping into a smile. They had become a family, the four of them, as Chi Ta had passed away and Khan was away fighting the war. Could Vuthy and I eventually become a part of this family to?

Mteay awoke me early the next morning.

"Come." She shook my shoulder, and I climbed from my hammock.

I looked at Vuthy who was still asleep, my throat tightening. When would I see him again? I remembered the fear I had felt when Mteay had abandoned us, leaving me to find food for us both. Also when Aupouk had worked all day and we had built leaf huts together. I remembered my constant panic at the temple, wondering if he was being beaten by one of the monks and I could do nothing to protect him. Fear churned in me. Who would take care of him now? Mteay tapped my shoulder, motioning for me to follow her, impatient for us to be on our way.

I followed her out of Chidaun's home into the early morning dawn. We walked in silence through the darkened streets of Battambang, the rising sun threatening the eastern horizon.

"My cousin's husband, Sal, has offered to hire you." Mteay's face was trimmed with a straight jaw and unwavering eyes "He'll bring you back with your payment in a couple of months. Hopefully enough to buy a few bags of rice. I'll have somewhere else for you to go by then." I nodded, unable to express the feelings swirling through my brain. Yet, she did not seek an answer.

This was what all Khmer boys did. Kiry had been working as a hired laborer when he was my age, but I wanted to stay with Vuthy. I even wanted to stay with *her*. I wanted us to be part of the family too. To know what it was to have a mteay again.

When we made it to the edge of town, I saw an ox cart coming through the dim light, the rising sun beginning to emerge.

"Soosdey." Mteay bowed her head, her palms joined, in respect. "Sal, this is my son, Rindy. He'll work hard for you."

He looked me over. "He's a bit small for nine. They're massive beasts—"

"I'm sure he'll be suited." Mteay's words were quick as if she feared he might change his mind.

After assessing me for another moment, he nodded his head, indicating for me to get on the back of the cart. Obediently, I climbed inside.

"See, you're so big and strong." Mteay beamed, but her eyes weren't smiling the way I had seen them the night before. It was a forced pleasantry. She hoped she wouldn't be stuck with me any longer than necessary.

I picked at a splinter from the cart that had just poked its way into my palm.

The cart began to roll away, the big wheels bouncing over rocks and ruts in the road.

The golden sun cloaked Mteay and played in her hair as we drove away. The blackness of her hair contrasted with the brightness of her surroundings, she was like a shadow on the ground. Her shoulders stooped a little, and her hands hung loosely at her sides, brushing the faded flowers on her skirt. Her eyes stared unblinking in my direction, like endless, black tunnels into the dust the cart made. She never waved. She didn't flinch. She merely stood there as if it was all she could do. I watched her until she disappeared into the blinding horizon.

I wanted her to run after me, pull me from the jostling cart and take me home again. I wanted her to find a way to pay for us to live without me going away. I wanted her to need me more than she needed money. I wanted her to say she'd never send me away again, even if she didn't mean it. I wanted her to *want* me.

Instead, she stood there like a tree, rooted to the ground, bearing on her tired shoulders the burden of living. My eyes stung in the sunlight, and the heaviness of the previous night's meal churned in my stomach.

Swallowing hard, I turned to look up the road. What type of beast had the man meant?

19
WAR BIRDS

"That is how I learned about the war." — Rindy

JULY 1973

I learned that the beasts I would tend were massive water buffalo. I worked for Sal for nearly a year, herding them to graze from place to place. They were as gigantic as he had said, and they had hooked horns. I was nearly gored several times, but after a while, I didn't fear them so much and got better in handling them. Although strict, Sal was kind to me. Kindness was the currency though as I often went hungry. I relied on frogs, snails and the fish I could find while herding the buffalo to supplement what he provided. After Sal no longer needed help, Mteay sent me to live with her other cousin, Boran, to plow and plant corn.

Remembering my time with him made me shudder as I dumped water into low troughs, thankful to be working for someone new. It was an unwelcome memory full of words that lashed and work I struggled to do. My utter uselessness was a constant companion from well before dawn to after dusk. Thankfully, I had just been sent to my new work assignment—for a man named to tend his Brahman cows and help in his orange orchard. The cows were white with floppy ears and large humps on their backs, but they weren't half as intimidating as the water buffalo.

"Come eat with us, Rindy," a young female voice called. Phala's daughter? I emerged from the small, grass-roofed shed where the animals were kept and found her standing at the open door of their hut.

"Father sent me to get you." She opened the door further as if to beckon me in, an inviting warm light flickered within. I closed the distance between us, walked up the stairs timidly and entered. Eating with those I worked for was unbroken ground, making me feel unsteady.

It wasn't as large as Chidaun's house, but it had wooden floors and a metal roof, with a few pieces of furniture scattered about. Phala, his daughter and his young son sat on the mat as his wife placed steaming bowls of soup in front of them. My face grew warm as I approached, retreating from the open doorway and the sound of crickets already filling the night air. Taking a seat on the woven mat, I took up a wooden bowl filled to the brim with a broth of fish that smelled of lime. The woman smiled at me warmly.

"My name is Yan. I have fond memories of your mteay as a child. She is my cousin."

I smiled and nodded. Yan continued serving the rest of her family, handing a bowl to Phala, next. Phala watched me, causing the side of my face to flush. It wasn't a gaze of disapproval but of curiosity. It made me uncomfortable all the same.

"You worked with Boran for the planting season?" Phala asked at last, giving voice to his inquisitive gaze.

I nodded, having just taken a mouth full of soup, the slightly sour taste of the broth smarted my tongue and warmed my throat.

"What type of work did you do?" he asked without waiting for more of a reply.

"Plow and plant corn, *Bong* Phala." I was careful to address him respectfully as an elder. I used my chopsticks to pile some fish and spinach onto my spoon.

"Was he kind to you?" The question surprised me. I looked up, meeting Yan's eyes, swallowing hard. "I have memories of him as a young boy too." Her eyes sparkled with understanding. "But they weren't such fond memories as the ones of your mteay."

I hesitated, not knowing how to speak truthfully of Boran. I winced at the memory of his spit on my face and the beatings as he told me how worthless I was for falling off the plow. But the handles had been eye-level, making it difficult to see where I was going, and I wasn't heavy enough to push it deeply into the soil. The truth was, he had dismissed me sooner than he had told Mteay, but seven months under his employment had felt like an eternity. Shaking my head, I dislodged the bad memory.

"Bong Boran knows many interesting curses." I spoke the words into my bowl, ashamed of my truthfulness.

Phala chuckled, so I looked up. Yan nodded knowingly.

I wanted to change the subject. "I never had soup like this while with him though." She responded with a pleasant smile and offered another bowl, which I accepted gratefully.

"In addition to taking care of the cows, as you know, you'll also be helping me in the orange orchard, which is a short walk from here. The oranges are nearly ready for harvest, and you'll help haul the cow and cart to the market for Yan to sell."

With the harsh treatment of Boran still fresh in my mind, this unusually kind treatment, along with the rich soup, left my stomach unsettled. Phala had even given me a hammock below the house, instead of sleeping with the animals as I was accustomed to. Somehow, I didn't think adjusting to this life would be as hard as it was to adjust to the last place I had lived and worked.

The next morning, as I pulled the cow to the orchard down the snaking cow trail Phala had instructed me to take, I heard a curious buzz carried on the morning breeze. It started off as quietly as the buzz of a fly, but grew louder and louder until it became deafening, reverberating through the air. Panicking, I ran for cover beneath a low hanging tree, pulling the cow by a ring in its nose behind me. Peering through the leaves, I searched the sky. When the sound hung over my head, shaking the ground beneath my feet, I caught sight of three black machines soaring overhead. They had two arms that cut through the sky like black bird wings. They thundered, waking even the nocturnal creatures with their roar. The lazy cows stood alert, feet prancing in agitation. Pulling my knees up close, I clapped my hands over my ears and pinched my eyes closed, waiting for the sound and shaking to cease.

An eternity was trapped in a few seconds, as I held my breath. To my relief, the buzz lessened until it disappeared altogether. Standing up, the faint outline of the flying machines were still visible, heading in the direction of Vietnam, leaving the sky ripped open in streaks of white.

"What are you?" I asked the air quietly, risking barely a whisper.

Later that evening while we ate a bowl of noodles and beef, I asked the question again, describing the sight and sound of the morning.

"They were B-52 bomber airplanes," Phala replied before I had hardly gotten the words out.

"They've been flying over for months now," he continued, slurping the rest of his noodles down. "The United States is bombing eastern Cambodia to cut off the Vietnamese supply routes and destroy the Viet Cong sanctuaries. You'll probably feel them hit sometimes."

"Whole villages are being destroyed in the process, with thousands of people killed or fleeing to the jungles to join Khmer Rouge forces." He looked up, his eyes shone with hatred. "Lon Nol is a slave of the U.S. government now and isn't smart enough to figure out how to get out of this bad relationship. He lets them do whatever they want. They've been bombing the countryside for three years now, and instead of stopping they are increasing in number. Lon Nol has gotten us into a mess we will not get out of without many wounds. He's a fool. Everything Norodom Sihanouk tried so hard to achieve, the island of peace, he is destroying."

I stared at the noodles in my bowl, remembering the similar words Mteay had said about Lon Nol. Not wanting to ask more questions, I left the house as soon as I could, Phala's anger still sparking like the cooking fire. I felt bad for angering him with my question. Laying in my hammock, looking at the night sky, my mind was consumed with the image of the bomber plastered in the sky. I could almost hear its roar and see its arms reaching outward with its nose cutting through the clouds. A great, yet terrible, war bird.

I would see that sight and ponder this B-52's paradoxical existence many times that year, as it often roared through my morning and consumed my thoughts. Sometimes I could feel the earth beneath my feet shake, as Phala had said, from bombs being dropped on the countryside. The war had seemed far away, being fought in obscure cities, but the presence of the bombers brought it closer to home.

I didn't fully know what war was, but gathering from the evening talk, it was something like that B-52; somehow glorious to behold yet terrifying at the same time. The women would talk about this war with fear creeping out between their words, but the men would talk in voices crackling with excitement, eager to jump into it. Each time I saw the bombers flying overhead, I wondered how one thing could yet be two.

20
THE KILL

"Every time I walked past that place, I was afraid." — Rindy

OCTOBER 1973

The morning dawned just like every other during the dry season. It held a pallid heat that only hinted at what was to come: a burning weight that suffocated me with each breath as the day wore on. I set off for the orchard like usual with the lazy cow in tow. The meandering path veered off to the left, and the tall heads of grass flicked in the breeze. The sights were familiar, but something felt different. With each step, my unease mounted, and I was startled by the most routine noises, like a cricket chirp or a bird taking flight.

Then a peculiar smell stung my nose. It twisted into my stomach, making me want to vomit. Looking around, I couldn't tell where it was coming from, but it hung in the air like a putrid haze, coating my lungs with each inhale, melding with the heat pressing on my lungs. Covering my face with the crook of my arm, I continued to walk down the path, pulling the cow behind me. Taking my arm away, I tried to see if the stench still lingered, but it was even stronger than before. I gagged as it accosted me at full force. The stench reminded me of the place behind the temple, where human waste was dumped, but it also smelled of the meat market in the heat of the summer. The combination was overwhelming. It was a heavy, metallic smell. Even the sun looked murky through its haze.

To escape, I ran further up the trail with my face in my arm, dragging the annoyed cow behind me. The usual number of flies was multiplied by the hundreds, speckling the landscape like chicken pox. Swatting them out of my way, I continued up the path, my vision blurry from holding my breath as I tried to escape the stench.

Then I saw the source of the smell.

A body lay prostrate across the path just a few steps in front of me.

Black blood soaked into the hot ground beneath it, nearly reaching my toes. The air was dense with the suffocating smell of rottenness and the swarms of flies were thick and black.

Shaking in horror, I stared at death for the first time. Seeing a dead body is different from seeing sun-bleached bones. This was a man who had been walking around—I leaned in closer—maybe two days before. His hair waved in the breeze and his skin was grey and blank, but still mostly intact. The flies and the oppressive heat would take care of that soon. This was not an old, peaceful death; this was a killing. The difference between the two was a chasm. A bloody hole was drilled into his back. It looked like a bullet hole, or what I imagined one to be from the stories I'd heard.

I recognized him as the leader of the nearby village.

It took only seconds for me to see all I needed, leaving my mind whirling. Getting up to run, I stumbled past the corpse, pulling the cow as fast as I could toward the waiting orchard. When I got several paces down the path, my stomach revolted. I doubled over, vomiting into the bushes. The stench clutched at my throat and nostrils, clawing its way into me. Would I be able to get it off? I pulled the cow faster.

I couldn't get away from the smell and the memory fast enough. I could still see the dead man's eye staring at me with each blink of my own. I ran faster and faster to forget, to block out the horror. Gasping and trembling, I made it to the orchard and searched for Phala or his wife. I needed to tell someone. Would that help ease my horror? I didn't know.

Running to a murky water bucket, I plunged my head in, hoping to erase the smell and the memory that clung to me like a cobweb, weaving its way into my skin. I emerged from the bucket soaking wet, the smell still clinging to me.

"Hello?" I called, desperate for contact with another living being. No one replied.

I sat by the bucket, staring at the ripe, green oranges weighing down the tree limbs. They were normally beautiful, but today they were the color of death, bound in a cluster. I tried to listen to the birds, but I only heard the flies feasting on the corpse. I tried to nibble on an orange, but I only tasted the smell of rotting meat. I began to pick the oranges I could reach, piling them in the cart. When I picked as many as the small cart could hold, I started back, but I dreaded the trip, so kept picking until they began spilling over the sides.

When the sun was high overhead, I forced myself to return. I took the long way back, through the village, careful to avoid the area of the corpse altogether. When I reached the village streets, a group of men were talking heatedly in a circle in the middle of the road. Phala was at the center, talking excitedly. He had also found the corpse on the way to the orchard.

"It was the Khmer Rouge," a young man said, his hands waving in the air. "I heard three of them trying to recruit the village chief the day before yesterday. They said something about wanting to 'take part in the glorious revolution.' They walked past my hut to his. They went down the water buffalo trail. I had no idea they would kill him."

Multiple voices began to chatter. "How do you know it was the Khmer Rouge and not the Viet Cong?"

"They wore dirty black clothes from head to toe, except for the checkered red and white *kramas* around their necks—who else would it be? They also were dark skinned. They didn't look Vietnamese at all. They were pure Khmer."

"But why would they kill him?"

"Because he wasn't sympathetic to their cause and didn't pledge his support. I think they wanted him to recruit members from our village—when he refused, they wanted to send a message." A chorus of voices murmured, everyone drawing their own conclusions.

"But how could Norodom Sihanouk allow this?" A woman's timid voice cut through the male voices. "Isn't he their leader? He surely could not be part of an evil regime."

The crowd nodded their agreement. Phala saw me and cut through the crowd.

"Better get the oranges and cow home to Yan."

I obeyed as he rejoined the conversation, pulling the cow from a clump of grass alongside the road, careful not to lose any oranges with Phala watching.

"My cousin just left for the jungle to join their forces," a new voice said.

"My brother just left too," another called. "But I didn't know the Khmer Rouge behaved like this."

"Are their forces near here?"

No one seemed to know.

I yanked the cow harder, eager to return to Phala's home. I remembered how the Khmer Rouge used to try to recruit Aupouk with fancy words, but never this type of force. They had yelled and cursed, but they hadn't shot him, and I was grateful for that. Clearly, they had grown much more violent in their tactics since those early years in the jungle.

"Their spies are everywhere." A male voice followed me as I left, filling my mind with questions. "Anyone could be one of them—anyone could be the Khmer Rouge slipping from the jungle to scope out a village. All they would have to do was get a change of clothes."

I shuddered at the thought.

The route where the man was shot was the most direct, and I couldn't afford the time it took to walk through the village or else Phala would grow impatient. So, each day I walked in fear of being shot by the Khmer Rouge, even long after the villagers carried the dead man away and the rain washed his blood into the dirt. The bamboo trees, which used to be friends, had become a threat as they could shelter a hiding Khmer Rouge. Each bird that sang, which used to be a welcomed sound, harkened impending danger. With each step, I imagined a company of crouched men, waiting in the shadows for the perfect shot. The words replayed in my mind like water caught in a current: "Anybody could be the Khmer Rouge...Anybody...Anybody...."

Every day I walked through my fear and back again. This is how I learned the meaning of war.

21

THE RUNAWAYS

"At that time my family had some issues." — Rindy

AUGUST 1974

After helping Phala and Yan harvest and sell oranges for most of a year, I returned to Phom Sampov with the money I had earned. I caught a ride on an ox cart and then on the back of a motorcycle. I was sad to leave Phala and his family, but I was glad to escape the fear of my walk to and from the orchard every day. My experiences as a boy of eleven years old, who had witnessed bombers flying overhead and had seen death up close, had stolen something from me. I no longer craved my mteay's love and protection. A deep-rooted streak of independence became ingrained in me, like a wheel track driven deep into the mud. This did not go well with Khan, my stepfather.

Khan had been traveling to and from Phnom Penh for the last several months as the war was waging in the capital city. He had joined the Lon Nol soldiers a few years before, but it was rumored that he snuck into Vietnam to trade supplies and sell weapons whenever he could. I had heard some of the villagers talk about the things he brought my mteay, fancy things.

I hadn't yet encountered him on any of my other trips home, bearing the money I had earned to help buy rice.

But when I returned from Phala's, he met me at the door of Chidaun's house, a dark scowl on his face. He bent over, gripping his stomach, and a pallid yellow hue coated his skin, nearly matching his muted green uniform.

"Why aren't you away working?"

I wanted to ask why he had come to the door and not Chidaun, but thought better of it.

"Phala has finished the orange harvest, and they have nothing more for me to do. So, he sent me home."

Khan pushed past me out the door, muttering and cursing down the street.

I found Mteay working at Chidaun's loom, but no smile softened her face. Ly and Sotha ran to me, hugging me tightly, abandoning their spinning wheels and cloth. "They said they would need you for at least a year. It's only been eight months."

I looked at my feet and dirt rimmed toenails. "The harvest was not so good."

"Girls, come back to work." Sotha and Ly obeyed. They had to be about six and five now, but they had grown much since I had seen them last.

"Where's the money you earned?" Mteay didn't pause to look up.

I reached into my pants and untied the pouch Phala had given me, which I had kept concealed inside my pant-let in my travels.

"I don't have anywhere else for you to go yet. Work is hard to find right now." She stood, took the money from my outstretched hand and placed the riel into an old can on the shelf.

"Where's Vuthy? Kiry too?" I added as an afterthought.

I heard a rattling cough from the next room. Mteay paused her movements to listen and shook her head.

"Your Chidaun is sick. She's only fifty-four, but you'd think she was a hundred. It's from all the betel she chews, horrible stuff."

Mteay continued to move her shuttle. Had she heard me?

"Kiry is working for my uncle in the rice paddies, but Vuthy is out collecting wood."

Vuthy was home. It had been over two years since I had seen him last.

Before Mteay could protest, I bolted out the door to find Vuthy. I revisited the small patch of jungle Vuthy and I had foraged for Chidaun years before. I soon found him there, his back was to me as gathered branches.

"Vuthy."

Bolting up, he turned, his face showing a mixture of shock and then joy. We collided in a rush of sweat and dirt. I pulled him back to look at him, a smile spreading my own face.

"You've grown. You're nearly as tall as I am now."

"I'd say I am taller than you, but that doesn't take much."

I hugged him again. Why wasn't I crying in relief? Tears had evaded me for years now. He was safe. He was here.

"Where have you been?" I took his face in my hands, turning his chin from side to side.

"I worked on a cassava farm and then a rubber farm, but the fighting was so bad in the area, they couldn't afford to pay me anymore, so they sent me back. What have you been doing?"

"First, I tended water buffalo, then plowed and planted corn, and I just now came back from one of Mteay's cousin's where I was harvesting oranges."

I sobered. "Were they good to you—the men you worked for?" I asked.

Vuthy dropped his gaze, kicking a rock loose.

"Not all were bad," he said.

I turned him around and searched his back. Three scars ran along his lower back, mocking me.

"Where did that happen?"

"The rubber plantation."

I dug my nails into my palms. I wasn't surprised, as beatings were common for all boys in Cambodia, but the blackness that began to spread inside as a result lasted longer than the initial sting. I wondered if Vuthy had been eaten by it too.

"They weren't much worse than Khan though." Vuthy spat the words. "He's going to be mad you're here. He raved for days when I came home unexpectedly with less pay than expected."

"Yeah, I already saw him. Is Chidaun really sick?"

Vuthy scrunched up his face. "Yes, I think so. Sometimes she coughs up blood. I miss her. Mteay doesn't want us."

I put my arm around him. I was back. We had each other.

Later that night after we ate, Vuthy and I tied our hammocks outside on the porch to catch the cooler night air and to avoid Khan. I could feel the rain coming. Through the closed door, we could hear Mteay and Khan fighting.

"I'll keep asking around, but it's going to take some time." I heard Mteay's voice, tired and strained.

"They can go find work. They're old enough." The agitation in Khan's voice was evident.

"How will they eat if they don't find work?"

"They are not my sons." His yells pierced the air. "They are not my responsibility."

"I'm sorry for that." Mteay sighed. I imagined the tired lines around her eyes deepening and her dark eyes narrowing in frustration. "But there is nothing to be done for the time being."

"There is always something to be done." Khan smashed his hand against something inside the hut. Would he hurt Mteay? I sat up, searching Vuthy's face. He shook his head as if to caution me.

"I still think sending them on their way is the best idea. They aren't legally my responsibility. You were supposed to have taken care of that years ago, yet here they are again—both of them."

"We've talked of this before. How could I stop his aupouk from abandoning them on my mteay's doorstep?"

"Where is your mteay now? She's bed ridden!"

"Hush," Mteay's voice hissed. "She'll hear you."

"Well, I just hope her inheritance holds." Khan exited through the back door; I could hear his military boots clomping down the backstairs. How long would he be here? Surely, he would return to fighting in the war soon.

I relaxed, back into my hammock, heart racing. Their words didn't hurt me as badly as they once had. Mteay had never wanted me. But Khan's words seared into my soul, bursting something inside. It tasted bitter and dark, yet familiar. Hatred.

Over the next week, Vuthy and I did our best to avoid Khan, helping Mteay with whatever she needed us to do. We collected firewood, hunted for snails for her dishes and washed laundry in the river. Ly and Sotha helped Mteay spin and weave silk to sell at the big markets in Battambang. But Khan spent most of his time at the Khmer *Kru*—the local witch doctor. He provided herbal medicine, gave out amulets, spoke meditations and scariest of all, practiced black magic. I had heard stories about this black magic and how he could remove someone's clothes from their bodies or kill a chicken by reciting a chant. Mteay told me Khan was trying to relieve the pain in his abdomen and his inability to eat much, so he could return to the war. But I suspected he cared more about going back to Vietnam to trade weapons and supplies than anything.

Khan practiced *neak ta*—spirit worship—like many people did in the village, bringing offerings to the tiny house near the pagoda. It looked like a mini temple, beautiful and carefully made, unlike most of the houses around it, and people brought food, flowers, incense, alcohol or cigarettes as offerings. No matter how hungry I was, I knew to never steal food from one as the spirits would haunt me. Khan worshiped these spirits and believed he had to live in a way that didn't anger them, which caused him to do strange things. One time, Vuthy and I had witnessed him cutting his tongue with a long knife while chanting, a ritual I had seen others who practiced neak ta do while parading through the streets. The sight made fear curl in my stomach, so we didn't stay long, retreating into the safety of the trees.

Several days later, when returning from the river with washed laundry, yelling poured from Chidaun's house. I glanced at Vuthy, and we began to run.

"You'll just have to get it another way, but I'm not giving it to you." It was Mteay's voice. She was strangely calm, despite his raging.

"Where is it, woman?" Khan slammed around.

"I'm not telling you. We don't have any to spare."

"If I don't get something to drink soon, I will tear this whole house apart."

I had never trusted Khan or his darkness and didn't know what type of violence he was capable of. His anger often took over his body, and his words slung like mud, coating anyone within hearing distance. This was especially true when he'd sit around with the other men who didn't leave to fight, sipping drinks out of bottles for hours into the night. But I hadn't yet seen him beat my mteay. Would he start today?

The door swung open, catching me unaware.

"What are you doing, you little spy?" Khan asked, emerging from the hut.

I shoved Vuthy behind me to walk away, turning to follow.

"I'm talking to you, you little beggar." He spat out the words, interlaced with curses. "You have no right to turn your back on me." He marched up behind us, his boots pounding on the floorboards. I pushed Vuthy harder, and he began to run. I was afraid, but anger elbowed out my fear. I turned to face his blazing, black eyes. The disgust I felt mirrored his own.

"Do you think you can disrespect me"—he leaned in close behind my ear—"without a beating?"

I remained silent, even as fear bubbled up in me.

"Just leave them be, Khan," Mteay called from inside the house, the thudding of her loom not subsiding.

"Not until he learns to respect me as his elder," he yelled back, his finger in my face.

"You're a little leech, trying to live off of me," he hissed, his spit hitting my face. "I didn't want you then, and I don't want you now. You expect to live off me because your Aupouk left you. He left you because you are worthless. Even your own father didn't want you."

I shook in anger, my whole body growing hot.

"Why don't you cry, little boy?" He taunted me with laughter. "You worthless—"

"Leave him alone." It was Vuthy's voice. He hadn't run safely into the trees like I had hoped he would.

"I'll start with you." He pointed behind me to Vuthy. "Your brother can watch."

Khan's fists were clenched at his sides, and his wide mouth was stretched across his dark face in a leering grin, eyes blazing black holes. His steps pounded toward Vuthy, but I lunged forward too, feet pounding, heart racing.

I grabbed Vuthy's arm, and we ran. Khan was sick and weak and he was no match for us, but the sound of his curses chased us, a rabid dog snapping at our heels. I hated Khan. I hated him for stealing my mteay, for joining the Lon Nol, for his spirit worship and his curses. Vuthy and I ran until we were panting and the hate eased.

"You want to leave?" Vuthy turned to face me.

"Yes, but where?"

"Remember Pou Kim? From the stilt hut?"

I nodded. Memories of the uncle who had helped hold Aupouk, Vuthy and me together after Mteay left. Memories of him saving my life when he pulled me from the river. Memories of him visiting me in the hospital. I hadn't seen him after Aupouk dropped us off at Chidaun's.

"He's not working with Aupouk anymore?"

Vuthy shook his head. "No, I saw him when I was sent away to work. I jumped off the ox cart I was riding on to talk to him and then caught back up before the cart was out of sight. He said he left shortly after we did, to farm his own rice paddy. It's about a morning's walk from here. I remember the way."

"Think he'll have any work for us?"

Vuthy shrugged. "It's worth a try."

"What if we run into soldiers and people fighting?"

Another shrug. "They wouldn't hurt two boys, would they?"

I didn't know, but we couldn't stay here. Looking up at the sky, the rain I had been smelling in the air was coming.

"We'd better hurry. It'll be dark in a few hours."

Without looking back, we walked east, the sky rolling in clouds.

22

RICE

"Rice paddies are mud." — Rindy

AUGUST 1974

As we walked, the sky pelted us with rain, but we didn't stop. Uncertainty churned in my gut, but the freedom of going where we had chosen was as exhilarating as running in the rain. We walked past huts built closely together and through villages. All the roads were dirt, leading in every direction. When it got too dark to see, we huddled together in a vacant shed. We only had our soaking wet shorts and cheap sandals. We owned nothing else. In the morning, the rain stopped, and we continued the rest of the way. Hunger gripped our stomachs and sometimes we heard bullets rippling in the distance. Once, they appeared to be only a few miles away, but we couldn't turn back.

I doubted Vuthy knew the way, and I told him so every few hours, but he insisted he did, so we continued on. We walked until the huts melted into farmland, stretching in endless paddies for as far as I could see.

It was four months into the rainy season. The land had already long been plowed with oxen or a motorized plow, to prepare to plant. It had already been smoothed and flooded with water and the rice seedlings had already been planted and were knee high, swaying like grass in the wind. I knew when they reached that height, they were ready to be transplanted into another paddy, farther apart so the grains could develop free of all the weeds that had grown up with them. We walked past paddy after paddy. The process of pulling up the seedlings had already begun and workers were knee deep in the mud, with their rice hats covering their faces. The rice seedlings were so green they almost glowed in the sunlight, each stem holding the ability to sustain a nation. Would Pou Kim still need our help now that transplanting had begun? Had he already hired workers? The thought prodded me onward.

At last, Vuthy pointed to the rice paddy in front of us.

"This is where I saw him."

"Are you sure this is the place?" I searched in every direction, but everything looked similar.

"I'm sure, Rindy. Stop doubting me. I saw Pou Kim knee deep in water, with his water buffalo right here."

A row of huts sat along the road, spaced out unevenly, belonging to those who farmed the rice paddies. Each one was a little different in style, but they were all made of bamboo poles and coconut leaves with metal roofs. Workers were scattered throughout the fields. Their straw hats looked like little, peak-roofed huts from a distance. We trudged toward them, hoping one of them was Pou Kim. Our feet sank into the mud up to our knees, but it was soft and cool.

"What are you two doing in my paddy?" a man asked, standing erect.

"Pou Kim?" My voice cracked. What if he turned us away?

He shielded his eyes against the sun.

"What do you want?" His voice was stern. He didn't seem in the mood for visitors.

Vuthy and I made our way to him, tripping through the muddy water.

"We're Vuthy and Rindy, remember us?"

"What are you doing here?" He came toward us, his arms out wide, a smile creasing his eyes.

Vuthy looked sideways at me, remaining silent, but I could feel him gloating.

"Things are not good with Khan, mteay's husband. He's a soldier in the Lon Nol army, but he's not fighting right now." I lowered my head, pulling my foot from the mud. "We've finished the jobs we were given, but we have nowhere else to go."

"Mmmm," Pou Kim murmured. "I see."

"We were hoping—hoping we could maybe work for you?" Vuthy began.

"Only for a place to stay and food, you don't have to pay us." I spit the words out quickly, the fear of him refusing clutching around my throat.

Pou Kim chuckled, slapping our backs. "You can help me with the rice then." He waved us toward the bare patch of land where he had already begun the day's work. "This is good fortune that you have come—maybe we can farm more land." He shot a look over his shoulder. "That is, if the fighting doesn't come too close and drive us away."

I sagged in relief. He would let us stay.

Bending at the waist, I pulled gently at the first seedling, and it released itself from the saturated soil easily. Its tiny roots looked like white worms clinging to its stalk. Soon a I felt a stinging on my ankles and feet, and I found leeches tightly attached. I ran a fingernail along my skin, breaking their hold on my flesh, and went back to work, but they continued to reattatch and soon I ignored them. After getting a large bundle of seedlings, I tied it with a string and set it aside for gathering. We repeated this process a thousand times that day.

The sun sank behind the horizon of palm trees, casting a pinkish hue over the luminous green. We gathered up our bundles and placed them on the side of the road. There were hundreds of piles, and we carried them on poles across our shoulders to be transplanted in a paddy nearby. My back was stiff and my toes numb from where the leeches had sucked my blood, but there was nowhere else I would rather have been.

23

BULLETS

"I can still hear the sound..." — Rindy

DECEMBER 1974

We stayed and worked with Pou Kim for the following months. He was kind to us, buying rope for us to make our own hammocks with, which we hung beneath his stilt hut. When the transplanting came to an end, we worked for some of Pou Kim's neighbors, helping them plow and fertilize their fields. Sometimes we heard the *"tu, tu, tu"* of machine guns firing in the distance, but we didn't see any soldiers and rice planting ensured life. At night, Pou Kim talked late into the night with his neighbors. They talked of the fighting in Phnom Penh and the imminent defeat of Lon Nol and the rise of the Khmer Rouge and how they had begun to rival the dreaded Viet Cong soldiers. Who would win in Cambodia? What would happen then? Everyone had a different opinion, and sometimes the conversation erupted in yelling.

Some of the younger men even left to join the Khmer Rouge forces, as most of the villagers' sympathies laid with them due to their loyalty to Norodom Sihanouk. Some agreed with Lon Nol because they hated the Vietnamese as hotly as he did. But I remembered the shot man on my route while working for Phala and feared the Khmer Rouge most of all. I kept my thoughts to myself, as no one would listen to a boy, but I wished all the armies would quit fighting and return home, so we could live in peace without the constant talk of war looming over the horizon.

When harvest time came, we still didn't see armies marching through the rice paddies, so we continued to work. The sun burned hottest when the rain didn't fall, and the rice had ripened from vibrant green into a golden hue. It swayed in the breeze, up to my armpits, its plump kernels bursting from each head. Hundreds of workers labored in the paddies around us, bent at the waist, hacking close to the ground with a sharp machete. We all swayed in the same rhythm; danced the same dance of rice.

After we chopped it down, we bundled it. It took a month before we began to extract the rice kernels. Laying a thick tarp on the ground, we stepped on the heads, rolling and crushing them beneath our bare feet or beating them against the beams that held the hut in the air. But they were not yet ready to eat. When thousands of golden kernels scattered the tarps, we laid them out in the sun to dry. Vuthy and I hewed out bowels in a log and charred the indentations with fire to make them smooth. When the kernels were dried, we crushed them with a stick into the bowls we hewed into the log, to make the outer shell release the hard white kernel inside. Last, we carefully scooped the rice into burlap bags.

When we finished, Pou bought extra food from the market: pork, vegetables and *prahok*—fermented fish paste—to celebrate. We prepared for a feast.

"How long did the rice take from start to finish, Pou Kim?" Vuthy asked, adding rainwater to the pot.

"About six months from planting to harvesting." Pou Kim scooped rice with his hands from one of the bags into a pot to boil. "Now that it's all harvested, we'll need to prepare the soil to do it all over again when the rains come. If the armies don't come before then."

We had all grown used to searching the horizon for the black uniforms of the Khmer Rouge or the green colors of the Viet Cong or Lon Nol soldiers, but so far, bare paddies lay as far as the eye could see. The sound of gunfire had increased, but we had grown used to it. War was with us while we worked the dance of rice. We all felt a strange tension. It caused us to constantly look over our shoulders, but we couldn't stop or it would mean starvation.

I shook my head, dislodging those thoughts, because tonight was for feasting. I grabbed a squash and a machete, using the log I was seated on to chop against.

"Why don't you get a wife to cook for us Pou?" I thought joking might lighten the mood. "So, we can just sit back in our hammocks after working all day."

Pou's face grew serious, and I squirmed. I hadn't meant to offend him.

"I once had a wife." He leaned forward, placing the pot on the stones over the flame. "But she died while having my son. My son died too."

"I didn't know, Pou, I'm sorry." I lowered my head, ashamed I had carelessly brought up such a painful memory.

"I came to work with your aupouk shortly after it happened. Then I found out his wife, your mteay, had left too. It felt like we all had lost someone. You three helped me with my grief."

I looked sideways at Vuthy. He remained silent. "You helped us during that time too. Aupouk often forgot about us until you came to remind him. He never wanted us after they got divorced, you know."

He nodded and looked up. "I know it doesn't seem like it, but your aupouk did love you."

"Why did he leave us with Chidaun then? He promised—he promised he'd come back for us." I was surprised at the heat of my words as I stared into the shifting and sparking fire.

Pou was silent for a while. "Have you ever seen a dog that's been hurt?"

I nodded. Cambodia was full of stray dogs that people beat and threw rocks at.

"Are they friendly to you if you try to get close?"

I shook my head. "They snap and snarl."

Pou nodded, looking deeply into the fire. "Hurt just keeps hurting."

I nodded, understanding his meaning. That was just the way in Cambodia. Hurt people hurting others was what I had seen in my family. My chidaun had hurt my mteay, by forcing her to marry someone she didn't want to. My mteay had hurt my aupouk by leaving him. My aupouk had hurt me by leaving me.

I looked up at the sky, wondering if there was anything beyond it, anything that truly controlled the endless cycle of death and life. What could possibly fix a world so full of hurt if we just kept reincarnating into it again and again?

That night, before drifting off to sleep, a memory I thought I had forgotten flittered across my consciousness. It was a picture of the man in the clouds on the pamphlet the boy had given me, the one who told me about Mr. Thach's Jesus. I wished I hadn't dropped that pamphlet so carelessly, while walking along the road.

After the harvest season, when the rice is cut and the farmers are not flooding their fields, the water recedes. Throughout the year, small silver fish swim through the paddies and spawn in the shallow water, feeding on all the bugs that thrive there. But sometimes, huge catfish swim from the canals too. I wanted to catch one of these, so I dug a big hole in the paddy on the farthest end of Pou's field, then went to check it every morning to see if a big fish had found refuge there.

When morning dawned, I swung from my hammock and set off. I looked over my shoulder when Vuthy called and waved to me, who hadn't awakened yet when I left. I waved back, calling for him to join me, but he shook his head and climbed atop one of Pou Kim's water buffalo instead, which he liked to ride for fun. The morning was still groggy and steamy, barely yawning itself awake. The water was cool on my bare feet and ankles, so I began to run. I stopped every few feet to search the water with my hands, hoping I would find a fish or two. No luck. I continued, until I had walked nearly a mile to where most of the water lay in pools across the stubbly ground. There was an elevated road that boarded the opposite end of the paddy, backed by trees, but I didn't know what was past it. We had heard bullets coming from that direction, but today, all was quiet. I searched the fields in both directions, I appeared to be the only one out today.

When I reached the hole I had dug, I plunged my hands into the muddy water. To my delight, something slippery brushed them. I couldn't get a good grip on it, so I continued to search the brown water, plunging my hands deeper, but again coming up empty. I plunged them in again, feeling the smooth skin of the fish, and I clamped my hands around it. It felt big, and I couldn't wait to pull it into view.

I grappled with it, trying to secure a good enough hold to lift it into sight, but it was slimy and kept flopping around. At last, I pulled out a catfish that was as long as my forearm. I inspected its snake-like head and slender body, almost tasting the delicious and spicy soup that it could make.

Rising to my feet, I began to walk back with my prize when a dull thud erupted behind me. Looking over my shoulder, I saw four men walking down the road flanking the paddy, toward me. They wore the muted green uniforms of the Lon Nol army and carried the black guns I had seen Khan with. I stared, wondering why they were walking through a muddy rice paddy at sunrise, when one raised his gun to his shoulder and shot.

I ran, the fish flopping at my side.

A bullet landed several feet away from me, burrowing into the mud. Then another, closer than the last. I ran faster, my mind screaming with the realization that the men were aiming at me! Another thud sounded. Another splash. A bullet whizzed past my ear and dove into the ground, splashing me with mud. Panic clouded my vision, as I sloshed through the water, my legs caked in mud. My foot caught on something sharp. Ripping it free, I continued to run, and the guns continued to fire. They rippled through the air like laughter. They were getting closer. I lunged face-first into the mud, but there was little to conceal me.

I looked over my shoulder, and the soldiers were following me into the paddy, their knees bobbing up and down as they waded through the canal. What did they want? Why were they trying to shoot me?

I looked toward Vuthy. I still had a half a mile to go. He stood staring in my direction, still mounted on the water buffalo.

"Rindy." His voice cracked in panic.

"Get off there!" I screamed.

Pushing myself from the ground, I lunged forward, crouching low as I heard the bullets darting into the mud all around me. I winced with each one, expecting to feel metal pierce my flesh at any moment.

With each shot, I blinked back the memory of the dead man's eyes, staring blindly into mine. With each splash of mud, I saw the blood oozing out of his lifeless body. With each second that passed, I smelled the stench of his flesh. He was coming for me, trying to pull me into the mud with him. I could feel his fingers curl around my bare toes as the cool mud splashed my legs.

I ran faster; my eyes locked on Vuthy who had dismounted and stood next to the mud-caked water buffalo. I had almost made it to safety. I could see the terror reflecting in his eyes. I was almost to him. The bullets continued to sound, but they had begun to thud behind me. I had made it.

"Run for the hut, Vuthy. Get Pou Kim!" But he wouldn't move. He just stood there, frozen to the mud, until I reached him and pushed him toward the hut. We ran the remaining yards toward the open door, where Pou stood with his hands on his head. We lunged up the ladder and into the shadows of safety with our chests heaving. Every inch of my frame shook uncontrollably.

"What have you done to have the Lon Nol soldiers after you?" Pou screamed at me, as he threw the door closed behind us.

"I was only collecting my—my fish," I stammered, realizing I had dropped my prize in my flight. "Then they started shooting out of nowhere."

"Why would they shoot at you?" he mumbled, pulling back the rice sack that covered the window and peering out.

"Here they come." He growled.

I stood frozen to the bamboo floor, but my pulse danced in my clenched palms. I could see a glimpse of an eye, a green uniform, and the black barrel of an M16, approaching through the floor. Pou cracked open the door.

"You house a Khmer Rouge spy." One of the soldiers hissed.

"There are no spies here," Pou Kim retorted, opening the door to reveal Vuthy and I. "You were shooting at a boy."

I heard their fists clench around the stocks of their guns, as they motioned for Pou to exit the hut. He stepped out, his movements uncertain, yet obedient. I could hear a few other soldiers going down the road, likely to our neighbors. What did they want?

"Spies are everywhere." A soldier climbed up the ladder and entered and stared at Vuthy and I, our legs caked in mud. His eyes were black; his gaze relentless. He shuffled through Pou's meager belongings, taking some riel and several bags of rice, before exiting.

"What about those inside?" one of the soldiers asked.

I melted into the thatched wall, as I hid behind the open door.

"They're just kids—let's go." Their boots shuffled through the dirt. I peered out the window, my heart pounding with each step the soldiers took as they walked away with Pou Kim. The barrel of their guns, pointed at his back.

24

ENLIST

"At that time the war was full blown, and they were getting closer to the main cities." — Rindy

THE NEXT DAY

I sat staring into the shadows of the hut until the sun began to sink, Vuthy beside me, silent. My foot, which had been sliced in my flight, had finally stopped bleeding. I must have caught a hoe blade, forgotten in the mud. The old blood had mixed with the dried mud, encasing my skin and making me itch. At some point, I fell asleep, escaping fear. But my skin began to itch so terribly that when I could stand it no longer, I got up to scrape the mud off my body. It was dark outside except for a sliver of moon.

Not daring to venture to the canal, I walked to the water bucket. Splashing my face in the warm liquid, I scrubbed until I didn't feel the roughness on my skin any longer. With my head lowered, dripping into the bucket, I heard a noise coming from behind the hut. Where was Vuthy? I had left him inside. I froze, heart pounding as I imagined the soldiers hiding there, waiting for me to emerge before dragging me off. The idea that I had gotten away from them so easily suddenly seemed too good to be true.

What if they really do think I'm a spy?

Sneaking into the hut, I crept toward the back window, careful to tread lightly. Vuthy stared at me, eyes wide. The noise grew louder, then stopped. Crouched beneath the window, I tried to quiet my quivering breath to listen, hoping all would return to silence.

Scrape, scrape, scrape. The noise started again, like digging in packed dirt. Had one of the soldiers returned to kill me? I pinched my eyes tightly, trying to breathe normally. Then the noise stopped. I waited in breathless silence, wondering what to do next. Minutes passed before I summoned up enough courage to creep up the wall and peek out. I was certain I would look into the eyes of a Lon Nol soldier, holding a gun to my face. My hair stuck to my forehead as my body broke into a cold sweat. Raising my eyes just past the windowsill, I peeked out. My heart pounded. My knees felt weak.

To my relief, I met the nose of the water buffalo, which hadn't been tied up. He rubbed his horns on the beams of the stilt hut. Laughing and embarrassed at my irrational fear, I reached through the window and grasped the rope tied to the ring in its nose and hooked it inside, just to make sure it didn't go anywhere. It was comforting to know it was there. Collapsing onto the dirt floor beneath the window, I escaped in sleep, exhausted.

Pou Kim returned the next morning before sunrise, and I woke to him slurping rice porridge.

"They determined I'm not a spy." Pou sighed, the sleepless night showing on his grim features.

Vuthy and I sat beside him. He handed each of us a bowl. I stared into mine.

"Did they hurt you?" I squeaked. "If I had known they were out there, I wouldn't have gone to fish."

"Apparently they were out patrolling and saw you, crouched in the rice paddy holding something that looked like a gun."

"It was a fish—a huge catfish. They all must be half blind."

"Well, most of the Khmer Rouge soldiers are boys only a little older than you. But I suspect they just wanted to steal from me and make a scene. I saw them taking rice from our neighbors too."

We sat in silence for a while.

"Did they hurt you?" Vuthy asked this time, as Pou hadn't answered before.

Pou rubbed his sides. "They were rough and interrogated me, hoping I would talk, but soon they realized I had no information on the Khmer Rouge."

"The Lon Nol soldiers are all over the village." Pou Kim looked grave. "They are moving into this region, and I have no doubt, into the paddies to camp. That's why they were out patrolling the area. The Khmer Rouge will pursue them. It's no longer safe here."

We heard someone call from outside. "Are you home, Kim?"

Soon all the neighbors had congregated to argue their side of the fight and grumble about their stolen property. The soldiers had taken rice and riel from everyone. Pou Kim squatted in his doorway, listening, but I knew he had a lot to say.

"The Khmer Rouge will restore the king to his rightful place," an old farmer speculated, his eyes surrounded by a million, tiny wrinkles.

"They will do more than that," a younger man interrupted, face ablaze with passion. "They are leading a revolution to restore Cambodia and cut out the corruption that has sunk into its heart."

"Lon Nol is the corruption," another man yelled, slamming his palms on his knees. "He's in the pocket of the Americans and is not looking out for the good of Cambodia. Look how much they just took from us. They'll rob us all blind before the war is done. Then what?"

The crowd erupted in shouting.

Pou stood to his feet, face weary. "Our lives are all about to change. The Lon Nol soldiers are settling into the area, being pushed back by the Khmer

Rouge who have been beating them at every turn. Soon fighting will be all around us."

"Yes, but what would they want from us? We just want to farm rice," a woman cried. Another shouted a retort.

Pou raised his hands. "I talked with someone in the next province, where the fighting has been. He said dead bodies fill the paddies, all the animals have been shot and eaten and women are being raped by the Lon Nol soldiers. If you don't think they'll steal everything we have or harvest, you're fooling yourself. If you think we can just go on planting and harvesting like normal, you are wrong. War is here and we can no longer look away."

He paused, looking at the faces before him. No one spoke. No one breathed. "I'm done just sitting by, hoping Cambodia is restored to Norodom Sihanouk—the rightful ruler. I'm joining the Khmer Rouge to make it happen."

I looked at Vuthy, and his frightened eyes met my gaze. We both knew what this meant. Life was changing again. I needed to get Vuthy somewhere safe.

25

CHIDAUN

"She was the backbone of the family." — Rindy

JANUARY 1975

"**M**teay?" I called at the closed door, feeling uneasy. "Is anyone here?"

I glanced at Vuthy. He shrugged. We had not been back to Chidaun's since Vuthy and I had run away several months earlier. My stomach clenched with nerves at the thought of seeing Khan again. Would he allow us to come back? I didn't want to return, but I had no other choice as everyone else we had visited to seek work had turned us away. They had no riel to pay us and no extra food to feed us. We had no other option, except to join the Khmer Rouge. I couldn't allow Vuthy to be put in harms way.

I knocked on the door again. Then I heard footsteps. A pretty, young woman opened the door.

"This is my Chidaun's house." I didn't know what else to say. "Is she here?"

"Yes, but she's not well." The last time I had seen her she had been in bed with an illness. Had she not recovered?

Chi Ta had always nagged Chidaun when he was alive to get a maid, as they made plenty of money to be able to afford one and many people had them. But she had always retorted with, "I can do the cooking and laundry myself." If Chidaun had accepted help she must be very ill. Vuthy and I followed closely behind her, the boards familiar beneath my feet along with the scent of incense. We reached Chidaun's room, darkened against the afternoon sun.

"Is my mteay here?" My voice sounded hollow in the echoing walls.

"Your mteay is no longer here. She left for Phom Phen with her soldier husband a few months ago."

I let out a breath, relieved. I wouldn't have to face Khan, yet. The maid knocked on the door. "Visitors for you."

"Who is it?" Chidaun's voice sounded forced and hollow.

"Some family." She looked over her shoulder, her eyes creasing, as if she enjoyed bringing happiness to my Chidaun. I just hoped happiness is what we would bring to her, and that she wouldn't send us away.

"Come," Chidaun wheezed.

Vuthy and I came around her mosquito net, bowing in a *sompeah*—our hands placed together and heads bowed—to show our respect. Chidaun's eyes had a strange yellow tint, void of all the usual sparkle. She was especially thin, and her cheeks were shrunken into her face.

"Rindy and Vuthy." She stretched a knobby hand out toward us. Her whole body wracked in a coughing fit. "I'm so glad to see you here." I couldn't help but let the pent up sigh escape my lips.

"Are you still feeling unwell, Chidaun?" Vuthy went to her side and took her hand.

"I'm just an old lady with a cough." She waved her hand to dismiss his inquiry. "You've both grown tall. Rindy you must be twelve now and that means Vuthy is about ten?"

We opened our mouth to respond but she sped on." What are you doing here? Your mteay said you both left when I asked about you."

She patted her bed, and we sat down and told her all that had happened since we had last been there. We told her about Khan's angry words, transplanting rice, Pou Kim and me being shot at by the Lon Nol soldiers. Several times, Chidaun coughed into her rag, her frail body wracked by the force. When she pulled her hand away there was blood. Vuthy and I looked at one another, grief settling over us. We were boys, but we knew what the road to death looked like—this was a slow one. A road Chidaun had been traveling alone.

"It's good you've come to stay with me. It will be nice to have young life in the house again. It's grown lonely since your mteay left to follow Khan, taking Ly and Sotha with her."

I smiled, so relieved she wanted us to stay.

"Why did Mteay leave when—"

Another coughing fit wracked her body.

"She hadn't heard from Khan and worried for him"—more coughing—"I'm sure she will be back for the inheritance though. I'm sure all my sons will return as well. Your mteay has resented me since the moment she drew her first breath. She wasn't going to stay and take care of her dying mteay." She coughed, blood trickling out of her mouth.

"Chidaun, you said you were going to be all right. That it was just a cough." Vuthy squeaked. I looked at him, his face was pale. I grabbed his hand and squeezed. I couldn't protect him from this.

In response Chidaun gave a sad smile and began to speak, but only another fit of coughing came out.

"Come boys, let me get you some food." The servant grabbed our shoulders and led us from the room. "Let's let your Chidaun rest."

I waited until we were out of earshot to voice the question burning on my tongue. "What's wrong with her?"

"The doctor says it's lung cancer, but it has spread into her whole body. It's just a matter of time until she passes into the next life." The servant's face was grave. She appeared to care about Chidaun, and I was glad she was looking out for her. "It's good she will have some family around her in the end."

She led us into the kitchen and prepared a delicious soup, one like Chidaun used to make before she sent us to the temple, with rice noodles and beef bones. I looked at Vuthy, slurping up his broth, and smiled. We knew where our next meal would be coming from and the following ones after that. Relief mixed with the broth in my stomach, warming me to my toes.

Over the next few weeks, I watched Chidaun grow thinner and thinner, while the wheezing plagued her every breath. She chewed betel root almost continually, to cover up the blood she coughed up and to ease her pain. Vuthy and I would sit with her and tell her stories of our adventures. We only told her the good ones, never speaking of the cruelty of the monks or the fear of the war. Each day she grew weaker and weaker. The time of her death was skulking in the corners of the house, creeping ever nearer to her bed at night. I struggled because I loved her, but I also hated to watch her die slowly.

A monk from the nearest pagoda visited Chidaun every evening with chants to chase away the bad spirits that haunted her, blessing her to recover. Buddhism was like a necklace Chidaun wore that her mteay had tied tightly around her neck when she was born. Some people wore it outside of their clothes for all to see, but others wore it hidden beneath. Chidaun had tied the necklace onto me, but I wore it hidden because I did not understand it but also didn't know how to remove it. Buddhism was supposed to be about enlightenment, but to me it was like staring into a muddy pond, murky and unclear. Yet I was Cambodian, and Cambodians were Buddhist, as Chidaun had reminded me often.

I watched as Chidaun's skin changed from yellow to a dull shade of blue, as if the disease was eating her body from the inside out. Her breath sometimes rattled around in her ribs and other times it seemed to stop all together. I couldn't decide which sound was more terrible.

The monks frequented the house much more often, waiting for Chidaun to die, so they could assist her soul in its journey to the next stage of life. They circled like vultures, draped in orange, waiting for her last breath. Whenever they were around, Vuthy and I retreated into the jungle and waited for them to leave. As they left, they chanted against the evil spirits, but the feeling of darkness seemed more present than ever before. Even in the silence of the night, their chanting haunted my dreams and took the shape of a tiger, pursuing me through the darkness. I awoke each time, gasping and trembling.

About a month after Vuthy and I came home, Chidaun fell into a deep sleep and never woke up. I watched the struggle of pain leave her body with the color that drained from her face to the chorus of chants and wails.

We would wait seven days to begin the burning ceremony, according to the custom, to give her soul time to be reborn. I wondered what she would come back as or if she had enough good merit to escape the cycle and reach *nirvana*—when the cycles could stop. If she hadn't, I hoped she wouldn't have pain in her next life. A strange combination of relief shrouded in sadness wrapped around me.

Later that night, alone in our hammocks, I heard Vuthy sniffling.

"You all right?" I looked straight up at the ceiling, futilely wishing tears would come for me too. Would they help lessen the throb in my chest?

"She took us when neither Aupouk or Mteay wanted us anymore." Vuthy sobbed. "There is nobody alive now who cares if we live or die."

I had thought of this but had hoped Vuthy wouldn't.

"We'll take care of each other as we always have."

I reached over and swung his hammock, trying to distract him from his pain.

"I can't be brave like Chidaun told me to be. I can't stop crying."

"I think sometimes crying is brave, Vuthy."

Except I couldn't cry, even though I wanted to more than anything to release the pressure within me. Vuthy continued weeping as we swung softly in our hammocks, wrapped in grief. We were boys of twelve and ten, experiencing the pangs of death amidst a war, trying to learn to be men.

26

THE SAVIORS

"People were rejoicing, I rejoiced. I thought the war was over."
— Rindy

APRIL 1975

When the seven days had passed, the women from the village covered Chidaun in a white cloth and scattered incense sticks around her corpse to make her spirit happy, but I could still smell the decay. Vuthy and I avoided the house as much as possible, sleeping on the porch like we used to, with the chanting and the mourners crowding the place.

A neighbor sent word to Phom Phen with her teenage son, to retrieve Mteay, and she made it in time for the ceremony, with Ly, Soth, and her new baby, Tang. So did Chidaun's other children, three sons, including Pou Ponlok, who I hadn't seen since the temple. I avoided him, not even venturing into the house if he was inside, afraid he might instruct me to bow and then beat me if I didn't do it right. The night they arrived they stayed up late and discussed the inheritance. Vuthy and I heard them from the porch, shouting late into the night. I didn't understand all of it, but I gathered that they were upset with the meager amount of money Chidaun had, after Chi Ta's passing. He had been a wealthy landowner, they said.

Why was this all that was left? They fought until each seemed satisfied, but it was decided that Mteay would get Chidaun's house.

It took Vuthy and I nearly all the next day to gather enough wood to make her funeral pyre. I stacked branches in a pile in front of the house as instructed. Chidaun was placed in a long wooden box on top of the pile, and Pou Ponlok, along with three of the local monks, lit the dry bark, chanting in a shrill pitch. I hid behind an old lady, so he wouldn't see me. Minutes passed before the flames licked at the wooden box, but soon the blaze leapt into the sky.

Looking through the flames I watched Mteay's face distorted in grief, her tears streaking in soot. She held Tang to her chest as she slept, shaking in a rhythmic, unbroken motion. Sotha and Ly stood nearby, their faces ashen as they cried silent tears. Their white dresses curled around their legs like the fire curling in the air. In Cambodia, white is the color of death. Chidaun's death left us all feeling weak.

I studied Mteay as she mourned. She sounded like she was also slowly dying. There was something else weighing on Mteay though, a deeper darkness reflected terror in her eyes. She looked even thinner, and her face was engraved with premature lines as if etched in by force instead of wearing in naturally with age. After what seemed like hours, her body became still. She no longer convulsed, and her tears stopped falling. She and the baby, Sotha, Ly and some of the women from the village went inside. And my uncles, including Pou Ponlok left, with their share of riel tucked securely away. Vuthy and I sat in our hammocks on the porch, not knowing what else to do with so many people about.

"It has been hell." Mteay's voice slipped through the open door.

"What has happened in Phnom Penh?" a woman's voice asked.

"The fighting has been so bad. Khan and the other Lon Nol soldiers have been fighting against the Khmer Rouge near the capital and the Lon Nol are no match. There is so much death, so much suffering. I've volunteered at a hospital outside the city, but it's just a tent really. We've run out of supplies and morphine to stop the pain. Most of the dying and suffering are trapped behind the Khmer Rouge, and no one can get to them."

She paused, taking a breath, as if even the memory was suffocating her.

"About a month ago, the Khmer Rouge surrounded the Lon Nol army a short distance from the city. They cut off all the food and supplies coming and going. I keep hearing stories of soldiers starving to death. I've been trying to get Khan food, but I can't."

"I haven't heard from him in six months." I could hear her crying again, her words shaking and unclear. "I don't know if he's dead or alive."

The women cooed and soothed.

"It will end soon, I think. There is nothing else to fight over, no one can resist the Khmer Rouge."

The burden of the war sat much heavier on the backs of the cities, where most of the population lived, rather than the rural parts of Cambodia. I tried to imagine what war looked like and how it felt to those enduring it for the past five years. Mteay knew. It haunted her. She couldn't scrub the look and feel of horror from her face.

An elderly man, head bowed in respect and sorrow, walked from the group of men congregated outside to the open door. I knew he was Mteay's Pou, Chidaun's younger brother. He was the family member Kiry had gone to work for.

"It was good of you to come." Mteay's steps sounded toward the door. "Please come in and eat; we have food prepared for you."

Obediently, Mteay's uncle removed his shoes and disappeared inside.

"Please, Pou, tell me of my son, Kiry."

"I'm sorry to bring this news, on such a sorrow filled day, but Kiry has joined the Khmer Rouge. He left one night and didn't return, but some men from the village saw him going with the Khmer Rouge recruiters."

"How long?" Mteay's voice was cold, void of all emotion.

"He left about six months ago."

Moments passed, no one said anything. I looked at Vuthy, his eyes large and frightened. We knew what this meant; Mteay's son and husband had been at war—with one another.

Within the week, the Khmer Rouge took Phnom Penh. News spilled from the radios of the black clad troops marching into the city filled with white flags of surrender and the Lon Nol soldiers surrendering their guns after the nearly five-year struggle. Then the radios went oddly silent. Had the Khmer Rouge stopped the broadcasting on purpose? Had they cut the power to the city? Nobody knew. The uncertainty did little to quell the general celebration, as Khmer New Year was approaching. Vuthy and I could hear the neighbors as they drank and played music late into the night.

"What does it mean that the Khmer Rouge have won?" Vuthy asked, unable to sleep from the noise.

"I don't know. But it means there won't be any more fighting and that's good."

He didn't seem convinced.

"Will he come home now?"

I knew he meant Khan. I had been avoiding the question, like pretending rain wasn't coming.

"I don't know if he survived. You heard Mteay. The war was bad where he was. Maybe all the Lon Nol soldiers were"—I swallowed—"killed."

I was conflicted. Mteay relied on him, and his death would devastate her, but I had never liked Khan, and I hated the words he constantly spewed at Vuthy and me. I closed my eyes against the bad thoughts.

We waited for days. The returning soldiers brought stories of death, destruction and the brutality of the Khmer Rouge, speaking in hushed tones and looking over their shoulders. Each day that passed we wondered. Would Khan return too?

The wondering stopped a few days later when we returned from gathering wood for Mteay's dinner fire and saw Khan leaning on the porch. He wore his green uniform, but he didn't have a gun. Mteay was talking inside with some of the village women. The cigarettes the men were smoking cast eerie shadows across their faces. Khan's cheeks were sunken, and his frame balanced against the wall as if that was the only thing holding him up. I pulled Vuthy down, and we squatted outside the circle of men, keeping to the shadows to catch what bits of the conversation we could.

"We've put our weapons down." Khan's tone was flat and low as he exhaled the cigarette smoke. "I didn't think I'd ever smoke one of these again." He cursed. "It tastes so good."

"Is it true the Khmer Rouge have captured the capital?" one man asked with eyes shining in the orange glow. "Lon Nol is completely powerless now?"

Khan scoffed. "Phnom Penh was his last hope. He lost every other territory, including the one he held on the border of Thailand. He had declared himself Marshal over all of Cambodia and had dismissed the General Assembly, seizing all power. He said he wasn't going to 'play at democracy during times of war.' In the end he had nothing left but his Buddhist beliefs. He sprinkled some sand at the entrance to the city while saying a chant before admitting defeat and running like a scared dog. Every soldier who didn't get shot is making their way home I'm sure."

"How did you get away?"

Khan paused, staring into the darkness. "I hid in a rice paddy until I could get away undetected. Most of the Khmer Rouge entered the city."

"The Khmer Rouge are the saviors," one man whispered to his companion, being careful to keep his voice low enough that Khan couldn't hear.

"What was that?" Khan asked the whisperer, his frame popping in agitation. He didn't respond.

"You may think you know the Khmer Rouge, but they're a bunch of kids with guns, boys and girls who aren't even teens yet. They were recruited from the poorest villages and trained for years in the jungles to be brutal, little war machines. I thought they were simple villagers, but they are full of tricks. One time, our battalion snuck up on what we thought was one of their 'talking meetings' where they rehearsed their code of ethics and played horrible music. But we found loudspeakers hooked up to a tape player, hanging from a tree. They had planted so many bombs that we lost almost half of our men."

He paused, taking a long drag on his cigarette. "They are not what you think."

Later that night, I heard Khan asking how much money we had made while he was away. He grumbled and huffed, and Mteay assured him she would find somewhere to send us to work soon, especially with the rice planting season coming. Then he asked about Kiry, and I held my breath, knowing Mteay's answer would enrage him. Would she tell him the truth about her son's disrespect for joining the opposing side to Khan, his stepfather? Or would she lie and leave it up to someone from the village to tell him?

"You just got back, let's leave this for another time." Mteay's words were soothing.

"You'll tell me now. Give me the answer to a simple question."

"I don't know…"

"Is he not still working for your pou?"

Mteay hesitated.

"Speak up, woman."

"He's joined the Khmer Rouge."

Khan rose to his feet.

"What? How long ago?"

"Maybe six months?" Mteay's voice was even and calm, lowering in pitch with Khan's mounting one.

Khan cursed, his voice booming. "How could the worthless boy—your worthless son—do such a thing? How could he disrespect me in this way? He probably hid in the jungle and laughed with the rebels, firing his rifle like a big man."

Khan's fists crashed against something inside, and Tang woke with a cry. I stood up. Would he hurt Mteay in his rage? Vuthy grabbed my arm, shaking his head.

"What are you going to do, Rindy? He'll kill you."

Khan's voice rose in pitch.

Regardless of our past, she was still my mteay, and I didn't want anyone to hurt her. Least of all Khan. I shrugged Vuthy off and walked toward the door.

Khan's voice continued to rage. "He probably tried to kill me. Well, if I ever see him again, I'll beat him to it. He was too slow, and I outsmarted him and the rest of them."

"Please, Khan, let us be until you are calmer. Please come back then." Mteay's voice was no longer calm but was laced with sobs. I reached the door, my hand trembling as I pushed it open.

I watched Khan disappear down the back steps with his curses. Relief flooded me, I wouldn't have to face him this time. Mteay sat holding Tang, rocking back and forth, tears streaming down her face. I approached, but she waved me back outside. She was no longer the woman I remembered when she was married to Aupouk, full of spunk and fire. She was worn down like an old pair of sandals.

I felt bad for her and how hard she had tried to find Khan and smuggle him food while he was fighting in the war. How she had endured months near the battlefield with all the death and starvation for a cruel and brutal man. He had survived the war, but his rage and demons had grown, and he couldn't drown them in his spirit worship or alcohol. The war might have been over, but it was just beginning in my family.

27

THE EVACUATION

"Then reality struck." — Rindy

TWO WEEKS LATER

For the next few days, the atmosphere in the village was like that of New Years. People rejoiced, got drunk in celebration, smiles plastered across their faces. People cried and hugged each other in the streets, anticipating the return of their husbands and sons and the restoration of their homeland. I got caught up in the excitement, enjoying the lively conversations and the look of relief on each person's face. Until I encountered a lone Khmer Rouge soldier, sauntering down the road toward me.

Unlike Khan, this soldier had not laid his weapon down, but carried it closely against his side. His checkered red *krama* —scarf— was tied tightly at his waist, contrasting the dingy blackness of his pajama-like uniform. Glancing up into his face, I expected to see the relief of a soldier who belonged to the winning side, but instead I saw cold, dark eyes and tightly pressed lips. He didn't appear to be celebrating.

I continued to walk toward the river, puzzled by his behavior but hoping to catch a fish or two for dinner. Soon, I encountered more soldiers on their way to the village, wearing their guns and the same hardened expressions.

There were men and women, boys and girls, some around the same age as me. They all looked the same. Even the women had short, unfeminine haircuts and wore the same black pants as the men. Very unlike traditional Khmer women. The road was crawling with them, like black ants, seeping up from the underground. They made me uneasy, so I cut back through the trees, avoiding the main road.

I expected to find the village in full celebration when I returned with my fish, as the victors were in their midst. When I approached though, I didn't smell pots of soup boiling or freshly lit cigarettes. Instead, panic filled the air. I passed one hut as a woman hurriedly gathered up her clothes from the trees surrounding her house, even though they were still wet. Finding her behavior odd, I checked the sky, expecting to see rain, but there wasn't even a cloud. Another woman called to her children who were playing in the street. Her tone was sharp and her eyes frightened as she pulled them inside and slammed the door. The Khmer Rouge were going door-to-door further down the street, so I picked up my pace, hoping to hear what they were shouting. I ran, the air suddenly becoming hard to breathe as I heard their words.

"You all must evacuate now," one soldier shouted as he banged on a closed door.

"The Americans are going to bomb this village."

I ran faster, shooting past him and the other soldiers, my mind ricocheting from one of their shouts to the other like a rock over a pond.

"Go anywhere but avoid the main towns and roads."

"Move quickly or you will all die."

"No need to take your belongings or lock your houses, we will take care of everything you need."

"You will be returning in just three days."

"We will keep you safe."

Their shouts rang through the streets, causing a haze of panic to hang over the village that had just been celebrating.

"There's no time," Khan yelled as I approached the house. He grabbed me by the arm and thrust me inside. The force caused me to lose my grip on the fish, and it fell to the dirt outside the door.

"Gather Chidaun's sarongs and clothing." He began to shove clothing into an old rice sack. "We can use them to trade if we need to." That's when I noticed Khan's Lon Nol uniform smoldering in a large pot, the flames already eating away at its green fabric. He tossed another match in and covered the lid. We never burned things indoors like that, and his behavior was strange.

Ly was roughly dressing baby Tang, who wailed in protest. Sotha was clawing through her clothing. Vuthy was rummaging through the pots and pans, shoving food as quickly as he could into his pockets. Mteay was gathering food and supplies, quickly throwing what dried fish and prahok we had into a basket. Fear shone from each of their eyes and echoed in their voices as they yelled at each other.

"I don't understand why we need to go. Can't we just hide here and leave if we hear the bombers?" Mteay pleaded, stopping to look at Khan.

"They are the ones with the guns, and they're telling us to go. We must go. We have no choice." He went to the window and peered out. "Don't think they won't shoot everyone in this house, because they will. I know what they are capable of."

"But we aren't at war with them. We are just innocent villagers."

"I've seen them kill innocent civilians just to make an example of them and frighten others into obedience." Khan grabbed the can of riel and emptied it into a pouch he tied around his waist, concealing it inside his pant leg.

"But it doesn't make sense. Why would the U.S. bomb Phnom Sampov? Haven't they left Cambodia after Lon Nol's defeat?

"Cambodia is already filled with U.S. bombs, more than can be numbered." Khan was growing impatient, but Mteay wouldn't relent. She had just been left Chidaun's home as her inheritance and didn't want to leave it, even for three days.

"But what if the Khmer Rouge loot—"

"No more protesting, woman." Khan slammed his fist on the table. Tang screamed. "We're going to leave."

"You carry this." Khan shoved a bag of rice into my hands.

Brup-Brup-up-up-up-up. A quick ripple of machine guns fired outside, and for an instant we all stilled, sucking in our breath.

"We're leaving, now," Khan yelled, pulling everyone from their trance. "Anyone who isn't ready will be left behind."

Mteay began to protest, but Khan grabbed the belongings that were already in rice sacks or baskets and threw them out the door, pushing us out with them.

"Where will we go?" Ly clutched her sack close to her chest.

"Just out of Phnom Sampov," Khan mumbled, grabbing the strewn bundles and slinging them over his shoulder. Mteay followed behind him holding Tang close, tears gleaming in her eyes as she looked back at Chidaun's home. Its finely thatched roof, real wooden floors and front porch shrine made it of great value. It was now Mteay's home, but she was leaving it behind. It was the one thing she hadn't bargained and scraped for, she and Khan could never have afforded it if Chidaun hadn't left it to her. Pain beat in the soft spots near her temples as she peeled her eyes away to follow Khan. They'd said only three days, only three days. I repeated the thought in my head, a silent chant in the pressing of those on the street.

"Come, run," Khan called from a short distance up ahead. The rice was heavy, but I picked up my pace. Villagers were everywhere, running through the streets in panic. Some were calling out for their loved ones, and others were taking flight like we were, their belongings strapped to their backs, carried on their heads or pulled in carts. Khan led us through the maze and into the thickness of the jungle. We ripped through the trees and onto a snaking road, clutching our belongings, joining other families trudging down the road. Our lungs burned with hot panic, but we kept running, searching the sky for the dreaded airplanes.

Crack! The air echoed with the sound of a gunshot. The crowd stilled. I sucked in my breath. Our heads swiveled trying to locate where it had come from. Then we saw a woman kneeling on the ground, her hands covering the wound in a man's chest. A Khmer soldier stood nearby, his weapon drawn. Had he just shot the man? The crowd parted around her, hurrying past.

"Why? Why? Why?" the woman screamed, her words almost inaudible, drowning in shrieks. "We're just merchants."

The woman had paler skin and more slanted eyes than most Khmer women. I knew she was of Chinese descent, it was clearly written in her features.

"Why?" the woman screamed again, her hands covered in blood as she clenched the hair spilling over her face.

"You're Chinese, it is enough." The Khmer Rouge soldiers raised his machine gun and gripped its trigger.

Brump-up-up-up.

The woman crumbled forward, falling on her dead husband. The soldier continued onward, yelling at people to keep moving and that he'd shoot anyone else who stopped.

I stared without seeing, unable to move. All was silent, the birds not even daring to sing. Or perhaps I couldn't hear them over the pounding in my own head. The woman and her screams were dead. But I couldn't take my eyes off her.

"Rindy, come," Vuthy cried, pulling my arm, pointing to our family that was already disappearing into the crowd. We continued to run down the road, the woman's screams ringing in my ears, and the bag of rice pressing into my shoulder. We all kept searching the sky, but I couldn't help feeling that the threat was on the ground, among us.

28
YEAR ZERO

"They always came at night..." — Rindy

LATER THAT DAY

We walked east, away from Phnom Sampov and away from the main roads as instructed. Not being forced in any direction, other than out of the villages. Mteay suggested we should go to Chi Ta's land, since she knew the way and thought it should only take a couple of hours to get there. The road was so clogged with people and water buffalo, cows and motorcycles that the Khmer Rouge kept waving their guns in the air and shouting for everyone to keep moving. Due to all the traffic, after four hours of walking we still hadn't reached our destination. The bag of rice hurt my shoulder, but Vuthy and I took turns carrying it. One Khmer Rouge soldier, who had no teeth and wore a tattered black shirt, matching pants and bulky sandals that looked like they were made from a tire, yelled at the crowd. He held a battery-operated loudspeaker, which squeaked and cackled, adding to the confusion and noise.

"April 17, 1975 is a day of great victory and tremendous historical significance for our Cambodian nation and people. It is the day when our people completely and definitely liberated the capital city of Phnom

Penh and our beloved Cambodia. Long live the Cambodian people—" The radio went into static and the man beat it against his leg, not realizing he had accidentally changed the station, until another Khmer Rouge soldier yanked it from him and tuned it to the correct channel.

"Long live the line of absolute struggle, independence, self-reliance and overcoming all obstacles of the correct and clear sighted Cambodian revolutionary organization." This time it was a woman's voice shouting from the speakers. Music took the place of the shouting through the speakers. It was ugly music, not like the traditional Khmer music I had always heard.

"The resounding victory cries of our people and army have put an end to the existence of the enemy, liberated the beloved motherland, and definitely ended the war of aggression of the cruel US imperialists, who have all been expelled from Cambodia."

The farther we walked, the more Khmer Rouge I saw. Ever since I had seen them the first time, trying to recruit Aupouk, I had assumed they were a small number of jungle dwellers who no one took seriously. Now, they were the ones in charge, and it was clear that their hearts were full of kum—the revenge of Cambodia. Some looked as scared as we were, but each had a gun and each one instantly became the authority. I had seen them kill, and all doubt was crowded out of my mind. They were not the saviors of Cambodia.

I wondered if Kiry was still alive, and if he was waving a gun in peoples faces too. I looked for my brother among the black hoard, taking a quick glance into the faces of the soldiers I passed. I wondered if he killed as ruthlessly as the soldiers I saw had. Wincing, I tried to shut the image out of my mind, but with each checkered krama that I saw, it reappeared, like the dead man's blood spackled shirt.

Some travelers had oxen pulling carts and they held up everyone else because the great, lumbering beasts couldn't move quickly enough. Others pulled along the sick and elderly. The road was a maze of tuk tuk's, wheelbarrows, bikes and travelers on foot. Everyone had the same scared eyes and bellies full of dust. If we stopped for too long, a soldier would bark at us to keep moving, but eventually so many people sat down that they let us rest. They seemed less concerned about the threat from the sky and more concerned with us following orders. I was tired, and the sun began to set, but at last we reached the rice paddies. Mteay pointed to a plot of land that had belonged to Chi Ta. The moon hovered over the landscape, casting shadows across the weary travelers. It wasn't yet the rainy season, so plowing or planting hadn't begun yet, which meant the homes and temporary shelters were deserted.

"This way," Mteay called, snaking her way through the crowd to the rice paddy and a vacant rice storage shed that had belonged to Chi Ta, before her Chidaun had sold the land with his passing. When we reached it though, it was already crowded with people. Khan began to shout and claim that it belonged to him, but a Khmer Rouge officer stalked over and declared that fighting was not allowed, and we needed to respect that others had gotten there first. We would have to camp somewhere else for the night. I was exhausted, and my sisters were too, even though they didn't have to carry the rice sack. Sotha cried, hiding behind Mteay's legs.

We walked deeper into the dry rice paddy. We approached a paddy next to a canal when the Khmer Rouge began to direct the crowd off the road. The land already sparked with hundreds of glowing fires and makeshift shelters. Some of the shelters were made of blankets, bamboo leaves and clothes, thrown together out of desperation. Each structure shivered in the midnight breeze, displaying the desolation everyone felt. There were already hundreds of people huddled beneath the cloudless sky, clutching their belongings, drunk with exhaustion, their faces reflecting in the pathetic fires they had managed to build. Even the stars hid in the blackness of the sky.

Khan led us through the maze of people until he found a vacant space large enough for all of us. Mteay laid blankets down, not bothering to make a shelter, as it was already almost morning. We collapsed into a patchwork of blistered feet, dirty clothes and exhausted faces.

"I'm hungry," whined Sotha, once all fell quiet.

"Shh," Mteay whispered, slipping her a piece of dried fish when she thought no one was looking. As she handed over the pathetic nibble, her movements were quick and almost unnoticeable, and there was hesitancy in her eyes. I knew she wanted to hoard it back, reserve what she could as she didn't know what the future held. I knew better than to ask for some fish too. I didn't want to see her hesitancy turn to a shade of panic. She didn't have enough for all of us to eat our fill. No one else said a word. We merely stared into the black sky, ignoring our stomachs.

I had not seen a single airplane the entire day, and I had stopped even looking for them. My focus was on the soldiers and their black uniforms and checkered krama's. Even though no one voiced it, we all knew we had been lied to. I tried not to think about it as I drifted to sleep listening to Mteay's song, swelling in a mournful tune.

The soldiers' barking commands woke us in the morning as they snaked their way between the people scattered across the ground.

"Every man is to come and receive a piece of paper. Write down your heritage and every job you have held, so we know how you can best serve *Angkar.*"

What was Angkar? No one seemed to know. Maybe Norodom Si-hanouk was Angkar. If so, why was he being so secretive about it? If they gave his name, everyone would be excited to cooperate.

"Everyone has a place in Angkar. Each will do his part to serve. If he cannot serve, he will not be a part. If you cannot not work, you will not eat."

Mteay and Khan had been fighting almost continually in quiet spats so the soldiers wouldn't hear.

"Will they let us go home after this?"

"I don't know what they will do."

"Are we just going to sit and do nothing?"

"In case you didn't notice"—Khan stood, unable to sit still—"I am not the one with the gun."

The rumblings were on everyone's lips. How long until we will be allowed to return to our villages?

Obediently, the scores of men lined up to receive their piece of paper and nub pencil, before peeling off to begin their homework for the day. Khan returned to the rest of us, still huddled together on the blanket. He clutched his paper nervously, his face matching in color.

"They must want to know each of our capabilities and the level of education we've reached," a man next to us whispered excitedly to his wife, his eyes large behind his wire-rimmed glasses. "Perhaps they want to offer us positions. The Khmer Rouge will need qualified people to help manage everyone. I may get a high position because I am a schoolteacher."

"What if it's some kind of trick though?" His wife looked scared, her eyes darting from side to side.

"How could they not want educated people? What benefit would it be to punish those who could be the greatest asset to them in building a new society?" the man said, already beginning to write.

"I don't know, I just don't have a good feeling about it."

The man stopped and looked up at his wife. "But what choice do I have? Should I lie and risk being pointed out by one of the children later if they do have ill intent?"

His wife didn't respond but bowed her head in submission.

The man's pencil scribbled across the paper until he had transcribed the extensive details of his education, which spanned the entire page.

Khan continued to stare at his blank paper, and I wondered why he was not as excited as our neighbor was. Then he began to write slowly, as if weighing out each word before putting it down on the paper. I noticed the words "banana farmer" scribbled in bad handwriting at the bottom of the page, before he pushed himself from the ground to shuffle back into the swelling line. I was puzzled, wondering why Khan would lie about his former occupation. Then I remembered the smoldering uniform. Curious, I followed him.

A soldier, who sat behind a makeshift table, scrutinized Khan as he handed them his piece of paper with a forced smile.

"I'm sorry for the poor handwriting," Khan began. "I hope you will be able to make it out."

The soldier's eyes inched down the page, his face blank and eyes narrow.

"Where did you sell your bananas?" he asked, looking up quickly.

"At a small market in Phnom Sampov," Khan replied, but his hands clutched the side of his pant legs. "It was a bad year for them though." He shrugged. "I hardly made half of what I did last year. Had some problems with the monkeys." Khan laughed, but I couldn't help but notice that his hands were still clenched.

"Did you have any involvement with the fight between the Khmer Rouge and Lon Nol?" the soldier asked, his eyes absently scanning the page.

"None at all." Khan responded, his knuckles turning white. "I live a long way from Phnom Penh and have a large family to take care of, three daughters and three sons. My oldest son, Kiry, is a Khmer Rouge soldier, but I do not know where. He's a good boy, and I raised him to love Cambodia."

After glancing one more time into Khan's face, the soldier nodded his head and waved the next man forward. It was the man with glasses. The soldier took the man's extended paper and began to read it, his eyes darting from one word to the next as he consumed them like a starving man consuming food.

"Oh, you are an educated man." The soldier hummed approvingly, nudging the other soldiers nearby to look at the man's paper.

I didn't wait to find out why they were excited as I hurried back to rejoin Vuthy. I couldn't help but wonder what position they would give the man though and decided it must be one of authority from how they were acting.

Later that night, hours past sunset, I was awoken by voices coming from where the man with glasses slept.

"Angkar wants to meet you and your whole family." A soldier said, instructing the man to follow him. The soldier's black uniform blended into the moonless sky.

Getting up the man with the glasses followed them without question. Glancing over his shoulder, he stared at his wife, regret written across his features. The moon glinted off of his glasses as he turned to go, his wife following, as they disappeared into the blackness of the night.

I never saw that family again.

29

THE COLOR BLACK

"The grip kept getting stronger and stronger." — Rindy

MAY 1975

"You are here because Kampuchea is starting over," the short Khmer Rouge official shouted, his voice shrill in the evening air thick with smoke. "All the 'new people,' the city dwellers, and those who have moved away from the land have been invited back to the land to learn from the ways of the 'old people'—those who have always been our comrades. Here is where you will stay. There is nothing left for you in your former homes, and everyone is invited to be a part of this new Kampuchea. If you try to leave, you will be brought to Angkar or face disciplinary action."

I had seen a few people try to take their belongings and leave by the road, but they were turned back by the soldiers positioned at checkpoints further down. Some had even tried to escape through the rice paddies, but they had all been caught. A few of them had been shot as an example of the "disciplinary action."

"What you have been taught in the cities is wrong, and you must be re-educated. Capitalism is evil. We are all brothers and sisters; all equal, all the same. No one is a *lok*. No more '*Srey*', we are all the same class, the same level."

He paused, taking a deep breath for emphasis. "There need not be division amongst us. The imperialistic west has tried to eat Cambodia up with its false ideas and with its propaganda. They say the rich and educated are the ones who should be in control. That is not true. Cambodia has been made prosperous by the hard work of the lowest classes, not those who benefit from them. If we do not have rice, we do not have life."

I blinked my eyes, trying to stay awake. The Khmer Rouge instructed us to go to meetings every evening, after we worked in the rice paddies, to prepare them for seed planting when the rainy season arrived. The rain was coming, I could feel it in the air. We didn't all have oxen, but they gave us each a hoe to dig up the clumps and ready the land for planting. The ground was hard and dry, not softened by rainfall, but they yelled all day repeatedly, "if you do not work, you do not eat." I looked down at my hands and picked at a blister.

"This is why none of us can have personal property," the speaker continued to shout, his voice mounting in pitch. "We are not different from each other. There does not need to be a separation between what is mine and what is yours. It all belongs to Angkar."

The wind blew out of Mteay's lungs, as she sat just behind me in the grass holding Tang. She was scared. The Khmer Rouge had set up a cafeteria and several small huts for their soldiers to live in near the road, made of bamboo poles, thatched walls and metal roofs. We were given two meals a day, one of mushy rice porridge and another of a salty broth with bits of rice. The soldiers who served us said our meals were provided by "Angkar," but I still didn't know who or what "Angkar" was. After we ate, Mteay secretly cooked a meal inside our tent with a tiny fire and a rice pot because we were always left hungry. We had been rationing the little bit of food we had brought for the last few weeks and were on our last cup of rice. Hunger had begun to grip my every thought and every movement, as the portions grew less and less with each passing day.

"We are Cambodia. We are one. We will demolish the division." The man's voice cracked.

With fresh zeal, the Khmer Rouge soldiers commenced to purge the camp of items of personal property, inspired by the speakers' ideals. No one dared to risk being taken to "Angkar" or being shot on the spot. They explained that they were not "stealing" but were "collecting for the corporate good of all." Extra blankets, food, dishes and jewelry were all confiscated to serve the larger purpose of Kampuchea. Thick tarps were distributed to provide shelters, appearing to have been stolen from the villages. Each family was searched, and no one was spared. Some of the soldiers were kinder than the others and some were so young, their guns seemed too heavy for them to carry.

I watched as the soldiers rifled through the belongings of a wealthier family who camped a few rows away from us. The children sat crying as they handed over their belongings. One of the women soldiers eyed them greedily when the old woman's hands trembled as she handed over a necklace of elaborate green, bracelets of blood red and rings of starry yellow. The bright droplets of color disappeared into the black pockets of the soldiers.

"We are not stealing but are collecting these items for the good of all."

When the soldiers approached our tent, I knew they wouldn't find anything so costly or alluring because Mteay had pawned anything of value long ago to buy food.

"Hand over any supplies you have," a soldier droned routinely. "Any jewels, books, additional clothing, pots and food."

We sat and stared, wondering what we possibly had to offer.

"If you don't produce anything, we'll search you," the soldier barked, unable to bite back his impatience. A young female soldier stood beside him. She looked about my age, her arms weighted down by the machine gun she carried. She had deep brown skin, and she looked at the belongings like she had never seen such beauty and color before.

We searched our things, realizing how very little we had brought with us. Ly produced a bundle of clothing, Sotha tearfully handed over her doll, and Vuthy grudgingly placed a pocketknife and extra pair of sandals on top of the small pile of belongings. Khan emptied his pockets, revealing a few crumbled riel, a photo of Buddha and a watch. I reluctantly handed over the writing pad Mr. Thach had given me. There wasn't any space left, and the paper was nearly worn through, but I had kept it so I could remember and practice what I had learned by drawing characters in the dirt. I had also kept it because of Mr. Thach and his kindness.

We all looked to Mteay next. She relinquished her pot and the last sack of rice with trembling hands. After poking around our campsite for anything else, the soldier tossed our belongings into an ox cart and moved on. The young female soldier eyed Sotha's doll like she wanted to touch it, but her hands clutched her gun instead. Had she ever had a doll before?

"Everyone come, wash and dye your clothes," was the next command to be shouted. Large pots of murky, black water were positioned throughout the camp, and each family was instructed to dye their clothing to match the Khmer color—black. Every mteay helped their children strip off their dirty clothes and wash them in the black water, with stained hands and sullen faces.

When our turn came, Mteay helped us out of our outer garments and plunged them into the pot, scrubbing briskly, as if she was trying to scrub the color away. The small pile of colorful garments at her feet turned into dripping lumps of coal, as she was careful to wash each piece of clothing we had gathered in our hurried departure from the village.

"Why, Mteay?" Sotha asked, as she watched her yellow sarong become engulfed in the black water. "They said we would only be here for a few days. Why do we have to look like them?"

"Don't ask questions," Mteay responded quietly, while scrubbing violently. A tear fell from her eye and ran down her nose, splashing into the dark water. As I watched Mteay's tear fall, I realized the truth. We were not going home. The dying of our clothes meant there was no turning back, no separation between us and the nightmare that plagued our every waking moment. Fear attached itself, like a leech. It showed on every face, in every word whispered and every movement made. The camp became blanketed in black, as if ash had rained in the night. It was a blackness that was not only seen but felt.

30

HUNGER

"I was a young kid. I didn't know much about anything and
I was scared." — Rindy

MAY-OCTOBER 1975

The realization that we weren't leaving soaked into our bones. It
rained on our heads and ate our feet like mud. It started with a few
panicked whispers then turned into an exchange of blank stares and the
sound of starving stomachs. Each person sank into his or her fate like a
bug realizing the spider has caught it in its web, a binding too tight to
escape. The meager food rations of porridge or salty broth with a little rice,
dwindled. The portions became too small to sustain any of us. Those in the
camp began to faint from hunger and some couldn't walk to get the little
bit of food that was allotted to them.

"Angkar has just won a great victory and is poor because of the great
losses and the struggle," the soldiers would say as we lined up to get food.
"But only for a short time. Angkar will provide food for us, but sometimes
the food will be late. That is why we must plant rice. With rice we will be
wealthy and happy. Rice is life."

Later that night, Khan and the man who had built a shelter next to us spoke in whispers.

"There just isn't rice." The man looked around, making sure a Khmer Rouge wasn't patrolling.

"What do you mean?" Khan spat.

"Keep your voice down,"the man hissed. "I heard the typical rice crops in Cambodia had been affected badly by the war, but I never could have expected it to be this bad."

"Yes," said Khan. "I heard soldiers talk about tramping through rice paddies while they fought for the Lon Nol, destroying crop after crop." Khan was still concealing his identity, but I knew he had tramped through rice paddies himself. "Many left planting rice to fight in the war on one side or the other because they couldn't farm their fields in peace and needed an income. Looks like most joined the Khmer Rouge."

"It's true, but the Americans drove them there." The man's tone was laced with barely suppressed rage. "I had a brother in Kandal Province who was killed by the B-52 bombs—he and his whole village were destroyed. The bombs took out rice paddies for miles around, and I doubt they will be farmed for years to come. That was just one small village. It happened in hundreds of villages."

Khan and the man stopped talking when the patrolling soldier stopped nearby to light a cigarette. I heard the click of his lighter and then silence. I fell asleep and dreamed of a tiger, crouching in a rice paddy, creeping closer and closer to me, but I was unable to move, unable to flee.

The days passed into weeks, which passed into months of plowing and planting the rice paddies. Soaking rain fell most nights, so the Khmer Rouge allowed us three days to build stronger shelters. Vuthy and I helped Khan cut bamboo poles and weave together palm leaf strips to make the walls and a roof for our shelter. We draped tarps over the top to keep out the rain. It wasn't large, but when we laid down, we all fit. Khan yelled at us several times for not doing it right or cutting the poles too short, but he didn't beat us because the Khmer Rouge came over and yelled at him to quiet down. He feared them, and I too had found some one to fear far more than I had feared Khan.

Water flowing through the paddies brought life. But when we tried to gather snails or frogs from the rice paddies as we worked, the Khmer Rouge would bark, "Do not stop to get snails. Plant rice. Rice will sustain us. If you have time to pick up snails, you are not working hard enough. If you do not work, you do not eat." So we got better about collecting them when the soldiers turned their backs.

Some tried to fill their stomachs with rice seeds as they planted, but anyone who was caught doing that was shot. Because "stealing from the collective to feed the individual was a grave offense," according to the Khmer Rouge.

When we weren't working in the paddies or at the talking meetings the Khmer Rouge gave each night, the sound of suffering was worse. One old woman near our camp lay so still that I thought she was dead, but someone came and slapped her face repeatedly until she sat up. A piece of mango peeling was produced, and she quietly nibbled on it, with shrunken cheeks and knobby fingers. Another man had such swollen legs that he couldn't walk and began to moan so loudly that the soldiers yelled at him to keep quiet. He could barely make it back and forth from the hole he had dug to relieve himself. Vomit and diarrhea were all over the ground in stinking piles.

So far, sickness had not touched our family, but soon Mteay's milk dried up and Tang began to cry ceaselessly, always clawing at her shrunken breasts. We each reserved some of our food for her, but she only got sicker. The baby's formerly chubby frame was riveted with hunger and her stick-thin arms and legs writhed through the air as if being prodded and poked. Starvation sunk its fingers into her tiny frame, refusing to let go.

Mteay rocked her in her arms as she wept through bloodshot eyes, teetering from side to side. At night when it was worse, I snuck to the edge of the rice paddy to look for fish or snails for her to eat, but they were hard for her to chew, even when Mteay cooked them and mashed them up.

Crying, coughing and desperation settled over the camp like an inescapable cloud. The soldiers became even more severe. They gripped the stalks of their guns tightly and paced down each row to discourage any ideas of rebellion. But starving people had a difficult time following rules. Panic began to slither amongst us and bit some harder than others.

Early one morning, a commotion started in the far end of the camp. I watched as a large truck pulled up to one of the houses the Khmer Rouge cadre's occupied. The soldiers began to unload supplies. I stood, knees shaking with hope; the desperate hope that the truck contained food.

The colors of sunrise brought the smell of rice cooking with prahok an aroma I hadn't smelt in the months since we had moved to the camp. One man, unable to quell his hunger any longer, lunged toward one of the caldrons cooking the rice and plunged his hand into the boiling water. The soldiers reacted quickly, pulling him back and casting him into the dirt as he clutched futilely at the few grains sticking to the blisters already forming on his hand. Every eye was glued on the pots, and the camp was filled with the sound of empty stomachs, clamoring for food.

Some of the Khmer Rouge soldiers stood around the pots, smoking cigarettes and laughing as the sun cast long shadows across the ground. The smell of food mixed with the smoke of their cigarettes nearly drove me mad. When the rice was done, the soldiers lined up on both sides of the pots to take turns eating their fill while others patrolled the camp. My mouth was dry, but I managed to summon enough moisture to wet my lips as I looked longingly at the soldiers with rice grains dribbling from their chins as they ate with their bowls and spoons. They often kept their spoons in their pockets, being as dear to them as their guns, but with each meal, we had to leave ours in a big pot at the end of the food line. We all stared, our eyes clapped on the men eating.

At last, the barking command came for us to line up in two rows, and the whole camp sprang to life. It exploded in desperation, like a beast awakened from a deep sleep. I grabbed Vuthy's arm, and we propelled our weak legs forward as everyone began to push their way to the front. The soldiers shoved us into a single file line with the butts of their guns. Some got hit harder than others, and I passed one man who bled from a cut in his head, lying dazed in the dirt.

We were so far from the front of the line, that I could hardly see the pots of rice through the jutting elbows and shuffling legs of the starving. The line inched forward. I focused on Vuthy's hair in front of me. It had grown long and matted in the months we had been here. Vuthy turned and looked at me, his eyes dark tunnels of hunger.

"We'll make it Vuthy, almost there."

I tried to think of a joke to distract us, but I could only think of hunger. In front of Vuthy stood a tall man. I couldn't see past him, and a bare foot collided with my heel as the line crept forward.

Spoons clinked as they were snatched from the pot. Desperate throats gulped. I trembled. My mouth salivated at the close proximity of food. A tear slid down Vuthy's face, and I wiped it with the back of my dirt-smeared hand before the guard to my right could see. Crying was not allowed by Angkar. The boy behind me stepped on the back of my heel again, but I didn't care. I was focused on the sound of eating.

At last, I could see the front of the line around the tall man, but the sound of spoons and pots had stopped. My stomach clenched in panic as I came face to face with my worst fear. Vuthy turned around, and we locked eyes for a single, agonizing moment. The unspoken panic asked the question I dared not voice. His black eyes brimmed with tears, and he nibbled at a black fingernail as if it was all he could do to keep from screaming. Our eyes only locked for a moment, but the fear in them bore into my chest like a hot poker.

What if they ran out of food?

Catching a glimpse of an old woman eating out of her hands as she hurried past to enjoy her much anticipated meal caused warmth to wash over me. I stumbled forward, blind with relief.

"There's still food," I whispered, hoping Vuthy heard me, but I couldn't tell if my voice had escaped my throat.

"Vuthy there's still food," I said again, louder this time. Vuthy's feet danced in anticipation. He knew it too.

The tall man in front of us peeled away from the line, holding rice in his cupped hands, devouring it in large mouthfuls. Vuthy stepped forward and received his rice. My knees trembled and dizziness swam in my eyes. I willed myself to remain upright, to make it one more step. At last, I extended my hands shakily as a female soldier dumped a glob of rice into them. The rice felt cold in my clammy hands, but I lifted it to my lips and gulped it down in several large bites. It stuck to the roof of my mouth and clung to my throat. I sat down beside Vuthy and he looked at me, mouth full of rice but hands now emptied. A few grains escaped from between my fingers, so I searched the ground to find them. The dirt was so sifted that it made it difficult to locate such a small object, but at last I found the two grains and popped them into my mouth. I tasted mostly the dirt, but the rice was in there somewhere.

With a satisfying heaviness in our stomachs, we returned to our family's camp. But as I neared, the air was heavy and oppressive. I looked at the sky. It was about to rain. My stomach twisted around the rice I had just eaten. I found Mteay clenching a handful of rice to Tang's lifeless, purple mouth. Mteay sobbed as she stared at Tang's tiny body, lying limp on the filthy blanket. The wails coming out of her didn't sound human. They pounded my eardrums like the wind. She didn't touch the baby, just stared with wild eyes as she pulled at her hair, rice clinging to the black strands.

"What have I done in my past lives to deserve this, Buddha? How do I right the wrongs?"

I had heard others ask this question. It ran like a current through every whispered conversation, a fact and inescapable fate. We were being punished for bad karma, and we must endure it.

Rain poured from the sky, pounding the tarp over our heads as my family wept, concealing our grief from the watchful eye of Angkar. A question pounded through my brain. How long must we pay for sins we didn't know we had committed?

31

THE PURGE

"I felt a conflict of feelings."— Rindy

NOVEMBER 1975

The grip of Tang's death didn't release after Mteay put her emaciated body in the hole we had dug with our hands. It continued to cling to me for days, chasing me in sleep and staring at me each time I looked into Mteay's bloodshot eyes. It felt like cold darkness and tasted like dirt, always sitting in my empty stomach.

Weeks passed, and Mteay didn't leave the blanket where Tang had died. She grew so weak that Ly and Sotha had to force drops of the salty broth between her cracked lips. The rest of us worked in the rice fields each day, harvesting rice. We snuck bites, eating them with the husk still on, not daring to take the time to extract the rice grain. With each movement of the sickle, our thin and shaking arms brought us one step farther from starvation. While we worked, we thought about eating rice with meat and what it would feel like to eat until we were full. As we harvested, we had it in our hands, it was the feeling of life and a future.

But as we bundled the grass, the Khmer Rouge brought trucks and took it away. Anger and panic rumbled through the camp, but no one dared resist. How could we? No one had the strength or the will because the Khmer Rouge had the guns and now the rice too. They held our lives in their hands. With each passing day, the Khmer Rouge would tell us about the greatness of Kampuchea and what our role was. They mostly told us about the evils of western thought and how we were to root it out in its every form. Then they began to talk more about the evils of the Vietnamese, Cham and Chinese and how they had corrupted Kampuchea as well. Anyone of foreign descent, even if their grandparents had been born in another country, meant they were a part of the corruption that was destroying the purity of Kampuchea.

"We must always maintain our voluntary attitude, and we must keep in mind the guiding principle of the Three Mountains," the Khmer Rouge soldiers often said at the daily meetings. "They are: Attain independence-sovereignty. We do not need any outside forces; Kampuchea can stand on its own and does not need foreign help or influence. We will scrub it from our midst until it is completely gone. The second mountain is to rely on our own strength. Last, we take destiny in our hands. We did not win the battle by negotiations or by the polite sompeah—we won by fighting with our own hands. Destiny is now ours."

While living in the corporate village, we were under constant scrutiny. The Khmer Rouge soldiers would patrol the camp day and night, but I never really knew what they were looking for until one day I noticed a soldier stop his patrol to stare intently into a woman's face. Bowing her head, she hid behind her black hair.

"What is your name?" he asked loudly, causing everyone to snap to attention and stare at the woman.

She didn't reply.

"What is this woman's name?" he asked the man sitting in the next tent, raising his voice even higher.

"Nguyen," the man replied quickly, spitting the words out as if hoping to avoid scrutiny himself. We all knew that was the most common surname for a person of Vietnamese descent. She was a foreigner.

"I thought so." The soldier nodded approvingly. "You have the look of a *Yuon*—a Vietnamese swine."

The soldier seized her by the arm and marched her out of the camp.

One evening while waiting in line for my food, I heard one of the soldiers begin talking to a man in front of me in a language I didn't understand. Surprised, the man looked up and responded in the same language. The soldier who dished the rice grinned, eyes gleaming blackly from their sockets as he shouted to a soldier near him.

"This one's a liar." He pointed to the man holding out his empty tin. "He's Chinese."

A rush of soldiers surrounded the man and tied his hands with a rope.

"I'm not Chinese!" he kept shouting as they drug him away. "I just understand the language."

A soldier was talking to one of the children who had come from Phnom Penh as I walked past. He looked like he was being friendly, holding out a piece of sugar cane. The girl's eyes lit up as she reached for it, yet he held onto it firmly.

"Did your papa give you this treat at home in Phnom Penh?" He bent low and investigated her face.

The little girl bobbed her head up and down, eyes locked on the first sweet treat she had seen in months.

"How about your family in China?" He looked into her eyes keenly. "Do they give you sugar cane when you visit?"

"I don't know." She reached for it. "I've never visited them because my aupouk says it's very far."

"Where is your aupouk?"

The little girl pointed to a man nearby who was pulling weeds between the rice rows. The soldier smiled at the little girl and nodded approvingly, then gave her the sugar cane. Scampering away, she nibbled at it in delight.

That night, the entire family disappeared.

A few weeks later, a soldier shouted through the darkness. "Everyone is to join us in the cafeteria." He paced down the rows of people. I sat up, rubbing the sleep out of my eyes, when the smell of cooking meat caught my attention. My stomach growled with excitement as Vuthy and I hurried toward the cafeteria in hopes of catching sight of what was cooking, along with the hordes of others who followed the tantalizing aroma. We were told to sit in rows, with the children in the front and the adults in the back. A Khmer Rouge soldier stood in front, with his chest puffed out and his checkered krama tied neatly around his neck.

"We are the future." He paced in front of us. "Angkar is our Aupouk, and he will make Kampuchea prosperous again." Stopping, he stared at us intensely before continuing. I squirmed.

"In order to accomplish this great task, all corruption must be purged from our great society. We must change it; we must make it right again. The Vietnamese Yuon, the Chinese, the Muslim Cham, the religious and the intellectuals are part of the disease wishing to corrupt pure Kampuchea. These are our enemies. They implement foreign ideas and foreign religions to rob Kampuchea of its authentic way."

My mind began to drift with the aroma on the early morning breeze. I had heard this speech many times before, but it had never been coupled with the smell of cooking meat.

"The Yuon and the Chinese wish to corrupt Kampuchea and steal it from us." He went on to explain, drawing me back to reality. "They do not respect our rights and they steal from our economy. Think about your own villages. Is not the foreigner always the opportunist?"

Murmured agreement rippled throughout the audience as men looked from one to the other, reminiscing on the experiences they'd had. No one liked the Vietnamese. I remembered the horror stories and the anti-Vietnamese marches in Battambang. Inspired by the common consensus, the orator continued with gusto.

"The Yuon are just like the Chams who are wealthy and do not share in our common struggle, and the Chams set themselves apart by their Islamic faith. They want to divide the spirit of unity in Kampuchea. They refuse our pork because it is not good enough for them. They call it unclean. There is to be no Yuon, Chinese or Cham, but one, single, nationality."

"We are one Kampuchea," he shouted, raising his fist. "We need to unify. We must expose corruption. We must engage in this revolution!"

The speaker stood tall and dignified as he continued to spout the Khmer Rouge belief.

"Angkar will take care of your every need." He motioned to the pots, steaming in the morning air. "Join us for a hearty breakfast of porridge and pig."

We quickly dispersed to receive our morning portion, and I reveled in the idea of eating meat. When my turn came, I extended my empty bowl and received a watery porridge with a few chunks of floating meat. My mouth watered at the sight of it. We had not received such a delicacy for six months. Slurping with delight, I savored the sensation of warmth on my tongue and the feeling of meat between my teeth.

Above the rim of my bowl, I noticed a soldier watching each person as they ate very closely. He was not the only one, however, for after looking around, I noticed a whole company of soldiers scrutinizing each person as they ate.

"Are you not hungry?" one soldier asked an older woman, who sat, staring into her bowl.

She did not respond.

"I asked you a question," he demanded more firmly this time.

"I'm not feeling well." Her voice was barely audible.

"Does the pig meat make you feel unwell?" His tone was mocking. "Are you too good for it? Too far above humble Kampuchea?" He bent down lower, looking into her face. "You must be a Cham." He seethed.

She looked at him with pleading eyes, but he met her gaze with a hardened expression.

"You are an enemy of Kampuchea." He spat into her face. Yanking her from the ground, he tied her hands and pushed her through the sea of eating people. The old woman barely protested, but merely stumbled in front of them, eyes locked on the ground.

Glancing around, I wondered who else in our midst were enemies of Kampuchea. I remembered the Chinese merchants who were shot in Phnom Sampov. Were they killed because they were Chinese? Did the soldier do a good thing? That question would fester in me day after day as we sat in the meetings, hearing the dangers of the foreigners. The Khmer Rouge wanted a better Kampuchea, a pure Kampuchea and I wanted it too. With each bark of the Khmer Rouge orator, I wanted it even more, so that maybe life could return to normal. Maybe Cambodia could start over.

"Kampuchea alone is great," the soldiers would say. "She does not need the help of foreign blood to make her stronger. We reject the foreigner to allow Kampuchea's blood to run clean once again. We must remember the three-mountain principle."

This made sense to me. I wanted my country to be strong and prosperous on its own. Sihanouk had secured its freedom from France, but Lon Nol gave it to the Americans, and the Vietnamese set up sanctuaries. It had been invaded and needed to be reclaimed.

Day after day, night after night of listening to the soldiers talk, the beliefs began working their way into my mind like a worm into mud, creating a pathway of thought that had not been there before. With each foreigner the Khmer Rouge rooted out, my shock and dismay began to mingle with relief. With each cry I heard as they drug a man, woman or child out of the camp, I felt a little safer. With each enemy exposed, Kampuchea became a little stronger. The Khmer Rouge were the most suited to lead Kampuchea with a strong hand, out of the days of darkness and into the light they promised.

32

RELIGION OF ANGKAR

"If they were secretive, they survived." — Rindy

MAY-JUNE 1976

"Religion is corruption."

The Khmer Rouge soldier stood before us. He was the one who usually talked at the meetings each night, which had started earlier and lasted longer since the rice had been harvested and taken away. To where? We didn't know, but a numbness crept over everyone, the way it starts at the toes and works up. No one was untouched by its chilling fingers. We heard rumors we would be moved, but we didn't know where.

"Religion creates division in Kampuchea."

I refocused on the man's words. Glancing around, I looked at those around me, their hollow cheeks and sunken chests flickering in the blazing fires the Khmer Rouge had built around the camp. I knew each had grown up in Buddhism just as I had. Each face reflected a helplessness I felt. The customary orange garbs of the monks had been long discarded as we all wore the same black clothing, but I wondered if some of their hearts were still cloaked in orange. Could Angkar steal someone's beliefs too?

"Religion steals from the unified heart of Kampuchea." His words were severe and clipped. His krama wrapped around his head, his eyes felt like they pierced my chest. "We are the laborers who work for our food and should never expect others to feed us with alms and donations. We are all the same and no one is greater than the other. Religion tricks the Kampuchean people into being weak and submissive."

My mind flashed back to the abbots house, as I lay prostrate on the ground, and he thrashed my back with the whip. I could still see the broken glasses and almost feel the lashes, with my cheek pressed against the cold stones. He had beaten submission into me. Shivering, I refocused on the orator.

"The Buddhist monk is a leech and worm." He raised his fist. "They beg for their food and do not work but pray all day and steal from those who do. They use other people's noses to breathe for them. They take, but do not give."

He was met with silence, but he raged on.

"The Christian is the corruption of the west and Kampucheans who bow to their God are frauds. They steal from our pure culture with their false ideas of servitude and dying, instead of fighting. They allowed their God to be killed and they didn't lift a finger to stop it. Like Buddhists they believe in a next life, but they are all wrong! We only have this life to live, no other. To believe anything else is to believe in children's stories."

He paused, looking out over the crowd of exhausted people. I noticed a small boy asleep near his mteay. Would the Khmer Rouge chide him? I watched his eyes rove, but he didn't seem to notice. I relaxed.

"Angkar will make one unified thought, one unified belief and one unified people. Do not tolerate the religious in your midst and report them to us! Kampuchea is a great democracy and is made up of you!"

"Angkar is our Aupouk,

Angkar is our Mteay,

Angkar is our future!"

I feared the name Angkar above all else; more than starvation or disease combined. Whenever the name was uttered, the hair on the back of my neck stood on end and a loud silence fell on everyone in hearing distance. Angkar was the reaper, the one who stole people in the dead of night. The one in control of us all. When Angkar summoned someone, I never saw them again. Many believed Angkar wasn't made up of people or even our former ruler Norodom Sihanouk anymore, but was a god that demanded sacrifice and worship for the bad karma in Kampuchea. They believed we were being punished for a past life and that we all had very bad merit. The belief sat on everyone's shoulders like a brick they couldn't shake off. It was an inescapable burden of shame, a collective, suffocating shame.

Finally, we were allowed to go. As I walked back to our makeshift hut, the moon cast eerie shadows across the ground. I encountered an old woman by her tent, as she swayed to and fro over her husband, who lay on his back, not appearing to breathe. Had he fallen and died while she was at the meeting as he was too sick to attend? I didn't know.

"Give him peace, give him peace, give him peace, Jesus." She moaned the words over and over again, between sobs. "Only in you do we have peace."

Should I tell the Khmer Rouge? I had never heard a Khmer pray to anyone other than Buddha or to the spirits as Khan did. She didn't pray prostrated like a Buddhist or in a bowing motion like a Muslim but just mumbled to herself. How could this swaying and mumbling even be prayer? I continued walking.

I played the name 'Jesus' over in my mind, trying to remember where I had heard it before. It was a strange name on my tongue and didn't sound like a name of a god or spirit. Then the encounter that I had as a temple boy flashed into my memory. I was standing near the market, on my way to sell water. I could feel the pamphlet in the sweat in my palm, and see the smiling face of the man in the picture as he descended from the clouds.

Jesus was the God of Mr. Thach. The one who was rumored to be alive. What was peace? I didn't know, because it didn't seem to live in this place. But what if it was out there somewhere? What if I just hadn't yet learned how to break free from the prison of karma? I carried the thought in my heart over the next weeks.

That old man wasn't the only one to get sick, as a wave of dysentery moved through the camp. I had to be careful where I walked so as not to step in a pile of excrement or vomit that lay scattered across the barren field. The air was heavy with stench and flies.

Soon Ly was struck by the illness and pale-yellow spots crept across her skin. She lay still for days, staring up at the tarp-covered ceiling. Not being able to watch her suffer, I grabbed the can long-emptied of evaporated milk and went to get water.

Emaciated bodies crouched throughout the camp, with empty looks in their eyes. They didn't seem like humans anymore, but more like animals trying to survive. I watched a soldier dash to the small patch of trees near the road to relieve himself, his gun clanked against his sides as he ran. Even the soldiers couldn't protect themselves from the sickness.

The food rations had dwindled and sometimes there was only salty broth, with no rice at all. Frogs and snails had become hard to find and with the rice being harvested and with no heavy rain in months, the rice paddies had dried up and the fish had all been eaten too. The sun beat down relentlessly, making the horizon dance like water. I shielded my eyes. Bending down to the murky canal, I dipped the warm water into my can. Many others were doing the same, as it was the only water source for miles.

When I returned, Ly was laying on her back with her head tilted sideways, staring absently. Being careful not to spill all the water on the ground, I dribbled some into her mouth with my fingers. Only moments passed before she rolled onto her stomach and retched into the dirt, but nothing came up.

Mteay dipped the edge of her krama into the water and washed down Ly's frail body, her stomach was sunken and her arms stiff. I looked away, but as I did her squinted eyes caught mine. They peered out of their puffy lids and said only one thing. I knew the look. I had seen it on hundreds of faces before. *Death.* The look haunted me as I went to look for something for her to eat.

Time passed slowly and with nothing else to do after eating a meager portion and attending the meetings, we watched over Ly each day, wondering if it would be her last. Everywhere I looked I could see bodies strewn throughout the camp, with flies crawling all over their frames. Some bodies had someone with them, mourning their stillness, others lay all alone under a bush or a tree.

To escape the world outside, Vuthy and I slept as much as we could. I lay face down, my forehead resting on the fraying and ragged blanket that used to drape Chidaun's bed, wishing for sleep to come. The blanket had once had beautiful swirls of reds and pinks, with tiny strands of yellow throughout, but it had become sun bleached and colorless. I stared at that blanket for hours, remembering what colors had been. I avoided Vuthy's eyes, because they asked questions that I couldn't answer. I couldn't protect him from this. I hadn't been able to protect him from any of it.

"Would it be better to die from hunger, sickness or to be sh-shot by the soldiers?" He whispered, one night, when everyone else was asleep. At first, I didn't answer, wishing he hadn't asked.

"Rindy, what do you think would be a better way to die?"

I turned toward him, barely seeing his face by the light of the moon. I saw the desperation there, hidden behind the tears.

"You are not going to die, Vuthy. I won't let you die." I grabbed his arm and wrapped my palm around its thinness. "I promise you won't die."

"What if there really is nothing after this—after we die, like the soldiers say?"

I thought for a moment, my mind leaping over ideas, over ways to comfort him. "But what if there is? What if there is a place —" I motioned to the sky — "up there."

He shrugged, not understanding me.

I told him of the man called Jesus, the one in the clouds who smiled and reached out his hands toward temple boys. I made up a story of his kingdom in the clouds that we would get to visit one day. My words drowned out the moans of the dying and wails of those left behind. I talked until Vuthy's tears stopped falling and his breathing slowed in sleep, until I escaped in sleep too.

Startling awake, I blinked into the darkness of the night. Vuthy stirred. I looked out of the shelter. The air felt different; it felt fuller and alive, like it held a secret. Where had the moon and the stars gone? I crawled out of the hut, being careful not to step on Khan's foot, Sotha's hand. I let the breeze kiss my face. Suddenly, a thunderbolt shuddered across the sky, lighting up even the darkest shadows of the camp. Rain, in the same instant, began pouring down with a force like fists. Soon everyone else joined me outside, as we looked out at the sky. Mteay cried and put out every vessel that we had to catch the rain. There were cans, sandals, cups and bowls scattered across the ground, showing up with each lighting strike.

I lay face up, letting the rain soak my body. Opening my eyes, I stared into the black sky. I didn't care that the rain stung my face, my eyes. After a year of being in the camp, the pain was proof that I was still alive.

33

THE SEPARATION

"The second year, the Khmer Rouge got more organized."
— Rindy

JULY-DECEMBER 1976

Over the next months, I watched Ly's life return to her slender body. Instead of lying limp each day like she had, she began to sit up, smile and move her legs. Mteay only allowed her to drink the rainwater she had collected, instead of the water from the canal. It returned life to her dried-up body like it did for the thirsty ground. With the rain came the planting of rice, then transplanting the seedlings and then the harvest. With the ripening and harvesting of rice, our confidence grew. Rice meant life. We hoped that with the harvest, we would get more food to eat as the portions of watery soup and porridge over the last year had not increased with the labor.

The coming of the harvest also stirred a confidence in the camp that ran like an undercurrent in each person's veins. The Khmer Rouge addressed us with renewed energy and authority. The meetings were riveted with passion, their guns were gripped with zeal and their eyes shone with a deeper sense of purpose. It was a gradual change, rather than all at once, like steady drops of rice grains into a bucket before they began to spill over. The once rag-tag company of soldiers had become more organized in their execution, their commands flowing from Angkar, which were delivered by soldiers who came and went by the trucks on the road. The cadres who brought orders from Angkar were higher in authority, their uniforms cleaner and they looked well fed and healthy.

The Khmer Rouge were feared not only because of the guns they wielded, but because they clearly believed in their vision so fully that nothing could stand in their way. We all knew what they were capable of, what Angkar was capable of. The previous year had been a brutal lesson.

I watched a convoy of military vehicles leave by the road, and it made me uneasy as I stood in line to receive my meager portion of rice porridge. What change had they brought for us?

Soon, a female soldier wove between the lines of the hungry, giving a command to each person. A number to a battalion. What could it mean? Glancing to each side of me I could see a soldier doing the same to each line. Uneasiness sank into my empty stomach.

"You join battalion three." She motioned to a man in front of me.

"How old?" She narrowed her eyes on me. I froze.

I was thirteen, wasn't I?

Irritated she barked, "you're battalion five," before moving onto Vuthy. "Is this your brother?"

How should I answer? Why did she need to know? I needed to protect him somehow.

"Yes," Vuthy answered for me.

"You're seven," she told Vuthy and moved on.

Did this mean we would be separated? Vuthy looked at me, his eyes panicked. "I should have lied and said you weren't. Maybe they would have let us stay together that way."

I squeezed Vuthy's shoulder, trying to quell my own dread. "We don't know what this means yet, it could be nothing," I lied. This couldn't mean anything good. After receiving my portion of porridge, I peeled away from the line to find battalion five. I cast a reluctant gaze toward Vuthy as he went to find his own group.

Everyone began to segregate themselves. One group was made up of weary looking old men, another of middle-aged men, and then a group of women Mteay's age. Every age group was assigned a different group, and everyone in the camp shuffled into their places placidly.

"Is this battalion five?" I asked a boy who looked to be about my age. He nodded, and I sat on the ground beside him to eat. Frightened faces of other boys gathered around us, mirrors of my own. We ate in silence, licking the food from our grimy fingertips as fear clamored in our chests.

"Welcome to battalion number five."

A tall soldier towered over us. He was a foot taller than most Khmer men, but he looked to be pure blooded with dark skin and unruly hair.

"My name is Vichet, and I am your leader."

He motioned for us to rise to our feet as his eyes danced over us. His eagerness was evident. He began to pace with his checkered krama tied around his waist, fluttering out behind him.

"You are the youth mobilization unit and the future of Kampuchea. You all have been selected to serve your country—a great country."

His teeth clicked against the sounds rolling off his tongue as he uttered each word with conviction.

"You are the workforce assigned to the irrigation systems. This is an important job because without free-flowing water, there will be no rice seedlings planted and no harvest. Angkar has instructed us to plant more rice this year—three crops instead of two. This will be an incredible feat. Your new task, your new great purpose, is to help provide the waterways in Kampuchea for the rice. Kampuchea is becoming the most prosperous, independent nation because of your hard work and dedication. So, you should know"—he paused as he looked at each of our faces, his brow furrowing—"you are vital to this revolution."

His words sank into my chest and swelled like rice does as it cooks. I had never counted myself as a member of this revolution. I was a mere evacuee who was forced into this shroud of blackness. I had endured months of meetings and fear, drawing me closer to the revolution out of necessity rather than desire. Yet in a few sentences, Vichet had made me want to believe as he did. Believe the Khmer Rouge really did have great plans for my country and that they could bring them about. Maybe such a heavy hand was necessary when undertaking something so great? Perhaps the future could be different? As I listened to Vichet, he made me want to be a part of the revolution in which I had found myself. I no longer wanted to be a mere spectator; I wanted to be a soldier.

"Everyone gets a shovel." Vichet walked to the back of one of the parked army vehicles and began to pass shovels to each one of us. He smiled as he went, as if he were dispersing presents, instead of tools. Each shovel was crudely built with a small bamboo pole for a handle, but I was confident it would do the job.

"This is your weapon." He ran his broad hands over the handle of a shovel. "Use it with care and never leave it idle. We will dig ourselves to prosperity."

An especially emaciated boy next to me slunk to the ground, melting into a puddle. Bracing myself, I prepared for the onslaught of insults that would no doubt be hurled in our direction by our new leader as I had never seen a soldier pass up an opportunity to scorn one of their subordinates. But when Vichet's eyes landed on him, they softened and didn't harden as he continued speaking.

"We are on schedule to leave immediately, as each battalion has now been assigned their new position. Everyone to a job. Everyone to a purpose." Vichet motioned for us to follow him.

In an instant, my calm resolution raged into panic. I searched the hundreds of swarming people for Vuthy, realizing that the last time I had seen him might have been goodbye. Peering through jostling arms and shovels I searched frantically, trying not to panic. Pushing my way to the outskirts of our battalion, I struggled to see anyone I knew. Finally, I spied Vuthy.

"Vuthy!" My voice sounded weak, lost in the confusion, but I waved my arms frantically. "Vuthy, goodbye."

I watched as a woman screamed while her daughter, maybe three years old, was ripped from her arms. A man and woman collided, tears streaming down the woman's face. Everyone was being separated. Children from parents, husbands from wives, brothers from brothers. Vuthy fell into line with his comrades. I waved, calling his name again, but he couldn't hear me. His head swiveled from side to side, he was looking for me. For one moment, our eyes locked. I waved my hand, forcing a smile. He smiled, wiped at his eyes and lifted his hand.

"Get back with your battalion." A female soldier shoved me into line, my shovel clanking loudly with the boy's next to me.

I looked back to Vuthy, but he was already marching north with his battalion. The air was thick with the rising dust from thousands of shuffling feet. I reminded myself this was not the first time I hadn't been able to watch out for Vuthy, that he could look out for himself, but it didn't help quell the panic in my chest.

I jostled along with the rest of battalion five onto the elevated road, as we began our out-of-sync march. Pushing through to the edge of the group once again, I tried in vain to catch a glimpse of Mteay, Ly, Sotha, or even Khan.

A group of men stood gathered in the field as a soldier shouted at them. "We will achieve great rice harvests—more than any other country. We will no longer only have two rice harvests, but we will have three. We will never go hungry again."

He pointed to several idle plows, which were being unloaded from a truck. Grabbing one man from the crowd, the soldier positioned the leather straps around the man's neck, motioning for him to pull the plow. There weren't any cows or water buffalo in sight. The men took their places, straining against the strap across their shoulders as they pulled the dull blade through the hard earth. I saw Khan among them, his head raised and eyes indignant. Thousands of skinny workers plodded across the landscape, trying to make the dirt breathe life. To make rice when usually the land rested, waiting for rain. We were separated from those we loved so we could make more rice for Angkar—our mother, father and brother.

34

THE COOK

"Sometimes you have rice and sometimes you have rice soup."
— Rindy

DECEMBER 1977

We marched in lines, with our shovels over our shoulders. I tried to keep in stride with those around me. Sometimes I stumbled, but I tried to regain my momentum quickly so no one noticed. I couldn't see where we were going, so I moved forward blindly, focusing on my own shuffling feet. We marched like soldiers, and our shovels were our guns. The air was thick with dust.

"March together," one soldier barked.

"Knees up!"

"Keep your shovels secure!"

We marched until my knees felt like they were on a hinge. It felt like days, but the sun was still hovering over the horizon. How had night not yet come? We came upon many canals and paddies waiting for rice. The boy next to me wheezed, his breath squeezing out of his tired lungs like a frog being squished into dry ground.

"This is your assignment." Vichet stopped at last, turning to face us. "Each one of you is responsible for doing your part in creating a prosperous Kampuchea with industrial waterways."

He paused for effect.

"Water is important for the future, and you all will have a hand in making it a good future." Vichet looked across the desolate field as if he was seeing an oasis teeming with life. I tried to see what he did, but I just saw dirt. I didn't know whether to fear him or admire him, towering over us, his shadow casting long and lean into the barren field behind him.

"This is a great task." His eyes shone. "You are a part of something great, something bigger than you or me."

I glanced around, feeling the atmosphere of the group change. I was no longer hearing the tired breathing and groans of hunger, but each face was studying Vichet intently, eating his words as if they were filling their empty stomachs. I felt it too; his words awoke something dead inside my chest, making it quiver back to life. It felt like eating soup, and it tasted like hope.

Several soldiers went over to a parked truck and began unloading black bundles before passing them to each of us.

"This is your clothing allotment for the year." Vichet began handing out the bundles. "You are blessed to wear the colors of the Khmer Rouge. You are a part of this revolution."

I sighed in relief at the new clothes as my shorts were full of holes and had gotten tight. I opened the bundle and found a pair of sandals made from old tires, black trousers, a loose black shirt and a red and white checkered krama. This was the first thing I had received that was my own to keep in over a year. I hugged the lump of belongings to my chest.

After everyone received their clothes, we walked toward one of the canals for a bath.

"Everyone bathes." Vichet waved us into the canal, and he followed. The water was low, but it was cleaner than back at the camp. We cupped our palms and dumped it over our heads, trying to wash ourselves the best we could without removing our shorts. I watched Vichet out of the corner of my eye. He didn't seem like the other soldiers. His eyes crinkled at the sides, enjoying the water too. The murky water cascaded over his strong shoulders. He reminded me of my aupouk before life had made him hard.

"Everyone put on your new clothes and come learn your new assignment." Climbing out of the canal, I shook the water off and put on my new clothes as quickly as possible. "Everyone, except"—his eyes roamed over the crowd of black headed boys—"you." Uncertain if he was referring to me, I froze, thankful for the black clothing that made us all look the same.

"Yes, you." Vichet stared me straight in the eyes, his intense gaze chased away all doubt that I was the one he was talking to. Swallowing the lump in my throat, I stepped away from the others.

"Follow me."

Obediently I followed him and another lower ranking Khmer Rouge soldier. My feet felt heavier with each step and my eyes didn't leave the heels of their heavy boots.

"How old are you?" It was Vichet's voice.

My mind whirled, panicking over the answer. I wasn't certain, but I had been around twelve when the Khmer Rouge took over. Had it been two years yet? Or only one?

"Don't you know?"

"I—I'm fourteen," I stammered, "I think, comrade Vichet."

"Hmm, I would have guessed you were younger."

"I think I'm small for my age." The humiliating fact washed over me, warming my face.

"Well, I'd say that worked in your favor for the first time in your life."

What did he mean? I tried to keep up with his long strides, showing that I was capable of anything.

We walked up the road until we came to where a small village had been. It housed several large structures and former homes, as well as several larger structures that looked like they had been recently thrown together, each one leaning slightly with poorly made palm thatch. They were open walled, held up by tall bamboo poles and topped with grass roofs. Groups of bamboo poles tied tightly together and put on posts, sprawled beneath them, forming large communal beds. Next to it, was a large structure with nothing much inside. Vichet and the soldier stopped.

"This is where we eat." A giant pot, several bags of rice and a small, white bag sat alone in the dirt, staring at me as if they had been waiting for my arrival.

"This is how you will serve." Vichet bent down to my level. "You are the cook for your battalion."

Stunned, I opened the lid of the pot and saw a small pack of matches.

"Do you know how to make rice?"

I nodded.

"Good." He smiled. "How about finding snails or fish?"

Nodding, I smiled this time. I was good at that. The other soldier ambled over to a shady tree and sat down, leaning his gun over his body.

"I'll leave you to it then!" Vichet stood and stalked back down the road to the rest of my battalion, leaving the soldier reclining in the shade. "I'll be back to check on your progress."

After shooting a glance at the napping soldier, I looked around. I was *almost* alone. I hadn't been alone in nearly two years while at the corporate village. I stared at the pot and rice, overwhelmed at my good fortune. My job was food; I would live.

Gathering twigs and branches, I lit a small fire outside the structure, blowing on the flames until they ate up the wood. Finding a bucket of rainwater beneath the eaves, I scooped the liquid into the pot and lugged it back, being careful not to slosh out any of the grains onto the thankless ground. The fire was larger when I returned, and I gathered four big rocks to balance the pot on. After casting one more look over my shoulder, I went in search of anything that I could add to the rice. I returned to the canal and found a few small frogs and several snails. I could see the rest of the battalion farther down, digging a trench from the canal through the rice paddy next to it. It was so strange to be allowed to look for food. Yet I was still afraid. Fear had become a part of me somehow.

I heard the water boiling when I got back, but the sleeping soldier hadn't moved. I removed the snails from their shell and pulled apart the frogs with a stick and threw them into the water. The rice grains had puffed up, but I had put too much water in, making it more of a soup. My mouth watered, and I couldn't wait to eat the rice. Could I eat my fill before the soldier saw? Would I get caught?

"Is the rice finished?" a voice asked behind me. I jumped, my heart racing. I was relieved I hadn't started eating yet and gotten caught. The sleeping soldier was awake now too, sitting as if he had been watching me the whole time. Glancing over my shoulder, I saw Vichet stalking up the road toward me, carrying a large crate of bowls. The soldier walked over and took the crate from him. Nervousness slithered down my face along with sweat.

"Almost." I lifted the lid to peek inside as a barrel of steam slapped my face.

Vichet peaked into the pot as he set the crate on the ground next to me. "What's your name, comrade?"

"R—Rindy." I stammered. No Khmer Rouge had ever asked my name.

"Rindy, it's good to meet you." His eyes were a deep brown, surrounded by tiny cracks which deepened with a flickered smile. He wasn't old, maybe the same age my aupouk was when we lived in the stilt hut. His eyes were framed by curving eyebrows, bushy and full. His hair stuck out at the back of his head in a comical way, catching in the breeze. Unlike every other soldier, this man wasn't intimidating. Could he kill someone as the other Khmer Rouge soldiers did?

"This is an important job you know." Vichet tapped the side of the pot with his fingers. "If you didn't cook for us, we wouldn't have energy to shovel. If we didn't have energy to shovel, you wouldn't have any rice to cook."

I grinned.

"As much as I would like to give everyone a heaping portion of rice, we'd better add more water, because we must make it stretch for every comrade. I don't want anyone hungry."

Heaving the pot off the fire, I opened the lid and steam barreled into my eyes.

"Do you understand, Rindy?"

I looked up, coughing as I waved the steam away. What did he mean?

"If you eat your fill before everyone else, then that would mean others would suffer. Cooks have been shot for eating before their comrades—" His voice trailed off with his eyes as he watched the soldier set the crate on the ground. "That's his job, to make sure you don't eat all the supplies."

He looked back into my eyes, his gaze narrowing. "I don't want you or any of your comrades harmed—ever. Do you understand?"

I nodded. I wouldn't get any extra.

He smiled, and together we peered into the pot of white swimming with specks of snail and frog. It stared back at me, drowning in water, but I added more until Vichet nodded that it was enough. Then I added salt and prahok, the thick fish paste in almost every Cambodian dish. It was salty and tasted like old fish by itself, but it smelled like home. Vichet rummaged through the bowls he had brought and handed me a coconut shell ladle.

"Everyone gets one ladle full. Better try to make sure everyone gets the same amount of rice or else there will be fighting." Vichet's smile melted into a thin line. Was he imagining all the skinny boys digging the trench into the dry paddy? They moved like starving skeletons but were the human machine of Angkar. He shook his head, and his eyes refocused.

"Let's get your hungry comrades."

35

THE TRENCH

"I had never done anything like that in my life." — Rindy

JANUARY 1978

"**K***ampucheans are a force for change,*
we swear to destroy all ,
harmonization makes us stronger,
we sacrifice our life for victory."

We sang the Khmer Rouge national anthem in monotone into the morning darkness, rotten with breath. The music crackled from the radio hooked to the loudspeaker hanging from a palm tree. Each day began with the anthem tuned to the Khmer Rouge radio station—the only radio station that seemed to be in existence. As hard as I tried each day, I never could like the music. I found it strange. It didn't sound at all like traditional Khmer music with soft trills and voices. Since we were purging out all foreign influences, it sounded like they had tried too hard and used too many gongs and strange clinging instruments throughout, especially at the finish when they raised their voices to an almost curdling crescendo. The radio squeaked, and I put an ear to my shoulder, trying to block it out.

Vichet stepped forward to turn it off.

I looked up at the gray sky. The sun was coming. It was the hottest part of the year, and the noonday sun had burned up the ground and any rain from the sky. I hadn't felt a drop in the four months I had been a cook for our battalion, traveling from place to place digging canals or building dams. Wherever we were, I was responsible for cooking the rice and scavenging for whatever else I could find. But as Vichet had warned, I tried hard not to eat before the rest of my battalion, failing a few times as I snuck some of the kernels that stuck to the edge of the pot.

The snails, fish and crabs had begun to disappear like the water, eaten by the cracked ground, making forging for food difficult. The uncertainty of where we would be next and whether I would be able to find food there, was all a part of the great game that Angkar was playing. I was merely a speck of dust clinging to the bottom of their boot. But I tried to do my part—we all did. Vichet inspired a desire within each of us, resurrecting pride and hope.

"We have been assigned a new project." Vichet's voice broke through the glorious silence following the anthem. He stood before us and beamed; his unruly hair flapped in the morning breeze like the feathers of a bird. "This is a great honor and I commend you. You all have outworked some of the battalions that are made of grown men."

Over the months, I was surprised by Vichet. He spent his days working beside the boys in our battalion, often taking the hardest jobs for himself. Every morning, he led every Khmer Rouge soldier in the area in a recitation of their "code of behavior." I had heard soldiers recite them back at the camp, but with Vichet it was different. When he recited them, he closed his eyes and swelled his chest, speaking each word with passion:

"You shall love, honor and serve the workers and peasants.

You shall serve the people where you go with all your heart and mind.

You shall do nothing improper respecting women.

You shall behave with great meekness toward the workers and the entire population. Toward the enemy, however, the American imperialists and their lackeys, you shall feed your hatred with force and vigilance."

I had even heard him reprimand other soldiers who were lazing in the shade of a tree while their battalions worked with one of his favorite lines:

"You shall continually join the people's production and love your work."

I watched what he said, how he said it and the way his eyes were more often soft and kind, rather than black and angry like every other Khmer soldier I had encountered. It was as if a pot of amber sugar was always bubbling in his pupils, keeping them warm and alive. Although we had been under Vichet's command for months, I still couldn't quite understand him. He wasn't cruel and brutal like every other Khmer Rouge soldiers I had encountered. I had seen other soldiers kill workers who couldn't work, but Vichet was true to his word, and he never harmed one. It was as if Vichet was serving in the true revolution, while the others only sought power. He really believed in what we were doing, and he made me want to believe too.

"Battalion five is moving to Kampong Pouy Reservoir, not far from here." Vichet's words brought my wandering mind back. "Your hard work and dedication have not been unnoticed by Angkar. Kampuchea is becoming great because of each of you."

We lined up shoulder to shoulder with our shovels sticking into the cloudless sky, ready to go to our new assignment. We marched past fields of barren earth and destroyed villages. The road was gouged with ruts and potholes, making the marching difficult. We passed a toppled pagoda which had once stood tall atop a hill. Its large bricks were strewn to one side, with charred fragments of wood sticking out of the rubbish. It looked like a beheaded man, left to die in his own misery. We marched most of the day, entering the deserted streets of Battambang. The once busy main street was completely vacant. Every shop had either been looted or burned. The bright prayer flags commonly seen flapping in each entryway hung in burned strands, making the street shops look like gapping, toothless faces.

Staring at the wreckage, I wondered if Angkar had burned away the good in addition to the corruption. Looking down I closed my eyes tightly, trying to stifle the nagging doubt clinging to the tail of every promise Angkar made. I looked from side to side, afraid the doubt in my heart might be detected.

Since year zero—the year the Khmer took control— I had been instructed in their dogma and how they were righting the wrongs of the past generations. They were drawing a new line in the dirt—a new way forward that gave those long oppressed by foreign powers a future of hope and optimism, ruled only by their own countrymen.

"Angkar is good...Angkar is good," I often found myself whispering, blind to the realization that I was the only one I was trying to convince. Angkar was Kampuchea and in order to survive, I had to be an obedient tool of the revolution. Only the obedient and resilient were alive, haunted by the memories of those who were not.

Through the wreckage of Battambang, we continued to march toward a mountain shaped like a sleeping man with his arms crossed over his chest. I hoped we would reach wherever we were going soon because my shoulder throbbed from carrying the shovel for so long. The road narrowed, forcing us to march two abreast. The sun peeked over the mountain. It barely cast a light over the valley, when the sound of digging shovels and the dumping of dirt reached my ears. Dozens of soldiers lined the road, looking downward as if into a deep hole.

"Welcome to the Kamping Puoy Reservoir," Vichet shouted over the sound of people digging. Dust curled in the air over our heads.

Approaching the edge, I looked down, unprepared for what I was about to witness. As far as I could see, black-clad workers were digging a trench into the valley between the two mountains. Their emaciated arms gripped bamboo shovels as they thrust them into the dry earth, moving like an endless, mechanical machine. They didn't seem human, just skeletons with dust for brains and empty crates for eyes.

"Keep marching," a soldier commanded, and I pulled my eyes away reluctantly. We continued skirting our way along the lip of the trench. Gulping through the dry feeling in my throat, I marched onward, forgetting the pain in my shoulder.

When we reached the small village erected to house all the workers, Vichet was led away by a high-ranking cadre into one of the nicest huts. A female soldier ordered us to follow her toward a vacant piece of ground, backed by scruffy trees.

"Here are your supplies." She motioned to a pile of bamboo poles and twine on the ground, her feminine voice unnecessarily gruff and forced, like all the female soldiers. "They are to be used to build your own personal hut."

"Angkar supplies all your needs and sees that you have your own hut to keep you safe and comfortable. This is your designated area." She drew a line in the dirt, encircling the group of us — the couple hundred boys of battalion five.

"Begin your task." She gripped her gun tightly as she waved it at us, then sat against a tree to watch.

I grabbed a pole and drug it past the line. I chose a patch of ground near a bamboo thicket, hoping the already planted poles could serve as additional support. I looked around at the other boys who had already begun. We had all built our own structures, but hadn't stayed in them long. Getting on my hands and knees, I began to dig holes in the dirt with my fingernails. The ground was hard beneath the top layer, so I jabbed a bamboo pole into it, loosening it enough to continue digging. I buried one of the bamboo poles, and it reached into the sky, just taller than me.

"Is there any water?" I asked the boy next to me, my voice scratching through the dry caverns of my throat. I tried to lick my lips, but no saliva came.

"I heard there isn't much water here," he responded, his black eyes taking up most of his emaciated face. "They're rationing it pretty tightly."

I kept digging. I was so thirsty. I had grown used to hunger, but thirst was a new sensation.

We worked on our huts until darkness snuffed out the sun. Hundreds of huts stood where dirt once had been. They were barely large enough for two boys to lie shoulder to shoulder. Most of them were crooked and lacked any real roof, except for the palms we stuffed between the bamboo poles, which we tied together. If rain ever did come, they would be beaten into the ground, but for now, they would do nicely.

I lay down on the dirt and dried leaves and looked up at the sky, visible through large patches of the roof where I hadn't yet thatched, and smiled, stretching my arms wide and placing them behind my head.

36

THE GIRL

"At first they gave us plenty of food, but we had other problems." — Rindy

FEBUARY 1978

"The bright red blood

Was spilled over the towns and over the plain of Kampuchea, our Motherland,

The blood of our good workers and farmers

And the blood of the men and women revolutionary combatants..."

The words filled the blackness of the sky, and I knew the sun would not rise for hours. We were awoken at 2 am to begin the day's work. I coughed, trying to croak through the morning anthem, but my voice failed me. I could only think about water.

"Their blood produced a great anger and the courage,

To contend with heroism.

On the 17th of April, under the revolutionary banner,

Their blood freed us from the state of slavery.

Hurrah for the glorious 17th of April!

That wonderful victory had greater significance

Than the Angkar period."

Unable to focus on the words, I tried to focus on keeping strength in my weak knees. But the anthem continued.

"We are uniting

To construct a Kampuchea with a new and better society,

Democratic, egalitarian and just.

We follow the road to a firmly-based independence.

We absolutely guarantee to defend our motherland,

Our fine territory, our magnificent revolution!"

The words spun around in my head like a fly caught on a string, moving faster and faster and faster. The boy next to me shoved me in the ribs, causing me to cough and stand at attention to finish the anthem. I moved my mouth, but no sound came out. The anthem raged on in a swelling crescendo.

"Hurrah for the new Kampuchea,

A splendid, democratic land of plenty!

We guarantee to raise aloft and wave the red banner of the revolution.

We shall make our motherland prosperous beyond all others,

Magnificent and wonderful!"

At last, the music crackled into silence, and we were left standing at attention, the anthem still ringing in our ears.

"You should count yourselves as the most fortunate in the history of Kampuchea." A man's voice rang, I looked but couldn't see him through the bobbing heads.

"You are responsible for being a hand that digs in this great dirt and a heart that holds the pride of Angkar. This dam is not just another task, it will bring electricity like we have never known in our history. We will build factories and give power to even the small villages. It will ensure three rice crops per year—"

Not able to focus, I tried to swallow again, hoping the dryness would go away.

"...Soon water will pool in your efforts and enrich the soil..."

I closed my eyes and imagined water, the feeling of it and the taste of it on my tongue. I began to tremble, the vision in my head overtaking my senses.

"...let us work with one common goal..." The soldier continued, drawing me back to my parched reality. I could hardly hear anything he was saying. I just begged inside my head for him to stop talking.

"...Angkar is responsible for this greatness, never forget that. They are causing the waters of Cambodia to run in purity and strength once again, being freed from western imperialist thought and action..."

I imagined the water again. I plugged my ears and tried to shut out the droning voice. I just wanted to drink water and never stop drinking. Faintly, the voice echoed in the background.

"It's time to begin. Every section is to dig 100 feet a day or you will be punished."

We marched in single file into the trench, digging our shovels and hoes into the red clay, then dumping it into a basket and passing it to the *met*—the comrade— beside us, who passed it on up the line, until it was dumped at the top. We took turns digging and hauling. We could barely see, but dirt is dirt, so we shoveled blindly. I tried not to think about being thirsty but failed. Thirst curled around every thought like the smell of cooking food, distracting and captivating me. At last, the silhouette of the soldier walking back and forth on the lip of the trench was visible, the butt of his cigarette glowing.

"Keep working" and "shovel harder," he barked down a few times an hour, when we lulled in work. I looked through the dim light creeping into the trench and saw Vichet hoeing the dirt beside a row of especially thin boys. He would call to us too, but he usually said, "keep going, boys, you're doing it." One voice spurred us on, the other we ignored.

Ding, Ding, Ding!

It was the lunch bell. The sun had climbed high overhead. We shuffled out of the trench and joined the hordes of dirty people, excited to eat. I wanted water more than anything I had ever wanted before.

Lining up, we shuffled into the cafeteria. I did not want rice; I wanted water, but I held out my bowl and received my portion anyway. The idea of refusing food was unthinkable. Walking over to my battalion, I sat down and put my bowl on the ground between my feet. The same watery broth stared back at me, and I could almost taste the overpowering saltiness.

"I'm so thirsty." I looked to the speaker of the words, a met who sat beside me. His bowl was also untouched.

"Why aren't they letting us go to one of the canals?" someone else asked.

"I don't know, I heard the guards say it was almost dried up," another chimed in.

I nodded and looked back at my bowl. I slurped up some of the broth, trying to imagine it was water, but the saltiness made me gag.

"I'll eat yours," a skinny boy said, his eyes locked on my bowl.

I shook my head and continued to force it down. After I was done, I rested my forehead on my knees. I hoped it would ease the pounding between my ears. I let my jaw hang loose, knowing no saliva would come. The talking around me began to throb to the pain in my head. The sound swirled like a million waves, crashing into each temple. I could nearly see the deep blues, light greens and faint yellows of being caught underwater like I had experienced when I almost drowned as a boy. It was tantalizing and kept calling me deeper into the water and further away from the present. Between the crashing, someone shook me.

"Look, Rindy. Look."

Lifting my head, I squinted at the speaker. His mouth moved, but it took a second to understand what he was saying.

"They have water!"

I lifted my head, rubbing the numbness with my thumbs and tried to find strength in my legs to push off the ground. People had already begun to flock to the three lines that were forming. Staggering to the nearest one, I waited, heart thudding inside my chest. My heartbeat was slow, it felt odd.

A girl next to me leaned against a pole, looking like she might not be able to make the short trip forward. She made me think of my sisters. Where were they now? Where was Vuthy? I hoped they had enough water to drink.

The line began to move without her, so I helped her stand, and we inched forward together, my arm supporting her elbow and waist. She was only bones. I took a step forward and closed my eyes, imagining the sensation of water on my tongue. An elderly man groaned nearby, his legs so swollen I doubted he could walk. It was strange, starving people sometimes got bigger, not smaller. I had heard some say it was from a lack of nutrition in our food and because of our high salt intake, but I didn't know. I shifted the girl, and she pushed away slightly, after giving me a brief smile.

"Arkoun," she offered her thanks.

I smiled in return.

Minutes passed, and I took another step forward, then another, then another. I stared at my sandals in the dirt; they looked blurry like I was seeing them through water. I watched them take another step forward as if they weren't my own.

Glancing up, I saw that there were only three more people in front of me. Then there were only two, then a mere one. I stood with shaking knees as my turn came. A soldier stood before me with an outstretched ladle. I trembled as I reached out my hands, numbly cupping it and lifting it to my lips. For a moment, I knew what the afterlife tasted like, felt like. It was endless and took me somewhere no sensation ever had before. From the darkness of my eyelids, I became lost in the sensation of water. I opened my eyes the clouds drifted by. It was gone. Three gulps. It wasn't enough.

"That's all."

I stared at the empty ladle, rimmed with a hint of rust. I looked back up at the soldier pleadingly.

"You've had your potion, move on. Move!"

I turned to go, my head feeling like it was full of feathers. Turning around, I made sure the girl got some water. I watched her drink, unable to move, completely mesmerized. She trembled as the water surged down her throat, she coughed and sputtered.

"That's all. Move along."

She shuffled aside, and our eyes met. I smiled, and she smiled back. Or did I just imagine it? She turned to rejoin her battalion, legs moving with a bit more steadiness.

I licked my lips. I was thirstier now than I had ever been. I closed my eyes and thought of drinking again, the feeling of it tumbling down my throat. I wanted to sink into the dirt and wait away the hours until we would get more water, but the bell began to sound for us to report to our battalions for work.

I found my group and stood in formation among the other teenage boys. Their eyes were strangely glassy. They too were fantasizing about water. Vichet stood before us, the afternoon sun beaming behind him, making him appear even taller than he typically did.

We grabbed our shovels, hoes and baskets, but a commotion rippled through our ranks. Every boy's head turned to watch as a group of girls marched toward us with shovels over their shoulders, a female soldier leading them.

"These are your new work partners," Vichet answered our questioning glances. "You are to assist each other in the work, so it will not become too burdensome. Everyone plays an important role in Angkar's revolution—you must remember that."

We glanced sideways at each other, knowing they had paired us up with the girls because they couldn't handle a whole section on their own. The soldier began assigning a girl to each one of us. I watched in dread as they worked their way down the line toward me, anticipating who would be assigned to me, growing more and more nervous with each name called. Working alongside a girl was not only uncomfortable, it was also dangerous to our assigned quota because they would slow us down.

My eyes dropped to my dirty toenails. Without moving my head, I felt a girl take her place in the line next to me. Even without seeing her, I could feel her presence and how small she was. Her smallness wasn't only in her frame, but she was small on the inside too, as if every part of her was tucked away in some corner of herself, scared of even the sunlight. I cringed. Her hands trembled. Unable to quell my dread any longer, I looked up into a pair of massive black eyes. Fear curled in them like water, and stringy hair framed her face.

It was the girl from the water line.

I smiled weakly when Vichet drew our attention back.

"I believe in you and in the greatness of Kampuchea." Vichet lifted his shovel. "Let us begin the day's work."

We followed him, past the soldiers patrolling with their Mks' and filed down into the trench. Dust drifted into the sky, with each step of the boy in front of me, coating my lungs. I tied the krama around my face a bit tighter, as did everyone else. I coughed and my shovel clanked into the girl's shovel next to me. Gazing through the haze, I could see that other battalions had already begun their work. Reaching the bottom, I plunged my shovel into the dirt.

"Here." I handed the basket to the girl. Our eyes met and I could see her peering out of herself, as if just for a moment, quelling fear. She took the basket and handed it on up the line. I couldn't help but notice the tremble in her arms as she did, as if it took every ounce of strength that she had. Her arms were thin and seemed to be stretching to an impossible length as they strained against the weight of the dirt. Checking for the soldier that patrolled at the top, I hoped they didn't see how slowly she moved. We repeated this process a few dozen more times, before I thought her arms might pull out at their sockets.

"Are you okay?" I croaked quietly, trying to ignore the dry feeling in my mouth for the thousandth time. She nodded, but her eyes betrayed her, and she looked like she might cry. I made sure the soldier took another turn away from us, before speaking again.

"You're doing good. We'll help each other." I plunged my shovel in the dirt again. I could feel her smile, even though her eyes didn't light up. A wind blew over the dry earth, causing a dust cloud to rise into the sky. Coughing, we tied our kramas tighter, dropping our shovels.

"Keep digging!" The soldier yelled down into the cloud of dust. I was irritated. The dirt cloaked my hair and clung to the line of sweat under my black collar. The sun beat down on our black backs, making it seem even hotter than it was. I wiped my arm across my face and swallowed, trying to chase down the feeling of mud in my throat. Then suddenly, a sound caught me off guard. It was a giggle! The girl's giggle. I looked up, surprised.

"You just smeared mud all over your forehead." She cast her eyes to the ground apologetically.

I smiled and began to say something but caught sight of the guard pacing toward our section, so I bit my tongue. Filling another basket to the brim, I set it a little farther up the embankment, so she didn't have to struggle so far. How far could I set it before someone would say something? She looked at me with massive, relieved eyes and smiled. Then she took her turn digging, but she couldn't dig fast enough and kept stopping to cough. I helped her fill the bucket.

"What's your name?" She whispered, our hands colliding on the basket handle.

"Rindy." I kept my face down so as not to attract the notice of the soldier.

Minutes passed and I wondered if she would offer me her own name, or if I would have to ask. I opened my mouth to ask —

"Mine's Chivy."

Chivy, I thought. Her name meant "life."

The name curled in my mind like the dust in the air.

37

RAIN

"Only Angkar will provide your needs." —Rindy

APRIL 1978

One evening, I felt a change in the air. I looked at the sky. It was still pale blue and cloudless, but somehow it wore a mystery. We had begun that day like every other: at two in the morning during the time of night when spirits walked around as shrunken men and hallow-eyed girls. It was growing dark; the sun had risen and set, but we weren't nearly done.

Dust clung to every inch of my body and swept its fine fingers through my hair like a comb, leaving every strand tainted. Running my tongue over my teeth, I felt dirt between each tooth. The dust had eaten me that day, but it was my stomach that seemed full of it. I felt like a walking sandbag.

I wanted water. The two cups we received at mealtime only teased me, like a feather to my nose. I wanted to swim in it—be engulfed in it. I hadn't had a bath in months, as water was a luxury not wasted on bathing. I didn't know where the dirt ended and my skin began, as each day my sweat pulled the grime further into my body.

"Keep shoveling," the soldier called in his strained voice, his boots sounding over my head. I didn't bother to look up.

I glanced sideways at Chivy. I sensed her suppressed giggle, even without turning my head.

"It's as if he has a lump of rice stuck…" She didn't finish her sentence before carrying the basket up the embankment. I smiled. Making jokes about the soldiers was our favorite thing to do while in the trench, the single star in the otherwise black night sky. Whenever we glanced up the embankment, his double chin was especially pronounced and jostled slightly with each step. His chubby fingers were white and clenched around his Mk-47 and his checkered krama had a lot less flapping at the end than most of the other soldiers' had. We were careful not to get caught talking, because the soldiers would yell at anyone who opened their mouths except to sneeze or cough. Even that could be risky. Chivy and I exchanged about a couple dozen sentences each day, so as not to try our luck. I would replay each sentence she uttered over and over again in my mind until the next one came. Hearing her voice was a luxury.

On days of especially brutal work and searing sun, I watched her eyes fill with hot tears. Somehow, they never spilled over, being locked inside the glass orbs of her eyes. Her eyes were black pools into her soul. They said everything before she did, and they couldn't lie, not even for a moment. Although she was thin and malnourished, she was beautiful to me. Her eyelashes were long and the color of charcoal, as if they were the only part of her that could afford to grow. Her timid smile, the way she made subtle jokes without hardly changing the expression on her face, always made me happy. Her ability to laugh, even when life crushed us to the ground, made her the sun to my world. The companionship I grew to find in Chivy was the reason I was able to endure each day. I even began to look forward to them.

"Do you think we'll ever be done?"

I looked up, but it had grown too dark to see anything. So, I just imagined it, the hole we were digging in the dirt that stretched for miles around us. The hole that was supposed to fix all of our pain and suffering. The hole that was going to give us three crops of rice per year. I feared we would eventually hit the underworld of the spirits, and they would start pulling us through, deeper and darker. Would it be much worse than this though?

"Rindy? Did you hear me?" Chivy's question pulled me from my dark thoughts.

"I suppose we will have to be done sometime. It's not like we can make all of Kampuchea into a giant hole." I tried to be funny, but my voice fell flat. I wasn't convinced that the Khmer Rouge weren't destroying everything they touched, as we had never known such drought or desolation before. They used all the water to irrigate the rice fields, as they forced them to grow during the dry season. But I kept that thought to myself, like all the others rattling within my chest.

Grabbing the last basket full, I uncurled Chivy's fingers and carried it up the bank. The soldiers hated when any of the girls received special treatment as "everyone was supposed to carry their own weight in the revolution."

"Are you okay, Chivy?"

"Yes, I'm just tired." I could see the outline of her shoulders and the dragging of her feet as we made our way back to camp.

"See you tomorrow, Rindy."

"See you tomorrow, Chivy."

I watched her disappear into the darkness, to the girl's sleeping quarters. I worried about her, as the soldiers were known to force themselves on the woman while they were sleeping. I had heard some of the older women whispering about it in the food lines. Would they bother Chivy? Thin Chivy, who could barely support her own weight? I picked up a rock and threw it. The stone thudded dully into the trench, now quiet and still. I would kill someone if they tried.

I walked to my section of the camp and sat around the blazing fire, as a Khmer Rouge orator filled the night sky with the glories of Angkar and how we needed to "trust the plan." I had heard it many times and wondered if they could come up with anything new, before nodding off, my head on my chest and my back resting against a palm tree. I dreamed of a tiger jumping from the fire, and I awoke with a start. How had I managed to sleep through the screeching man's voice? It must have been only a moment. At last, he completed his tirade, yet I couldn't recall a word. I strolled groggily with the rest of my battalion to my little hut, which I had improved slowly over the months. I lay down and rolled on my side, instantly falling asleep and cascading into a darkness too deep for dreams.

Awaking with a start, I rolled onto my back. Looking up through the little peep hole I'd left in the roof of my hut to see the stars. The stars that had filled the sky when I'd fallen asleep had vanished. A difference stirred in the air and it was familiar. The sky rumbled, rolling like giant black cobra, making the earth tremble beneath me. Sitting up, my heart began to race. It was here. It was finally here!

"Did anyone hear that?" I sucked in my quivering breath to listen.

Excited voices echoed through the night.

Lying flat on my back, I closed my eyes, waiting for the sensation to hit my skin. Then a drop splattered on my face. Then another.

"It's here." I crawled out of my head and reached toward the sky. Relief fluttered in the cage of my chest.

"Quick," someone shouted. Others exited their huts, and we flung ourselves into frenzied digging, so we could catch the rainwater in holes. Then it started to pour. Lying down with my face to the sky, arms outstretched, I let it wash over me. I couldn't tell if I was crying in relief or if it was the rain dripping off my nose, but either way I didn't care. The rain pelted me, coming in sheets. It stung my skin at first, but it was the best thing I had ever felt.

After a while of lying still, I decided I had better get clean. I wrung out my clothes and hung them on the poles of my hut, before letting it pelt my bare skin. Someone passed around a homemade bar of soap, made from kapok fruit and fire ash. My hair was clumped like muddy seaweed as I scrubbed it, hoping to erase the months of dust clinging to every strand. I traced a pulsating vein in my arm, as the layers of filth dissolved, leaving only my skin. I felt clean. It was a clean that went past my skin and into my soul, filling in all the cracks and smoothing all the rough places.

I don't know how long I sat naked in the rain, but my body, long baked by the sun, began to grow cold. So, I slunk back into my hut, dripping wet and exhausted, to try to warm up. The roof barely kept out any water, so I crawled into the corner and mounded up the straw around me, not even minding the hordes of bugs that lived there.

The rain didn't stop, and I sat shivering in my hut all night, my clothes sticking to my body. I awoke to the feeling of numb toes and the sound of my teeth knocking together. Where were the bells? I hadn't slept until sunrise since coming to the dam. The sky was cloaked like a crimson monk, showy and proud. Stepping out of my hut, I saw hundreds of holes filled to the brim with water. Being careful not to step on them, I bent down and slurped some of the water up. I wasn't thirsty, but I wanted some anyway, just because I could.

"Report for the national anthem of Democratic Kampuchea." The voice boomed from the speakers. I crept my way through the ground punched with holes and congregated with my battalion made of soggy and smiling boys.

"The rain has brought good fortune to the land of Kampuchea." Vichet shook his head, the rain pelting the nearest boys. "Now that it has come, we've been assigned to work the rice paddies."

A murmur of excitement drifted through the crowd.

"But I want to congratulate all of you—" He paused, waiting for everyone's full attention. "This battalion—a youth battalion—completed our assigned section before anyone else!"

My smile faded with the sound of excitement. I wanted to work in the rice paddies, because anything would be better than working in the trench, but would Chivy be there too? I looked through the crowd, craning my neck in every direction, but I couldn't find her from where I stood. I wandered through the hordes of black clothed people, their clothes dusty and bodies frail, but their eyes full of something wild, something intoxicating. The rain had resurrected something I thought had long died.

A will to live.

38

RICE

"Only Angkar will feed you." — Rindy

MAY-DECEMBER 1978

My battalion was moved, along with many others, to the rice paddies surrounding Kamping Pou Reservoir, to transplant the rice seedlings into the paddies now flooded with water from the rains and the canals. We did this to expand the rice production and reduce the number of weeds that grew with the seedlings. While working in the paddies, the soldiers didn't usually bother us, as they lazed around the road or washed themselves in the canals, giving us the glorious feeling of freedom. Except for Vichet, who always worked beside us, his broad shoulders bent in work like ours while he told jokes to anyone working around him.

I felt like a new person, washed clean and reborn. I loved the feeling of the mud squishing between my toes. It reminded me of my time with Vuthy as we worked in Pou Kim's rice paddy. Was Vuthy okay? Was he getting enough food? Had he survived this long? The worries buzzed in my stomach. I couldn't drown them with water or the little bit of food we were allowed, no matter how much I tried.

Then, without fail, my mind would always drift to Chivy. Thoughts of her drifted between everything else like the fish swimming between the seedlings, filling me with a will to live and a confidence that I wanted to. I had even asked Vichet where she was, but he didn't know. Worry for her was different than worry for Vuthy, though I couldn't quite understand why. I had always worried about Vuthy because it had been my job as his older brother to protect him. But with Chivy, the worry pulsated deeper through my veins. I wasn't just worried whether she had enough to eat, although I was. I was worried that maybe she didn't have anyone to share her questions with or that she didn't have anyone to make her eyes light up with laughter. Memories of Chivy felt like the sunrise, glowing and burning through the sky. I looked up at it, allowing my back a moment to stretch unbent, before plucking another seedling from the ground. Did she think about me too?

I heard a commotion of feet in the mud behind me as more workers filed in to begin the work of rice. My battalion had been moved earlier that morning to a larger field, and we were barely making a dent in the acre upon acre of rice seedlings ready to be plucked from the soil. I was relieved to hear them approach because I had been hoping more workers would join. After barely a glance over my shoulder, I continued to work, not because someone was barking commands at me, but because I wanted to. Rice wasn't like digging a reservoir; rice I knew. I didn't like much of what the Khmer Rouge said, but I did like that "rice is the lifeblood of Kampuchea," because it was. It gave us confidence in tomorrow.

Something hit my neck. What was that? I swiped at it before continuing to pull and bundle the seedlings. Then something bigger hit my back. Spinning around, I expected to find one of my smiling mets with a grin smeared on his face. But I didn't. Chivy stood shyly before me, ankles sunk in brown water and a smear of mud across her face. She had never been more beautiful.

I took a timid step forward, then another, before I felt my arms around her slender body, encircling her. I touched the skin on her arms, reveled in the feeling of her closeness. I had never embraced her before, and I lingered a moment, catching the smell of her hair before releasing her. I stood back, awkward after my forward display of emotion. Her eyes shone up at me, asking so many questions I didn't know the answer to.

"I've missed you, Chivy."

She smiled in reply, her large eyes eclipsed. There I could see it. She'd been thinking of me too.

"Get to work little, love birds, before you get us yelled at," one of my mets called, grinning at us. "We've got a good thing going here without the soldiers breathing down our necks."

We began to work, Chivy and I, side by side. I couldn't stop looking over at her though, and she caught me many times.

As the weeks passed, I could tell she was enjoying being near me too. Transplanting seedlings was different from shoveling. It was still back-breaking, but it felt more natural somehow. Dust didn't choke us; instead, mud ate our feet.

"Ay!" Chivy jumped as I splashed water onto her neck.

Smiling, I lifted my fingers to my mouth in mock surprise, and she responded with shining eyes, before resuming her work. I stole a couple of quick glances at her, bent at the waist. She was still thin, but the inside of her seemed to expand somehow. Nothing made me happier. Working in the rice paddies was much better for her than hauling dirt, as it didn't weigh on her arms or her soul as much. Breathing in the fresh air, I continued to pull up the tender rice seedlings, deciding I had better focus and work. I caught sight of a plump snail crawling up a rice plant. Grinning, I pinched it carefully and brought it up for Chivy to see.

"Look what I have prepared for you." My face stretched in the biggest grin I could manage.

"How kind." Chivy smiled, but her eyes devoured it hungrily. I handed it to her quickly and watched as she chewed it as if it was the best thing she had ever eaten. We hunted for snails as we worked for the rest of the day, never growing tired of the taste of them on our tongues.

By midday, dark clouds began to roll in the sky like a fish caught in a trap. By evening, we were running back to camp as the sky poured. Instead of dirt eating my skin, rain began to. It seeped into my veins and seemed to water down my blood. The deluge battered our thrown together huts, and each morning I tried to improve mine with whatever I could find in the jungle, but it didn't help much. As soon as my black clothes dried out, more rain came.

The rainy season lasted five months, until the sky was satisfied, and the earth began to bake beneath the sun again. The rice seedlings we had transplanted in the fields grew tall and began to ripen, with acres upon acres of the golden grass swaying in the wind.

Then harvest began, and Chivy and I waded into the field to begin hacking away at the plants, along with the hundreds of others who had previously worked on the reservoir. In the meetings each night, the Khmer Rouge said our hard work would soon be rewarded with heaping bowls of rice—not the watery soup we had eaten for the past years with only a few slimy kernels. I dreamed about what a bowl of plain, white rice would taste and feel like on my tongue. The weight of it, the flowery aroma rising to my nose. Chivy and I even began to talk about the different foods we remembered from our childhood that we would prepare with it. She talked of her mteay's coconut fish curry, and I spoke of my Chidaun's *Lok Lak*—a savory beef stir fry on a bed of fresh cucumber and tomato.

As I gazed out over the acres and acres of rice, the pregnant plants waved back at me like flags of surrender from the enemy camp until the fields in all directions were laid bare by thousands of workers. We had survived, and the seeds we had planted in the mud had survived. The worry of starvation that had long plagued me like a vulture flew away over the stubble of the golden fields. For the first time in three years, since the Khmer Rouge's takeover, I had confidence in the future. A future that saw flesh growing on Chivy's bones, a future that held more than enough and a future where we could reap the benefits. Bending at my waist, I continued to gather the felled rice grass scattered over the paddy that had been harvested. Chivy walked beside me, bundling what I handed to her before placing it on the cart we'd take back to the massive storehouses that had been built. Storehouses bursting with rice that had been threshed and processed until it was ready to be cooked. Hearing a commotion, I glanced up and saw a brigade of large military trucks roll down the road. The ground trembled beneath my feet, and every person nearby stopped to stare.

"Keep working," a soldier barked, waving his gun in the air.

Rubbing my back, I bent over to gather a small bundle filled with the last of the rice harvest. My back burned under the heat of the sun, and my muscles were tight, but the tightness in my chest expanded as a fear I had talked myself out of resurfaced in throbbing victory. It throbbed until minutes turned into hours.

"They're taking the rice." Chivy grabbed my shoulder. I stood to face her. Her eyes were wild with panic. "All of it. They're clearing out the entire storehouse."

I froze for a moment, staring at the peeling skin on my hands, refusing to look and see for myself. I didn't want to believe Chivy. I was afraid to look at the trucks again, but I knew the truth. I had known the truth since I had heard the cheerful Khmer Rouge soldier spout lies every night for months, but I had refused to believe it. We all like to believe in fairytales, after all. They had said, "This time is different. This time we'll get to reap our reward—eat the rice we worked hard for. The days of starvation are over." I looked at Vichet, who stood farther back in the field, pulling a mostly empty cart of gathered rice grass. His face was bleak, his lips pressed together in a frown as his eyes moved with the trucks. Was he beginning to doubt Angkar?

I watched as a naked-headed vulture circled in the pale sky, casting a shadow over the ground we stood on.

39

MATCHMAKING

"Angkar didn't want you to love." — Rindy

JANUARY 1979

The bell clamored, causing everyone working in the reservoir to pop with anticipation, like they were lit on fire. The bell was obnoxious and loud, but it produced a thrill in each breast. The sound of that bell was one of the things I had grown to live for. It was a source of security and comfort, and a daily assurance that I was still alive.

Falling in step with my battalion, we marched to the cafeteria and lined up for our portion. Inching forward in the line. I sniffed the air. Where was the smell of cooking food? It had been years since I had smelled Prahok or rice. Holding out my bowl I grimaced, knowing what to expect, but hoping I was wrong. The usual watery bowl of broth with a few indistinguishable, floating vegetables was slopped in. The vegetables were a nice addition. They must have been grown in the communal garden, tended by the elderly women unable to work. It was patrolled night and day though, so few people could steal food.

It was more painful to see Chivy grow thin each day than it was to feel my own arms and legs wither. Somehow, I didn't fear for myself, but my fear for her had become a torment. With each meal, I watched her devour her food with a ferocity that took more energy than the food gave her. She was not alone. As I glanced at the faces of those around me, it was impossible not to see their starved and shrunken frames, as if they lived on the salt of their sweat alone. A blanket of listlessness settled over those of us working in the reservoir. We merely existed like a speck of dirt on the back of a shovel that was being driven deeper and deeper into the earth.

I slurped slowly. Chivy squatted next to me, staring into her empty bowl. I dreaded seeing her despair. The hope I'd had for her growth and health had withered in the sun. Her knobby knees were supported by thin legs, void of muscle. Looking up, she caught me staring. Her dark eyes took up most of her face, and her black hair hung like dried leaves over her forehead. Her collarbone protruded through her skin, and her clothes hung from her body as if no one was inside them. She looked like an old lady trapped inside a girl's body.

"Please take it." I handed her the rest of my soup.

She shook her head, dropping her eyes.

"Chivy, please—" I raised the bowl to her lips. Her throat contracted, allowing the liquid to go down. Her eyes met mine again; a tortured thanks, brimming with tears.

Glancing at the sky, I squinted into the sun. The rainy season had passed, and we were again working at the reservoir. My back felt as black as the shirt covering it, charred beneath the rays reflecting off the red dirt we were digging. I missed planting and harvesting rice. I missed the confidence I felt working around food. Looking back down at my quickly emptied bowl, I remembered the golden field of rice, bursting with promise. It had been three years since the soldiers drove away in their trucks with our food. We hadn't eaten rice in ten days.

"Everyone assemble for a celebration." A soldier waved all those eating around the cafeteria to assemble out front of the longhouse. "Angkar has great things in store for you today."

Standing at attention, we waited and watched, uncertain of what "celebration" meant. One of the leading Khmer Rouge cadres sat at a table surrounded by his subordinate soldiers. The soldiers were assembling young men and women from various battalions. "There is nothing to fear, this is a glorious day," the cadre told us.

But I was nervous. With each darting glance and each muffled whisper, the feeling deepened into my stomach, like termites eating holes into a tree.

Standing, the cadre approached us, a notebook in hand, making little marks as he went along. He looked intently into each face and then briefly from head to foot before strolling onto the next. His eyes lingered over some, while barely brushing others. I trembled, thinking about my approaching turn to be inspected. He seemed to pay special attention to our faces, which was odd because Angkar didn't seem to see us at all. We were merely instruments in his hands. We were diggers, planters, and cooks, but we were not humans. I could feel him approaching on my left, and I held my breath as he stopped to inspect the comrade next to me. He was a tall boy, probably about twenty years old, with fine straight teeth and broad shoulders. The leader tarried, writing in his notebook.

I could hear the crunch of his boots as he approached. He took a step forward. His shadow covered me before I looked into his face. I held my breath and began to grow dizzy, his eyes and hair blurring into one. My fingers shook as I extended them at my sides. But he barely paused before moving past me quickly, going to the next comrade. Relief flooded me along with the air I let into my lungs. Out of the corner of my eye I watched him continue farther down the line. With each step he went I breathed easier.

Then a thought crept into my mind like the shadows extending over the ground from the surrounding palm trees. I licked my lips, hoping to make the sudden dryness in my mouth disappear, but the fear continued to swell. What if it was bad that the soldier didn't pay much attention to me? What if I was of little use? What if I was about to walk into the night?

These thoughts rushed through my mind like a landslide of dirt into the trench, and I completely lost track of the cadre and his routine movements until he was standing back in front of us. He set down his notepad and cleared his throat. I trembled.

"You are the blessed youth of Angkar who will uphold the purity and future of Kampuchea. Today you will begin an important phase of the next step of the plan." He glanced down at his paper briefly. I didn't hear a single breath expel around me.

"Angkar is both Mteay and Aupouk to each of you and provides you with every need and desire. Today Angkar allows you to marry—for those of marrying age." A commotion rippled through the crowd.

My mind began to race, new fears replacing the old.

Was I old enough? How old was I?

While living in the camp we never knew what day it was. Every day was the same. I didn't know how much time had passed since I had left my family, and it felt like a lifetime ago since I had seen their faces. The Khmer Rouge owned even time. I didn't know how many years it had been since becoming a child of Angkar. Frantically, I tried to count from the last comment I remembered Mteay making about my age.

Fifteen.

I thought I was fifteen, but I knew I was small for my age. For the first time in my life, I was grateful for that fact. I didn't know what "marrying age" was, so I stood there, holding my age on the tip of my tongue like a drop of water, hoping I was not called. Then a new thought shrugged across my consciousness like a slow, morning sunrise.

Could I marry Chivy? I thought about her midnight eyes, the little hairs that stuck to the back of her neck and how she could make me laugh at anything. Marrying her would be a way I could ensure her constant safety. I could be with her always, watching over her and making sure she got enough food and always had someone protecting her.

Stealing a quick glance over my shoulder I looked for Chivy. I found her standing a few rows back, like a slender willow, swaying in the breeze of uncertainty. Her large black eyes locked on mine, as if she had already been staring at the back of my head. Was she thinking the same thing? Could she want to be with me in the same way I wanted to be with her?

I turned quickly back around before I was caught by a soldier, questions burning in my chest.

"When I call your name, come forward." The cadre drew a long line in the dirt with the heel of his boot. "Males form a line on this side and females face them."

He began to read off the names scribbled into his notebook.

"Darany Keo."

I could hear the tall boy next to me catch his breath, before taking a tentative step forward. Would anyone dare to resist? The buzz of flies and mosquitos filled the air, but no other sound stirred.

"Vanna Moul."

A quiet sob sounded behind me. Turning quickly, I saw a beautiful girl with tears spilling down her face, her hands over her mouth so as not to let another sound escape. Her hair was shorn short like everyone else's, but it was thick and healthy. Her eyes were large and oval shaped, rimmed by long eyelashes that dripped with tears. The look on her face haunted me. It was sad, but also panicked, like she was being slowly cut in two while standing there.

Vanna emerged from the crowd and stood where the officer pointed—directly opposite of Darany. She was a short girl with a round face. Her eyes were close together and her nose was large and wide. Anyone could see the striking difference between her and Darany. One had apparent dull and unattractive features, and the other was strong and handsome. Vanna stood looking terrified and ashamed. Darany stood at attention with a set jaw, not looking at the girl standing opposite him, his fists clenched at his sides. Unconcerned by the apparent mistake in the match, the soldier continued to call names, first a male's then a female's.

"Bona Mey." He called next.

"Kayna Em."

The beautiful, sobbing girl emerged from the crowd and stood across from an impossibly thin boy, who had large ears and teeth that looked as if they were crammed into his face, each one shoving the next, until a few were bruised black.

More names were called and the solemn procession of a boy, then a girl continued until about fifty couples stood beneath the trees in the clearing: each one facing the other, their toes behind the line drawn in the dirt.

They were pieces in a game, being moved at Angkar's command. Their emaciated frames were especially noticeable as they stood there like lone blades of rice grass, vulnerable and alone without their comrades beside them. As I looked over those facing each other, I couldn't help but notice the mismatches that seemed to be made. Those who were tall were paired with someone short, those who had well-spaced features were paired with someone whose features were all crammed together and those who had straight teeth were paired with those who had no teeth at all.

The head soldier looked over the group approvingly, like a man looking over his chickens, determining which one to eat for dinner. The girls bowed their heads, letting silent tears wet their dusty feet. The boys stood tall, but they looked frightened. Darany looked indignant. Kayna looked as if someone was burning her back with a hot poker. I looked away.

"Today you meet the one you will marry." The soldier smiled at those assembled in each line. "Be good couples and have many children—this is your highest service to Angkar."

Then music began to sound out of the speakers, with loud clanging and lighthearted singing. It was meant to be a celebration, but the music felt like laughing at a funeral. The joyless notes clashed onto my eardrums making me wince, and the loud voices only added to the sick feeling in my stomach. At last, the song died away, eaten by static.

"To validate this ceremony, each of you will exchange your krama," the soldier continued, clapping his hands as if to speed up the process. "This will make you legally married in the eyes of Angkar. This is binding for life."

The boy across from Kayna held out his krama apologetically as she fumbled with her own. Her fingers shook, her eyes on the ground. Darany stood still, his back stiff, his jaw clenched, his krama still wrapped, untouched around his neck. The girl across from him held her krama out awkwardly. We all stared at it in her trembling hands.

"Remove your krama," a soldier barked at Darany. "Are you deaf met?" He paced over to Darany, prodding his back with the barrel of his gun, the veins on his neck looking like stretched leeches. Darany didn't respond. Grabbing the butt of his gun, the soldier jabbed him in the back of the leg. Darany collapsed onto his knees in the dirt, hands still clenched at his sides. Kayna shrieked in a strangled voice.

"Oh, I see how it is." A smile dawned across his face, cold and menacing, as he looked from one to the other. He strolled over to Kayna, his movements slow and dramatic, as if he was relishing the new turn of events.

"Is she the reason you will not exchange your krama with your new bride?" the officer asked in an oozing tone, and the leeches retracted back into his neck. Kayna's head was bowed, but her shoulders trembled.

"You must love each other, mmm?" He yanked Kayna out of her place in line. Darany's eyes followed the officers every movement, his eyes black tunnels. If eyes could kill, Darany's would be shooting bullets.

"Bring him here," the soldier yelled to another, who jumped into action as he shoved Darany onto his knees next to Kayna.

"Illicit love is forbidden by Angkar, as it makes people weak and vulnerable." The commanding officer stood from behind his table and walked over to the couple, droning on routinely. He reached inside his boot and pulled out a knife. I watched helplessly, wanting to look away, but unable to tear my eyes from the two kneeling in the dirt and the blade glinting over their heads. I had seen the Khmer Rouge do many things, but this was a first and even while living in their nightmare for almost four years, I had no idea what they would do next. Love wasn't something that had been addressed much. We were often taught what to think and what to believe, but not yet how to feel. Angkar had stolen our bodies, our work and our pride, but they had not yet stolen our hearts.

"Let this be a public spectacle to everyone." The cadre stood; blade drawn over the heads of the couple. "This corruption must be sliced out."

In a single motion, he ran his knife blade across Kayna's throat, cutting short her scream. Blood squirted out of the wound. Darany screamed, lunging forward to grab her body as it fell into the dust. Reaching out and grabbing him by the hair, the cadre pulled him back to his knees and sliced his throat, in the same, single motion. Darany's lifeless hand still clasped Kayna's black shirt. My stomach revolted, churning like a raging storm. I poked my fingers into my eyes, trying to erase what I had just seen and trying to punish them for not turning away.

"Let us congratulate the new couples," the cadre shouted, triumph oozing out of his every sweating pore as he wiped his knife on Darany's limp krama. The krama that was still wrapped, untouched around his lifeless body.

The alarm sounded, and we dispersed into our battalions and marched back to the trench. Fear over what we had just witnessed was mirrored in each passing glance. "Angkar owns us. Angkar owns us," played like a song over and over in my head, as we shoveled and dumped, shoveled and dumped until the moon shone overhead. Chivy and I barely spoke, but I had so much I wanted to say. The words just stood in my throat, dammed behind horror.

That night after being released from the trench, I was unable to sleep, replaying the events of the day over in my head. Then I heard a woman's scream, piercing the night air like a missile. Then another. Then another. I couldn't tell if it was the same woman, or if it was multiple women screaming. Then more screams rang like a chorus, layering one over the other, revealing dozens of voices, each coming from a different location in the camp.

"Do it, you fool," a soldier yelled, barely audible over the screams. "I'll hold her down."

Grabbing lumps of the dried leaves, I stuffed them into my ears.

40

PANIC

"A person is not worth a bullet." — Rindy

TWO WEEKS LATER

We trudged along in the blackness of the morning. It was the time of day that was even darker than night, as if the night was attempting to fight the sun from rising. I was tired, but this tiredness went deeper than my lack of sleep. My heart throbbed as if it was even weary from beating in step.

In the weight of darkness, I flirted with the panic that had slowly been infecting the rest of those in the trench like dysentery. Workers whose past identities had been discovered as being schoolteachers, doctors or a part of the Lon Nol were often led away to "Angkar," and never seen again. Sometimes in groups of one, three, five or by the dozens. I watched them walk by, their faces panicked or reserved and dignified. The Khmer Rouge had gotten better and finding their victims among us.

There had been many runaways too, as there had been rumors of freedom fighters on the border of Thailand. I don't know how many escaped or how many were killed. I just never saw them again. On the outskirts of the camp, I could smell those who got caught, as the stench of their eroding bodies wafted through the palm trees accompanied by the sound of feasting flies. I had heard there was a shortage of bullets, so the soldiers started to suffocate those caught running away with plastic bags. Since my nightmares were snuffed out by a death-like sleep, the images haunted me during the day as I shoveled and dumped, shoveled and dumped, with the flies drinking my sweat and the dust eating my lungs.

Chivy stumbled next to me as we marched to the trench, jolting me out of my own darkness. It took her a moment to regain her footing, so I braced her with my shoulder. Her bones dug into mine, her flesh stretched tight over her skeleton. Her knees were like the knots on a thin tree, out of place and too large to be supported by her frame. Her eyes stared at me from the black holes sunk into her face, as if they too were eating into her like a puddle eats into the ground. I pitied myself, but the sight of Chivy broke me. Without words, I wiped the tears on her cheeks, smearing mud in its place.

Filing into the trench, we began. Taking up a shovel, I thrust it into the hard dirt, glancing into the dim distance. We had completed our assigned section of the reservoir, and Vichet praised our work, but the light had slowly been dimming in his eyes and the passion leaking out of his words, like the air from a bike tire. He couldn't believe in the ideal of Angkar any longer, the cracks had become too large, and he'd seen beneath. If Angkar was a man or god I didn't know, but I did know it was evil, and no good could be found there.

Plunging my shovel into the dirt one more time, water sloshed in my hollow stomach. My stomach had grown tired of grumbling for food because I had stopped responding to it. I had stopped feeling constant hunger, which had dulled to an ache. Yet every once in a while, I would feel that little slosh of water and remember that I still needed food. We had had no more than a watery bowl of soup since they took the rice away, but

I would swallow the panic of starvation along with my soup, hoping the liquid would quell the other in my stomach.

"I have to go."

I looked up. It was as if Chivy spoke to the fly crawling into her mouth. I nodded and watched as she struggled out of the trench, her black uniform flapping off of her body like a flag of surrender. I was afraid Chivy was surrendering herself to the hunger that was eating her from the inside out.

I trudged out of the trench, carrying a basket to dump at the top. I could see Chivy squatting in the dirt behind a pathetic little bush. Falling over, she propped herself back up again before shakily standing to her feet. Shame had been steadily vanishing each day, blown away with the wind that continued to peel a new layer off the ground. In its place was left something almost animal. We relieved ourselves wherever we could. I didn't have to go much though, because there was nothing for my body to discard. It hoarded everything it got.

"Get back to work," a soldier shouted at Chivy, as she paused, staring at the ground absently. Chivy struggled back into the trench, not bothering to swat the flies speckling her face. I poked at one crawling into my ear before waving them off of her. My hand lingered, as if drawn like a magnet to her waning cheek. I touched her for a mere moment, but the feeling of her skin beneath mine sent a ripple of life through me. Chivy just looked at me, eyes void of the usual mirth and wittiness. I cringed when returning her gaze, but it captured me, and I couldn't look away. Breaking the trance, Chivy grabbed the shovel and went back to work.

Think of something to cheer her up. Think!

"I've got to go." She caught me off guard, because she had just relieved herself. I looked at her questioningly, but Chivy didn't begin her climb out of the trench as I expected. Instead, she kept shoveling, her hands loosely gripping the bamboo handle.

"Didn't you say you had to go?" I whispered after a while of digging. Chivy looked up and stared at me. Her black eyes didn't only look sad, they mirrored something else. *Panic.*

"You're going to be all right, Chivy," I whispered quickly before the soldier caught us talking. "We're going to get through this. Don't lose your love of life. Don't lose your laughter."

I don't know what made me say it, but the look she wore drug it out of me. She didn't respond, but merely kept digging, elbows jutting in lifeless, mechanical movements. She wore the look all day and worked like she was the shell of a human. At last, the darkness of morning wore into the darkness of night and bells clamored for us to return. We marched back, dusty and hungry prisoners of Angkar.

"Goodbye, Rindy." Chivy turned to face me, before returning to her section of the camp. "Thank you." Her eyes were alive with moonlight. The panic was there too, staring, but so was something else. What was it? Turmoil played out across her features like wind rippling over grass, making it sway beneath its power. It was as if she was struggling between the options of giving into panic or continuing to swallow its bitter drudge. I wanted to reach my hand out toward her in a feeble attempt to touch her, to draw her in close and make her feel safe. I wanted to whisper into her ear that we were going to make it out alive and she was going to grow happy and strong. I wanted to curl my arms around her shoulders and knees, to add my flesh to hers and to shield her from the cruelty of the world. I wanted to draw her close and never let go. I reached out my hand—.

"Move," a soldier shouted, jerking me back to reality. He sharply motioned with his gun for Chivy to go her way and for me to go mine.

"Goodnight, Chivy," I called, taking one more glimpse as she walked into the darkness.

The morning bell began to sound, it was static over the speakers, and I struggled to hold onto sleep, ignoring the bell for as long as I could.

"Everyone up." a soldier called, forcing me from my denial.

Uncurling myself, I grabbed the shovel and basket outside my hut and joined my battalion, which was already marching toward the reservoir. Scratching the back of my head, I tried to pick at the lice dancing on my scalp. The smell of rotting teeth and body odor rolled around in the air between those of us marching. I hadn't cared in a long time if it was mine or someone else's as it was all of us in varying degrees. Then I noticed that something was out of place.

Chivy. Where is Chivy? I craned my neck to search for her, the question pounding my brain with each marching step.

"Chivy?" I whispered, not caring about the attention I was drawing.

"Chivy, where are you?" I called louder, panic mounting with my voice.

"Silence," a soldier yelled routinely, his cold, unconcern showing on his every taught feature. My comrades responded with blank stares and shrugs. She wasn't among us. My stomach clenched around last night's supper. I wanted to vomit. I couldn't march in sync and kept stumbling around, whispering "Chivy, Chivy, Chivy" into the black, morning air. We filed into the reservoir, but it was too dark to see far.

"Has anyone seen Chivy?" I asked the other girls, but no one even knew the name. She was just another skinny girl who moved dirt.

"You are all equal and all the same," the Angkar orator played in my head, stuck on repeat. "Each one of you is a grain of rice: the same in value, trait and purpose."

Chivy was just a lost grain of rice in the sea of sameness. But she wasn't just another person to me. She was my reason for enduring the past years of torture. The one I shoveled with, the only one I dared talk to, the only one who knew my name, and the only one who didn't see me as just another grain of rice. I loved her with everything in me. I would have given her every ounce of soup I was allotted, would have transferred her weight to myself and I would have died a hundred deaths for her.

"Chivy!" I screamed, until my voice grew hoarse.

"Shovel," the soldier yelled down at me, the blackness of his frame barely distinguishable from the blackness of the sky. I let the blackness take me to its depths. I pleaded to cry, wanted to cry out the anguish in my soul, but nothing would come. My mind was wild with fear, but like a robot I continued to shovel, unable to stop my limbs from mindlessly moving. No one joined in my sorrow, because no one replied. Each one was fighting their own darkness and trying to swallow the panic into the pit of their own empty stomachs.

"Rindy." I turned my head, surprised to hear my name among the nameless horde as we left the trench to get the little bit of sleep we were allowed. Vichet wound his way through the battalion. I stopped, letting the boys flow around me until he stood before me, his face illuminated by the torch made from palm branches he carried to guide us back.

"I heard you calling for your work partner, your friend." He dropped his gaze.

I waited, my knees trembling like the firelight. My heart thudded to the sound of its flicker.

"I asked her battalion leader—" Vichet swallowed, his eyes meeting mine once again.

"She was caught..." He exhaled the words. "She was caught trying to run away with some of the older girls."

"Was she—was she—" I stuttered, unable to ask the question, unable to set myself free from the weight of it.

"Yes, Rindy." He looked at me, eyes squinting in suppressed emotion. "She was."

I tried to remain upright, tried to think clearly through the words coming out of his mouth, but my mind was unable to soak them in.

"I'm sorry." His voice faltered, then began spilling out like water through his hands. "I'm sorry. I thought I could keep everyone in my battalion from dying if I proved I was dedicated to the Khmer Rouge and if you all worked hard. I've fail—."

"Why aren't you all moving?" A soldier stalked up from behind us, emerging from the darkness. "Move!"

I stumbled forward, jolted by the soldier's command. I cast one last glimpse at Vichet as he walked behind me, his form slumped and face gaunt in the firelight. Something glistened down his face and disappeared into the hard ground. Then his eyes met mine and they blazed with fire.

41

THE FALL

"I knew I could not survive it anymore." — Rindy

NOVEMBER 1978

Even though I had learned her fate, I continued to look for Chivy with each passing day, whispering her name in the trench, searching for her around the cafeteria and in the shadows of the palm trees. The girl I had worked next to for the last three years had disappeared into the air as if the wind had carried her slight frame away. Yet I knew her fate was neither so mystical nor merciful because I lived in Angkar's world. Sudden disappearance was normal. Death was normal. Grief was normal.

Glancing at my hands, I tore a loose callus so hard it made me bleed, but it brought a strange relief. The dust on my shovel mixed with the blood on my hand, making a deep red mud. My life had become like that mud. It was mixed with so many things that I had ceased to exist. I was a child of Angkar, a soldier, a worker, but the human had long disappeared. Chivy's disappearance had sealed my fate.

My head pounded with the words she had last uttered, "Goodbye, Rindy. Thank you." They played repeatedly, with each shovel of dirt and with each step I took. Her voice said them, whispering into my brain. I clenched my eyes closed, trying to escape in the darkness because her eyes stared at me from each hole I was digging in the dirt. They stared at me with the look of panic and the turmoil of whether or not to run like she had, knowing my fate would end in the same. But would that be so bad?

I tore at my hair. I hated myself for not throwing my arms around her that last night, for not whispering that I loved her and for not holding her close. To make her want to fight; to make her want to live. I would have tried harder to help her see that I needed her, that she was the only reason I made it through each day.

I love you.

I love you.

I love you, Chivy.

I breathed the words out, over and over and over again, until I yelled them in the air curling with dust. They were the words I wished I had said, the words that haunted me and throbbed in my chest. But it was too late.

In nightmares, I could see the plastic bag clinging to her head greedily when I closed my eyes, with her lifeless body sunk in the mud. Then a tiger leapt from her frame, chasing me until it pinned me and tore at my flesh. I always awoke gasping and unable to sleep again.

I had seen Angkar kill countless times, but I had never felt the death so personally before. Each death had horrified and haunted my mind, but Chivy's death haunted my heart. There was no way to regain the illusion I had willingly lived under. It was shattered into a million pieces and had already blown away into the dust filled sky. Angkar was not the savior; it was the demon of death. Angkar killed us in a million different ways every day, while continuing to create new ways. The anthem that had echoed in my head with pride now caused me to cringe in rage. The checkered krama tied around my waist no longer signified freedom. It was spilled blood. The black clothes hanging limply from my emaciated body were not the color of revolution, they were the color of death. When I looked around, I stared into the unblinking, glass eyes of the others who were prisoners in the same way.

I had known the truth about Angkar for a long time, but it was easier to ignore it and live, than acknowledge it and risk being overheard by one of their many spies and sent to one of the prisons. I had never seen anyone return after being summoned by Angkar. I had kept this realization in the back corner of my mind, hidden from sight, buried in the ground of my subconscious, carefully tended, but never unearthed. We were all puppets in a play called the death game. The soldiers were merely a deader version of myself. This reality weighed on me more and more heavily with each basket of dirt I dumped. I continued to dig, but I sank deeper into the panic that was slowly consuming me too.

Three days came and went, and I knew that I could not endure another one. I had reached the point Chivy had, and I was willing to face the plastic bag if it came to that. Being left lifeless in the mud would have been better than continuing without a living heart. I dug like I always had, but my mind was sharp for the first time in months, maybe years, as if a cool breeze had blown all the dust of confusion away, allowing me to see clearly. It wasn't a feeling of excitement, but that of resolve.

Placing my hoe carefully on the ground, blade sticking upwards, I climbed out of the trench with my full basket. I reached the top with wet palms and shaking knees, but I tried not to look suspicious. My heart began to pound, and I dumped the dirt and placed the basket on the ground. Then, without turning, I backed up slowly, one foot behind the other. I looked around to make sure no one was watching, before I took another step. Dirt crunched beneath my sandals, flies buzzed through the air, a soldier barked at an emaciated form not moving quickly enough. Visions of what was about to happen paraded through my mind, but I took another step. My heart raced, and I took another. Wincing, I dreaded the drop off, yet welcomed it grimly. I took another step. Then the ground crumbled beneath my heels, and I fell backwards.

I groped at the empty air and brought a landslide of earth down with me. The wind was knocked out of me, and the force of my body crashing against the dirt surprised me. A rock hit my face. My body gained momentum as I tumbled backwards. I hoped meeting the sharp hoe at the bottom wouldn't be too painful, yet I also hoped it would be successful in creating a wound. I had to choose my escape from the trench by death or injury, as they were my only two ways out.

Rolling to a stop, I felt a sharp pain in my hip, and I winced. My consciousness disappointed me, but the amount of pain I felt was a small consolation. Trying to stand on my feet, I grimaced, pulling up my shirt to survey the damage. My waist was gouged with a cut larger than my hand, already turning purple with blood. Those around me paused their work, staring absently, but not moving toward me.

"Get working," a soldier called down, seeing the others standing around. "Vitchet, you've got one down. Deal with him or I will!"

Through the dust, Vichet emerged. His face had aged, but his eyes still held something the Khmer Rouge had not yet stolen. *Pity.*

"What happened?" He helped me to my feet.

"I fell."

"Can you walk?"

"A little."

I tried to limp, exaggerating the pain. Would he notice?

He inspected the gouge, the blood already soaking my shirt. Yet black doesn't show blood. Maybe that was by design? His movements were inexperienced and awkward but gentle. "It's really deep and is bleeding pretty badly."

I waited in damp nervousness, chewing at a dusty fingernail, wondering what he would decide to do with me. I felt bad lying. It was surely bad karma, but I no longer cared. Karma was a cruel taskmaster. I had seen it punish mercilessly. I had seen it kill. I just wanted to escape the trench, escape the pain in my chest for a little while. I wanted to sleep forever.

"You probably can't shovel for a bit." Vichet stood and grabbed me by the arm to help me out of the trench. I swallowed down a lump of guilt, like mud, as I struggled up the embankment past the others still working. With my arm slung over his shoulder, I marveled at him. How had he put on an act so well? How had he seemed to love Angkar with such zeal, when it had all been a ploy to save more boys from a leader who would have been like the others—cruel and evil? Had he ever believed in their cause? Yet when the Khmer Rouge took over the country, there had never really been any good choices. It was either join their sham revolution or die. We had all been playing the game ever since, in one capacity or another.

We walked toward the camp slowly enough for me to keep up. His gun hung over his shoulder like a costume piece rather than a weapon. When he carried it, I felt safe. When any other soldiers carried it, I felt like I had a target painted on my forehead.

"I've been trying to get as many out as I can." Vichet's voice was low, his words sparking with life. "There has been enough death here. The ground can't take it anymore." Then as if to himself. "I can't take it anymore."

I was stunned. What did he mean to get people out?

"The revolution is crumbling; they just don't know it yet—" His voice lowered to an inaudible growl as we passed a group of soldiers playing cards. They looked at us absently, seeming curious why a soldier would help a worker rather than just kill him.

Vichet motioned for me to sit at the base of a palm tree near the longhouse where we ate, which was now vacant.

"Wait here, a truck will be coming for you soon. There's a place I've been trying to get people to, but it's easiest for those injured or sick. No one asks questions that way. The work isn't as hard, and there's more food."

He turned to go, his shadow blocking the scorching sun for a moment. My throat twisted with the unlikely taste of relief, guilt and gratitude all swirling on my tongue. Yet I didn't know how to swallow. I didn't deserve to escape any more than anyone else did. Why me? Yet here I was, sitting by a tree waiting for a truck to carry me away from hell. While the man who had arranged my escape, walked back to it.

"Arkoun, Vichet." I voiced my weak thanks.

Vichet turned and looked at me, his eyes raging in amber flames, sparking with renewed purpose. For a moment, he held my gaze unblinkingly, as if he peered into my soul. It was as if he saw my dead baby sister, my worry for my family, my heartbrokenness over Chivy and all the horror locked inside of me. He saw it, and he was sorry for it.

"Arkoun." I whispered again.

"This won't last forever, Rindy. Dawn is coming. You must live to see it." With those words, he turned and walked away.

42

ESCAPE

"They always did everything at night. Night is evil." — Rindy

LATER THAT DAY

I sat bracing myself against the jostling truck. My head throbbed and my open gash continued to ooze blood, making me grit my teeth against the pain. Looking around, several pairs of glassy eyes stared back at me. There was an older boy whose face was pale and eyes were placid as he held a poorly splinted arm, and three girls, who shrunk into the shadows, away from the dying sunlight. One girl was so thin she couldn't sit up. She lay flat with only her head propped up against the side of the truck. She stared absently, and I wondered a few times if she were still alive. I didn't know what was wrong with all of them, but I held onto the hope that where we were going was better than where we had been. I had heard rumors of people being chosen to work on a farm surrounded by food, but it seemed too good to be true. How had I been chosen to go? The possibility still didn't seem real.

It felt so odd to sit idly with my back resting against the soft canvas as my battalion was wallowing in the dirt. Guilt clung to me with every memory, inescapable even in exhaustion. I dipped in and out of sleep, the warm sun and the sound of the truck motor lulling me.

We drove until the sun began to set and dark shadows hollowed out the faces of those around me. No one seemed overly hopeful. I wondered if each person was past the ability to hope. They seemed like dead people with blinking eyes. Was it already too late for them? Death had been gnawing on them for days, devouring them one painful bite at a time. What horrors had they witnessed? Who had they lost? How many times had they feasted on panic? With the falling darkness, fear began to mount inside of me, replacing the hope I had felt with the sun.

What if this was an execution truck?

What if Vichet didn't know?

The truck ground to a halt, and one of the soldiers slammed the door and stalked into view. His face was a graveyard of shadows and sharp lines, with his cold eyes reflecting the moonlight. The thoughts continued to circle in my brain faster than I could even comprehend them. My heart pounded, and my hair stuck to my forehead.

What if I was about to be shot?

Or suffocated?

I hoped I would be shot rather than suffocated.

The more I looked around at the half dead people in the truck bed, the more I became convinced that we were not headed to a farm but to our deaths. I had seen the Khmer Rouge soldiers kill many who appeared to be able-bodied, and I had no reason to believe they would spare four half-dead ones and one with a wound.

"Everyone out." The soldier's voice seemed overly loud, as if we were deaf as well as dead.

I was closest to the back, so I slid out, careful not to hit my side. I limped to the right side of the truck as the rest were unloaded. The boy with the splint climbed down, but the girls could hardly walk. I watched as they lowered themselves down with shaking arms, barely capable of holding their own weight. Their feeble feet crumbled to the ground upon contact. I moved toward them, supporting their arms across my shoulder, forming a tangle of limbs and fear. I wished the soldier would just kill us here if this was our final destination. The effort it took for these fluttering pulses to continue living was exhausting.

"Follow me. Move quickly." We walked and limped down a winding path through the woods, trailed by the soldier and his friend as they gripped their AK-47s. It was dark except for the moonlight shining occasionally through the thinner trees.

"Move."

I pulled the girls harder, feeling one girl slump between us, her bare feet dragging. The girl on the opposite side stumbled into a slice of moonlight. Our eyes locked, and her fear did the speaking. I could feel my side throbbing and bleeding, but my pain was the lowest in the group. I glanced grimly at the soldiers' guns, hoping they would be merciful and use their bullets, even if they were their last ones. But I feared we were not worthy of bullets.

One of the girls stumbled and fell, her face hitting the dirt with a thud. She got up quickly and continued behind me, wiping her bleeding nose into her filthy sleeve. Even the drag of her feet sounded ominous. As we continued to walk, I shrank at every shadow, and my heart raced at every noise. The trees were alive with the sound of frogs and bugs. It was as if the jungle itself was anticipating the fate of those shuffling by, already familiar with the march of death.

Would my death be fast?

Would it drag on?

The thoughts pounded behind me, in unison with the soldiers' heavy boots.

Approaching a clearing, I anticipated the feeling of bullets ripping into my flesh. I wondered what it would feel like for my heart to stop squeezing blood and for my own breath to strangle me. I had already been dying for months. I hoped that would qualify me for a kind death. Qualify me for a death by bullet.

What would come next?

Did I have good merit to secure a favorable rebirth?

That single question clouded my mind, lodging there like a stick in a current, causing every other thought to make a path around it. Words from the monks began to swim in my mind along with memories of Buddha. Death was supposed to lead to rebirth into another form or being, be it a demon from hell or a human or god. But I didn't want to come back. I wanted to be done—finished with the dust, the hunger, the sweat and the hopelessness of the world that Angkar had created. Reentering the world I had known seemed like the worst form of punishment, the cruelest joke, and the most unimaginable fate. I didn't know what to fear more: living or dying. Both seemed equally grim. I could no longer believe in building up merit by good deeds, that system was broken for me. I had seen too many perish who didn't deserve to. What had Chivy done to deserve such a gruesome death? Why had her merit condemned her? I had no alternative, no answer to the riddle. How could we right the wrongs that were pressing us into the fires of hell? How could I make up for such a chasm?

We approached a dimly lit hut on stilts, nestled amongst the trees. A dim fire burned beneath, and the palm trees rustled in the breeze.

How fitting that the end of my life should be much like its beginning—in a jungle surrounded by growing things.

"Halt."

We stood there, lined up in the orange light, counting the seconds. Another black-clad soldier emerged from the hut, and he and the soldier who had led us through the jungle exchanged muted words. One of the girls slunk to her knees, unable to stand any longer. I sucked on my quivering breath, as if it was my last meal. My stomach clenched searching for remnants of the broth I had eaten the night before. I squeezed my eyes closed, losing myself in the sounds of the jungle.

"Come."

My eyes flew open.

The soldier motioned to us and then waved into the shrouded distance. My eyes traced the density of shadows, seeing varying levels of greenery. It looked like a garden. I imagined vegetables growing just on the other side of the clearing, lush and ripe.

After several minutes, the soldiers who had brought us sauntered down the trail without even looking back. The other soldier remained standing; half-illuminated by the light from the doorway. He eyed us. Half of his face was hidden, indistinguishable in the darkness, the other half eerily starring. I knew how this story went.

They always killed at night.

The soldier fumbled with something at his side. I braced myself for the impact. Where would he hit? I hoped he wasn't pulling out plastic bags from the folds of his black trousers. I closed my eyes again, determining that I didn't want to watch it happen. I hoped he'd be fast, and I hoped he'd kill me first, so I didn't have to watch the others die. My heart thundered in my ears. The girl beside me began to cry, her breaths sharp and constricted. The moon emerged from behind the clouds, casting silver light over us.

Dusty memories shrugged across my mind, nearly forgotten, nearly forsaken. A man standing in the clouds with a smile on his face and arms stretched wide, a woman praying to the God of peace, a God who was still alive. Would I meet him now? The thought filled me with warmth.

"This way." The soldiers' words clapped onto my ears like thunder. With quaking limbs, I walked behind him, trying to keep in step with the others staggering blindly ahead of me. He led us past the garden and past a vacant area of dirt, then toward a communal hut draped with palm branches, which flapped slightly in the night breeze. What was this?

"This is the girls hut." He waved toward the structure. The girls shuffled toward the shadowy doorway, each holding up the other between their spindle-arms, their movements quaking with relief. They disappeared inside.

"Boys, this way." The soldier yawned and led us further down the path toward another hut that was a little smaller, with densely thatched walls. After the soldier waved us inside impatiently, we tentatively stepped through the door.

The boy with the splint shuddered, and I bumped into his back. I could hear faint snoring and heavy breathing. I brushed against a hammock, heavy with a body. I inched along, feeling my way forward, trying to find an empty hammock to crawl into. My fingers stuck into the loops of a limp hammock, and I crawled inside, exhaling the breath I'd been holding. The feeling of being suspended in the air, as opposed to lying in the bug infested grass and leaves, was a sensation that wrapped around me and ran through me. I stared unblinkingly at the dark ceiling, swaying gently until my hammock stilled and my heart slowed. We had made it. We were still alive. We would live another night.

I woke up the next morning to sunlight touching my face. Jerking awake, I swung my hammock, accidentally bumping the hammock beside me.

"Ho!" A chubby boy's face emerged, and he waved a handless arm at me groggily. I was so stunned that I didn't even respond. I hadn't seen such a healthy-looking boy in years, and I searched my body for any bullet holes, making sure I hadn't been reborn into another place, free of Angkar's reach.

"Isn't there a bell here before sunrise?" I chewed on a jagged fingernail.

"No, now shhh!" The boy responded annoyed, lying back down with a grunt.

I looked around the small hut, made of thatch with a dirt floor, seeing two-dozen or so hammocks with limp bodies weighing them down. I stared back up at the roof, unable to believe we were allowed to sleep so late.

"Do you get food here?" I asked the boy again, but he was already snoring softly. I was wide-awake without feeling the pull of exhaustion for the first time since I could remember. I reveled in the morning sunlight and put my hands behind my head, smiling widely.

Soon I heard a soldier calling for us to assemble outside. I lifted up my shirt and inspected my wound, it was angry and swollen, but it wasn't bleeding anymore. I rolled out of my hammock, careful not to reopen my wound, and followed the line of boys of various ages and injuries out the door. Boys with one arm, one leg, mangled hands and twisted feet stood at attention in the morning light. Other boys were gaunt, with lucid looking skin and shallow, wheezing breath. Yet their eyes looked alive, reflecting the sun. How had I ended up here with only a scratch? I closed my eyes trying to erase the guilt I felt for all those whose fate had not been so merciful.

"Today is for bananas." A man wearing a krama wrapped around his head and no shirt, squatted in the dirt before us. His words were void of the typical Angkar impregnated dogma I was accustomed to. I twitched in nervousness. He opened a sack next to him and pulled out a banana plant. I blinked, not believing my eyes. I smiled. I knew bananas.

"This is the banana plant." His voice droned on. "You dig a hole big enough to put your head in, loosen the dirt below the roots the length of two heads and place the plant on top of the dirt, burying it lightly."

"Plant them in the land you plowed last week." The man paused, scratching his head, before sauntering off to a patch of shade to catch his morning nap. I continued in single file to the cleared section of the field that we had passed the previous night, to begin the day's work. I bent down and touched the rich soil, lifting it to my nose.

"What happened to you?" I looked up and saw the one-armed boy from earlier that morning. I lifted my shirt and showed him my wound.

"Lucky." He tilted his head toward his stub of an arm.

I nodded, avoiding his gaze and my own shame. Bending over I dug a hole and dropped a mangled banana seedling into the loosened earth, ensuring mine was in line with the boy's beside me. I looked up at the sun and smiled. This work made me feel alive again.

Before long we were called to the communal kitchen by a woman beating on a pan. Would there be more than watery soup? Falling in line I held out my bowl shakily and received a heaping scoop of rice with cooked vegetables and—could it be? Pork!

I stared at my bowl dumbfounded, hardly able to believe my eyes. There was sliced squash and taro root with a bit of pork, topping my white rice like a fine hat. I put a bite on my tongue and closed my eyes. I hadn't had anything so delicious or with so much flavor, in the past four years under the Khmer Rouge. I shoveled in another bite, then a dozen more so quickly I barely chewed. As soon as it hit my stomach, I vomited it back up again.

My stomach continued to refuse anything I put in it as if it had forgotten I needed food at all. I was determined I would teach it again. I made myself eat slower the next meal. It was torture to chew one bite at a time, then swallow, before eating another, but I began to taste the food I was eating: the slight zing of the lime, the sourness of the Prahok and the bite of the salt on my unsuspecting tongue. My stomach was kinder to me then, as it allowed the food to stay awhile, without evicting it with force. I began to remember what it felt like to have a full stomach. The heaviness, the contentment, the hope it brought.

The days passed quickly, and I met each one with anticipation and a tinge of disbelief. We cleared the jungle to plant more vegetables with a sharp machete, and I tore through the vines and trunks to expose the soil beneath. It was still hard work, but compared to the trench, it didn't feel like it at all. We even snuck some of the corn, cucumber, giant taro and sugarcane that we tended, while the lazy guard wasn't looking. I began to watch my arms grow wider and my stomach began to expand. I fell asleep each night swinging in my hammock and awakened to the sun kissing my eyes open each morning. I began to forget the gnaw of hunger that had been a constant companion. I began to walk easily, without looking over my shoulder. I began to talk to those around me, without fear of them being executed. Between it all, like water filling in every crack, guilt flowed freely. It haunted my nights, taking the constant form of a tiger that tore me to pieces, leaving me shaking and sweating.

The world of Angkar remained a distant nightmare until the day I heard the rumble of trucks invade the peaceful air. Then I remembered, I was still alive in Angkar's world.

43

THE PRISON

"They left them in the jungle, that's how I know." — Rindy

THREE WEEKS LATER

The sound was coming from the other side of the trees. I sucked in my breath as I began to tremble, fearing that Angkar was coming to get me. Had they learned of my dishonesty? That I wasn't injured badly? Sinking to my knees, I quickly began to dig around a stubborn tree root. If they were coming for me, they would find me working. One truck rumbled past, then several more, the sound of rusty metal bumping over the potholes. I let air back into my lungs, but continued to hack at the root, my heartbeat lessening.

The rumble of the trucks came and went all that day, the dust rising into the blanched sky. The trees stood still, barely moving in the breeze. Even the birds were mute; they were waiting too. What would they do? We worked in silence, fearing even the sound of our own breath, but the trucks kept rumbling, unaware of the terrified boys working on the other side of the trees.

The next morning, the rumbling resumed, but we worked less nervously, happy their mission was unrelated to us. Another day passed the same way.

Weeks inched by, and the rumble of the trucks became common as we hacked our way ever closer to their path on the road. Until one day, there were merely a few feet between the wheel-smashed path through the jungle and us. Curiosity ate at me the way I ate at my dirt-rimmed fingernail. I hated the invisible pull to go see, because I feared what was on the other side of the trees, but it continued to lure me anyway.

"Sokna." I looked at the one-armed boy. "Sokna," I said a little louder.

He looked up, annoyed.

"Let's see what's past the trees." I twitched my head toward the guard who was quietly snoring with his chin resting on his chest.

"Don't be stupid." He continued to drag a large palm branch towards our pile. He waved his stubby arm in the air at me, its jagged scar stared at me with a frown, mirroring his disapproval.

I continued to hack away at a bamboo stalk, but my mind was consumed with what was on the other side of those trees. The trucks typically rattled along the road in shifts, with several hours between their traffic. The road had been quiet for hours. I knew because I had cautiously counted each one, flirting with the idea of an expedition.

"Sokna, the trucks have stopped for a bit," I said, unable to let my curiosity die.

He rolled his eyes and grabbed one of the hacked bamboo poles to drag it from the clearing.

"We'll be really fast," I coaxed.

With one more glance to the sleeping guard, I headed towards the road. Sokna reluctantly followed.

Creeping up to the edge of the tree line, we searched the road as far as we could see. It disappeared in a zigzag line in both directions, only tire tracks were in the dirt. No traffic. I nodded to Sokna with confidence and stepped into the clearing.

"Hurry." I beckoned as he hesitated in the shadows.

We crept down the road to the south. It was exhilarating and terrifying, like eating a fire ant. Picking up the pace, we rounded a bend and came face to face with a massive structure. Dodging into the jungle we peered at it, hidden in the greenery. It looked like it had been a school once, but had been transformed into a prison. Its cream-colored walls were scraped and confined by the barbed-wire web clinging across its windows and doorways. The jungle had become one with it, as vines and trees latched onto its roof and walls. Several soldiers lumbered about the exterior, smoking cigarettes and laughing, their black uniforms dancing against its face. Sokna jabbed my shoulder and started crawling backwards toward the road. After stealing one last glance over my shoulder, I followed.

Breaking through the trees we quickly began to work again, ignoring the questioning stares we got from the other boys. Grabbing my machete, I hacked my way into the bamboo patch one swing at a time, the eerie image of the building in the jungle settling on me like a shadow over the sun.

The next day, Sokna and I worked in silence, never discussing what we had seen the day before, afraid that even speaking of it would somehow summon its darkness into us. It haunted my dreams as I slept. I saw myself wrapped in barbed wire in a dungeon-like room, the sound of a tiger roaming the halls coming nearer and nearer with each heartbeat. But always just before I awoke, a speck of sunlight would shine into the darkness, snapping the chains one by one. I'd awaken, trying to understand the peace I felt, but unable to put it into words.

The day began with the rumble of trucks through the thin line of trees like the dozen before it, but I shuddered as I watched them go by. I caught glimpses of their green metal siding between the smooth line of bamboo poles lining the road and crept closer to see, leaving my machete behind. Then something else caught my attention through the obscured movement on the road. It was the color black and red in the truck bed and the glint of silver chains. Squinting my eyes, I waited for the next truck to roll past. What I saw made my mouth go slack in disbelief. The truck bed was stuffed with Khmer Rouge soldiers–both male and female–and they were bound. The light caught on various pins of distinction that flapped languidly from their collars. They weren't merely soldiers, they held high ranking positions. The hands that had once gripped their guns were bare and idle as they bumped along in the open vehicle. Their faces, painted with disdain, were chiseled with crevices of confusion. I counted eleven trucks, all carrying the same cargo. Sokna's eyes reflected the question burning on my tongue.

Why was Angkar imprisoning its own soldiers?

The thought sat in my mind all day, as hard to extract as a thorn buried deep in my skin. I hardly noticed my work as I hacked through the rows of the bamboo poles. Instead, the faces of the prisoners stared back at me from the hollow places of the hacked bamboo.

I had feared Angkar because I was a lowly worker, the lowest rung of the ladder–dirt beneath their heels. My place was clearly established; it had been beaten into my head for years. But the men and women in chains rumbling past on the road were different. They were the enforcers—those with authority. They didn't merely exist under the weight of Angkar's commands; no they were the battering ram that forced all of us to keep going. They were the ones who wielded the guns. The ones who rationed the food. The ones who did the killing.

What I had seen turned the world on its head, and I suddenly realized everyone was under someone. Even those who towered over me, shrunk under another. The hierarchy of cruelty that had been squishing me, and those like me, into the ground had toppled in my mind, and I was left to pick through the wreckage of a shattered ideology.

This unraveling persisted over the next few weeks. The disruption began to simmer in the soldiers stationed over us. They became less concerned with us and seemed uneasy and more concerned with each other.

While walking to the place where we relieved ourselves, I saw two soldiers talking loudly and so violently that they spat into each other's red faces.

"I'm leaving tonight," one soldier said, face taunt with fear. "If we don't get killed by the enemy, we could get killed by Angkar."

"Our orders are to stay here," the higher ranking one hissed. "You are letting your head rot with conspiracy."

"That prison isn't filled with conspiracy." He waved toward the prison behind the trees. "It's filled with breathing men and women who used to be in command."

"The maggots are eating at your brain again," the other shouted before turning to walk away. But as he turned to retreat, doubt clouded his face. Fear slithered through the camp like a snake biting the soldiers one by one. Even the lazy guard, who wasn't even a soldier but just a local peasant, began to move with urgency for the first time since I arrived. They all stared into the woods toward the prison with shifting eyes.

Then one morning, I awoke late. How hadn't I been awoken? Swinging down from my hammock, I exited our sleeping hut. Stillness settled over me as I stared at the sun, already high in the sky. Spying Sokna rummaging in the center of the planted corn, I made my way over to him.

"What are you doing?" My voice squeaked, as I glanced over my shoulder, nervous that he might have already been seen.

"Eating." He mumbled the words around a bite, the silk hair from the corn sticking through his yellow teeth. I gapped in disbelief, fearing he had finally lost his mind along with his hand.

"They're gone!" He gulped hard. "All the soldiers—they're just gone!"

"What?" My ears heard, but my mind was unable to comprehend.

"What?" I repeated, stumbling out of the garden to look around. Other mets were milling about without any sense of purpose. Most were eating because free reign on food was not something we'd ever had before, even when well fed. There were no soldiers in sight. Not even one.

"Come on, Rindy." Sokna waved his stump of an arm, the other one stuffed with corn. In a fog, I turned and walked toward him, picking up the half-eaten piece of corn he had dropped.

"Don't eat that." He smacked the back of my head with a fresh ear.

Taking it from his outstretched arm, I pulled back the leaves and bit into its juicy flesh. Glancing over my shoulder, I expected to hear a soldier screaming at me, but nobody came. No one cared. I ate five ears of corn before making my way to the cucumbers. I ate three of those and continued on. Sokna was ever ahead of me, enticing me with more food.

"There are loads of bananas." His voice bounced off the big banana leaves like a grasshopper. I ate six and a half bananas in record time before my stomach revolted. Lying down in the shade of the banana leaves, I stared at the sky, trying to make sense of what had happened and what to do next. I drifted to sleep, my stomach so full I didn't even want to think about food for the first time in four years.

I jerked awake from a nap I didn't know I had fallen into, expecting an order, a rebuke, someone to be standing over me, but there was no one. I wasn't certain if I was awake or in some beautiful dream. A strange noise came through the trees. I got up to explore and plan my departure.

The noise rumbled and roared low to the dirt, almost like a military truck sputtering and sucking in water.

A slight breeze blew at my back and rustled its way through the trees. I was nervous to be out in the open, but I kept walking. Something crunched under my foot, and I glanced down to see a watch smashed into the dirt.

The noise was growing louder, accompanied by a chorus of squeals and throaty grunts. Ignoring the watch, I continued closer. As I approached a ravine, I slowed my pace. The sound became deafening, and a stench rose from the ground and roared into my nostrils like fire. The stench seeped through my skin and churned in my stomach.

I knew the smell. Death. Human death, which was so different from the smell of animals.

There, scattered throughout the ravine, were bodies. They were a feast for hairy pigs and pregnant flies. Together, they created a roar of delight over hundreds of corpses; corpses with black uniforms and checkered krama's still clinging to them.

I shook my head and turned to flee from the nightmare; I didn't need to see more. I couldn't bear to see more. They were the bodies of those who had been taken to the prison. Angkar had killed them because that was what Angkar did best. I then knew I was not dreaming.

But then something welled up in my chest, a feeling bubbled up like water from an underground cavern deep in the jungle. It was cold and sent a chill through me, yet I welcomed it. It was a mixture of relief, but also happiness. I was glad they were dead. The only thing I regretted was that the other Khmer Rouge soldiers weren't there too, in one rotting heap. The realization startled me, but I didn't extinguish it. I let it burn.

44

THE INVASION

"That is how I survived, because I was not with them."
— Rindy

JANUARY 1979

Chaos reigned like the loose end of a rope caught in a hurricane. The whole camp erupted in a frenzy of greed and confusion, as we all rushed to hoard as much food as we could. We anticipated the desolation of our family members and wanted to have something to offer when we found them—if we found them. The gardens we had carefully tended were ravished, every plant scoured for whatever growth it had produced. I fought like the rest, trying to scrape together whatever I could find. The cafeteria was also ransacked, and those who got there first confiscated the rice stores and prahok. The air stirred with excitement and confusion as we relearned how to navigate a world free of orders and demands.

I had longed for independence since the beginning of the Khmer Rouge takeover, but once it was upon me, I shied from it. For the past four years, I had been told how to work, how to march and how to think. I had forgotten how to make decisions for myself.

Freedom was frightening.

As I walked through the rooms the soldiers had occupied, I could hear the echo of their bark and feel the sting of their words calling from the shadows. Angkar had owned me, and suddenly I was floating through life without meaning.

Filling a jug with water and gripping my hammock stuffed with unripe bananas, sugar cane, cucumbers and corn, I ran down the winding path through the jungle, the way I had come on the truck. I hoped I would find my way to Mteay by backtracking, and she'd be the link to Vuthy.

As I ran down the winding path through the jungle, I heard the sound of hurried feet, trampling through the trees from the opposite direction. Instinct took over, and I hid. Peering from the thick underbrush, I watched as black cladded soldiers ran passed me. I had never seen so many guns. All were gripped by white knuckles. Every Khmer Rouge soldier had a gun and wore a mask of terror. Their faces were worn with lines, and their eyes darted as they marched. Their backs hunched toward the ground as if fleeing invisible bullets. They had been the tigers, but suddenly they had become the prey.

"What are you running from?" I asked the air. The soldiers had already disappeared down the road.

The answer to my question came soon enough. The sound of soft padding boots of a different army filled the air a few hours later. It slithered in pursuit through the jungle toward the running Khmer Rouge. They were the worst of all tigers. They wore camouflage-green uniforms, their red collars stamped with gold stars. Their eyes narrowed at the horizon of trees. Their guns were held with confidence and ease. Their faces were painted as black as their guns. They were what nightmares were made of.

They were Vietnamese.

My fear of the Khmer Rouge was dwarfed by my fear of this army. My mind flooded with legends of torture; legends pressed into my mind by the Khmer Rouge loudspeakers day after day. I was told the Vietnamese used the skulls of their enemies as the stones of their fire pits, roasting them alive. I could almost smell the stench of the burning hair by just looking at their brazen expressions. Even though some of the soldiers were no older than me, they were hardened and savage. I crept back into the shadows to hide until they passed, barely daring to breathe.

Then I continued to run through the jungle.

As dusk settled over the trees, I heard the feet and panting breath of someone running toward me. I dove into the underbrush, waiting and listening. I recognized him. He was a member of my own battalion, but now he was holding a gun instead of a shovel. His chest was heaving, his eyes were bloodshot and wild, and his blood-soaked krama was wrapped around his leg.

"Hallo, met!" I wove my way through the trees toward him.

His eyes roved madly as he raised his gun to shoot.

I lifted my hands and yelled. "I'm a met, I'm your met—don't shoot!"

He lowered his gun, but his eyes were still wild.

"What is happening?" I kept my hands raised, uncertain of him.

The boy lowered his body to the ground, leaning his back against a tree. I handed him a piece of sugarcane and corn, and he ate them like a wild animal.

"The Vietnamese army came and our whole battalion was given a gun and told to fight. The Khmer Rouge soldiers put us on the front lines." He chewed loudly, spitting his words out between bites. "I barely got away. So many are dead—" his words trailed off into the dusk. I sat there, staring into his foggy eyes. What horror had he just endured?

"Our whole battalion was wiped out. We were not trained to use weapons and to fight Vietnamese guerillas. We were trained to dig."

"Where did it happen?"

"The Khmer Rouge had gotten news that they were coming towards the trench, so they started handing out guns and told us to stay on the outskirts of the trees while they hid deeper. We had the guns of the Khmer Rouge at our backs and the guns of the enemy in front." He took in a ragged breath. "Everyone around me had their heads dropped to the ground like fallen coconuts. Their bodies were ripped full of holes." His voice broke, and he stared blindly into the trees behind him.

I watched him silently.

"I don't know how I survived." His haunted eyes met mine. "Where have you been?"

I dropped my gaze and picked at the ground. I swallowed back the bitter taste of grief and shame before answering.

"I got hurt. Vichet sent me to work at the banana farm."

"You're lucky. I don't think anyone else from our battalion is left—except you and me."

I didn't want to hear more, but he continued anyway, unable to stop reliving the terror of what he had just seen.

"When I got shot, I crawled into the trees as the Vietnamese trampled the bodies of the dead, charging after the fleeing Khmer Rouge. The bullets were so loud and there were so many of them." His tears came in streams down his face. I envied the relief this brought him.

"Our battalion was massacred." He wiped his nose on his sleeve, snot smearing across the black fabric. "Vichet, our fellow mets, they're all dead. I watched them fall."

"Vichet?" My throat tightened around the words.

"Yes, I watched him die shielding a group of girls who were too terrified to even fire their gun."

My mind was too busy picturing Vichet lying lifeless in his own blood, surrounded by those he had tried to protect. He had saved me, but he had sacrificed himself alongside his battalion. He never tasted the freedom he had given me.

A part of me died along with the news of the death of my battalion. I could feel it, break off inside me. Agony was the silent chord that had bound us together. Now it was a severed chord. Agony didn't need words. Despite standing beside the other survivor, I felt more alone than I had felt before. My mind flashed images like a rock skipping across a lake. Images of the eyes, the legs and the stomachs of my mets being punched full of Vietnamese bullets. Images of those who surrendered being used as fire pits for the cooking pots of Vietnamese, and images of the trench we had dug being filled with thousands of slain Cambodians.

"I—I'm glad I got to see you." I handed him another ear of corn, but I dropped my gaze; I just couldn't look into his eyes that were so full of accusation. I stood to leave—to grapple with my own shame alone and to drown out the cries of my fallen mets with the pounding of my feet.

"Where will you go now?" he asked, between bites.

"To find my family."

45

BULLETS & FIRE

"I know I was afraid, but we were so busy running." — Rindy

THREE DAYS LATER

"Mteay," I called to the back of a woman.

"Mteay!" Her shoulders were sharp ridges, and her spine protruded from the back of her black clothes, but there was a hint of the familiar. She was swarmed by a mob of other black clad people, pressing in panic. The commune where I had last seen my family was in a frenzy as the half-dead occupants grappled with their newfound autonomy while trying to find their lost families.

"Mteay!" I hoped I wasn't shouting at the back of yet another woman who was not my mteay. The woman turned; her black eyes stared at me from the dark hollows of her face. I recognized the remnants of who had once been my beautiful mteay. Her frame was withered and frail. Her hair, which had once been a lustrous black, was streaked with gray and matted. Her eyes were as starved as she was, as if they too had only feasted on disease and loss for the past four years. My chest throbbed looking at her. How had she survived?

"Rindy," she gasped as if coming to life in a fleeting burst of energy. She wove through the mob of confusion toward me with groping arms, eyes locked on mine.

"I'm so happy! So, so happy—" she whispered over and over again as she clutched me to her sunken chest. Her breath rattled like a rock clinking into an empty canyon. Her heart throbbed against my cheek. Weak but relentless.

"Have you seen Vuthy? Anyone else?" I asked, still pressed against her cheek.

She shook her head, trembling. I couldn't tell if she shook from the shock of seeing me or if her frame always quaked like a dying leaf barely hanging onto a branch.

It was hard to breathe, hard to think in an embrace that was so unfamiliar. I didn't feel safe, even in Mteay's shaking arms.

I had been running with the constant fear of the Vietnamese shooting at my back, and it had consumed me—every step—for the last three days. The face of Vichet and my fallen mets stared at me from puddles in the dirt. Their voices called out to me in the night. The ideology of the Khmer Rouge was crumbling around our heads. Ironically, I felt the need to help support its teetering stilts for fear a greater oppression would replace it. I feared the Khmer Rouge, but it was a fear I had grown comfortable with. It had rocked me to sleep each night, awoke me each morning and held my hand with each step of the day for the last four years. It was familiar to me, and I knew every corner of its massive temple. The Vietnamese were a new fear, an unknown fear. Unknown fears are worse.

I couldn't stop the feelings in my chest—feelings of guilt, panic, and rage that played tug of war with my senses. Why had I been spared when everyone else had died? I could only see one way out. To help fight the green typhoon ripping through my country. Maybe it could help redeem the bad karma sticking to me for being a coward. It seemed like my only logical option. I had rehearsed it over and over in my head for the last three days as I made my way to find Mteay.

"I'm joining the Khmer Rouge forces—" I wheezed; my voice muffled in her shirt.

"What?" she rasped, bending down closer to hear me.

"I'm going to join the fight." My eyes met hers. "We must fight the Vietnamese. They're going to kill us all." Each word I uttered made her face contort in pain.

"No." She shook her head, moaning. "No, no, no!"

As she clutched me closer to her chest, I realized how much I had grown since I had last stood beside her. I now stood taller than her. I was still short for a sixteen-year-old, but I welcomed the realization of growth. Despite the starvation and overwork, my bones had managed to stretch themselves upwards. My feeble body's determination to live surprised me. Feeling Mteay shaking me, brought me back.

"Rindy, you will not go that way." Her voice was pregnant with resolve. "Do you hear me? You are not going that way. I need you with me now."

It was strange to hear the words from her tongue. Words I had wanted to hear for as long as I could remember. I had often imagined what it would feel like to be wanted by her, to be needed by her. But now that it had come, I didn't know how to feel. The deep pleading in her eyes made me relent on my decision to join the Khmer Rouge. I could at least help her get someplace safe before leaving. Maybe I could find Vuthy on the way.

"Let's go back to Phnom Sampov." Mteay summoned me with her words and her strong grip on my arm. "Everyone will know to go there. Everyone who—" She left the words unfinished, but I knew what they were.

Everyone who was still alive.

It was the unspoken current throbbing through the air. Who was left? Who had survived?

I helped her onto the road with the mob of others who were fleeing the hopeless camp where we had been held prisoners of a twisted ideal, which was crumbling all around us.

Mteay gripped onto me as if she were holding the only thing she had left in the world. As far as we knew, that could be true. Loss and fear have a way of making life constrict, leaving only the necessary in its clutch. Everything else blows away like chaff in the wind. Family was a concept she now clung to. Desperately. Hopefully.

Bullets exploded in the distance, endlessly shooting. We picked up our pace and ran east with thousands of others. We weren't sure if we were running from or toward danger. We just ran.

Several miles from the commune, the landscape opened into rice paddies, ripe and golden. The farther we walked, we found dead bodies slumped over on the road, swollen and days old. I passed one, not thinking much of it, but then I passed three more. The road and paddy were littered with bodies. As we got closer, we could see their stomachs were swollen by the sun and crawling with maggots. Decay had disfigured them past recognition, and the hot earth had already begun to eat their eroding flesh. I didn't know if they were fallen Khmer Rouge, Vietnamese or those caught in between. The flies feasted without discrimination. I had never seen so many dead in one place before. As my gaze traced the horizon, I found thousands laying amidst the ripe rice. Life was interlaced with death.

Carefully, we tiptoed around them, with our krama's covering our faces. It felt like it took days to get past them all. The very soil was full of death and I wondered how it could possibly hold another bite. My lungs burned from the putrid air, but they continued to suck it in. We kept going until the air was cleaner and the stars began to glimmer in the night sky.

Near a large paddy, I left Mteay to sleep for a few hours, while I gathered rice and threshed it beneath my feet. Finding a plastic jug, I poured the rough rice grains in, making them easier to carry. I was thankful the paddies were dry, crisp and ripe for the taking. And that there was no one to stop us. The Khmer Rouge were too busy fighting the Vietnamese.

Mteay awoke, and we continued on, tripping at last into the shrouded village I had once called home. It was barely recognizable. Mteay clung to me in shock at the devastation. The formerly neat streets of Phnom Sampov were polluted with ashes and toppled structures but alive with stray animals and birds. It looked grotesque in the darkness, like a face broken and bruised. I had known these streets well, but the disarray erased all familiarity.

"I think it's this way." I turned down a road, trying to trust my instincts when my eyes were no help.

We wound our way through felled bamboo poles, crunching and gray amidst abandoned carts and supplies, until the surroundings offered a hint to my memory. The farther we went, the bleaker it became.

We approached the place where Chidaun's house had been, desperately hoping it hadn't been burned or torn down. Hope is a resilient thing, and I marveled that we were still capable of it. Standing on familiar ground, we looked to where the house had been, with its fine walls and roof, seeing only a few charred stilts and broken water pots. That was all that remained of Chidaun's once grand home. I stood where we had burned her corpse, but the memory felt like it was from another life. And it was.

"Why would they do this?" Mteay asked feebly.

"Because they could."

Even in the darkness I bent down and saw the vibrant colors of baby clothes and one of Mteay's vibrant skirts, half buried in the dirt. I reached out to touch it, letting my eyes linger on them for a moment. I had almost forgotten what color looked like. Following Mteay, I walked to where the porch had been.

"I wonder if there is anything the Khmer Rouge has not taken," Mteay whispered as her tears fell. She didn't bother to wipe them away as she surveyed the wreckage.

Soon, the smell of smoke choked the air. I ran down the road to see what was on fire.

The horizon danced with firelight. My stomach twisted, disbelief churning in my gut. They wouldn't do this. How could they do this?

At the edge of the trees, the rice paddies were engulfed in flames as far as I could see. The sky was alight with an eerie glow. The dry rice cracked and popped as it was consumed. The trees around Phnom Sampov were green with vegetation to ward off the flames, but not the paddies. They were miles upon miles of kindling.

"If I had known, I would have gathered more. Now it's all gone," I mumbled to myself, looking at the jug I still carried, tied to a string over my shoulder.

"How did this happen?" I said again, aloud.

"How do you think?" a voice answered.

I jumped, turning toward the shadows behind me.

"Why do you think?" The voice asked again, as a form emerged with it. He was an old man. His body was blackened by ash, but his eyes glinted in the firelight.

"The Khmer Rouge soldiers. They set fire to all the rice before fleeing that way—" he pointed absently in the scorched distance toward Thailand. "I tried to stop them, but what could I do? What could any of us do?" He continued to mumble.

"Why? I don't understand!"

"Because they hate us." The words dropped from his mouth and thudded into the ash, spitting and sparking. "The Khmer Rouge say the Vietnamese have come for our rice and that they will starve them out of Kampuchea, but I know it was because they enjoy watching their own people starve. Angkar is the king of death. They've sent us all into hell, and we must pay for what we have done. We've all become *pret*. We will never get out."

Without another word, the man turned to walk down the road, muttering to himself about us being pret: the tortured souls of the damned. They were the ones destined to endure torment because of bad karma. I knew I had bad karma, and the reason wasn't a mystery to me. It haunted me with every step.

How could I be set free from myself? The question burned in my lungs as I went back to Mteay. Turning back one last time, I looked over the ashen fields, the graveyard of rice resurrected my fear of hunger.

46
WAITING

"I wanted to look for my family again." — Rindy

TWO WEEKS LATER

Once we made it to Phnom Sampov, Mteay's legs gave out. It was as if her legs had carried her as far as they had to before collapsing beneath her meager weight. Was it malnourishment or disease? I wasn't sure. I hung a hammock—the one I used to carry the food—between two trees and helped her into it.

As I held her close, I couldn't help but notice her swollen stomach. It protruded, and her ratty blouse was pulled tight across her midsection.

I looked up questioningly.

"Yes. I'm pregnant."

Dread oozed through me, and I swallowed back the question that burned on my tongue, fearing the answer.

Mteay sighed, when breath rattling from her chest was interrupted by coughing.

"Who's baby? You weren't—"

"No, it's Khan's. There's no fear of whose."

I slunk to the ground, relief squeezed my lungs.

"I didn't know you had seen him."

"After you left, we were allowed to be together until the Khmer Rouge sent him to work in another paddy. I haven't seen him since. I must have conceived the last night…"

Her voice broke and she turned her head, unable to meet my gaze any longer. She fell asleep, and I left her in peace, swinging gently in the hammock. How did a child survive while the body housing it wasted away? It was a mystery to me how new life emerged in a place so pregnant with death.

I cooked some rice, and when she awoke, I gave her some.

"Can I take you to a hospital? For the baby?"

"No," she said. "We will not leave here until everyone returns. Because everyone will return here—to our home."

Then her knobby knuckles gripped the front of my shirt, and she pulled me close.

"Promise me, you will stay with me and not join the Khmer Rouge."

I averted my eyes in shame. The often-present throb in my chest rushed back with the mention of joining the Khmer Rouge. My frame, which wasn't as sick or shrunken as hers, was my shame. I had gotten more food over the past few weeks while being at the farm than she had had over the past four years. I didn't deserve it. I hadn't really been injured or sick. Mteay deserved to be sent to a lovely place to plant bananas—not me.

"Rindy."

"I promise," I breathed the words. "I wouldn't leave you like this."

She drifted to sleep again, her face contented and a look of victory softening her severe features.

I sat and watched her face for a moment, fighting emotions I didn't understand. The lines around her mouth and beneath her eyes were ruts like water etches into mud. My memories flew through the years, ticking over the disappointments from my childhood. I was a grown man now.

Wasn't I seventeen years old? Did I still need a mteay? I had long outgrown my need for her. But hearing her insist on the promise that I would stay and feeling the desperation in her grip filled me with something new. It was warm and inviting, a flavor on the wind that I had always sought but never quite found. Is this what it is to be loved, to be valued by a mteay?

Then a cool wind blew, bringing me back to my senses. No, she just needed me. This was not love. This was my duty. I worried about Vuthy and wanted to go look for him myself and learn of the others, but I could never leave Mteay in her condition. She didn't need me to promise her that. Mteay cradled her tiny stomach in sleep, thankful for the child that would replace the one she had lost in the first year of the takeover.

Had she lost everyone else too? Everyone but me—the son she had never wanted, but now needed? The question rolled through my mind.

To keep my mind from feasting on this fear, I busied myself with finding additional food to add to my waning supply. After scouring the jungle nearby, I dug up some taro roots, bamboo shoots and found some snails. Then I scoured the desolate village and found a dented rice pot, a rusted machete and some ragged sarongs, which I thought Mteay could wear or one of my sisters, if they returned. We waited, unable to move forward or go back to where we had been, with a singular question haunting every moment: Would they come?

After four days had passed, Ly and Sotha emerged with the dawn, entangled in each other's emaciated arms.

"Mteay, look," I cried.

They were barely recognizable. The sunlight shone harshly behind them, almost shining through the holes in their souls. The cruel years had eaten away at their growing frames, making their bodies look younger than the last time I had seen them, while their faces looked centuries older. When I hugged them, they felt like wax between my hands, as if they would crumble to pieces. I helped them to Mteay. Each one collapsed in a sobbing heap on Mteay's chest as she lifted her shaking palm to their faces, cradling their tears. No one spoke a word, they just sobbed because words weren't enough. They had lived through the unspeakable.

I turned aside, allowing them the space to be together without the need of words. I hoped no one would ask where I had been, as I didn't look as bad as they did. No one seemed to notice my silence. We absorbed our memories, into ourselves, swallowing them. It was an unspoken rule of karma—you don't talk about the bad things that happen. The bravest thing you can do is swallow them into the pit of your stomach. Sometimes it felt like swallowing vomit though, but that was far better than allowing others to hear about my cowardice. It churned my stomach night and day.

With the return of my sisters, I felt even more obligation to ensure their safety. But I worried about Vuthy. Would he come as Mteay promised he would? Lured by the memories of Chidaun? Lured by the memories of the closest thing we had had to a home? I continued to wait.

After a week had passed, I looked up from chopping wood to find Khan walking through the jungle, a broken man with a gimp. His frame was hunched and starved, but his jaw was muscular, as if he had spent the last four years gritting his teeth for food.

I stood as relief, for Mteay's sake, surged through me. Khan's eyes narrowed on me first, then on Sotha and Ly who were cooking rice over the fire.

"Your mteay?"

I pointed to where she lay, sleeping in the hammock.

Without another word, he stumbled over to her and collapsed beside her. They looked at each other, eyes full of questions and memories they weren't yet ready to share. They sat together like that for hours, occasionally talking quietly, but mostly sitting in silence with Khan's hand on Mteay's stomach. I left them to it.

As the days passed, I wanted to be alone in the jungle. I needed to be alone. I had left the food for Mteay, my sisters and now Khan, whose leg was mangled and sore from an apparent gunshot wound.

It was strange to all be together again with so much history flowing between us. Most of my memories were away from them, so I didn't know how to pretend to belong among them now, especially with the past looming. I was so relieved they had survived, but I shied from their presence. I wanted desperately to know their stories, how they had survived, but when they looked at me, I felt like a rat caught in a trap. I couldn't share mine without shame. My memories hurled themselves around in my stomach, making me want to vomit, but they crushed my throat when they attempted to escape.

I became obsessed with fear for Vuthy. I told myself over and over again that if he returned, my brokenness might be made whole. My family would be with me again. But would he? Was he even alive? I needed to know. But Khan was injured, and I couldn't leave him to care for Mteay, Ly and Sotha alone.

I chopped bamboo, and the steady stream of worry that had flowed through me for the past four years became a raging river. Vuthy was strong and brave, but could he have survived the Khmer Rouge? For they targeted those like him. The memories of the last time I had seen him played repeatedly in my mind: Vuthy, waving goodbye to me, the dust and confusion curling around his frame. My mind told me there was no way he had survived, but my heart held onto him. My eyes refocused on the bamboo I was chopping, the sound of the blade slicing through the stalk reminded me of my childhood with Aupouk.

"Rindy?" a voice emerged through the stillness, a voice that also belonged there, in that memory. The voice was deeper now but was somehow still the same.

I spun around, as a tall boy walked through the underbrush toward me, his smile wide, his hand raised.

"Vuthy!" I lunged toward him. He ran toward me. Our bodies collided, and my heart pounded. I pulled him away to look at him. He had become taller than I was. I felt the muscles on his lean back and smelled the sweat clinging to his overworked body. It was the smell of life. He had survived.

"Are you all right?" he asked at last, searching my face. That's when I noticed a curling scar behind his left ear.

I nodded, my voice failing me.

"You look just about the same." He grinned, eyes shining. "Somehow, I've gotten taller than you. But maybe I was born taller."

I laughed, and it surprised me, as it rattled around in my ribcage, wanting to get out. After my sides stopped heaving, I looked Vuthy in the eyes again.

"Where did you come from? What did you do? How did you survive?" The questions burst out.

"I worked in a battalion that repaired bridges. We were working on a bridge in western Cambodia, before the Vietnamese came." His answer was absent as if it was already a distant memory. "Command fell apart, and I got away as quickly as I could."

We stood in silence for a moment, reliving our nightmares.

"What about you?" His eyes refocused to the present.

"Let's not talk about it any more today." I waved his question off and began to pick up the bamboo, happy to change the subject. "How'd you find me?"

"I found Mteay, Ly, Sotha and Khan near Chidaun's home—or what's left of it. They told me you were here, gathering poles to build a new hut. I can't believe we've all survived. Everyone but baby Tang."

A clouded look entered his eyes. Was he wondering if it were all real? If this was some strange kind of dream we hadn't woken from yet? Because that's what I wondered.

"Yes, everyone but Kiry has come. Have you seen him? He joined the Khmer Rouge before the takeover."

Vuthy shook his head. "I always expected to find him over the years, but I think he joined in a different region."

I nodded.

"Do you think he killed people?" Vuthy asked. "The way the others did?"

I shuddered, feeling the nightmare of the past four years gnaw at me again. By the look on Vuthy's face, the memories were eating at him too. I nudged his shoulder, and we walked back to camp, holding the bamboo poles that would help us rebuild our lives. Vuthy was here, he was alive, and we would continue to survive, together.

47

THE VIETNAMESE

"So, the people starve again." — Rindy

MARCH 1979

"Wake up." I heard the words float fuzzily through my sleep. But whose voice? I ignored it and drifted back off. I wanted to sleep forever. To forget. To heal from the past. But this night had been fitful and filled with haunting dreams. Again.

"Come on Rindy, wake up," the voice said again, and someone shook me. Squinting, I saw Vuthy standing over me in the murky darkness. It had to be early morning, the moon still hanging in the western sky.

"We've got to move. There's about to be fighting in Phnom Sampov, I'm sure as soon as it gets light. There are Vietnamese troops camped a few miles away in the paddies. Their camp fires are everywhere. We've got to leave now, before it gets light." I blinked, hoping this was just a bad dream, but the air smelled like smoke and panic.

Several days before, while cutting bamboo for our hut, I had snuck up on some Khmer Rouge soldiers camped just inside the jungle, but I hadn't anticipated the Vietnamese soldiers pursuing them this far into Cambodia. They must be pressing farther west, inland from Vietnam, following the

Khmer Rouge who were retreating toward the Thai border or fleeing to the Cardamom mountains in droves.

I wanted to believe we could be done running and swallow my fears of the Vietnamese, but that wasn't possible.

"We look like the Khmer Rouge soldiers." Vuthy's brow furrowed. "Do you have a change of clothes? Do you think they'll wait for us to shoot at them before they shoot at us?" Vuthy ripped at his clothes, the remnants of the Khmer Rouge revolution still clinging to him. I looked at my own tattered, black pants and krama, and bare feet—my black shoes had worn out long ago.

"We were a part of Angkar, remember? They won't see us as victims but as supporters of the regime."

I sighed. He was right. Rumors had been running rampant from every starving and displaced child of Angkar. Our liberators were our greatest fear. We'd heard from other refugees who were looking for their missing family members that the Vietnamese troops had been seen tying refugee's hands with their own kramas and leading them into the trees. I knew how that story ended. Why had Vietnam invaded Cambodia to begin with, if it wasn't to liberate us? What did they have to gain?

Our campsite stirred, Ly and Sotha waking. Khan came running down the road, and Mteay called from her hammock sleepily. Vuthy stood and threw some sticks on the fire, rousing its embers, so we could see to gather our belongings.

"Mteay can't walk." I sat up, my voice croaking.

"We're going to have to carry her in her hammock." Vuthy shrugged. "Let's, get moving."

I nodded, pushing myself up from the ground to collect our food. In addition to the little bit of rice I had gathered before the paddy fires, I had also gathered wild yams, taro root, bamboo shoots, snails and even managed to catch a few fish in the canals before they ran dry. I placed what food we had left in a sarong and tied it tight. It wouldn't last us long, maybe a few more days—but if we knew anything, we knew how to conserve food.

I looked over my shoulder at the stilt hut Vuthy and I had nearly completed, as the flicker of firelight illuminated it's unfinished form. After clearing the wreckage from Chidaun's home, we cut and planted thick beams for stilts, fastened the floor with bamboo poles, made the walls with finely thatched palm branches and had just begun on the roof. We would have to abandon another attempt to make our home here.

"Now, we'll go to the Thai border. It's the only option." Khan heaved, as he leaned against a palm tree, taking the weight off his foot. Khan had been talking about a rumored "refugee camp" on the Thai border that had been set up by an organization called "United Nations." He had been relentlessly trying to sell the idea of going there for weeks.

Vuthy and I had no interest in going to the Thai border, and with Khan's bad leg and Mteay's condition, Khan's plans lived inside the confines of his constant grumbling and incessant prayers to his many spirits. However, with the approach of the Vietnamese army, we could not remain here any longer.

"It's got to be over 100 miles," Vuthy roared, jumping up to face Khan. I looked up in surprise, since we both largely avoided Khan and left him to his scheming in private.

Vuthy had grown bold in his time under the Khmer Rouge and would no longer cower to anyone—not even to Khan. I looked at my hands, tying the last knot in the sarong.

Vuthy came back strong, while I came back broken. He was the rightful one to take charge, although I was the oldest. He was braver, stronger and smarter than me. I wasn't fit to make decisions because I always seemed to make the wrong ones—the cowardly ones.

"Are you head of the family now?" Khan stood straight, meeting Vuthy's gaze, "Who are you to question my decision?"

Vuthy stood a few inches taller than Khan, which made me smile. Vuthy took after our Aupouk.

"You've got a useless leg and Mteay is going to have your child soon." Vuthy drug out the word "your" to further insult Khan for his carelessness. "You want us running toward the border—the place the Khmer Rouge are running to? You're mad as a dog."

"And you think camping here, waiting for a battle is a better idea?" Khan replied. "You know as well as I do that the Khmer Rouge are hiding in the jungle and caves around Phnom Sampov. Do you honestly think it will be that simple? We can just hide from the Viet Cong—the most dangerous and bloodthirsty soldiers ever to walk the earth? What will we eat when a war is waging around us? You're a—"

"Stop—just stop." Mteay pushed herself up on her elbows. Her hair streamed around her pale face, black eyes sparking in the firelight. "I know of a military hospital near Battambang. I think it's time I go there."

We all looked surprised at Mteay. She had known about this hospital all along?

"How do you know this?" Khan moved to her side, "Why haven't you said anything before?" His voice popped with agitation. We had wanted to tend to Mteay for weeks, but all the doctors had been killed during the Khmer Rouge rule, all hospitals disbanded, or so we thought.

"I heard that one hospital was allowed to remain and sometimes women who were having trouble in childbirth were permitted to go there. Most did not make it to the hospital."

Mteay's voice faltered. "I fear this one, I fear crossing the water..." Her voice trailed off. Women had referred to childbirth as "crossing the great water," for as long as I could remember. It was a journey many Cambodian women did not successfully make, even before the Khmer Rouge took over. Childbirth was always spoken of in fear and dread, as if shrouded in evil spirits. My stomach clenched. We couldn't lose Mteay. Not now. Not after all she had endured.

"We'll get you there." I gathered up a felled bamboo pole and laced it through her hammock loops. Vuthy ran over and picked up the other side. We would find this hospital. There was nothing left here for any of us. Grasping at normalcy during this strange war was as futile as spitting into the wind.

"My strong sons." Mteay's breath wheezed through a faint smile.

"You've become a very little woman." Vuthy grinned, even as deep lines squiggled across his forehead. He was malnourished and his strength was a fraction of what it could be on a full meal. I tried to shift most of the weight to my shoulders, but he was taller than I, which made it difficult. The girls huddled together behind us, black eyes revealing the fear they didn't dare voice. They carried the food, the sarongs and the rusty rice pot.

The open road was dangerous, so we kept to the jungle around Phnom Sampov as much as we could. The journey to the hospital should have taken about four hours, but it was hard to walk at a regular pace while carrying Mteay. My breath heaved, and my steps were awkward.

Before long, we heard gunfire ripple through the air. We stopped and listened. It seemed to be coming from behind us. Relief, thumped in my chest. I was glad we had left when we did.

As sunlight began to cut through the tops of the giant Doa and coconut trees, the fog curled around us, making it difficult to see far. Peering through the veil, I imagined Vietnamese soldiers emerging from the shadows, guns sticking out in front of them and their eyes wild.

Tripping over a root, I nearly dropped my end of the pole. After that, I was more careful with my feet, although still trying to fight back fear. The density of the fog trapped the gun's screams in its thick web, making it difficult to know where the gunfire originated. I couldn't tell if it was getting louder or farther away.

My shoulder ached under the weight of the pole, and my head pounded as beads of sweat dripped into my eyes. Then, suddenly, it went quiet. I only heard the heave of my own breath and the rustling of my own feet. I wished the fighting would start again, so we could try to gauge their location. In silence, there was no way to know if someone was sneaking up on us or if we were about to stumble upon a Khmer Rouge hideout.

We stumbled along. Something rustled behind us. A twig snapped; leaves breathed.

Vuthy slid his end of the bamboo to the ground, and the rest of us followed quickly. We held our breath. What had he seen?

Vuthy and I rolled Mteay in the hammock and concealed her under low-hanging rattan leaves, then crept under them beside her. Ly and Sotha slipped into a bamboo patch, their slender bodies disappearing in the shadows. The fog, once thick, now writhed over our heads, leaving us exposed as sunlight began to consume it. I rested my head on the dirt, clenched my eyes closed and waited.

Feet trampled through the underbrush. My eyes flapped open. Two-dozen Vietnamese soldiers crept toward us through the jungle. Their eyes darted and their guns were cocked and ready, twitching in their hands. One soldier supported another, whose blood-soaked pant leg flapped loosely as he walked, but everyone else looked sharp-eyed. Ready to kill.

First, they passed my sisters. Then, they moved toward us. I wished to still even my heart, but it beat like a thousand pounding raindrops. Vuthy's hand curled around my ankle reassuringly. We lay there, frozen to the dead leaves and the dirt. A boot landed near my head, so close I could see the bloodied mud caked on its heel. The boot paused. The soldier slapped at his neck. His cigarette smoke and body odor flooded my lungs. I hoped he couldn't smell my fear.

Then the boots kept walking. They crept toward Khan. To my dismay, Khan's foot was visible, barely protruding from under the leaves where he was hiding. I couldn't take my eyes off Khan's scuffed heel. I willed his foot under the leaf, hidden completely out of view, but it remained, taunting me.

The seconds hung in the haze, as trapped as we were. At last, the soldiers continued to walk. Slowly, they passed Khan. I let out half a breath, my panicked heartbeat only allowing that much. Then one of the last soldiers paused. I couldn't see where he was looking.

Why are you stopping? The question pounded in my head. A bug crawled on my ear. I didn't move. My heart thundered. The air was suffocating. At last, that soldier continued walking, disappearing into the jungle like the rest.

I lay with my cheek imprinted in the earth, Vuthy's charcoal eyes returned my stare. We lay there silently for what felt like hours, until the birds and monkeys forgot us and resumed their song. Eventually, my heart slowed to a normal pace, but my limbs still trembled. Mteay hadn't moved the entire time. I feared the fright of the morning might have done her frail body in. I put my hand on the hammock and felt her faint breath rising and falling.

The sound of bullets ricocheted through the trees ahead of us. The Vietnamese must have found a Khmer Rouge hideout.

Vuthy and I jumped up, hoisted Mteay in one coordinated motion and ran out of the jungle toward the main road. Avoiding the open road, we ran into the scorched rice paddies. We didn't stop, even when we heard gunfire in the jungle behind us. We ran until the sound of the bullets faded. The Khmer Rouge had burned this area as far as the eye could see. Total destruction of the "breadbasket of Cambodia." My stomach sank. The area around Tonle Sap Lake was demolished. It was an area with rich earth, where much of the rice was produced for the whole country. If the rice was destroyed here, Cambodia was doomed. There would be only starvation.

Around midday we stumbled into Battambang. The city that once rang with the sound of vehicles, people hawking their wares and the aroma of noodle stands, had been reduced to people rummaging through the wreckage looking for food. Stray cats and dogs that typically scampered through the streets were missing. They had either run for their lives or were being roasted over someone's fire.

I passed an old woman who lay crumpled in the dirt, like a cast-off garment. Her gaunt face and bony fingers were frozen. Merely being here had done her in. Why had I survived when so many hadn't? That thought was a relentless fly buzzing in my ears. I shifted the pole and continued onward, gritting my teeth to ignore the pain in my shoulder.

"We die with the Khmer Rouge, and we die without them," Mteay whispered through parched lips. She rocked from side to side, suspended and helpless.

We asked several people for directions as we sifted through the desolated city, and we finally found the hospital. We were told a western-trained doctor had been allowed to practice there for a short while after the Khmer Rouge took control. He was eventually killed, of course. When the Khmer Rouge's stranglehold collapsed, doctors who had survived were rumored to have begun practicing in the run-down hospital.

It was a massive structure with peeling stucco walls and the cloying stench of death. Could we trust this place? What if it was a trap? What if it was set up to lure the sick people in to kill them?

We camped in its shadow, trying to determine what to do next. We argued until Mteay once again spoke.

"I fear I will not be able to have this baby alone. I know it's coming soon. I can feel it, but it's too soon. If I die, then I will die at least trying to live."

We all were silent for a moment, sorting through what to do next.

"I'll take you. Sotha and Ly, you come too." We looked up as Khan lifted Mteay and hobbled inside with her. The girls followed obediently, but not before casting frightened looks at us.

Vuthy and I sat—alone once again. We looked at each other. A strange mixture of dread and relief squatted between us. We sat in indecision for only a moment, before I voiced the obvious, the continual need that drove us. "We've got to find where the Khmer Rouge stored last year's rice harvest."

Vuthy nodded.

48

CHASING RUMORS

"The currency was rice and gold." — Rindy

MARCH-DECEMBER 1979

Over the next several months, Vuthy and I chased rumors. We tracked down every whisper of rice that we heard. If we could have filled our bellies with these rumors, we would have been fat as kings. Most of them turned out to be as useless as the air they floated on, but in blind hope, we chased every single one.

Mteay safely delivered a tiny baby girl, with the help of a few doctors who had, indeed, survived the Khmer Rouge. She named the baby Selay. Our country was slowly rebuilding. The new leader, Hang Samrin, had apparently been a former Khmer Rouge official before defecting to the Vietnamese. Nobody trusted him, but we didn't have any other options.

With medical care and the little bit of food the hospital offered, Mteay began to regain strength, but they could only keep her for a short time. The hospital halls crawled with the sick and dying.

Rumors of rapes and looters were almost as common as rumors of rice. So, when Mteay left the hospital, Khan watched over the females as they camped inside the jungle and gathered whatever food they could find. We all took huge risks to find food because we had little left to lose. Those risks took us behind Vietnamese lines, amidst bullets, through minefields and mass graves—all to no avail. The area of the rumored rice was too entrenched in fighting between the Khmer Rouge or Vietnamese for us to reach it or, in most cases, when we reached the storehouse, it had already been swept clean.

In our pursuit, we found a sugar cane field the Khmer Rouge hadn't destroyed. Vuthy and I cut the stalks, then extracted and boiled the sugar cane. We remembered our aupouk doing this when we were children. We were thankful for this skill to help our family. When the process was complete, we brought the sugar to Mteay. She took it to sell at a market that had resurrected in Battambang. Slowly, the remnants of old Cambodia began to emerge—although in a broken and limping form.

For several months we made our way, by harvesting and processing sugar. In the evenings, Vuthy and I carried sacks of our amber-colored product over one shoulder, to our family's campsite, a shabby, makeshift tent. Inside the ragged walls, my sisters and Mteay would sit anxiously waiting for that day's yield. The sugar had become our lifeline.

Ducking inside the tent one evening, I was met with sullen faces. Even Khan was sullen rather than combative. I knew they had news to share. I glanced at Vuthy. His eyes held the same questions.

"Come sit with us," Mteay whispered, reaching her hand toward mine.

I obeyed, dropping the bag of sugar at her feet. Vuthy followed my lead, and we sat down beside her.

"We don't want to stay here anymore." She measured each word carefully before letting them escape her thin lips.

I took in a long breath.

"We want to leave," she continued. "Khan has heard that the camp on the Thailand border has rice and they are helping refugees. We paid smugglers we met at the market for a map through the Dangrek Mountains and into Thailand. There is no more rice to be bought at the market, but we have some gold left from the sugar we sold. Khan can't find any more game in the jungle, not even wild roots. There are too many others looking for food. There is nothing left for us here. We must all go together." She looked first at me, then at Vuthy. "Please."

I chewed on the edge of my lip. It was at least a hundred miles to the border, through an area infested with Khmer Rouge. I knew the rice for sale in Cambodia would eventually disappear, but I didn't know it had already happened. I had blindly hoped that if I did my part to get the sugar, the rest would sort itself out. Mteay was right, but I dreaded heading back into danger and the unknown.

"We're leaving tonight. We want you both to come too. We'll all be so much safer together," she said the words with finality. She stood, strapping the sleeping Selay to her chest with a cloth krama, and took the sugar cane to the market to sell.

I looked at Vuthy, and we both rose and exited the tent to talk privately.

"We could stay here and try to live off what we earn. We can replant the paddies." Vuthy's words sprang out quick and eager.

"With what rice seed, Vuthy?"

"They only want us now because they need us for protection," he spat the words, bitterness lacing each one. "Even Khan, with all his pride, knows he can't take care of everyone on his own. He's not done fighting either. I can see it in his eyes. He's desperate to join the freedom fighters at the border. As soon as we get there, he'll leave us with the women."

"You may be right." I nodded. "But is it such a bad thing that we're needed?"

He was silent—looking at the dirt at his feet, brooding.

"It's taken seventeen years, but we're now a family," I said. "Mteay depends on us. We must go."

Vuthy shook his head, unconvinced.

"Besides Mteay is right." I clapped him on the shoulder. "There isn't anything for us here anymore."

At two o'clock the next morning, we left. We headed northwest, expecting the rising sun to confirm our direction by day. We hoped to make it to the thick jungle surrounding the Dangrek mountains along the border of Cambodia and Thailand in two days. Everything we owned was strapped to our backs, but Mteay had a little gold concealed in her clothes. As we ran through the rice paddies, the shadows danced with other refugees fleeing their country, nameless faces, clinging to life. Their company gave me comfort because others were following the same route.

One day later, after running through the rice paddies at night and resting during the day, we reached the safety of the jungle on the edge of the Dangrek mountains. We trudged over the uneven ground, following the path snaking through the trees. The red clay had been worn down and smooth; many had gone before us. There was a tangle of vines and in some places it was overgrown, but we hacked our way through, helping the women over the difficult places. As we retreated deeper into its heart, relief bubbled up within me like cool water. I closed my eyes, hearing the birds overhead chirping and trilling in an endless melody. I brushed through the vegetation, rich and supple, feeling water on the leaves. I felt like I had come home.

The jungle took on a new form at night with the songs of tree frogs, crickets, and cicadas. The noise swelled, becoming deafening. It was relentless, throbbing through the air. And, eventually, its constant, deafening thrum became the same as silence to my ears. Our movements disappeared into that rhythm of sound, becoming one with it. It protected us. The jungle nurtured us. Fear evaporated from me like the sweat leaving my pores.

The nightmares I had of jungle tigers in my childhood had long been replaced by even worse realities: the human animals I had encountered.

Spider webs clung to us as we brushed past. The lemon eyes of rats stared at us from holes and trees, not running and not afraid. Vuthy and I had caught some to roast and eat the day before, but it was now night, and at night they were king. At night the vines came alive and slithered upwards at our approach, making Sotha scream.

After a few hours, the jungle melted into a river. It ran dark and deep and peaceful. We stood on the bank staring at the water gurgling past. There was no other way onward, so we waded through. Khan led the way, holding Mteay's hand. She clutched Selay. Then Ly and Sotha waded in next, their eyes reflecting the moonlight cascading through the opening the river made through the jungle canopy. They searched the water as they crossed. I knew what they were looking for and I hoped they didn't find it: a crocodile. As the water deepened, uneasiness mixed with the water licking at my slowly submerging body.

I continued to wade, until the water began to lap at my neck. I didn't like deep water. Stopping to listen, I distracted myself by joining my sisters in keeping watch for crocodiles. While I didn't necessarily want to encounter one in the dark, if I could catch one, it would provide meat. Not hearing the croaking noise that baby crocodiles make, I continued onward. My heartbeat quickened as I felt something against my shoulder, then my leg. My mind raced and I lost my footing. I wobbled, before regaining it.

"It was just me," Vuthy whispered with a chuckle.

Letting out my breath, I continued onward. One step after another, my bare feet sank into the silty bottom, then over slippery bamboo poles and rocks until the water finally started to shallow.

I watched as the others climbed out, liquid shadows onto the bank. I counted them as they emerged. Mteay, Vuthy and I were the only ones still crossing. Although the water was down to my waist now, I couldn't get out of it fast enough. In my peripheral, I caught movement several feet down river. It was graceful, a skilled swimmer, intent on its prey. In a rush, we pressed forward, propelling Mteay with the gold and the baby onto the bank, Vuthy and I scrambling behind.

"What was it?" Vuthy panted.

I searched the black water again, closer to the edge, but it flowed past peacefully without any sign of a crocodile. "Nothing, I guess."

We were out of the water, back in the embrace of the jungle. We rested for a few hours, our backs resting against the moss covered stones and tree trucks.

I awoke to sunlight tunneling through the canopy, illuminating circles on the jungle floor. Everyone appeared to be asleep. I counted, finding everyone but Ly. Where was she?

I pushed myself from the ground and went in search of her. She knew better than to wander off from the rest of us. I ran down the path, my feet pounding. My head swiveled. Was I going in the right direction? She wouldn't have gone back to the river, would she?

"Rindy, I'm here." I spun around, seeing Ly kneeling beside a small waterfall. Relief dripped from me.

"You really shouldn't have left the rest of us."

"I know, but I just had to come a little farther to relieve myself. Did you see the sunlight through the canopy?"

I nodded, looking around us. The jungle was aglow, following the stream trickling down its rocky path. I had never seen so many shades of green before, and I breathed in the musty, earthy smell. I never wanted to leave this place.

"Look at this."

I turned back around, to face Ly. She crouched next to the waterfall, pointing at the crevices. There were several tiny, orange flowers that looked like drops of glowing sunlight hidden in the shadow.

"What are they?" I moved in closer for a better look.

"They're orchids I think, just smaller than the ones sold at market." She reached out to pluck one.

"They never get sunlight here. I didn't know things could survive in complete darkness." I looked around at the thick underbrush.

She looked up at me, her eyes shining with tears. "Yet somehow, they do."

I smiled at her and wiped a tear from her cheek.

"We're going to make it, Rindy, aren't we?"

"Yes, you've all come too far for it to end here."

"We've come too far, Rindy. Don't forget yourself."

I looked away from her searching gaze. "I don't deserve to be here."

"Why would you say that?"

"There is much you don't know, Ly. It's better if you don't."

She was silent for a moment. "Well I know we wouldn't have made it this far without you, Rindy. Your whole life you've been looking out for Vuthy and now you're looking out for the rest of us too. I always feel so much safer with you around."

I met her gaze and smiled, before helping her to her feet. "We have survived, and we will keep surviving. Come, we better rejoin the others."

We walked until the darkness evaporated into light and the sun swallowed up the sounds of the night. We came upon a large group of refugees led by a smuggler who was kind enough to sell us a little rice with the gold we had brought— still safely concealed inside Mteay's clothes. We bowed gratefully in a sompeah, our hands together at our foreheads in the once outlawed gesture of respect. How could anyone share such a gift with us?

A group of girls with ragged clothes and tear-streaked cheeks huddled close to someone who appeared to be their chidaun.

"Did you make it through without"—the old woman's voice faltered—"harm coming to your women?"

"We all made it through safely." I responded, as understanding washed over me. Not all had been as fortunate as we had been. The realization caused me to shudder.

"Just know, the freedom fighters are nothing but bandits who rape and steal what they want. Keep away from them." The old lady lifted a shaky finger.

I instinctively stepped closer to my sisters. Vuthy and I exchanged glances, relief written across his face. We had not run into any trouble like this group had. We were a small group compared to theirs and had traveled mostly at night. Was that why we'd avoided detection? We had been spared, protected in the heart of the jungle.

"I've led many groups through the Dangrek Mountains," a thin man said, his eyes wild and black. "The closer you get to the border, the more you better watch your step." He paused for effect. "It's filled with landmines. More than you've ever seen. Watch for tiny, nearly invisible threads."

We stumbled forward into the unknown. We hadn't made it. Not yet.

49

THE BORDER CAMP

"It wasn't very bad, besides starving." — Rindy

TWO DAYS LATER

As we emerged from the density of the jungle and onto a road, land mines appeared on either side and sometimes in the middle, their coin-sized detonator buttons exposed by previous rainstorms that had washed out part of the road. I had heard about them and their tiny nylon threads, but we could not go back now.

"I'll take up the rear." Khan motioned us forward. Vuthy looked at me, and I stepped forward slowly and carefully.

"Wait till I get several paces in front."

Vuthy followed me, then came Mteay and Selay, then Ly and Sotha. Lastly, Khan. My eyes roved back and forth across the ground before each step. Pausing, I turned and made sure everyone was still with me. Their eyes were wide. Mteay clutched the crying baby. I couldn't see Khan, but hoped he wouldn't stumble on his bad leg and blow us all up.

Let me get blown, not the others. The words played in my mind over and over again as I took each gritted-teeth step.

We passed huge craters filled with bits of bones and shards of supplies, some appeared fresh but most were months old. Many had gone before us. Many had not made it. Someone stumbled. I held my breath. Nothing exploded and we continued on.

Let me get killed, not them, not them, not them.

We continued to walk, until the craters lessened and everyone breathed easier. I knew we weren't entirely safe yet, but I felt a whole lot better getting this far.

At last, Khan shouted and pointed. I stopped walking and lifted my eyes from my feet to see a hundred blue tents stretching through the trees along the road for as far as I could see. We walked towards them. Groups of soldiers walked by us, speaking a language I didn't fully understand. I caught only a few words here and there, recognizing the Thai language. They held guns and wore mismatched camouflage uniforms. They must be Thai soldiers.

"What's going on here? Is anyone allowed into Thailand?" Khan asked a group of congregated men squatting in the shade of the trees, smoking cigarettes made of rolled leaves.

"This is Nong Chan. We're stuck at the border," an emaciated man answered, his words flowing from a toothless mouth. "We're not welcome in Thailand."

"The Thai government has planted landmines all along the border so we can't cross, and just a couple of months ago they came in and fired on us, killing about a hundred people," another man said, gripping a bandaged arm, covered in dried blood.

"Why?" We all looked at one another, fearing we had made a terrible mistake in coming.

"Some rogue soldiers killed a Thai soldier because he raped a Khmer woman, and the Thai military commander Colonel Prachak Sawaengchit"—he took a break to curse—"retaliated by firing on a bunch of un-armed refugees. The Thai would be happy if we all died right here."

"We're stuck," the first man repeated in monotone.

"I've heard of these soldiers fighting for the refugees," Khan said, his eyes bright and every muscle tense and alert. "Where are they now?"

"I think they're digging a bunker," one of the onlookers responded, spitting hard into the dirt. "They call themselves freedom fighters."

"Why a bunker?" Mteay asked, swaying nervously as she patted sleeping Selay's back.

"In case we get bombed again."

"What are the freedom fighters doing about this?" Khan asked.

"Besides digging a bunker?" The man shook his head. "Well, they're probably shooting at the Thai or the Vietnames and then running to hide in our midst, drawing the fire right to us."

"Where can I find them?" Khan didn't appear to have heard all the man had said. I looked sideways at Vuthy.

The man pointed down the road and grumbled, turning back to the others.

Vuthy had been right. Khan had obviously intended to join these soldiers and fight the injustices inflicted on the refugees. Despite all he had been through, he still had a fire in his belly that only killing would quench. Joining the freedom fighters was his way of spitting in the face of the Vietnamese and the Khmer Rouge at once, but to me it was like spitting into the wind. Everything we could do was useless against a greater force.

Leaving the group of men behind, we continued, walking deeper into the jungle and closer to the border, weaving our way through the makeshift camps of war-torn refugees. People were everywhere, under trees and beneath shabby shelters built with blue tarps. They were huddled together and stared at us with sunken eyes as we passed. I didn't see anyone eating, and that worried me because we had been told there was rice in this camp.

I hoped we had not left our country of starving people to beg food from the starving.

"Are they handing food out anywhere?" Mteay asked a thin woman, who sat on the ground cradling her limp infant. I closed my eyes to avoid that image, only to be haunted by the memory of Mteay holding limp Tang in her lap as the hands of starvation tore her from us. I had seen this picture before, and once was too many times. The woman merely shook her head slowly as if she was mute. Sorrow veiled her face, along with strands of oily, black hair. At one time the woman had been beautiful, but her struggles had etched themselves into her skin, until nothing else remained. We walked and walked, taking in the scene at this border. Why had so many stayed after the massacre of their companions? No one said a word. We continued to weave through the mob of people. It felt like every time we went someplace new, it was a mistake.

We continued to wander our way forward, looking for a place to set up camp, when we heard a singular familiar voice call through the crowd. "Mteay, could that be you?"

We turned and searched the throng of people as an emaciated frame draped in shabby clothes, moved toward us. His eyes were wide in their hollows, his arms were reaching for Mteay.

"Kiry—is that you?" Mteay stumbled toward him. The two collided, baby Selay squalling between them, removing all doubt from our stunned minds. Kiry had survived.

"How could this be?" Mteay asked, clinging to her oldest son, head buried in his shoulder. Ly took Selay. "We thought you were dead."

"I've been looking for you for months. Chidaun's house was ransacked, and I couldn't find you." He sank to the ground, as if his heart couldn't take all the excitement. "So much has happened since I joined..." His voice trailed off, his eyes focused on Mteay, but his mind was somewhere else entirely.

"How did you escape the Khmer Rouge?" Khan spat. Khan's gaze was indifferent, his tone sharp. "When did you realize you chose the wrong side?" He was careful not to mention his previous involvement with Lon Nol. He had spent the last five years hiding that fact from the Khmer Rouge.

"Now is not time for that, Khan. Please." Mteay pleaded. Releasing Kiry, she grabbed Khan by the elbow and pulled him back before he took another step toward her oldest son.

"I think, if we could go back, we would all do things a little differently. Don't you?" Kiry's eyes went dark as he glared at Khan. Mteay took Kiry's hand, holding tight as he greeted the rest of us warmly.

But I stared at him from a distance, shaking my head coldly. It was odd to feel myself agreeing with Khan for once. What type of man had Kiry become? Had the Khmer Rouge propaganda eaten his heart? Was he now a monster? Had he barked orders with the same disdain they had? Did my brother force people to work until they collapsed from exhaustion? How many people like me had he killed? I wondered if he had suffocated people like the soldiers had suffocated Chivy.

When he sat down, talking to Mteay, I watched him. Seated beneath the gently swaying palm trees, with his skinny arms and haunted eyes, he looked just as broken as the rest of us. But it was hard to see through my hate colored haze.

50

THE WELL

"That is how I survived." — Rindy

DECEMBER 1979

We left the border and ventured deeper into the trees that grew in clumps along the road. We built a shelter out of palm branches and bamboo poles, hanging our single hammock for Mteay. A fellow refugee shared a blue tarp with us, which had been passed out by the mysterious "United Nations" before we arrived. I worried not only about our need for rice, but our more pressing need for water. We had arrived during the hottest season, and rain wouldn't be coming for months. When I asked around, I found that aid was sporadic, but sometimes a truck would come and pass out tarps, rice, and water bottles.

We sat in the shade of our new makeshift home, hungry and tired, wondering what to do next. Khan only talked about the Freedom Fighters, and I only thought about how to get food.

After a few days of waiting, it was evident that rice was not coming anytime soon, so I asked around and bought some with the remaining gold Mteay had made from the sugar. The rice was very costly, and I knew our gold would soon be gone, so I sat in a bamboo patch trying to figure out a way to make more, until I became too thirsty to think about anything but water. The need for water burrowed into my mind like an ant in the sand, completely consuming every ounce of brainpower. After asking around, I discovered there was no water for miles as the drought had been far-reaching, and the desolated area was teeming with those leeching every resource.

I had to remedy the situation, or at least try. Wracking my brain laced with thirst, I remembered how I had earned money as a temple boy.

Going back to the edge of the camp, I picked through items discarded by the refugees, likely because of their unnecessary weight. I found a small handmade shovel and a basket. I walked deeper into the trees and farther from the border, being careful of every step so I didn't set off a mine. A long-buried memory played through my mind. It came in Aupouk's voice like a forgotten song. "If you dig deep enough and in the right place, you will always find water."

Walking to a small clearing, I searched the surroundings, looking for any hint of where water might have been. Coming upon a dried-up stream with a few young trees clinging to its banks, I decided here was as good a place as any. I dug, surrounded by the whispering leaves, hoping I had chosen the right spot. The ground was rocky, and I jabbed the shovel deeper and deeper. My arms shook and blisters opened on my hands, but I kept digging. The digging reminded me of the trench. It reminded me of Chivy and all my mets who had died in my place. I dug and dumped, then I dug and dumped some more, crowding out the memories. Soon blood from my blisters mixed with the sweat and dirt, but I wouldn't stop. The words deeper, deeper, deeper, played in my mind until it became the rhythm I dug to. I was far too thirsty and too hungry to let myself risk slowing down.

In the waning daylight, I stood in a hole up to my armpits, but I still hadn't found water. The only mud I felt was inside my mouth. Now, even that seemed to be drying up. I swallowed hard, trying to clear my throat of the sludge.

"No water." The birds mocked, cackling at me from the shade of the trees. Ignoring their taunting calls, I continued to dig. At last, it became too dark to continue, so I walked carefully back to the hut, watching the way for landmines.

"Where have you been all day?" Vuthy asked, adding more branches to our makeshift hut and fastening them with twine.

"I...Water," I wheezed out, feeling like my mouth was full of chalk.

"You missed an eventful day. After a great fight, Khan and Kiry both left to join the Freedom Fighters—but not together because all's they do is fight." Vuthy's words sparked. "We knew he'd abandon us with the women as soon as he could."

"Khan didn't believe the woman we encountered in the Dangrek Mountains? The one who said they raped and stole?"

Vuthy shrugged. "I guess not."

The news didn't shock me, but it didn't please me either. I knew Khan would join eventually and I wasn't surprised that Kiry had either. I was too tired to worry about them and too tired to ask any more questions. Ly emerged from the hut and handed me a tin of water and a little rice on a leaf.

"This is all we got with the rest of the gold." Her eyes looked grave, but she attempted a smile.

The camp was bustling with people selling things: from rice, to home-made trinkets and even soda which boys rolled around in carts. It appeared that smugglers were bringing supplies from Thailand to sell to the refugees who hadn't had their gold stolen while making the journey there. The prices the Thai charged were outrageous, but the refugees paid them because they couldn't just go up the street and try another hawker's stand.

Those who had no gold were reduced to beggars, holding their cups out pleadingly near the market.

I savored the few sips Ly had given me, desperate for my plan to work. Now my stomach felt like mud too, and I fell asleep to its taste in my mouth.

The next day, I returned to my hole and continued to dig, but the earth's belly was dry and barren. I had dug deep enough that I needed to fill up the bucket before hoisting it over my head. My muscles twitched with the repetitive motion and soon operated without thought. So my brain was free to think dark thoughts, review the horrors of my past, and to wonder, "What if all this was for nothing?"

I dug for two more days, climbing in and out of the hole I was making in the earth. It was over my head by two feet now, and I had to climb out using small earthen steps that I left for myself, to dump the dirt at the top. The deeper I went, the longer and harder the process became. Dig, fill the basket, carry it up, dump it, repeat.

Climbing down into my hole again for the thousandth time, I jabbed the shovel into the bottom of the hole and heard a different kind of thud. It sounded warm and heavy, like someone breathing—like the earth was breathing. Sticking my hands into the loose dirt, I reveled in the way it felt, cool and lumped together with my touch. It was mud.

I scooped up another handful. And another. Frantically, I continued to dig, scooping out the dirt to get to the liquid. Soon it began to trickle from the depths, kissing my hot feet.

"Water," I croaked and, cupping my hands, I lapped some up. I got as much dirt as water, but I didn't care. I wanted to sit in it, take a bath in it and never crawl out of the hole onto the hot earth again. I sat there, soaking it in. I did climb out eventually, only to return with every castoff jug and can I could find and several pieces of twine.

I sat on the edge looking at the water for what felt like hours, in order to let the dirt settle before lowering a bucket down with twine. Pulling it up gently, I handled the water as if it was liquid gold. In truth, it was even more precious because this would keep us alive.

Trying to contain my excitement, I jostled all the water I could carry to Mteay, who accepted it gratefully with gleaming eyes. Then I returned, being careful that no one followed me. I drew up as much as I could carry and walked through the paths of people, happy to have something to sell or barter for rice.

Khan and Kiry didn't last long with the "freedom fighters" and returned after a few weeks, learning that the rumors of them pillaging and raping refugees was indeed true. They had helped them complete the bunker, but refused to join them in their other exploits. When they returned to the campsite, Mteay was elated. I dreaded seeing them. I despised Khan and distrusted Kiry. Now they both had guns, which they apparently had not returned to the freedom fighters.

Khan looked once again like a man who had watched his ideals fade away like a mirage before his eyes, and he was left with empty hands. He was angrier than ever. We had all heard the rumors about the exploits of the Freedom Fighters, but Khan had been so desperate for a cause—so desperate for a reason to fight—that he had been blind to them. The truth of who the Freedom Fighters really were hit him at a much deeper level than it did others. They had been his lifeline, his new idyll. The reality wrestled on his face, drawing sharp lines between his eyebrows and sharper words for the rest of us. When those lines were present, we knew it was not a good time to be around him. We all remained silent when he retreated sullenly into the hut, not wanting to get caught in any collateral damage. Kiry was aimless and brooding, and I avoided him as much as I could. I had no desire to rekindle a relationship with my oldest brother. I had never really known him, and now I had no wish to. Neither he nor Khan seemed interested in doing much of anything to contribute to the family's well-being. Some things never changed.

After several weeks of being at Nong Chan, I was making my rounds selling water when a commotion rippled through the camp. Rumors that food was being given out was passed from person to person until the whole camp was in an uproar. I gathered the rest of my family and pushed myself into a line at the border crossing. A line of trucks stood idling on the other side of the barbed wire, with the letters UNICEF painted on the side. When I received cans of rice and water bottles from one of the trucks carrying supplies, a lump balled in my stomach. There was no charge. I didn't understand. The Thai looking men who had given it to me didn't ask for anything. Not like the Khmer Rouge, who in turn demanded manual labor. It felt odd to eat rice I hadn't earned and to drink water I hadn't carried for miles from outside the camp.

I grinned, watching my family eat. For the first time in months, we filled our stomachs with food we hadn't scraped and saved for, and it tasted good. It was like eating sunlight.

51

SHELLING

"We were caught in the middle." — Rindy

JUNE 1980

Afetr nearly six months of being at Nong Chan, we had fallen into a rhythm of uncertainty. We had moved along the border and eventually continued deeper into the jungle near the river, building a more permanent stilt hut to keep us dry before the seasonal rain began to fall. Humanitarian agencies I had never heard of funneled food, rice seed, farming tools and basic necessities into the country. I couldn't understand this. Why would they help us? Who was UNICEF or ICRC anyway? How did the United States suddenly care about us now, when before they bombed us? I couldn't make sense of it.

The aid to the refugees had become more reliable, and those at the border were encouraged to take the rice seed and basic farming supplies back into Cambodia. However, we heard that the new government, run by Hang Samrin (the former Khmer Rouge), wanted to funnel all supplies through his authority in Phnom Penh. We couldn't trust it. We wouldn't trust it. Despite the supplies pooling life back into Cambodia, we were reluctant to move inland. We chose to rebuild our lives closer to the source of food. It was safer. We weren't certain if we would ever be allowed entrance into Thailand and were reluctant to trust the government there either.

Over the past months, we had heard stories that caused our blood to run cold. Before arriving at the border camps, over a hundred buses had pulled in and invited refugees to be relocated to a camp "with better conditions." It was said that 45,000 Cambodians had climbed in, eager for a new life, only to find that the buses stopped near the Dangrek Mountains at a temple called Preah Vihear. The Thai military then forced refugees down a steep cliff with rifles and whips, only to meet the minefield below. The few who survived had returned to the Nong Chan, bearing the scars of their blind trust. I was determined to never trust again; I had learned from my own mistakes and would learn from the mistakes of those who had gone before me.

We lived life as normally as we could, and I did whatever I could to make money so we wouldn't be dependent on any government. Vuthy and I fished, built a sturdier stilt hut and cleared land to plant vegetables, until one day, as I was digging out a root, the familiar sound of bullets cut through the morning air. I lunged across the field towards my family and heard more erupt behind me.

"What is that?" Mteay asked, instinctively grabbing my sisters, who were playing with baby Selay who had just begun to walk.

"They're coming!" Khan answered, springing towards his gun. "Everyone follow me to the bunker! Kiry bring up the rear!" The sound of hot metal colliding with earth rang in my ears.

"Are those bombs?" Mteay cried. The earth shuttered as if in reply.

Khan led us through the trees and onto the road. Vuthy and I ran behind Mteay, protecting her, Sotha and Ly, who was carrying Selay.

There were hundreds of other refugees running in the same direction. It wasn't the first time they had watched the tree line rain fire. I had heard of shelling in the border camps before, but in the months we had been there, we hadn't experienced it. We thought maybe we were safe.

The freedom fighters had helped dig a bunker-like trench deeply into the earth and I was thankful. I wondered who was shooting at us? Was it the Vietnamese or was it the Thai? The enemy changed from month to month and sometimes day to day. Our lives were like walking through a minefield, never knowing what was going to go off and who would try to kill us next. The sound of bullets ripping through the trees continued to thunder through the jungle after us. Chancing a glance behind me, I caught sight of the dreaded green uniform and red star of the Vietnamese soldiers. Had they come all this way just to kill us?

Dodging into the trench, we pressed our faces against the dirt and felt it tremble as explosions erupted overhead. Then more began coming from the opposite direction. The Thai troops were shooting back, their tanks firing at the Vietnamese as they tried to breach the border. Missiles exploded everywhere. The sound thundered through the jungle, thudding onto the earth like a giant's footsteps.

I wanted to crawl deeper into the dirt, further from the danger overhead. Our ears rang and Selay's frightened screams were barely audible between explosions. Huddling together, we counted the seconds between each blast. Some were closer than others.

The earth shuddered and groaned beneath the weight of explosions and the air was riddled with bullets. Our hands clawed into the dirt at the bottom of the trench, as if pleading with it to conceal us. I shielded Ly and Selay the best I could, but my body could only do so much to protect them. Ly's eyes met mine, her pupils were dilated. A vein in her temple was beating at an impossible pace. Her eyes asked the same question she had at the waterfall, deep in the jungle. *Are we going to make it?*

I pulled her down with me, pressing my forehead to the dirt next to hers and whispered, "We're going to be okay." I willed it to be true.

Someone fell into the trench beside us. He was missing limbs, now just a lifeless heap.

After several hours, the fighting moved north. We didn't dare to venture far from the trench. Selay screamed for hours until exhaustion allowed sleep to calm her away at last. When the sound of the fighting dulled and continued farther north, we crawled out, one by one. We stood up and together walked over the beaten earth with shaking knees. Dead bodies of those who didn't make it to the bunker in time littered the landscape. Everywhere I looked, loved ones cried and screamed.

Trees were shredded and smoldering; huts were smashed, unrecognizable. Great, gaping holes scattered the landscape. Several undetonated artillery rounds were partially planted in the dirt. We tiptoed past them, so as not to awaken their fury.

52

THE BUS

"My family was the first, but we were afraid because of the buses and their bad history." — Rindy

A WEEK LATER

"Come and see,"Mteay called, waving her hands over her head to Vuthy and me, where we were clearing the land around our hut. We stood erect and followed her, leaving our hoe and shovel behind. What was she so excited about?

Without an explanation, she disappeared into the hut. We found her gathering our meager belongings and shoving them into baskets and rice sacks before thrusting them into our hands. Last, she grabbed the last of the gold and Thai money we'd earned and shoved it into the waist of her sarong.

"Hurry! Let's go. The others are near the market."

"Where are we going? I don't understand."

"We're leaving this place, Rindy. We're leaving. Come now, there's no time."

We pressed our way into a growing crowd around the center of the market. Mteay pressed farther in, to where the others stood closer to the front. Everyone was pointing to several passenger buses, idling in a row. The once-white tin siding was yellowed and dusty, with muted red stripes running across their sides. Three foreign men stood around the first bus, dust covering their fine-laced shoes. One man had pale skin, huge glasses and a bushy mustache, and the other two had longer, sandy colored hair. I had never seen skin so pale before or hair so light. I couldn't stop staring at them. Standing with them were Thai soldiers who didn't look like they wanted to be there.

The pale man with the mustache spoke into his shiny loudspeaker, using strange words. I couldn't understand what he said, except for "United Nations." One of the Thai men translated the strange sounding words into broken and lurching Khmer. "A camp has been opened inside the Thailand border through the administration of the Thai Interior Ministry and the United Nations High Commissioner for Refugees."

A ripple passed through the crowd like a shiver.

The man continued, and the soldier translated.

"Huts, beds, food and a hospital have been organized for your benefit." A fly buzzed around his head, landing on his face. "The world has noticed your suffering and has sent aid." He paused, swatting at the fly. "The world sympathizes with you. Today is your opportunity to leave this war zone and move to a place of safety inside Thailand." My mind overflowed with these words, as I heard each one, it elbowed the next, trying to make room in my brain.

"We need volunteers to come with us." He motioned to his companions. "All your needs will be met."

His invitation was greeted with silence and the smell of thousands of unwashed bodies. A foul mixture of fear and skepticism showed on every face. The silence was long and heavy, like the humid air. Only the flies stirred. No one dared to move first. The memories of what had transpired only months before had left an indelible mark. How could anyone willingly climb onto a bus again?

"Please, you have nothing to fear," the Thai soldier translated.

We had everything to fear.

Then to my surprise, Mteay pressed through the crowd, and the rest of my family followed. Her black eyes shone, and her hands clutched Selay to her chest. Stunned, I watched as she inched forward into the open space between the crowd and the bus, as the man with the loudspeaker looked on approvingly.

She scanned the crowd and beckoned to Vuthy and me. As we walked forward, holding the sacks of supplies, the crowd parted. My face grew hotter with each whisper and sideways glance. At last, I stood beside the others.

"Anyone else? We cannot leave until the buses are full," the foreign man said, his massive height even more intimidating up close.

My hands shook. I leaned close to Mteay and whispered, "What if they are lying?"

"What if they're not?" Her eyes looked back into mine, reflecting a resolution I had never seen in them before.

She was going.

I looked at Vuthy, and he shrugged. Should we stay?

Then suddenly, as if a spell had broken, a mob of people rushed toward the buses and tried to cram onto them all at once. I was swept inward, my choice made for me. Our bus groaned beneath the weight of bare feet as people trampled to get a place inside.

"Not all at once, not all at once," the man with the speaker stuttered, his back plastered against the side of the bus. His cool demeanor sparked terror from the sudden rush of the crowd.

I slid into a seat beside the window and Vuthy followed, as dozens of bodies quickly filled the bus to the maximum. It wasn't possible to cram even one more emaciated body on board. The Thai soldiers sprang into action, beating people back. I looked behind me, and the other buses were filling in the same manner.

"Unfortunately, we cannot take everyone this trip," the man shouted, his voice muffled through the windows. "But we will be back."

The elbows, shoulders, and greasy hair of each passenger melted together until we became a single unit of desperation. Resting my head against the tiny window, I could taste the smell of rotting teeth and vomit swimming in the air. I exhaled, knowing I smelled just the same. Closed in on every side, the oxygen in the air seemed to evaporate. I tried to locate the rest of my family. I craned my neck and located Ly and Sotha, then Khan, Mteay, Selay, and even Kiry. They had made it. Memories of the forced evacuation, the guns and death, swirled in my brain. I couldn't tell if it was the odor or these memories that made my stomach tighten, but I wanted to vomit. I could feel it, like a string rooted deeply in my stomach, pulling upward. Closing my eyes, I tried to swallow it back down as the bus lurched forward.

I craned my neck to watch the border camp become eaten in miles of dust. My mind continued to flash through memories of nightmares like fire flickering into the night sky. With each memory, I could feel the string uprooting my stomach and sliding up my throat a little further. The big man next to Vuthy shifted his weight, forcing me up against the window, and I could taste the dust sneaking through a crack. I bumped elbows with Vuthy, and his eyes met mine, full of the same agony I felt. Were we going to our deaths?

"We're going to be fine, Vuthy."

His eyes darted around wildly. I grabbed his chin and made him look at me again.

"We're going to be fine."

He seemed reassured and slumped against the seat.

I pressed my cheek against the window and wondered what the future held, as the bus rattled down the Thai highway.

"We're not heading toward the Dangrek mountains, Vuthy. We're going into Thailand. We're really going into Thailand." Relief bubbled inside my chest, and I slumped against the seat beside Vuthy.

With our eyes locked on the scenery flowing past, of lush greens and mountains, came a tall fence made from barbed wire rolled in endless circles. Inside the enclosure were ponds—fishponds most likely. Hundreds of huts with leafy palm branch roofs, but no walls, stood in tidy rows as far as I could see. The ground was carpeted with red, hard-packed dirt. I stared through the sweaty marks my trembling hands left on the hot window. As the bus approached the entrance, a red and white striped gate slowly rose into the sky, and we rolled through and ground to a stop. The doors opened, and our group of refugees uncurled themselves from one another and shuffled to the exit. Filing off the bus, we walked in a single line. Everyone was silent, waiting for a command of what to do. The mountains around the camp stared down at us from its varying shades of green, and our bare feet mingled with the red dust.

"Welcome to Khao-I-Dang Holding Center," an official, wearing a Thai uniform and a wrinkled forehead, said in broken Khmer. "No person is allowed to leave this camp. If anyone attempts to leave, they will be punished severely. All your rations will be provided by the United Nations officials, and we will take care of all your needs."

We had made it out of Cambodia. I caught sight of Mteay's eyes, and they brimmed with tears. She had gotten us here. Somehow, she had known.

53

SMUGGLER

"The darker, the better." — Rindy

JULY 1980

I shuffled forward, gripping my plastic cup. It was bright yellow and had small bumps on the outside, like lizard flesh. I stood picking at it as the line inched toward the trucks and the light-skinned people handing out supplies. Since entering the camp, standing in lines had become a daily ritual. The lines were long, and as soon as I got out of one, I got into another. The camp was crawling with thousands of refugees who had no means to provide necessities for themselves as they waited for relocation to another country. We had heard that the visa process to go to another country was a slow one, and we should not to expect to leave anytime soon. Some in the camp had been there for months when we arrived. There was no end in sight. We were told there were only so many available spots and some were prioritized over others. From what we had heard, it could be years before we left.

My throat was dry, and I licked the beginning of a crack in my upper lip, anticipating the drink of water I would soon get. When I had started in the line earlier that day, the sun had barely been visible in the early morning sky, but now it bore down on my back. The surface of the red dirt was like a frying pan beneath my bare feet, and I shuffled them deeper to keep them cool.

The day wore on, and the line slowly inched forward, but at last my turn came. As I held out my cup, a clean woman wearing khaki pants and a flower shirt poured water from a bulky, white jug. The hole on the jug was big, and a few drops cascaded over the sides. I quickly reached out my hand to catch them before they hit the ground.

When I looked back up, the woman was wiping tears from her eyes. I stared at her curiously for a moment after taking the cup from her trembling hand. She looked so different from all the women I'd ever seen. She had light hair and white skin, but her eyes dripped like a rainy sky as they seemed to stare straight through me. Her eyes reflected pain. Was she in pain because of me? I blinked uncomfortably away from her gaze. Vuthy nudged me from behind, and I continued to the next person who handed me a can of sardines, a cabbage and a tin of rice. With full arms, I slurped my water in between steps as I walked back to our section of the camp, past row after row of huts, crammed full of those who had also survived.

Two times a day the trucks would come in and give us water and a ration of food. At first, I hid most of what I was given, only sneaking small bites at a time, but after a while, I trusted that the trucks would come. Sometimes, we even ate fish from the tilapia ponds inside the camp, as they were grown for the refugees. Whoever ran this camp kept their promises, unlike the Khmer Rouge. But it was still hard to fully depend on someone else, especially an obscure organization called the "United Nations," to provide for us long-term.

I couldn't. I had seen my family starve too many times to wait on others to feed us. I stared at the jungle through the barbed wire confining me on all sides and thought about the well I had dug to earn money for rice on the other side of the border. I missed it. I wanted to do more to pull my family away from the groping hands of starvation and release them from this state of dependence. I feared the fences for many reasons, but mostly because if the food stopped coming, we would all die, trapped inside of it. I began to grow restless, and boredom slunk after me everywhere I went, with its dreary, lazy step.

I began seeing supplies shuffled from hand to hand inside the camp that weren't provided by the aid workers. Cigarettes smoked in secret and elaborately printed fabrics, worn discreetly, appeared as if from nowhere. The mystery of it intrigued me, and I made it my mission to discover the source of the goods, chasing rumors around the camp and asking anyone who might know.

One afternoon, I sat staring at the soccer game taking place in the dust. I was bored. I watched the same group of boys play soccer day after day. My eyes staring, but not seeing.

"Why do you ask so many questions?" A voice startled me from behind. Turning around, I saw a boy just a few years older than me, walking with a tall, confident stride. I had noticed him before, standing in the shade, watching the game.

"Answer my question," he demanded, his voice low as he stopped next to me.

"I can't stand being locked up in here," I replied, still staring at the game, not meeting my companion's gaze. "I want to make my family's life better somehow."

"How heroic of you." He scoffed. "What we do is too dangerous just to do because you're bored. Two nights ago one of our boys got caught by the soldiers and was beaten like a dog. They almost cracked his skull in two. They can legally kill you if you try to leave." I didn't reply, but I squeezed a rock around in my hand until it became hot. Shrugging, the boy turned and began to walk away.

"I want to go," I called after him. "I don't care about the danger."

I lied. The fact was, I cared very much about the danger, and I didn't relish the idea of being beaten by the Thai soldiers. But I feared the inside of the fence more. The boy stuck out his hand and extended it to me.

"How old are you?"

"Seventeen." At least I thought I was.

"You look younger."

I shrugged, "I'm short, okay?"

He studied me for another long moment, his eyes squinting. I looked around, trying to appear cool and collected, before meeting his gaze again.

"I'm Chhay." His face twitched a smile.

"I'm Rindy." I shook his hand and smiled with all my teeth.

"Tonight, three of us will go out," Chhay said. "Meet me here and we'll sneak through the fence together." He turned to walk away. "You know, I am not responsible for you."

Excitement boiled like ants in my stomach as I walked back to the communal hut where my family stayed, along with hundreds of others. Mteay and baby Selay were the only ones there, the others were probably standing in lines or dozing somewhere in the shade. I began to lounge around, trying to drown the feeling of ants with a bit of water.

"What do you want more than anything?" I asked, trying to sound ambiguous, as I grabbed some of the gold from the pouch where mteay kept it, without her noticing.

"Hmmm?" Mteay asked absently, scrubbing the hem of her skirt in a pot of murky water.

"What do you wish you could buy, if there was a store that carried everything here in the camp?" I asked again, securing what I was looking for.

"Chicken," she replied, after a moment's reflection. "Just the way your Chidaun used to cook it." Rolling onto my back again, I imagined the flavors of chicken curry soup, with creamy coconut milk, tender carrots and bamboo shoots. I drifted to sleep, tasting the memory of it.

From the depths of darkness, I jerked awake. Had Chhay already left without me? I quickly grabbed an empty rice sack and a little gold. I crept away from my sleeping family and stole through the night. There wasn't a moon, and the clouds concealed the stars. Sneaking along the last hut near the makeshift soccer field, I nearly stumbled over Chhay and another boy, crouching in the shadows. Pulling me down next to him, he whispered hotly into my ear.

"What took you so long?"

"I'm here now."

"You, me and Samang are going to sneak through the fence. We'll go first, and then you follow. You must be fast, really fast, because the soldiers patrol the border all night."

A cold sweat rose to the surface of my skin, as we waited for the darkness to become a little thicker and to time the absence of the guard perfectly. We watched as the flashlights sprayed yellow across the ground, sometimes pausing, sometimes jerking around in an unpredictable way. Chhay crouched tensely next to me, like a rubber band stretched to its limit. Whenever he moved, I jumped. His glare bore into my forehead with each unauthorized movement. At last, when the guard was a hundred yards down the fence, he sprung from his feet, ran to the fence and crawled through the shards of wire. He was stealthy and soundless, calculating each step and movement like a well-practiced art. The yellow of the flashlight danced over the dirt inside the camp, the guards oblivious. Then Samang went. His body disappeared into the outer darkness of the jungle, hemming the edge of the wire. He was just as stealthy, just as soundless. Then I was alone with only the sound of my own breath.

What if they want me to get caught? The thought tapped me on the shoulder, lurking just behind in the shadows. I froze, waffling in indecision of whether to go or stay.

How do I even get through the wire? The questions in my mind called me to retreat into the shadows. Looking past the darkness where I sat, the fence loomed. It taunted me. I couldn't let it win. It would taunt me every day until I conquered it, leering at me with a thousand razor-sharp teeth.

Not allowing myself another moment of doubt, I sprang forward, keeping an eye on the dancing flashlight in the distance. My feet sprang over the dirt, faster than I had ever flown before.

Reaching the fence, I crouched low and maneuvered through the barbs, thankful for my small frame. But a few grazed my bare chest, back and legs. Grimacing, I pushed through, contorting my body like a snake until I made it past the last strand. It wasn't art and it wasn't stealth—it was pure willpower.

At last, I made it through, leaving only bits of my skin and hair behind, clinging to the teeth of the defeated fence. I dashed into the jungle, leaves and branches hitting my face as if they were flags of my victory.

"We thought you chickened out," Chhay whistled, running up next to me.

"I thought you left without me," I shot back.

"You sounded like a wild boar ripping through the wire." He laughed. "How bad did you get cut?"

"Not at all," I said. With hot adrenaline running like fire through my veins, my voice didn't shake. It sounded credible. I almost believed my own lie.

We ran southwest, not stopping for miles. I thought my lungs would burst. As the sun began to warm the sky, we stole into the deserted streets of Aranyaprathet, where the sleeping shops were barely blinking with life. Gripping the gold, my eyes wandered over the colors exploding before me. I rubbed my eyes, trying to take it all in. Had I ever seen such color? Had I truly forgotten? The street shops seemed to go on for miles. Fabrics with intricate patterns, bold images in hundreds of shades of every color waved at me, rows of shoes stared sullenly and the smell of hanging meat tantalized me. I wanted to scoop all of it up and carry it back to the dusty camp, so those who had been starved by black fabric could see color again. The shopkeepers stared at us like hawks on a perch. Three skinny boys who browsed their merchandise were anything but innocent. My hand pulsated around the money to remind myself to get only what I could easily sell for a profit. Chhay and Samang veered off the street to haggle with cigarette vendors, but I had my gaze glued to the naked chickens, hanging from their yellow feet farther up the road.

"How much...chickens?" I asked the old Thai lady, who slurped on her rice porridge.

"30 baht," she chirped back. We stared each other down. She knew it was an outrageous price as well as I did, but she just picked at a jagged toenail like she didn't have a care in the world. Haggling was an art, and one I had a few skills in. Wagging my head in a slow, exaggerated motion, I continued to walk past as if I was going to find another vendor, but the money burned in my palm.

"Haaa..." The woman waved me back into her tent. "I give you very good price." Her eyes twinkled. "Because you're a skinny boy. I give you two chickens for 40 baht." She shook the yellow foot in my face.

"Four chickens." I said firmly.

The woman gasped and muttered, countering my offer. The battle ensued, but in the end, I walked away holding six chickens for 60 baht and the victory.

After meeting up with Chhay and Samang in the jungle, we smoked cheap cigarettes and chomped on cooked crickets until darkness concealed our reentry into the camp.

54

THE ROBBERY

"The moon that night was bright." — Rindy

APRIL 1981

I was hooked. Sneaking out of the camp to smuggle in supplies became my reason for living. The money I was stockpiling was an added bonus. I slept during the day and escaped two or three times a week, coming alive with excitement when escaping the Thai soldiers. Each time became riskier, as the soldiers began to catch on, but we still outran them with ease. Hot blood pounded through my body as their flashlights and curses danced after us through the trees. We laughed and ran until several miles of jungle swayed between us. With the sound of gold in our pockets, we strolled into Thai streets to buy our goods like the king of men. I was no longer just a refugee who depended on others for a ration of food and water. I was the smuggler, the escapee and the one in control of my life.

The better part of a year passed quickly, and just like many nights before, Samang and I escaped through the wire and made our purchases, before returning to the camp.

"You get a bargain on chickens?" I asked Samang as he wove between the thick underbrush carrying a lumpy sack.

"The lady was an old hag." He spat. "She made me work hard for it."

"How'd you do with the cigarettes?" he asked in return.

"Fine. The man who sells them to me, you know the one near the fish market? He and I get along. He gives me a good price." I chuckled in satisfaction and looked at the moon through a clearing in the treetops. It bathed us in light for a moment, before we plunged back into the darkness. We were still a few miles from camp, but I always enjoyed the walk. My pockets were bulging with cigarettes, and I trudged with a sack full of vegetables. The night creatures were unusually quiet, but I attributed it to the noisy Samang and his jostling bag.

"It's so quiet—" I began, when suddenly, two Thai soldiers emerged from the underbrush with guns cocked at our chests.

"Stop!" They shouted, thrusting their guns at us.

Freezing in our tracks, we dropped our supplies and lifted trembling hands over our heads in obedience. I closed my eyes against the moonlight and regretted not relishing it sooner, because I was sure my eyes would never see it again. I glanced at Samang, whose eyes stared back into mine, large and black. I could see regrets running across his face too. With greed in the eyes of the soldiers, they elbowed each other as they searched our supplies. One of the soldiers pulled the packets of cigarettes out of my pockets and began sniffing them. The other collected all the money we had.

I'm going to die over cigarettes and vegetables.

I swallowed hard. For most of my life, I had seen death looking at me from afar, peering through the darkness. I always knew it was approaching because of its gentle purr and orange eyes. It had been my companion, sometimes walking closely, other times retreating into the distance. Yet I had managed to keep it afar and elude its advances. Until now. This time I didn't hear it coming, when I should have. Nobody will ever know how we died. The realization slammed across my consciousness like a door. I closed my eyes again, waiting for the click, waiting for the surge of a bullet.

"Pye, Pye!" The soldiers shouted in unison.

I couldn't believe my ears, so I stood there, staring dumbly. Did they really mean it? We could run free?

"Come on. They said run." Samang ripped through the trees like a madman as the gunshots ricocheted through the air around our heads. With each shot, I ran faster, expecting to feel a bullet embed itself into my back. Another bullet sounded, but I kept running, vines and cobwebs hitting my face. Then another, but I remained upright, legs flying. With every bound, we left the sound of the bullets farther and farther behind us as we ran up the mountain. After running for a few miles, we collapsed into sweaty and relieved heaps.

"They weren't going to kill us." Samang wheezed. "They were shooting into the sky."

"I'm not so sure," I responded, breath heaving, still terrified.

"They only wanted to rob us." Samang cursed. "They waited for us to hit up their favorite cigarette stand before busting us."

I laughed, but my mind was filled with the sound of bullets, so I swallowed hard and tried to forget. As I sat intertwined with the roots of a tree, I tried to hide from the moonlight that searched for us.

After a few hours lying still, we peeled ourselves from the tree line and slid through the barbed wire into safety, never so thankful for the ability to blend back in and assume our identities as refugees.

I didn't venture outside the camp for a week, the memory of that encounter still fresh. I resumed watching the endless soccer game, stood in line for my portion of rice and water, and tried to sleep at night. But I couldn't give up my nocturnal excitement, as I lay awake for hours dreaming about the jungle. I had tasted freedom, and I was unable to reason myself out of the desire to taste it again. It called to me when I did manage to sleep and visited me when darkness crept across the ground. I was no match for its allure. I returned to sneaking through the barbed wire to flirt with danger.

A few months later, under a black sky, a small group of us slipped back into the camp with our supplies. I was the last one inching through the barbed wire when a flood of flashlights blinded me. Hands grabbed my arms, pulling and shoving me into submission.

Voices in Khmer scoffed at me. I bumped against holstered guns and grazed against wooden nunchucks. When my eyes adjusted to the harsh light, I recognized my captors. They were the Cambodian police. They dragged me to their waiting vehicle and shoved me in, slamming the door behind me. Through the cloud of exhaustion and fright, I watched as we sped down the road toward Cambodia, leaving the safety of Thailand behind. I looked back and saw the taillights casting their blood glow over the already red ground and wondered if I would ever be free again. My mind shuffled through the past months of smuggling and all of the camp ordinances I had broken, as the officer's eyes glared at me through the rearview mirror. Arriving, we pulled up to a tiny white station, draped in a thick grass roof. It was remote, and it looked deserted. This outcome would not be good. I was pulled from the car, and they marched me into the glaring lights of the one room station.

"You've broken a camp rule." A leering officer sat behind a desk in front of me. His eyes squinted into mine. "And I know it's not the first time. You know this is a serious offense." He tapped his black stick on the table. "We could legally keep you locked up forever." He paused, his words swelling. "You would never see your family again. Never walk about freely. Never be anything but a prisoner. What you have done is a criminal offense." He stood, filling the empty space between us with his hollow words. Heat entered my face. I knew what these men wanted, and it wasn't to lock me in a cell.

"You have made quite a successful business extorting your fellow refugees, I'm sure." He walked toward me. "I'm sure you've gotten very rich from this."

With the officer towering over me, I knew the punch line was coming like drool from a dog's mouth. Bending down, he blew the smell of stale cigarettes and corruption into my face. "If you turn over your profit, we may overlook your treachery." I lowered my head and stared holes into my feet. "But you have to agree right now to pay us every coin you earn or no one will ever hear from you again."

I bit my tongue until I could feel the smart of metal.

"Lock him up," the officer sputtered at last, shoving me into a small cell and slamming the iron doors.

"We'll get what we want one way or another."

Sinking to a dusty mat on the concrete floor, I rested my head against the cool wall and let sleep take me.

"Get up," someone growled as I blinked into the morning light. A policeman stood with the cell door open, beckoning me out. I followed him out of my cell and into the small room. The fluorescent light glared angrily into the face of the morning sun, and a sticky flytrap hung from the low sealing, speckled with flies and mosquitos. Mteay stood there, beneath the flytrap, her eyes piercing and shoulders as stiff as wood. The officer from the night before sat with his feet brandishing his metal desk, a gloating expression stretched across his features.

"I told you; we would get what we wanted." He poked a pouch of money on the table with his finger. "Your kind and beautiful Mteay gave us what we asked for."

I recognized the pouch and knew it held every piece of money I had earned from smuggling. It wasn't just money, it was freedom. A way for my family to buy our independence. I turned my back to the man at the desk and walked away, fists clenched and a mirage of rage dancing before my eyes.

55

SUNDAY

"I was curious, because I heard He was alive." — Rindy

MAY 1981

The camp I had once escaped became my prison. I was penniless and had no way to make money to buy supplies to smuggle in and sell. It was as if everyone in the camp had heard of my arrest and avoided me, when before they had happily bought the supplies I brought.

My nights were mostly sleepless. When I did manage to sleep, nightmares plagued me of tigers with the face of men, chasing me through the clinging vines. During the day, I rarely talked to anyone. I stared through the barbed wire for hours, remembering what life was like on the other side. The endless soccer game was still being played in the dust, the same food portions were being given out and boredom walled me in on all sides. I had sampled an unquenchable taste of freedom and was left thirsty.

One Sunday morning, as I lay in my hammock, Samang approached.

"Rindy! What are you doing today?"

"Nothing," I responded, my eyes wandering over the grassy ceiling. "Always, nothing."

"Well then, let's take a walk." He poked my ribs with his thumb. I shrugged and followed him.

Our aimless feet took us to the north side of the camp, and it wasn't somewhere we had been often. Over the past year, the camp had been filling with thousands of people, sprawled out all over the dusty landscape inside the barbed wire fence. Within the camp, there were different sections dedicated to different ethnic groups. Despite this segregation, we were all in the fence together, a hodgepodge of displaced people who breathed the same dust-filled air.

We stopped in the shade of a Buddhist temple that had been erected within the camp for those who still wished to worship. I could hear the chants coming from inside, clashing with a very different sound coming from across the street.

"What's going on there?" I asked Samang, nodding my head toward a mob of people gathered around a building made of tall bamboo poles and a grass roof. The building didn't have any walls, so those who couldn't fit inside were sitting under trees and in the dirt, listening to whatever was happening within. There were hundreds of people there, all crowded around.

I looked at the temple beside us. It seemed to be nearly empty.

"I've heard of them," Samang said. "I think they're Christians." In the camp, I had heard it might be easier to gain a visa if you were a Christian.

"I know they're not Buddhists." I glanced at the silent temple looming over our heads. "But what's a christian?"

"They follow Jesus." He shrugged.

Jesus.

It was a name I had never forgotten. At it's mention, was back at the temple of my childhood, staring at the pamphlet of the smiling man in the clouds. I could almost taste the stale, castoff bread and smell the incense from the monk's coffers. I remembered Mr. Thach saying he was praying to Jesus for me. Praying that I could know Him. I remembered the story of Jesus in the cloud that I had told Vuthy to comfort him, a story I had forgotten but that hadn't quite left me, buried deeply in my subconscious.

"I've heard of Him," I whispered, more to myself than to Samang. "I've heard that He is alive—" I left the sentence unfinished, trailing off into the sweltering air.

In the temple's shadow, my mind spun through memories I had never reviewed before, like the unencumbered spinning of a bike wheel flipped on its side. I remembered the sting of the stick on my back as the monks beat me with hatred staring out of their eyes. I saw the golden statues of Buddha smeared with mud and sunken headfirst in ponds when the Khmer Rouge toppled the temples. I could still hear the ringing of the teachings and chants in my ears, like flies buzzing and crickets chirping, "bow, bow, bow, bow to Buddha." The empty chants filled my head once again. Something within me settled like a pond after a hard rain, and I saw clearly. I stepped out of the shadow of the temple, compelled forward or perhaps repelled from behind.

"What are you doing?" Samang asked, with puzzled zigzags running across his tan forehead. I shrugged, because I didn't know what I was doing or why I was doing it. I had an inner urge to walk away from the shadows, walk away from dark teachings, the abuse and the fear that had lurked behind everything I had known of Buddhism.

"They're waving at us." Samang whispered. A group of people sitting beneath a tree, waved to us as if they had been expecting us.

I walked toward them, and they crammed closer together to let us join. This was strange because in the overcrowded camp, everyone had to fight for his or her place. Sitting down, I looked around curiously. Those near us stared back with huge, smiling eyes that unsettled me. What did they know that I didn't?

I couldn't see much of what was going on inside the hut because of all the black heads bobbing in the way, but soon, singing sparked inside, and like a fire, it spread to the rest of us outside. The singing was off key and jumbled, but oddly, it was nice to hear. The words were strange and happy, unlike any other song I had ever heard before and very unlike the anthems the Khmer Rouge made us sing. Khmer Rouge songs droned on in choruses of superiority, fighting, and the inevitable success of their conquests. These songs talked about joy, love, and kindness. The songs rippled into quiet, and an expectant silence fell over the crowd.

A Khmer man began to speak, his voice projecting loudly and confidently. The Khmer Rouge had always said Christianity was a "white man's religion" of the despised Frenchman, not belonging in Cambodia. Curious, I listened intently to this khmer Christian.

"Jesus came to earth for one purpose: to make us right with God. He didn't come to kill his enemies. No, he loved his enemies. He left his home in the clouds, with his loving father, to join in the struggle we have on this earth because he loved us *that* much. He knew that no matter how much we tried, we could never be clean, never be made right by our own effort."

I was stunned. The words sank into my chest like rocks dropping into a pond, one by one.

"I feel like I need to say it again. Listen, friends, Buddhism has always taught that in order to have a good life, a life in right standing, you have to work your way to salvation—to enlightenment. You had to give sacrifices, pay monks and earn good merit in order to be saved, to escape the endless cycle of rebirth. But I tell you, Jesus does not require sacrifice or gaining good karma to redeem yourself. He knows we cannot. He knows that no matter what we do, we could never be good enough to redeem all the bad we have done."

I hung my head, shame filling my chest. The shame that had been my constant companion for as long as I could remember. The shame of knowing that no matter how hard I tried, my good karma would never outweigh the bad.

"But that is why Jesus is different. Please hear me, He is different because He made us right, He made us perfectly clean. He wiped out all the bad that we never could overcome by ourselves by taking all the bad merit, the sin and our shame onto His shoulders to bleed and die, so we don't have to."

I looked up. They killed Him? Desperation clawed at my throat. I felt like I was trying to grasp water that was spilling through my hands.

"Jesus, the Son of God, came to earth as a baby, grew into a man and lived a perfect life—because we could not, even if we had a million lifetimes to live. We are incapable of living lives without sin."

He paused. No one seemed to breathe, hanging on these words of life.

"But the world did not receive Him. No, they killed Him. They beat Him and hung Him on a cross to die. They killed the only sinless, spotless human to ever live."

I wiped at my eyes, not understanding the emotion swelling in my chest until it felt like it might suffocate me.

He didn't die. He couldn't have. I had heard He was alive!

"He died for your sin, and He died for mine, so we didn't have to. He died for Cambodia. He died for all the sin and destruction that has been waged here. He died for *us*. He died so we never again have to work our way into salvation because we never could. He died for us. He died for us. He died for us. Do you understand this?"

The man's voice cracked. People around me began to weep. If this perfect man is dead, the one who had no bad merit, then all is lost. There is no salvation left for us.

After a few minutes passed, the man began to speak again, his voice quieter. We all leaned forward to listen.

"But He rose from the dead, after three days of darkness and destruction, as He conquered not only sin, but *death*. He rose back to life again. He was reborn back to this earth for one purpose: to conquer sin and death for us because we could not. It's a lie that we are reborn in an endless cycle until we are released. We only have one life to live and know this Jesus before we die and can be reborn into His glorious kingdom or else suffer eternal suffering apart from Him in hell."

I looked at Samang, his brow furrowed in puzzlement. But I felt like my chest had just been split open and sunlight was pouring in.

What did He require—this Jesus who died in my place?

As if to read my thoughts, the man continued speaking, "If anyone is wondering what this God requires in order to follow Him, I'm here to tell you today that all He wants from you is for you to accept this gift. The gift that Jesus came to earth, lived a spotless life and died in our place—your place."

There must be a catch. There must be.

"Is there anyone out there who wants me to pray with them as they make this decision? Anyone who wants me to introduce them to Jesus?"

My heart pounded. It seemed like the crowd was suddenly aware of me—a single boy in torn clothes. I had so many questions, so many fears, but I rose to my feet and began to walk forward. I could hear Samang behind me, following. No one seemed surprised to see two confused looking teens make their way through the crowd. Instead, they too seemed happy we were there. Weaving our way to the front, we reluctantly lowered ourselves to our knees into the dirt with dozens of others. Some of them were crying and others were smiling.

"Do you want to give your lives to Jesus?" the speaker asked, bending down to look each of us in the face. He spoke softly, and something in his eyes looked familiar. They were ordinary brown, but something in them reminded me of Mr. Thach. Perhaps it wasn't the color at all, but something deeper than that.

What do I have to lose? I met the gaze of this Cambodian Christian.

"Yes," I responded, and so did Samang.

"Repeat after me then," the man said.

"Jesus, I know I have sinned, and I ask you to forgive me." I uttered the words, trying to understand them. The weight of my shame and my cowardice never more real, never more palpable. "I believe you, Jesus. I believe you died for me and that you rose from the dead." I smiled, repeating the words. I knew He was alive; unlike Buddha and every other god I had ever heard of. "I invite you, Jesus, to come into my life. I want to trust you and follow you only, as my Lord and my Savior."

Is Jesus the only God? I wondered, my thoughts sputtering. Do I follow only Him? My thoughts spilled out like water all over the ground. I thought about Buddha, all the spirits Khan worshiped and the host of other gods I had brushed shoulders with throughout the years. The idea of serving only one was a new thought—one I couldn't quite understand. Then a single thought scooped up all my scattered droplets of confusion and brought them back together again.

If He did all this for me, then there is no other god worth serving.

"I invite you to come into my life." I stared straight ahead, not understanding why some closed their eyes. "I will follow you—only you, Jesus." Stumbling over the words, I tried to remember exactly what to say. I looked up awkwardly because I knew I hadn't repeated the words just right, but the man smiled and nodded, placing a hand on my shoulder. Samang and I arose and walked out of the structure, through the mob of people who were now singing. What had I just done?

Something felt different in the air I breathed. A cleansing rainstorm had come and driven all the haze away. For the first time in my eighteen years of life, I saw clearly.

56

DEATH OF THE TIGER

"I was searching." — Rindy

LATER THAT NIGHT

I was in the trench again. Chivy and all my mets were alive, working beside me. When suddenly, I began to beat them, my hands pounding in their faces, unable to stop myself. I screamed, trying to pry my hands from them, but I couldn't stop. My hands were no longer my own. They cried for mercy, but I would not—could not—stop. Chivy tried to escape, climbing up the trench, but I yanked her back and raised my hoe over my head, screaming as I let it fall. When no one was left alive, I screamed and tore my hair. That's when I heard the heavy purr I could never forget. It emerged from the darkness of the trench, crawling over the lifeless frames of my mets. Its fiery eyes locked on me. I had nowhere to run, nowhere to hide. It crouched to leap and sprang toward me.

I awoke with a jerk, sweating and shaking. I crawled off the low bamboo platform bed and sat on the ground, careful not to awaken anyone. I looked up at the sky. The moon stared back, only an incomplete drop of water in the expanse. It was far from daylight. I walked to the fence and stared out. I didn't feel alone, and I remembered what had happened the previous day. The day I had given my life to Jesus. For me, it had been an easy exchange, as I had received something but lost nothing. But what about Him? What if He didn't want someone like me as a follower?

Absently, I walked through the rows of sleeping people and passed a few fires, dozens of men drank out of bottles and smoked smuggled cigarettes. I'm sure Khan and Kiry were around one of them too, just not the same fire. They couldn't be in each other's presence without an eruption. I didn't know where I was going, but it wasn't there.

After hours of walking, I went to the only place I felt like I could—the last place I had felt peace. As I approached the structure where the Christian had preached earlier that day, I was surprised to see a small fire kindled beside it and a single man sitting there.

"Come."

I approached uneasily.

"So, you're the reason I couldn't sleep." Firelight danced across his smiling features. It was the Christian who had spoken to the crowd. The one who had told me about Jesus. "I didn't get to introduce myself yesterday, but my name is Pastor Akara. What's yours?"

"Rindy." I squatted beside him. "What do you mean I'm the reason you couldn't sleep?"

"I awoke suddenly and felt that I needed to come here. So I did."

I gazed into the fire, not understanding, but comforted by his words.

"Did you have trouble sleeping?"

I nodded.

"Want to tell me about it?"

I hesitated, not knowing how to begin. "I have these nightmares almost every night. They're horrible, and I can't seem to escape. They are every night. They always have a tiger." I shuddered at the memories.

"I see. I have had similar ones."

My eyes met his, understanding reflecting there. "You have?"

"Yes, many times."

"Do you still?"

"No."

I spun toward him. "Tell me how they stopped."

"Jesus set me free from them after I stopped running."

"Stopped running from what?"

"From myself."

I didn't understand.

"Let me tell you a story. Did you know that there are nearly two hundred of us Christians that escaped Cambodia in Khao-I-Dang?"

I shook my head. "I thought the Khmer Rouge killed all the Christians."

"No, about twenty families survived and made it here. But do you want to know what keeps me up at night?"

I nodded my head, unable to look away.

"It's the ones that aren't here because of me."

Pastor Akara began to cry, gleaming tears running down his cheeks. I envied him for his tears and the freedom they brought. I couldn't remember the last time I had cried.

"Shortly before the Khmer Rouge took over, I met a Christian at my workplace, and he convinced me to come with him to church. I soon became a Christian myself. They welcomed me into their small circle, loving and caring for me. When the Khmer Rouge offered a little extra food to anyone who knew anything about any Christians, I exposed three families. Three beautiful families—with mothers and children. They were murdered that night."

I pulled my eyes away from him, staring into the fire as it danced and writhed.

"After I had eaten the extra bowl of watery rice, the guilt and hatred for myself, crushed me. The nightmares were unthinkable." He shook his head. "Until some of the Christians that remained, risked their lives to tell me, me"—he pounded his chest—"about forgiveness."

My eyes met his.

"About the forgiveness Jesus offered me when I deserved to die."

Warmth began to creep up from the pit of my stomach.

"Rindy, Jesus asks for your life not so you can lose something, but so you can gain everything. You can gain forgiveness, and He can teach you how His love covers every sin. Every single one. For the entire world. For you."

He paused, looking up toward the sky, seeming to mutter to himself. Then his eyes rested on me again.

"I'm going to make a guess here, but I think the sin you're carrying the most heavily is the sin of hating yourself for being alive when so many are not."

At these simple words, I broke. A torrent of tears flowed out of me, out of a place that was yet unexplored—my soul. For the first time, I mourned Chivy and all the mets who had died in my place. I grieved the brokenness of my country. The brokenness of my family. The brokenness of myself. The sin was great. Sobs wracked my body, until at last, I could see clearly again. My pulse slowed and my breath eased. The sun was rising over the horizon of trees, and Pastor Akara sat beside me, his eyes wet too.

"Why me? Why did I survive when Chivy deserved to live, not me?"

"Chivy?" Pastor Akara's eyes softened. "That's a lovely name. Chivy means life. If I've learned anything following Jesus so far, it's that death gives birth to life. No death is wasted. I know this will be your story."

He paused again, studying the horizon. "I can't answer the question of why so many died. I don't think we're meant to always know the whys behind the things that happen in this broken world that is bent on sin. But I do know that the enemy, this tiger named Satan who's been hunting you since the day you were born, will be killed once and for all. But until that day, Jesus has given us everything we need to overcome him."

He turned to me, his eyes reflecting the rising sun.

"Rindy, you have been spared because the world needs to know that God lives, even in Cambodia. Especially in Cambodia. He's seen what has happened here. His heart breaks over it; I know this without a shadow of a doubt. He's choosing you as His messenger to bind up the brokenhearted, to heal the sick and to proclaim that He still lives and will never leave us."

He turned to me, grasping my shoulders in his big hands. "If you hate your life and wish it away, God can't use it. He can't redeem it. He can't present it to the world that so desperately needs to know that He can restore, even out of this deep darkness we are all climbing from."

The sunlight was consuming the shadows, casting their rays over every place in the camp. Over every shadow in me.

"Rindy, do you want to be done running?"

I nodded, smiling.

I never again dreamed of the tiger.

From that day forward, his power was broken over my life forever.

57

CHURCH BOY

"Not that I was a smoker or drinker, I never did any of that, but I felt that my life was changed...I was no longer a 'temple boy,' I was a 'church boy.'" — Rindy

FOUR DAYS LATER

"Y ou've betrayed your family."

The words were like a slap to my face. I squatted in the dirt, looking up at Khan. I glanced at Mteay and Vuthy, who were the only other people present.

I had just returned from the Christian church, as Samang and I had been talking to Pastor Akara. He had read many of Jesus's words to us from a book he kept in his pocket, which he called "the Bible." One sentence, he uttered, had occupied every corner of my mind since.

"Are not five sparrows sold for two pennies? And not one of them is forgotten before God. Why, even the hairs of your head are all numbered. Fear not; you are of more value than many sparrows."

The thought had been ridiculous and clashed with my understanding of all the gods I had ever known. The idea that I was known not by just a god, but the only God, didn't seem possible. I chewed on the words slowly, savoring the sweetness but unable to swallow them. I had chewed on them all the way back to my part of the camp. When I found my family and told them I had become a follower of Jesus, Khan had not been pleased.

"Are you even listening to me, you fool?" Khan growled, the insults dribbling out of his mouth. "You have betrayed our tradition and our religion." The odor of incense mingled with the sweat evaporating from his body filled my nostrils. "I just got back from the temple, but I will return to ask the spirits to forgive your treachery. You're risking everything. Don't you want us to have the good fortune of being able to get out of this camp?" He stalked away, leaving his words to cling to me like mud.

I looked at Mteay, who sat thin and quiet on the bamboo communal bed. Her look of disappointment hurt worse than Khan's angry words.

"Mteay?" I whispered, walking over to sit next to her crumbled frame. "Mteay."

She looked up at me with eyes full of questions.

"Is Buddhism not good enough for you anymore?" she asked, her breath quivering.

"It never really was." My words come out softly and gently, so as not to hurt her. "I lost whatever faith I had in Buddhism long ago." I paused, reflecting. "Because of all that has happened to me. Because of all that has happened to us.

"What was so bad you turned your back on it?"

"When Chidaun put me in the temple, I was hit bad..." I sputtered into an uncertain silence, heat flooding my face with the old, unspoken memory. Her eyes questioned mine, but she never opened her mouth. Instead, her neck hung low, making her shoulder blades stick into the air. My words sat heavy on her, squishing her to the ground. She slowly stood and shuffled after Khan to the Buddhist temple, leaving Vuthy and me alone.

I looked into his eyes, seeing the questions there. I didn't know how to answer them, I only had this feeling inside my chest that I didn't have the words for. I stared into the sky, swirling in windswept clouds. Silently, I prayed what Pastor Akara had told me to whenever I didn't have the right words.

Jesus, help me.

"Vuthy, I've found the One who wanted us. The One who thought we..." I paused looking to the sky again for the words. "I found the Father we've always wanted—One who has never left us and promised to never leave us."

Vuthy's head shot up from the place in the dirt he had been absently scribbling at with a stick.

"What do you mean, Rindy? You're talking nonsense."

I looked at the sky again, searching for the way to tell him, make him understand.

"Do you remember those stories I told you about Jesus, coming in the clouds?"

Vuthy nodded.

"It wasn't just a child's story. It was true, but I didn't know how true until now. Jesus really did come from the clouds from His Father, to introduce us to Him. He's been watching us this whole time, just hoping we'll know Him and how much He loves us."

Vuthy's eyes narrowed in confusion.

"God sees us, Vuthy. I heard some of His words in a book today, and when I heard them, my heart beat so quickly, like they were just meant for you and me. I knew the words were true. I don't really know why or even how, but I know it's true—"

"What's true, Rindy?" Vuthy exhaled the words, frustrated.

"That He loved us even when we were worthless kids. That He wanted us when Aupouk and Mteay didn't. That He loved us, before we even knew He existed."

Vuthy stared into my eyes, and for a moment, I remembered being eight again. Vuthy was six, and he was crying. I heard the words I was never meant to hear:

"I don't need him.

I don't want him.

I have no use for him!"

They were the exchanged words of Mteay and Aupouk as they volleyed them back and forth at each other until my worthlessness was stamped on my eight-year-old mind. The words had buzzed around my head and landed on me, tipped with the poison of rejection. They had borne their way into my heart. I had always felt the sting of them, buried just beneath the skin; too deep to dig out but shallow enough to always feel. They had long since festered and had eventually calloused into an inseparable part of me. There, sitting next to my unsuspecting little brother, the words of Jesus slid deeper, past my brain and into my skin, burning into that calloused place.

"You are not forgotten.

You are intimately known.

You are of immense worth."

These words reverberated in my chest until they seeped into my whole body, flowing through me, mixing with my blood cells. For the entirety of my life, I had been worthless, but at that moment, the God above every other called me something different. It was a new thought, a completely new way of seeing myself. The lump under my skin smoothed, and the old fester stopped throbbing.

I put my hand on Vuthy's back. I wanted him to know *this* too. I wanted to help him and make him see what I saw, but I didn't know how.

"Following Jesus makes everything different," I whispered, barely seeing him through the tears blurring my vision. "I follow Him because He knows me. Giving my life to Jesus is not a risk at all. I've gained everything."

Surprised to hear Vuthy speaking, my eyes refocused on him. "Rindy, I want it too. I want to know this Jesus."

Vuthy and I and hundreds of others, followed Pastor Akara down to the water to be baptized. He said baptism was something Jesus had instructed us to do, so we could think back on an event, on a day when our old selves died and our new lives were resurrected. The only significant source of water in the camp was a tilapia pond, which supplied us with fish. It was closely guarded, but somehow Pastor Akrara had gotten permission. As we walked up close to it, I could see the water alive with the movement of thousands of fish.

"Are you sure you want to follow Jesus?" Pastor Akara asked me as we waded waist-deep into the water, the swimming fish bumping into our legs. "It won't be easy."

I nodded. I didn't know entirely what it meant, but I knew for sure that I wanted to find out. The murky, warm water enveloped my face. It smelled of fish being baked beneath the hot, Cambodian sun. When I emerged, the foul water left my skin streaked and feeling dirtier than before, but I didn't care. Something inside of me felt washed clean.

58

PERSECUTION

"...but I did not hate him like I did before." — Rindy

MAY 1981

The endless soccer game continued, they still handed out food portions, but life was entirely different for me. The world seemed opened to me for the first time, and I found a purpose for being inside the woven walls of the camp. I had been viewing the world as something outside the camp, but I realized how much was occurring within the rolls of barbed wire. With others from my church, Vuthy and I talked to anyone who would listen about Jesus.

Many ignored our words or scoffed at us, but others surrendered their lives to Him after a mere conversation. The hardship of the years under the Khmer Rouge had tilled up the beliefs that had been entrenched in Cambodian soil for generations. The belief that good karma and merit would save us had disintegrated like plastic in a raging fire as we had watched thousands of innocent people die. The belief in karma was broken for many, and they were willing to accept the gift of grace.

One day when I returned to our hut, I found Mteay crying as she stood waiting. Had she been waiting for me?

"Rindy, I've talked to Pastor Akara. I've become a Christian."

She came to me and held me to her chest, her tears falling on my shirt. "You were right. I can't describe this feeling—" she clutched at her chest. "I don't understand how I've lived my life this long while being so blind to, to" —her eyes searched mine—"to what it means to truly live."

With this victory for my mteay, came the ever-increasing opposition from Khan and Kiry too. They still viewed each other as political enemies until they both found themselves on the same side of hating me. Both were equally enraged at what I was doing to the family. I avoided them as much as I could. I felt guilty about this, but I didn't want to talk to them about Jesus. Not yet.

One day, I rounded the corner and was caught.

"You can't be a Christian." Kiry seethed. He stopped rolling cigarettes and stalked toward me. He had been smoking cigarettes and chewing betel relentlessly since entering the camp, but the supplies seemed to be disintegrating and so was his patience. "It's the western indoctrination and religious corruption."

I crouched in the shade of our family hut. I had just returned from church but was in no mood to hear his opinions. The Khmer Rouge propaganda poured from his mouth like foul water. It had been forced down his throat so often that he still believed it. He was a haunted shell of a man. His eyes were always cutting from side to side, and he acted like someone was always watching him, monitoring his every move. His voice had effectively adopted a tone of superiority, and he carried an unspoken command of authority wherever he went. Yet I could see through the haunted shell of a man to the quivering, small boy who stalked off through the rice paddies to join in a fight he was not prepared to endure. How differently it all looked now, how much death, destruction and desolation lay on the opposite side of that youthful ambition.

"You were born a Buddhist and a Cambodian and that is how you will die," he shouted.

"You're destroying this family," Khan added as he rounded the corner into view, no doubt returning from the temple and the spirits he worshiped.

"Your Mteay just told me she is planning on attending church with you this Sunday. She says she has become a Christian as well."

I gulped. I had wondered how long Mteay would wait before telling her husband. I knew he wouldn't take it well. I was so happy to see the newfound joy in Mteay's eyes that it helped subdue the fear.

"I've warned you and warned you," Khan growled, walking ever closer. "I've had enough." Uneasiness and sweat crept down my spine, and I stood up from my crouched position and braced myself, backing into the bamboo wall. I knew what was coming. Why had I come back just now?

"Khan, if you would just come with us, you would see—" Khan's hand landed a blow on the side of my head. My world spun, my ears rang, and dust rose into my nostrils. His fist plowed into my cheek next and then my eye, before I fell into the dust, sputtering out blood. Through the haze, I saw Kiry's boot come for my face, so I shielded my head and took the blows.

When they were finished, I got up and stumbled back to the church to find Pastor Akara.

"Rindy, what's happened to you?"

I waded through a small group of people talking at the church's entrance.

"Khan—my mother's husband—and my older brother beat me up." I slumped onto the ground, wiping my nose on the end of my shorts. "They hate that I'm a Christian. They say I'm destroying my family and our heritage."

"I see." Pastor Akara came and sat beside me, silent for what felt like a long time.

"I told you it wouldn't be easy." I looked up, Pastor Akara appearing fuzzy through my puffy eyes. "This is that 'not easy' part. It's called persecution, and we as believers are instructed in the Bible to expect it. It's a sure promise."

"But they're wrong. They're so wrong about everything!"

"They are, but we all are before we learn the truth."

"They'll never learn, I can promise you that. They will be the last ones to become Christians—if the whole world follows Jesus, I bet they still won't."

"Rindy, I need to ask you a question, and I need you to answer honestly."

I looked down at my hands, afraid of what might be coming.

"Do you want them to become a Christian?"

I scratched at an old scab on my arm, avoiding his eyes. I sighed.

"No, I really don't want them to become Christians. Being a believer means something special to Mteay, Vuthy and me. I don't want them to ruin it. They're such horrible men, I haven't even told you or anyone, who Kiry—"

"Rindy, this hatred and unforgiveness is only hurting you. Not them. You're allowing their sin to crawl inside you and fester. Don't allow it a place to stay."

I pushed myself from the ground and left.

Why had I expected him to understand? He probably hadn't ever been beaten up by anyone in his life. I seethed and vented for hours, but as the sun began to sink behind the trees, my anger cooled and something new began to bubble through my veins in response to Pastor Akara's words. It wasn't as solid, or as easy to hold in my hand as hatred and anger were, but it flowed around and through me. It was like dropping a rock to run my hand through water instead. The words of Mr. Thach came back to me like that water, "Kum is like a sickness that gets into your heart. As it grows, it takes over a person with plans to destroy the person who caused them pain. Revenge. Bitterness. Hatred. Murder. Kum hurts you worse though. It'll eat away at you until you become sick with it. It's a sickness that runs rampant through the streets of Cambodia, like it's part of her soul."

Mr. Thach had prayed for me and that my heart would be free from the weight of Kum—that Jesus would set me free from it. Did he know it would take nearly twelve years for it to become a reality? I watched the sun explode on the horizon and something shifted in my chest. I wanted to forgive or at least begin.

I didn't want to return to our communal sleeping spot because Khan and Kiry would be there, probably drinking around the fire again, and I wasn't ready to face them. With a lowered head, I shuffled back to the church. Pastor Akara was just finishing a Bible study with a new group of people when I approached.

"I'm glad you're back. That didn't take long." He smiled.

"Me too. I know you're right. I was just so mad. I still am."

"I know you are. You'll deal with that feeling the rest of your life, but *how* you deal with it makes all the difference."

I nodded. I knew he was talking about forgiveness.

"Forgiveness is a serious issue. Very serious in fact. Jesus says that if we don't forgive, then we won't be forgiven. Have you been forgiven, Rindy?"

I nodded my head.

"I'm not saying you must be perfect at it now or even begin tonight. The Lord knows forgiveness is still hard for me. I'm just saying, let God work in your heart. Let Him consume any darkness that lingers."

"No, I'm ready tonight. I want to forgive tonight. Or at least start."

Pastor Akara smiled, his weary face softening.

I closed my eyes, still not sure why, but I found comfort in it. For the first time, I prayed for Khan and Kiry and asked God to reveal the truth to them.

"Did you truly mean the words you just prayed?"

I looked up, sheepishly.

"It's okay, pray every day until you do mean them, soon you will. Soon you'll truly desire that they would come to know the saving power and forgiveness of Jesus."

I nodded, deciding to do it regardless of the outcome.

"Can I sleep here tonight? I don't want to get beat up again."

Pastor Akara nodded, retreating to his own section of the camp to bring me back a blanket. As I watched him leave to join his wife and children, I prayed another prayer, one that I truly meant.

"God, make me like him one day."

59

KHAN'S ESCAPE

"He was afraid that if he became a Christian the spirits would hurt him." — Rindy

SEPTEMBER 1981

Lying still on the bamboo slats, I listened to Mteay and Khan talking by the fire as they had many nights before. They didn't see me, lying in the shadows while everyone else slept. Their words crackled too, as emotion gripped them.

"You became a Christian because you thought it would help you to get an education and get out of here," Khan scoffed, his words sizzling. "You can't deny it. You told me the advantages yourself."

Mteay was silent for a moment. "That's what I thought before I understood." Mteay's words were like cool water on his fire.

"And what don't I understand?" Khan asked, his tone mocking. "This Jesus is the son of a God and is still alive today, did I get it right?"

Ever since I had become a Christian, I had watched Khan cage himself in like an animal, biting at the hands of his family members who tried to reach him through the iron doors he hid behind. I was accustomed to his constant attacks and jabs because he had always been like that. After becoming a Christian, I was the one who changed, though. So had Vuthy, Mteay and even Ly and Sotha, who had also become Christians. When Khan and Kiry were off trying to locate cigarettes or alcohol, we had started praying for them, always careful they didn't catch us at it. I had even come to mean every word I prayed. When confronted with Khan's outbursts, Mteay never recoiled into timidity like she always had either. When Khan got angry and lashed out, she remained quiet, but not cowering. This both intrigued Khan and angered him.

"I'm ashamed of the way you have thrown away everything you've ever known to chase after this God." He continued, reiterating his point for the hundredth time. But somehow, his words didn't hold the typical amount of passion and spite. He sat by the fire limply, as if Mteay wasn't the only one he was trying to convince.

"He isn't a god, He is the God, and that makes all the difference." Mteay's words were barely audible over the sound of the fire cracking and popping. I smiled to myself. I knew the truth of her words. They had worked their way into my heart and sat there glowing and diminishing every other thing I thought to be true. I rolled over on my side to look at them, wishing I could offer help. I began to pray.

"How do you know He's the only one?" Khan asked, his voice strangled and oddly quiet.

"Because every other god is not like Him," Mteay quickly retorted, as if she couldn't swallow the words burning on her tongue. "He is compassionate, slow to anger, loves the poor and the weak—" her voice trailed off into the black sky like smoke.

"He knows me," Mteay added, her voice throbbing. "It's the strangest thing, but I know He knows everything about me. When I hear the words He spoke, it's like they peel back my skin and look into me." Her words danced in the air like fire, I could almost see them and taste them on my tongue. I braced myself, waiting for the curse—waiting for the slap of words Khan always hurled. But none came.

In the orange light, Khan hung his head between his legs, hands hanging uselessly over his knees. In his silence, I knew a war had taken over. It curled into every fiber of him and screamed into every crevice of his brain. The spirits he had welcomed in so eagerly held him captive, whispering to him at every turn—keeping him paranoid by fear.

Khan had practiced *neak ta* for as long as I could remember, always adding more rituals or new spirits to this black magic. He hung these superstitions like a bulky necklace around his throat, but they had been getting tighter and tighter with time. I had never met a man so burdened by living. Every decision he made and every direction he took was wrapped in ritual. He would visit the Buddhist temple every Sunday, mixing its beliefs with neak ta like a boiling, rancid soup. Buddhism was a black hole that married seamlessly with every spirit and every superstition known to man. But when Khan left the temple, he was more irritable and abusive than when he had entered, his cloudy eyes searching the shadows and his lips muttering some chant. The longer he lived, the more he embodied this darkness—the darkness I had sensed when I first met him. Since then, I had felt it a hundred times, surging out of him as he cursed or beat me.

As I watched him through the orange light, wrapped in shadows, I felt the strangest sensation for him. It wasn't pity and it wasn't empathy, it was something else entirely. It came from a place inside myself that I had never explored before—a facet of my being that was entirely new, entirely foreign. The sensation made me want to run to him, look him in the eyes and tell him I wanted him to know how it felt to be whole. To be free from the spirits that clawed into his flesh and bit into his heart at each step. The sensation lodged in my throat, making tears come to my unsuspecting eyes. I prayed harder.

"I'm—I'm afraid," Khan whispered the words, not lifting his head. "I'm afraid that if I give it all up, I will be killed." His voice was almost inaudible, I tried to scoot closer to hear. Reaching inside his loose shirt, he gripped the necklace I had never seen him take off. He believed it protected him, because it had been given to him by a witch doctor from Phnom Sampov.

"If I follow Jesus"—agony gripped his words—"I know the spirits will hunt me."

"Jesus is more powerful!" Mteay's voice was no longer quiet. Her words extended like a strong hand through the darkness. I could see him staring at them, wrestling with the desire to reach out, reach through.

"All right," he whispered the words quickly. "I want to follow Jesus too."

Hidden in the darkness, I laid as stiffly as the bamboo slats. My heart pounded with the realization of what Khan had just said, my mouth gaping in shock. I had wanted to hear him say the words—we had even been praying for those words—but when he said them, I couldn't believe he had.

"Say it again." Mteay's voice came unwavering.

"I want to follow Jesus from now on." Khan's voice grew louder as he spoke, revolting against the fear waging war within him. "He is the only God, the God above any other." With shaking fingers, he reached behind his neck and pulled the necklace from his throat, tossing it into the fire.

"Jesus, please protect me." He raised his head, his black eyes reflecting the light. Mteay reached out her hand and clasped his. Together they stared into the flames, warding off fear.

I rolled to my back, staring at the ceiling, believing God could, indeed, do anything He wanted to.

60

THE WINDOW

"I felt like the world had opened the door for me. I could see a better picture." — Rindy

OCTOBER 1981

As my hunger for the Bible grew—the book Pastor Akara read to us—my hunger for knowledge grew with it. I looked on with curiosity as the Bible was read, digesting every word, fascinated by the things I heard. I had barely learned to read Khmer, as Mteay had taken me from the school near the temple when I was young, but each day I continued to practice and learn, expanding what I could read. A school in the camp taught basic Khmer reading and writing, but I didn't want to just master Khmer, I wanted to learn English. I heard rumors of a class in the west end of the camp that taught English, and I was drawn to it, like a bug to a flame. The teacher was said to be important, being a graduate from an amazing place called "Oxford," but the class was only for those who had completed their formal education. Because I had not, I couldn't pass the entrance test. I was discouraged, but I wouldn't give up. Not after I'd tried everything.

On the day when classes were rumored to begin, I snuck up to the edge of the one room hut. I listened to the strange, muffled sounds coming through the thatch walls of the hut where the class was taking place. I sat in the dirt beneath the window, taking it in, chewing on the sounds of the words. I had no idea what they meant or what the words looked like, so I slid up the wall to look through the window. I was captivated as this "Oxford professor" wrote squiggles on a big board hanging on the wall behind him. Fearing that I would get caught, I only allowed myself glances through the duration of the class. I sat there for hours, learning what words I could and reworking them in the sifted dirt between my feet.

I continued to sneak up to the window for several weeks to learn what I could until one day, I found it closed. A thin board was tacked against the shabby building, blocking my view completely. The mosquitos were terrible, so I assumed it was to try to keep them out. I stared at the blocked window for a while, discouraged by the setback. Not willing to give up, I inspected the walls of the building. They were thin and thatched with palm leaves, so I poked through the wall to make a hole just big enough for me to see through.

Although I was still able to learn, the Oxford professor covered everything from the basics of English to advanced writing. It was hard to grasp the difficult material. The English language was like a stolen motorcycle—I didn't understand how it worked or how to make it take me where I wanted to go.

Soon, I heard of another class that taught English, and I was the first to scribble my name on the crisp, sign-up sheet. With the few words and phrases I had mastered, I shuffled into the classroom. It was like the others—a one room hut, and I took my seat on a rickety bench near the front. A chalkboard was tacked to the wall behind a desk, with numbers and English letters meshed together. It was odd, and I had only learned to read some of the letters so far. Soon the room filled with others, mostly older than me. A middle-aged man entered, with light colored skin, and strode to the front of the class.

"Welcome to Introduction to Engineering," the white man said, his English trickling from his mouth seamlessly.

Engineering class? I had thought it was an English class. I replayed the words in my mind, stumbling over each one awkwardly. I looked around, heat rising into my face, hoping no one would notice. I slumped in my seat, trying to disappear into the floor.

"An extensive understanding of mathematics is required for this class," the teacher continued, glancing over the faces before him. Remaining calm, I nodded and smiled along with the rest of them, hoping my charade would be successful. "This class will be offered in English and French." I swallowed. A ball of saliva tried to choke me on its way down, but I held it in so as not to draw attention to myself. I didn't want to be noticed. I had one job, and that was to learn, if I could stay in the class without my lack of education being discovered.

That day, when I walked back to my section of the camp, I grappled with an especially difficult word I had heard him say, "Geometry." I kept repeating it to myself, struggling over each syllable.

"How's it going?" Looking up I saw one of the students from class who seemed to have all the answers. "You can call me Tommy."

"Good." I answered, trying to make my English sound as effortless as his was, but knowing I failed terribly. "Rindy."

"That's great, Rindy." He walked in stride with me. The sun beat on my back and my palms soaked the piece of paper I carried with the few things I had managed to scribble on it. I hoped he would say something else, so I wasn't forced to try starting a conversation with my helpless English.

"I'm going to a friend's house, if you're interested in joining." He paused to look at me. "We read the Bible together, and we'd be happy to help you with English."

I nearly stumbled in excitement. He was a Christian?

I nodded, trying not to appear too eager.

We wove through the section of the camp belonging to those who had survived the Khmer Rouge who were of Chinese descent, a section I had never visited. It was hard to shake ourselves free from the world the Khmer Rouge had erected for us, but I wanted to start, especially if they were Christians too.

Nearly every day after class for the next six months, I stole through the Chinese section of the camp to join Tommy and his friends. After basic mathematics, they taught me English from a King James Bible that we huddled around, sitting on the communal bamboo beds. Soon we invited others to join our Bible studies, and we grew into a large group of young people. I started spending more time with these Chinese-Khmer Christians than I did with people who looked just like me, and I soon forgot there was ever a difference to begin with.

My English improved quickly, as well as my understanding of the Bible. But I was ever eager for more, the two being intertwined together, one enriching the other.

61
BREAKING SILENCE

"I thought my life was hard, but it was nothing compared to theirs." — Rindy

APRIL 1982

Tommy and I watched as a bus carried more of our fellow Christians to new lives in new countries. Some of my closest friends, including Samang, were among them, on their way to the place whose existence I questioned: America. Emotion choked me, but so did joy. It was unlikely that I would ever see any of them again. Khao-I-Dang camp was a mere stop, a world between worlds, where we waited, prisoners of expectation.

Many people in the camp were attempting to gain visas to travel to new countries, but only a select few were granted. The Chinese Visas were more likely to be approved because of the targeted persecution they experienced under the Khmer Rouge regime. This granted them asylum in other countries quickly. It was the same for the Vietnamese and the Cham in the camp.

For the average Khmer like me, it was more difficult to be allowed access out of the country. Only a few select government workers, teachers, or high-ranking Lon Nol soldiers were typically allowed visas. Life had significantly improved for me in the camp, but regardless of my newfound internal freedom, my life was still lived within the confines of the fence. As I watched my friends disappear through the rings of barbed wire, I wondered if I would ever step foot on the other side, as free as I felt on the inside.

"Will you help pastor your fellow believers?" Tommy asked, turning to look at me. I met his gaze, surprised. After several months of meeting in various homes in the Chinese section of the camp, we had gained the building materials to construct a small church. Tommy had even gained permission to travel outside the camp and preach in Bangkok. Many people in the camp wanted to learn or improve their understanding of English and would attend any occasion where it was spoken. So, Tommy began giving sermons in English, and I translated them into Khmer. We both wanted to spread the gospel message any way we could. We also began giving classes in basic English to anyone interested. But when Tommy traveled to Bangkok to preach, he left a gaping hole, which we all felt in his absence as the Sunday lessons lapped into silence.

"Your English has improved remarkably." He smiled at the look of shock on my face. "I can see how much you love God and the people of our church."

"I'm Khmer." I shrugged sheepishly. "Do you think the other Chinese Christians will accept me?"

"I guess we'll find out." The creases around his eyes deepened as he smiled.

Three weeks later, while Tommy was away in Bangkok, I stood alone at the front of a hundred or so people. Three Khmer women sang, *Amazing Grace.* One of them was Ly, who had discovered that she loved to sing. Singing had become her release and worship, and I had once come upon her alone as she sat with tears streaming down her face as she sang wordless melodies I had never heard before. I glanced over and smiled at her; she was becoming whole again. We all were.

My eyes scanned over those attendants who had begun from Tommy's Bible study. For the first time, I was the one speaking—not translating. I felt out of place, but I found comfort in familiar faces. Mteay was there and she held Selay on her lap beside Sotha and even Khan. Even Pastor Akara was there, grinning from ear to ear. I knew Kiry would not be there. He hated me more than ever before and believed I had turned everyone against him. The last time I had seen him, he had been in an alcohol induced stupor that lasted for days.

My eyes refocused on Mteay's, a feeling tightened in my chest as I saw them gleaming with pride. We had had many conversations since she had become a Christian and had wept her regret over our childhood. I had forgiven her, truly. Khan in contrast, looked tortured. He was trying to stop drinking alcohol, but it was taking everything he had not to bolt out of the church and find a smuggler. He was still having bouts of rage, but unlike the other times, he was repentant afterwards. I pulled my eyes from them, silently praying.

Give me the words to say to them, Jesus.

The song came to an end, and I stood from my small stool, wiping my hands on my new khaki-colored pants that Tommy had brought from Bangkok. I cleared my throat.

"Tommy said I should talk about something God has taught me," I began, my voice cracking to a slow start. "He said our testimonies of God are like a living book." I paused, nervousness choking me.

"Today, I want to tell you about my story." I was ashamed of the simplicity of my words. Stumbling through my message, I told the journey of my life through my childhood to the current time. I told them of the weight I had carried all those years, the weight of rejection, shame and hate. How I ran away just before my mets were killed, and how I carried the guilt of their deaths. As I spoke, my memories moved in front of me, like a grotesque charade, until I came to the camp and found freedom in Jesus. I paused, uncertain what to say next.

"For generations, we as Khmer have believed that we gain good karma by not talking about all the wrong that has been done to us and the wrong we have done. That it will somehow disappear if we swallow it. I did this. I thought my shame would disappear if I didn't tell anyone about it, but I can tell you, it grew instead." I paused, looking out over the crowd, my heart swelling with compassion for them before I continued.

"Jesus tells of a different way to handle our sin and the sin done against us. He tells us we should confess it to each other—not keep it inside." I paused, searching the small paper I held, my sweat making marks on the thin page. "I held onto hate for so long that on the inside I was no different from the Khmer Rouge or the Vietnamese who were my biggest enemies. I didn't just hate others, I hated myself the most for being alive when so many had died in my place. When I heard about the Gospel and how Jesus wanted to set me free from my sin and the sin that was done to me, I thought it was impossible. But the more I ponder His words and allow His spirit to work in my heart, what I thought was impossible is becoming—" I stopped trying to find the word. "It's becoming *real* in me. I no longer hate myself and think that what happened when I escaped from the trench was my fault. I am not ashamed to live the life God has given me, and I must accept that He was the one who spared my life. I still sometimes don't feel worthy of it, but I must trust that He knows what He is doing."

I thought for a moment over the years we had just lived through, looking into the faces of those who had survived in body, but were dying in soul. I paused before I spoke again.

"I don't understand why so many died in such horrible and brutal ways, but I do not for a second believe that it was God's plan. It was Satan's plan.

He wants to create hell anywhere we let him. We had a glimpse into his hell while living in Cambodia these past years. I pray it makes us realize we never want to spend eternity there. We've been given a chance to know God before it's too late. Satan will not win if we expose the darkness to the light. Jesus is the only reason I no longer carry the weight of sin. Because He was the only one to tell me how to be free from it. He said, 'my burden is easy, and my yoke is light,' and we have an invitation to accept His words. His words are true because I have experienced how very real they are."

I paused, hesitant about what I needed to say next. I swallowed. "If you feel like you have a burden, a hidden sin or a sin that has been done against you, I invite you to come up here. I want to give you an opportunity to confess it, and I want to pray with you. Pray that God would set you free from whatever it is. I know He wants to."

As I spoke, I watched the faces of those gazing back at me. Some softened and others hardened at my words. A few even got up and walked out. My eyes landed on two of my closest friends who I had met through Tommy, a brother and sister, who were the sole survivors in their family. The girl's eyes were a penetrating black, matching the hair framing her face. I winced away from her gaze because I knew her story: a story I wished I hadn't heard. A story of soldiers who had raped her on the border of Thailand, just before reaching the camp, after enduring months of starvation, sickness and death by the hands of the Khmer Rouge. I knew the weight she carried was heavy—heavier than mine had been. Tears blurred her eyes, but she squeezed a thin smile across her face. Forgiveness had already been working inside her.

Thank you, Jesus, for helping us forgive the unforgivable. My heart throbbed the prayer, unable to speak the words.

When I looked up, a man stood before me, his eyes shifting hesitantly. He had a tortured look on his face, but he began to speak despite his apparent apprehension.

"My family was Chinese descent, living in Cambodia." A calloused scar bobbed on his Adam's apple as he talked. "I lived with my wife and three daughters near Seim Reap. I was a fisherman and used to come home every evening to my family, bringing the fish for my wife to sell at market." His voice choked. "One evening, men in black pajamas knocked on the door." The creases in his face filled with tears. "They prodded me out of the house with their guns and bound my hands. My wife screamed after me, crying as she held onto our daughters. They led me into the darkness of the jungle, tied my body with a rope from my neck to my ankles and beat me with the butts of their guns and ox whips until everything went black." Turning his head, he revealed a bald spot on the back of his skull where the hair hadn't grown back, the flesh scarred and uneven.

"I thought I had died." He looked up, memories swimming in his eyes. "When I woke up, I couldn't feel my body at all. I could hardly move, but they had beaten the ropes that bound me into shreds, so I crawled my way back to my hut. When I got there, I found my family—" His voice lowered to a whisper. "It had been many days and the smell—" He couldn't continue.

After a few moments his tear-filled eyes met mine. "I haven't spoken of them all this time. I need Jesus to help me bear this. I feel hatred raging in me every second of every day. I can't bear it alone anymore."

I understood that hatred all too well. Did it make any difference who it was directed at? Hatred scorched everything in its wake like a consuming fire. I so desperately wanted this man to experience freedom from it as I had. I led him in a prayer of surrender to Jesus and then continued to pray over his memories and his future. That God would bring life from the deaths this man carried in his very bones. Only God could heal his anguish. I knew He had just begun the journey, but a beginning is a beginning, and that thought comforted me as I watched him walk away.

After praying with several others and hearing their stories and their sin, I sat on the small platform, praying that God would wash my memory clean. A rustling at the back of the wall-less hut, which I thought was vacant, caught my attention.

I looked up, alarmed. I had heard that some gangs in the camp had been formed and were beating up Christians for a bit of fun. But Kiry emerged from the shadows. I couldn't relax yet.

"I heard your talk from outside." Kiry stood, as if not knowing what to do next, his words slurring.

I nodded, encouraging him to go on.

"You know nothing of what it means to hate yourself." He pounded his chest. "You didn't kill innocent people like I did. Like I was forced to—" he mumbled incoherently for a moment. "But I had no choice, no choice. I thought I should like killing as the others did, like committing the final act on a life, but I didn't—" he muttered to himself again, his eyes roving the room. Then he looked up. "No one knows I was Khmer Rouge here except my family. They just think I'm another victim, but I know the truth. I know. I will never escape it."

"Some of us can never be forgiven." With that he staggered away.

I sat in the darkness for a long time, wrestling.

"God, I'm not sure I'm ready to forgive yet, not them. Especially not the ones who aren't even tortured by their horrible sins as Kiry is. The ones who killed Chivy."

The words I had just spoken to those gathered in the church came like sunrise over my soul.

My burden is light, and my yoke is easy.

It was time to let another burden go, by choosing to forgive even them.

For the first time, I prayed for every Khmer Rouge soldier I could remember. Each one by name if I knew them, and for the rest, I described them to God in detail. He knew them, I know He did, but I needed to remember them. I needed to be cleansed, and that didn't mean avoiding. That meant digging into the dirt of my memory, pulling each one out so I could be free. I prayed that they would find forgiveness and peace in Jesus. I prayed for Kiry and the guilt and self-hatred he carried. I prayed for the ones who weren't sorry for what they had done. Theirs was the worst prison of all. I prayed for every black-clad soldier, whose faces were burned into my memory like an indelible mark only God could wash away. I continued to pray that prayer over the following days until it became easier and easier. Until the hatred gave way to light.

62

THE APPLICATION

"For the first time, I felt like something was happening in my life." — Rindy

JUNE 1982

"Rindy Nong." The sound of my name seemed hollow next to all the others. I stepped forward, trying not to clench my fists in nervousness.

"Where did you learn English?" The question was asked by an American. His eyes were a startling blue. His tone was even and pointed.

"I learned in Khao-I-Dang refugee camp," I responded, measuring each word carefully before releasing it into the cool, stale air of the little white room.

In a progression toward a visa, my family and I had moved from Khao-I-Dang refugee camp to a visa processing camp, and then a transit camp, where we were awaiting resettlement. But I didn't just want to resettle, I wanted a job. All the waiting and visa applications had led me here, standing before a stern American, as I vied for the most coveted job that a refugee could obtain.

"How did you learn English?" he asked, his eyes not leaving mine.

"There was a man who graduated from Oxford who held a class for those with formal education," I responded, meeting his gaze, determined to tell the whole truth. "I listened to him teach from outside the window and then through a hole in the thatch wall. It was hard to learn this way. Then I met a Chinese man who taught me to read and speak English from the King James Bible. After a while, I began translating from English into Khmer for him during our church services." I gulped. The utter idea of me applying for this job was absurd. My story was met with silence. Again.

I had been standing in the room for what felt like the better part of an hour, recounting the major parts of my life. I had wanted to lie, to gloss over the portions I wished had never happened, but I could not. If I had any chance at getting this job, it would be an act of God and not on my abilities. So, I answered each question as simply and honestly as I could.

Glancing at the window, I wondered if the scores of other applicants who crowded outside were as nervous as I was. They probably weren't because nearly everyone was much more qualified than me. I was confident of that. Yet here I was, applying for a job that seemed laughable: Translator for the U.S. Embassy.

After they finished questioning me, I was permitted to leave. My agitated nerves made it hard to resume normal camp life, so I loitered outside the building used to conduct official interviews. Since being in the transit camp, I had been through three interviews: one with the United Nations, one with the State department and one with the department of immigration. Each one had been terrifying, as the officials collaborated with each member of my family, comparing stories to ensure we were telling the truth. Many refugees who sought visas lied about their histories in hopes of appearing to be more appealing candidates. Lon Nol soldiers' visas were typically approved because they were a target group for the Khmer Rouge regime, as nearly every soldier of the opposing army who was discovered was put to death. I now understood why Khan had burned his Lon Nol uniform the day the Khmer Rouge evacuated the city. If he hadn't, our fate may have ended in death. Now in the camp, the identity he had kept hidden for the years of Khmer Rouge domination became a point of prestige.

A few weeks after entering the transit camp, I heard that the Embassy was hiring refugees who could be translators for those who were seeking visas. It was a job opportunity unlike any other, as it took not only exceptional interpreting skills, but also skills of discernment. A translator was left to determine the authenticity of the stories being told, while helping the U.S. Embassy sniff out potential lies. As I dropped my application in the basket, I knew I was the most unlikely person to be chosen, but I submitted it anyway.

"They're about to announce the names," another applicant whispered excitedly. I assembled with the rest of the hodgepodge group of hopefuls. There were eighty in all. Cringing, my gaze brushed those of the Oxford man. I had unknowingly entered this competition against him. I hoped he didn't recognize me as the boy who had leached off his class. My face flushed as embarrassment climbed up the collar of my nicest shirt, which had been yellowed by sweat and the sun.

What am I doing here? I wondered. The apparent absurdity staring me in the face for what felt like the thousandth time that day. I held my breath as a secretary emerged from the small structure to stop outside, facing the crowd. She wobbled slightly in her pointed, high-heeled shoes, as the ground wasn't level. Squinting in the glare of the sun, she studied a small piece of paper.

"On behalf of the U.S. Embassy, I would like to thank each of you for applying for the translator's position." Her words droned mechanically. "We are very pleased with the turn out." She paused.

I didn't breathe.

"We are only in need of two of the present applicants at this time, a—" She paused again, studying the names on the list. "Khean Mock —" She looked up as if to question the pronunciation. I could feel my stomach clench around the soup I had eaten for lunch. Dread and hope sloshed around, each vying for the upper hand.

"And a Rindy Nong."

Unmoving, I stood with my mouth gaping slightly. Feeling dizzy, my mind sluggishly moved over what I was seeing and hearing. The floral blouse of the secretary, the dusty ground, the several pairs of eyes staring at me, chased away the nagging impossibility that I was the one called. I could feel their eyes on me, poking holes into me with their gazes. Perhaps it was admiration or disappointment that the onlookers wore; perhaps it was envy, but it didn't matter. I was the one called.

I was the one chosen, from amongst the eighty.

With each step I took toward the building, memories rolled before me. Memories of my childhood in the jungle, of Aupouk who didn't want me, of Mteay who didn't want me, of Khan who didn't want me. Yet all that had been redeemed, miraculously. They were like whispers on the breeze, blown into the distance, as I followed the secretary inside.

I stood shoulder to shoulder with the other qualifier, as we stared at the secretary who sat behind her desk, gazing at us over a mountain of papers.

"Being a translator for the U.S. Embassy makes you a target," she began sternly, looking from one of us to the next.

"Your safety is at risk. If a refugee isn't permitted a visa due to your interpretation of their story, you are in harm's way. Secondly, refugees may try to bribe you, so you would fix their outcome. You have been chosen for these positions because we believe you have a good work ethic and are men of integrity, able to withstand these threats. In order to minimize risk, however, we must separate you from the camp and relocate you away from the other refugees seeking visas. Prepare to leave for Bangkok, immediately."

She handed me an official looking packet containing my work documents and my freedom.

In a daze, I climbed onto a bus once again and sat next to a dusty window. I could still taste the hurried goodbye I had just made as I hugged each of my family members, their shocked faces mirroring my own. No one said much. Words didn't seem sufficient. Mteay's eyes spoke for everyone. They dripped like a late July sky, brimming with both pride and sorrow. Parting with Vuthy had been tough, but for the first time in my life, I had known God was watching over him and I didn't have to. He'd smiled back as I took his hand. His strong stature and good character would take him far. I was confident in this. Ly and Sotha had been tearful and so had four-year-old Selay, who'd run up and gripped my legs as I was leaving. Khan had shaken my hand solemnly. His eyes were clear, and he had escaped the grip of alcohol and had begun volunteering at the clinic in the camp. Kiry hadn't been there. He had gotten married and was still being processed in Khoa-I-Dang, due to his involvement with the Khmer Rouge. I didn't know what his fate would be, but I knew his eternity was sure. He had become a Christian at last, after the past years of praying for him. The last I had seen him, his eyes had shone with new light, free from the haunting of his past sin and shame. I continued to for him, though, and for the rest of my family as well, as I knew they were praying for me.

Out of everyone in my family, I was the only one who knew English, and it had become my ticket out. I hoped it could be their ticket out as well. I didn't know how it would be possible, but God had gotten us this far, and He could get us the rest of the way.

The bus wasn't half as crowded as it had been the day I climbed onto it in the border camp, unsure of what was next. There were a few embassy officials who had conducted the interviews, and I was thankful they didn't seem interested in asking me more questions. There were also refugees on board who had secured their visas and were being moved to other countries. Fear churned in me again, like the last time I was on a bus, but not for the same reasons. I still had an unknown future ahead of me, but I was certain neither execution nor starvation were a part of it. It was a future that wasn't cloaked in black. It was a future that didn't taste like dread. It was a future that was still unwritten. Looking out the back window of the bus, I watched as the red dirt road engulfed the rolls of barbed wire, and the walls that had trapped me for the past four years.

Getting a crick in my neck, I turned forward. The sky was cloudless, and the road stretched out in front of me for as far as I could see.

63

THE CITY

"It was a different world for me." — Rindy

LATER THAT DAY

The red, dirt road turned into one of cement, and the few lone motor-bikes gave way to hordes of tuk-tuk's and other vehicles, cramming onto the road. Buildings towered into the sky, their windows reflecting the setting sun. The ground was a patchwork of lines, arranged in a dizzying way, and I didn't know what any of it meant. People walking, driving and riding bikes swarmed everywhere at shocking speeds. The whole city was dancing a dance I had never seen before, each one knowing when to cut in and when to stop.

My eyes feasted upon it all, but my swiveling head could hardly take everything in. How could all this grandeur and advancement exist in a mere four-hour drive from war-torn Cambodia? Since the days of Sihanouk and his proclamations that Cambodia was an 'island of peace' and advanced beyond its counterparts, I had believed that Cambodia was indeed great. Instead, it had turned like a rabid dog, consuming itself in insanity. How had the world around us succeeded so greatly, when we were generations behind, despite the years of backbreaking work and lofty ideals of the

Khmer Rouge? As I looked around me, I couldn't grasp the reality I was seeing.

The bus pulled up to a tall building, and I shuffled out, along with the refugees who were on their way to new countries. The look of bewilderment on their faces told me they didn't understand the dance of the city either. Gripping a small paper bag containing a picture of my family, a few changes of clothes, a comb, and a small cup of dried bananas Mteay had snuck in between the layers, I walked into the lobby of the hotel.

I could feel the cold floor through my thin sandals, laid out in squares in front of my feet. Red fabrics draped the windows, and glass lights hung from the ceiling. A row of smiling women stood behind a tall desk, their lips painted red. I felt out of place and smaller than ever before in my malnourished, nineteen-year-old body. I looked years younger than I was, but I tried to stand up straight and appear capable for my new job.

An embassy official, who had traveled with us on the bus, greeted the women and chatted confidently, handing over the parcel containing my freedom. It had my ID with my new title stamped across the top: U.S. Embassy translator. He then handed over a large sum of Thai money in exchange for a room.

"How about some food, Rindy?" The man turned to me. "My name is Dan, by the way." His brown hair fell to his eyebrows, and he wore a flower shirt. He seemed to be perfectly at ease in all the chaos buzzing around. I nodded, trying to relax the expression of bewilderment on my face.

I followed him back out the door and fell in step beside him as he wove through the streets.

"I've been meaning to ask you, during the years the Khmer Rouge ruled your country, did you ever meet Pol Pot?"

"Pol Pot?" I wracked my memory but had never heard that name before.

"Yeah, the main man behind the Khmer Rouge. You've never heard of him?"

I shook my head. "We only knew of 'Angkar,' we never knew any names of who was in charge. At the very beginning, Norodom Sihanouk was said to be the leader, but after years, we didn't hear his voice on the radio. One man was behind it all—this Pol Pot?" The idea was shocking, but oddly comforting. A man, after all, could be defeated and driven out of power.

"Yes, apparently, Pol Pot just used Sihanouk to gain popularity and power, while Pol Pot was truly in charge. Pol Pot kept his identity and location a secret, not trusting anyone. He's even thought to be insane, but I thought maybe you'd met him or something in all your time in Cambodia. I never imagined you never knew the name of the man behind it all." Dan's face registered shock, and he shook his head as he watched his shoes, emerging and disappearing behind his big pants.

I shook my head. "Anyone who was called by 'Angkar' didn't survive. I never heard of anyone mentioning this Pol Pot."

We walked in silence for a moment, the city traffic deafening.

"Do you know what happened to him, to Pol Pot?"

"The last I heard he'd retreated to the jungle and is trying to reform a government. The crazy thing is, the U.S. are backing the Khmer Rouge and Sihanouk partnership because they're the only ones here opposing the Vietnamese."

"The United States are supporting the Khmer Rouge?" I couldn't believe my ears, the noise of the city suddenly dimming in comparison. In my mind, the United States stood for freedom. Why would they be backing the Khmer Rouge who destroyed freedom?

"Yeah. President Carter helped the Khmer Rouge keep its seat at the United Nations, saying they are still the legitimate rulers of Cambodia."

"But, why?" I swallowed, embarrassed at the squeak in my voice.

"You must understand that the United States are longtime enemies of Vietnam. They couldn't back them for power." Dan's tone became defensive. "I don't think President Carter wants to pick a fight with China either, who have always backed the Khmer Rouge."

We approached a little shop nestled on a quieter street. I was relieved to get away from the buzz of the city streets to think over all I had just learned.

Dan paused, stopping abruptly, as he lowered his voice. "But between you and me Rindy, I think if President Carter were here and could hear some of the stories I've heard, he'd change his tune." I didn't know what it meant to "change one's tune," but I hoped he would change.

"This place has the best fried rice." Dan opened the door wide and winked.

I took it all in, in an instant: the picture of peacocks on the wall, the colorfully scrawled wallpaper and tables covered in red cloths, rimmed with chairs. A young Thai woman approached and led us to a table next to the window, handing me a plastic-like piece of paper, with tiny words scrawled across it.

"This is a good restaurant." Dan gave me a reassuring smile. "I promise."

I forced a smile too and repeated the word under my breath until I could say it with ease.

Restaurant.

I had only ever heard of a restaurant, where food is prepared in a separate room and brought to you by pleasant people. The idea seemed strange, and it took a long time for me to rest my back against the padded chair.

"So," Dan began. "What looks good?" I absently scanned the page, trying to read the English words, but I couldn't focus, my mind spinning with all the new sights and sounds. The last thing I felt like doing was eating.

"I'll get what you get," I said at last, placing my menu on the table with a sign of relief.

"I won't let you down." Dan smiled, as he rattled off our order to the smiling waitress. Our food soon emerged from the back, carried on peculiar round, white objects. Glancing out of the corner of my eye, I watched as the table next to us ate their food off the white objects, shoveling it into their laughing mouths with chopsticks.

"Everything alright, Rindy?" Dan asked. I nodded mutely, still staring at the pile of food sitting before me.

"What is this?" I asked at last, touching the smooth corners of the shiny white object, my curiosity forcing the question.

"Well, that's a plate," Dan responded, looking like he might laugh.

"A plate." I dug into the steaming rice and vegetables with the chopsticks. It was the best thing I had ever eaten; flavors I had never tasted smarted on my tongue. The plump rice, the tender vegetables that all swam in a delicious sauce. After we finished eating and Dan paid for the meal, he led me back to the hotel. The lipstick ladies directed us to a hallway, crowded with doors, plastered with numbers, on each side.

"This one's yours." Dan held up a key, showing me how to unlock the door. He waited for me patiently and let me try it myself a few times before I got a hang of it. Swinging open the door, I walked into the room.

"Goodnight," Dan called, as the door closed by itself. "I'll come get you in the morning, so you can start your first day of work."

I was alone. My feet sank into the softly padded ground, and I bent down to run my hand over it, feeling its woven texture. Removing my shoes at the door, I took another step, letting my eyes adjust to the dim lighting of the room. Going to the window, I slid open the curtain. Light exploded into the room, and I looked around, my eyes darting, trying to take it all in. There was a bed, large enough for three people to lie down, side by side. I sat on it, feeling its softness, engulfed in the clean fragrance.

Sitting across from the bed was a funny little box with a glass front. I had seen one only once before, when I was delivering water as a temple boy in Battambang. It had sat peering through the opened door, propped on an old crate, singing and lighting up as I handed a jug of water to one of my wealthier customers. It had fascinated me at the time, even if I had only caught a single glimpse of it. Running my hands over the glass, I imagined the same picture, dancing across the screen. There were buttons on the front so I began to push them, and the mute box came to life. Sitting on the edge of the bed, I disappeared into the colors and sounds on the screen. It was mesmerizing. The people trapped in the box never stopped for a moment, but sang, laughed and talked endlessly. I watched until the sunlight began to fade and the pressure in my bladder caused me to pull my eyes away.

I continued my exploration to a small compartment with a porcelain toilet; another sight I had only seen once before. I knew its use, but I stared at it for a moment, uncertain how to go about using it exactly. Opening the lid, I climbed on top of it, balancing in a squat until I was finished. After climbing down carefully, I pushed a lever on the side and jumped back in surprise as the toilet gurgled and swirled water around before disappearing. I felt like a fool, as my heart pounded in my chest.

Pulling back a curtain near the toilet, I stared into a low basin with a spout sticking out of the wall. Wiggling a handle, I jumped back as water gurgled from the spout. Peeling my clothes off excitedly, I slid under the stream, as the icy water bit into my head and shoulders. Soon my teeth were chattering. I studied the handle and saw an "H" on one and a "C" on the other. What did it mean? I turned the one I hadn't tried at first, and the water turned warm. How could both hot and cold water come from the same place? I never knew such things were possible.

Once I felt warm water falling over me, I reveled beneath the stream. I let it fall all over my tan body, smeared with dust. Not just dust from a day, but dust from the years I had lived. I let my head rest against the smooth, cold wall, as my hair dripped onto my feet. I stood there for a long time, turning the water from hot to cold and back again. I scrubbed until it all washed down the drain, the black water disappearing into clear.

64

THE BRIBE

"They wanted me to compromise my beliefs." — Rindy

MAY 1983

I studied the book before me which had *Pass The GED* on the cover in bold white and red lettering. I was trying to read between bites of rice, while being careful not to soil my fine shirt in the process. I squatted in the shade of the building the U.S. Embassy used to conduct their interviews. For the past year, I had spent my days waking up early and bussing to the various transit camps to serve as an interpreter for the U.S. Embassy. I enjoyed the work, but the days were long, and I had come to cherish these moments of solitude so I could study.

Even though I had been translating for the Embassy for a year, I still dreamed of going to America. I was uncertain how long it would be before my family and I were permitted to obtain visas. Our only aid was that Khan had been a Lon Nol soldier, but even that didn't set us apart from the hundreds of other refugees who were clamoring for visas themselves. We weren't particularly persecuted as the Chinese or Chams had been, and we weren't elite schoolteachers or royalty who had lost everything. We were merely another family of base people, who were stuck in a never-ending line that inched into eternity.

Although it didn't appear that we would be permitted visas anytime soon, I couldn't escape the desire to prepare myself. I wanted to know as much about America as I could before landing on her soil, if I ever did. I didn't only want to master the language, but I wanted to master mathematics, English and Social Studies as well. I planned on gaining my GED as quickly as possible, in hopes it would help me get a job. I had expressed this desire to a friend at the Embassy, who gave me a brand new, GED testing book. Since having it in my hands, I hadn't gotten a full-night's sleep.

"Hello, friend." I looked up to see a fellow Cambodian saunter my way. My heart dropped. His stride was confident, but his smile seemed forced. I nodded a greeting as he squatted in the dirt beside me.

"It's quite a job you have," the man began. "You get to leave the camp and work for those guys." He nodded toward the building that was used to conduct official interviews. "You're almost like an American yourself!" I remained quiet, the last bite of rice growing bitter on my tongue. I knew what was coming because this wasn't the first time I had endured this type of encounter and it wouldn't be the last.

"Tell me what it's like out there." He wasn't deterred by my silence. "I've been dreaming about it every night—"

"What can I help you with?" I interrupted him, hoping he'd get to the point. I only had a few minutes left before I needed to get back inside. The man's gaze turned on me hotly, his eyes ablaze and his posture no longer amiable.

"I want the same thing you want!" He spat. "I want to obtain a visa to get out of this place!" I waited, knowing the man had hardly warmed up in his attempts. "I'm afraid that when I'm called for my interview, I will be judged for my past." He cast his eyes downward with his hands hanging loosely.

"My dark, humiliating and sad past. I want a fresh start so badly. I want to forget the hell we have endured. I want to be given a fair chance—" He shuffled in his pocket and clutched something in his palm. "You're the only one standing in my way. You're the only one who can help me." My pulse quickened, and I stood to my feet, unable to remain neutral any longer.

"I want to give you this!" The man thrust his hand toward me. His tone was desperate, but his eyes were threatening. "This is my gift to you. I hope you will remember me as I stand before the judges." Nauseated, I began to walk away.

"At least look at what I brought you," the man called after me, his words hitting my back like rocks. "This isn't something that you want to refuse."

I retreated to the steps, giving myself a moment for my pulse to slow. This had not been my first unpleasant encounter with a stranger. The memories of the past attempted bribes paraded across my mind. There had been the old woman, who was sent by her family and endeavored to gain a promised visa for all of them. There had been an older man who had called me "brother," and had asked me to help him by giving him the questions that would be asked. He had said "one Christian must help the next one." Most had been men who feared their true identities as Khmer Rouge soldiers would come to light. They all wanted the same thing though: in exchange for money or jewels, they wanted me to fix the outcome of their interrogations. They wanted me to tell the Embassy officials whatever was necessary to secure their freedom. Some just wanted to know the questions that would be asked, so they could prepare better.

It wasn't that I didn't have compassion for them, because I did. Anyone who I could help in good conscience, I tried to. I helped smooth over questions to people who stumbled with their nerves, and I even helped clarify when someone was presenting themselves in a wrong light unintentionally. Each time before going into the room and beginning a new interview, I prayed for discernment. Overtime, I had become known for that discernment, but some called me mean and cold-hearted. It hurt listening to their stories, knowing I could help make their dreams come true. But if it came at a cost to my conscience, I could not.

"You coming, Rindy?" The secretary's voice called, as her head emerged from around the corner.

"Coming," I responded, running up the last few steps.

I was at my usual place, seated on a chair, waiting for the next interviewee to enter. I glanced at the small, smudged and fly speckled window to my right. There was only one more interview for the day. The sound of the fan on full speed hummed in the air. Several Embassy officials were scattered across the room, and the stenographer was seated behind a desk, the clicking of her keys silent, waiting for the next interviewee. A few others stood against the opposite wall, endeavoring not to doze off in the "hellish heat" as they called it at least twenty times a day. The head interrogator, Mr. Powell, stood scanning a piece of paper in his hand. I heard the shuffle of feet, the heavy breathing and the feeling of fear entering the room. I looked up to see the same man I had encountered on my lunch break. The man who had tried to bribe me to secure his visa. My face flushed. I glanced down at my fine-laced shoes and endeavored to normalize my breathing, saying a quick prayer for discernment.

"Are you Mr. Let San?" Mr. Powell glanced up from his piece of paper. I stood to my feet and walked forward. The man looked at me. Our eyes locked, and I held his gaze. The events that had transpired just a few hours before hung like static in the air between us. My feet felt on fire.

"Are you Mr. Let San?" I repeated in Khmer, careful to translate the question as closely and precisely as possible, as I had been instructed.

"I am." His eyes flashed and his fingers twitched. Then the interview began like all the others. I asked Let San to verify his birthplace, family members and home region. He responded to all the questions quickly and confidently, with seemingly little thought given to each. Then the questions became more pointed and the subject matter more dangerous.

"What involvement have you had in Cambodia for the last four years?" Mr. Powell asked. I swallowed and repeated the question, paying special attention to not only what Let San responded, but how.

"I have been a poor rice farmer." His eyes darted from side to side. He was clearly uneasy. "When the Khmer Rouge soldiers forced me from my home, I migrated with my family to a corporate village just south of Phnom Penh. It was very difficult to be evacuated from my home and forced away from my livelihood. I did not want to obey them, but I felt I had no other choice. The journey was very difficult, and we lost my youngest child on the trek." The man's face saddened his eyes downcast. I had seen that exact look before as he had evoked mock sadness during his attempted bribery.

"Were the Khmer Rouge very cruel to you?" I asked directly, after glancing at Mr. Powell to indicate that I had a few questions to ask of my own. Somehow, it was never very difficult to discern who had been Khmer Rouge. I had spoken with hundreds at this point, and I had observed commonalities. In many cases, pride and hate still boiled beneath the surface, discernible even through their ruse. I may not have always been correct in my assessments, but I prayed that the next round of interviews would amend any mistakes I had made.

"They were not cruel, but they were disciplined," Let San responded, his eyes glaring into my own.

"Do you feel that what they did was unjust?" I stared steadily into Let San's face; his color rose.

"I think they went too far," Let San responded, meeting my gaze. His tone was defensive and his body language tense, saying the things his lips wouldn't dare utter. After several more minutes of questions, Let San was permitted to go. After he disappeared through the door, every eye in the room landed on me.

"Khmer Rouge?" Mr. Powel asked.

"Khmer Rouge," I responded.

Later that evening as I walked through the door, preparing to leave the camp for the night, I saw a group of men congregated near the exit, talking and smoking cigarettes. They laughed loudly as I walked passed, the shadows of the night clinging to them. Ignoring them, I continued toward the gate, anxious to leave.

"There he is," a voice called over the din. "He's the one who thinks he's too good for us and too superior to accept our humble gifts of appreciation. He's an 'Embassy boy' now, and they supply all his needs." I continued walking. Their words accosted my back, making color rise into my face despite my effort to remain calm.

"You're just like us. Except you're smaller and blacker. You'll never be a pale-skinned American, no matter how hard you try. You're just a little black man."

The taunting continued until I reached the gate and handed my information to the Thai guard, who quickly waved me through. Their taunts berated me in imagined whispers all the way back to the hotel and stayed when I arrived, making studying a difficult task.

65

THREATS

"Many people who failed the interview felt that I should do more to help them." — Rindy

July 1983

The bus pulled up to the gate that I had been through dozens of times—the same transit camp my family resided in. My mind was foggy, and sleep called to me from the steady hum of the engine, but I forced myself to stay awake. The red-and-white-striped arm heralded me in as I sat next to the dust-filmed window, clutching my identification papers and the GED book I had studied until two in the morning. As the bus ground to a halt, I was surprised to see Mteay's face peering through the fence, anxiously waiting for me to climb from the bus. I quickly climbed out and went to her. I missed my family and hadn't been able to see any of them for several weeks due to my busy schedule.

"Rindy," Mteay called waving her arm over her head as I pushed through the crowd of people congregated around the gate toward her.

"Are you well? Vuthy? The sisters?" I asked quickly, unable to shake the impression that something was wrong.

"We're all well." She embraced me. "But I'm afraid that you are not." I pulled away from her quickly to survey her face.

"Rindy, people have been saying horrible things about you throughout the camp." Her eyes filled with tears. "Everywhere I go in the camp, I hear people talking about you and how there are men who want to harm you."

I swallowed. The words sat on the top of my skull, refusing to sink in.

"Did you hear me?" Mteay asked, shaking me.

"Yes, yes." I pulled her away from the crowd to the shade of an over-hanging tree so we could speak in private.

"I have been afraid it might come to this." The past months of translating interviews, the threats, the angry faces everywhere I went, swam before my eyes. "I have had to translate some very difficult cases."

"Yes, I know," Mteay said. "People are so upset about the widowed woman and her family."

I sunk beneath the weight of her words. Although the interviews I translated were official and confidential business, it seemed that everyone in the camp knew everything that went on. I knew exactly which case Mteay was referring to, as it had haunted me since it occurred.

There was a particular refugee family petitioning to obtain visas to America. The woman was a widow because her husband was killed for being a schoolteacher during the Khmer Rouge takeover. I could still see the sad shape of her eyes and hear the hollow sound of her breath as I stood beside her, translating her heartbreaking history. When her verdict was announced, I was shocked and dismayed to hear that she and her entire family had been denied entrance to America by the State Department (the most difficult department to pass). I didn't know what would happen to them, as they would perhaps be sent to another camp or released back into Cambodia to fend for themselves.

"People in the camp are blaming you, Rindy," Mteay said, her eyes pleading with me. "They say you are responsible for their denial!"

"As if I have that much power." I ran my hand through my hair. "Don't you think I would have gotten us out of here long ago if I had the power to 'deny' or 'grant' anyone? I translate and help the officials understand each person's story, but I don't have that kind of power."

I lowered my voice, seeing the tears in Mteay's black eyes well again. "Mteay, you need to know I tried to do everything I could to help that woman and her family. When she got confused and anxious, I helped her sort out what she was trying to say, so she didn't sound like she was lying. I'm as upset as everyone else is about it."

"I know, I know." Mteay gripped my arm. "But the camp is in an uproar. They're calling for you. It's not safe for you any longer."

"Has anyone threatened any of you?" I asked quickly, gripping Mteay's shoulders. Her eyes avoided mine. I instantly knew the answer.

"Gather everyone together and try to avoid the main areas of the camp." I walked quickly toward the small, white building we conducted interviews in. Suddenly, it didn't seem so small and familiar any longer, but it loomed above me like a snow-peaked mountain. My breath was shallow and halting, my hands trembled as I walked through the door.

"Oh, there you are, Rindy," the cheery secretary called, her large-rimmed glasses and enormous curls greeting me. "Mr. Powell is waiting for you to conduct the next interview."

"I'm sorry I'm late." I shuffled through the door in the middle of the back wall. With each step I took, my fear mounted. I felt like a bug, crawling slowly, willing my tiny legs forward. The weight of all who had gone before me in similar trepidation was not lost on me. I was merely one of the thousands who had walked up to that door with the same anxious thoughts.

"Rindy, you ready to get going?" Mr. Powell asked, not looking up from his papers. That's when I knew I had an advantage over every other person who had walked through that door. No one else had been greeted with familiarity, with personal history and with trust. What a privilege I had been granted. What a blessing from God. I gulped, the weight of what I was about to do settled on me in a single breath.

"Actually, do you mind if I speak to you alone?" The words barely escaped the desert of my throat.

"Sure." Mr. Powell motioned for the others to leave the room. Shuffling feet and questioning stares filled my senses.

"What can I do for ya, Rindy?" Mr. Powell's broad smile stretched across his face.

"I don't want to break protocol or put you in a difficult position." My voice squeaked to a slow start. "But there's something I have to ask, for the safety of myself and my family." Mr. Powell's brow furrowed, and he leaned back in his chair.

"I'm being threatened because of the decision to deny the widow woman and her family visas. Men in the camp think I am responsible. My mteay has been hearing rumors of threats, and I'm afraid my whole family is in danger."

"This is unfortunate, but not an uncommon situation. Translators don't last too long for a reason, but we'll be sad to lose you—you've been one of the best." Mr. Powel drummed his fingers on the desk before bringing them to his mouth. "I'm glad you said something, because threats are not to be taken lightly. . ." his voice trailed off into silence. "We will get your family in for interviews as soon as possible. We will handle this situation with the utmost urgency."

I exhaled, not knowing I had been holding my breath for the last few minutes.

"Shall we begin?" Mr. Powell glanced at me over his tented fingertips.

66

AMERICA

"I never thought I would be here." — Rindy

AUGUST 1983

My freshly-polished shoes gleamed as I stepped onto the pavement. The air teamed with humidity and smells of the city, even at four in the morning. Cars honked and the sound of airplanes taking off filled my head—a sound so foreign, so exhilarating. I gripped my belongings contained in a small, leather suitcase and took a step forward, closing the taxi door behind me with a thud.

Winding my way through the mob of people, I looked for anyone with a familiar face. There were stewardesses, workers, and local Thai walking about, but most noticeably were the hordes of refugees who huddled together in dazed groups, trying to understand what they needed to do. Their ragged clothes hung from their frail bodies. Their eyes told stories of fear. Although I had on new clothes, toted my GED book and could read the English signs plastered everywhere, I felt as equally out of place and lost as the rest of those from the camps.

You're supposed to be here, Rindy. This is right. God has a purpose. I reassured myself, keeping a tight grip on the small bundle of papers that contained my freedom: a passport, a letter from the State Department, and a visa for the United States of America.

I scanned the crowd, my eyes stopping on familiar faces and emotion gripped me. I approached a group of people who looked especially bewildered. There, standing beside a single paper bag, was my family. Mteay rocked from side to side, trying to console Selay in her arms. Khan tried to get information from an attendant in pathetically broken English. Vuthy stood like a soldier at attention as he watched over Ly and Sotha, who stared around with eyes swollen full of unfamiliar sights. The only one who was missing was Kiry, who was still in the process of obtaining visas for himself and his new bride. As I gazed at my family, I breathed out gratitude, fighting the tears that entered my eyes. They had endured death and destruction, emerging victorious. Although the past had etched itself into the skin on their faces and eaten away at their frames, they were alive and on their way to a new life. A new life in the United States of America.

"God thank you for allowing me to be here to see this," I whispered to myself, wiping my eyes on my freshly ironed sleeve.

"Rindy," Ly cried, spotting me through the crowd. In an instant, I was enveloped in arms and slaps on the back as they welcomed me into their midst.

I hadn't seen them in months as they had been transferred to a different camp, amidst the threats, to await their official documentation, which would allow them to leave the country. Being surrounded by those I loved the most gave me the confidence to continue forward.

After winding our way through the airport, I sat nervously at our gate, fearing to even use the bathroom in case we missed our flight. I was surrounded by what seemed to be hundreds of other refugees who hadn't had the privilege of a proper shower in years, contenting themselves with buckets poured over their heads as they scrubbed with their clothes still on. Many of them were sick and decrepit, barely able to sit upright in the hard-backed airport chairs. It was painful to watch them board. Some had to be carried because there were not enough wheelchairs to accommodate the many who needed them. The Bangkok airport was an entirely new world, and their eyes reflected their uncertainty. I wasn't afraid, but a ball of electric nervousness buzzed in my stomach. The idea that I was departing for the land where all my hopes and dreams rested seemed too impossible to be my reality.

When it was my turn to board, I found my seat beside Vuthy who stared at me with wide eyes. I would have thought I was dreaming, except the smell of those around me brought me back to my senses. Despite their constant composure and plastered-on smiling faces, the beautiful stewardesses couldn't mask their nausea. They exchanged desperate glances at each other, as they took turns cleaning up vomit or helping a mother calm her screaming infant.

"They don't even know how to use the toilet," I heard one whisper to the other. "Some must have thought the sink was the toilet and others didn't even seem to aim for anywhere. It's an absolute mess. This is a disaster."

The atmosphere on the plane was one of desperation, hedged by varying shades of discomfort. I truly felt sorry for everyone locked inside. The majority of those on board weren't prepared for such a journey, and the stewardesses weren't prepared for what that meant. Regardless of our unpreparedness, we rose from the ground and lifted into the sky toward America.

As the plane glided into the air, the pressure rose inside the plane, and I felt Vuthy's hand on my arm, his palms sweating in panic.

"We're going to be okay, Vuthy." I nudged him in the side. "We've made it. We've survived. This is nothing."

He gave me a faint smile in return and eased his grip. A hush fell over all those on board. Even the babies seemed quiet in a moment of realization as we left the land that had held us as prisoners. I gazed out the window at the disappearing landscape, bathed in the early morning sun. The city gave way to the jungle, and rice paddies evaporated into clouds. The varying shades of green were captivating, melting from a deep emerald into a dazzling shade of neon. As the landscape became clothed in white, I knew that somewhere below my feet was a stilt hut and the tiger who roamed there. I pictured the stilt house and tried to ingrain its image into my mind, to somehow etch over everything else that had happened, so it became the Cambodia I would remember. I thought hard, calculating my age once again. I would be twenty in a few months.

Once the clouds completely cloaked my vision, reflecting the piercing light of the sun, I closed the window and faced forward. I was leaving Cambodia behind and embarking on a new journey, one that the past had no sway over. I had survived the night and was soaring into the triumphant light of day.

HISTORICAL NOTES

CHAPTER 4: ARRESTED

According to academics, the first 1967 Samlaut rebellion and the later one in 1968, set the stage for the political upheaval that would eventually give birth to the Cambodian civil war. For years, the rural areas of Battambang had grown to distrust the government, led by Prince Norodom Sihanouk. This destabilization paved the way for the emergence of a yet-little-known political organization known as the "Red" Khmer or the Khmer Rouge that would offer the disenfranchised much needed stability and leadership. Meanwhile, Pol Pot, a Marxist-Leninist disciple was climbing his way through their ranks.

Ben Kiernan, The Samlaut Rebellion and Its Aftermath, 1967-70: The Origins of Cambodia's Liberation Movement, Parts I and II (Monash University, Centre of Southeast Asian Studies, 1975).

CHAPTER 7: THE RECRUITERS

Since the early 1960's, U.S. Special Forces teams had been making secret reconnaissance and mine-laying incursions into Cambodian territory. In a series of operations, usually conducted by several American personnel and local mercenaries, a total of 1,835 such missions were undertaken, resulting in the capture of twenty-four prisoners, and an unknown number of deaths and injuries. Many of which were the result of "sanitized self-destruct" antipersonnel mines that those conducting the missions were authorized to lay, up to thirty kilometers inside Cambodia.

W. Shawcross, Sideshow: Kissinger, Nixon and the Destruction of Cambodia, London: Deutsch, 1979, pp. 65, 24; S. Hersh, The Price of Power: Henry Kissinger in the Nixon White House. New York: Summit Books, 1983, pp. 177-78.

CHAPTER 16: THE COUP

It was commonly believed in Cambodia that the CIA was behind the coup that ousted the beloved Norodom Sihanouk, yet the U.S. denies involvement. However, in accordance with their alliance, the U.S. channeled millions of dollars in military aid to the Lon Nol government, much of which was misused by corrupt military leaders. As the generals were said to have sold the weapons to the enemy, creating 'phantom soldiers' to garner the extra soldiers' pay for themselves and building extravagant houses for themselves. In exchange, their men went hungry while fighting the notoriously brutal and skilled Viet Cong army.

Haing Ngor; Roger Warner, Surviving The Killing Fields, New York: Carroll & Graf Publishers 2003. pp. 66-67.

CHAPTER 17: THE GLASSES

The action of Norodom Sihanouk, becoming allies with his former enemies—the communist Khmer Rouge—caused their forces to grow in sympathies and strength as many in Cambodia would follow the beloved leader anywhere. As a result, the Khmer Rouge became a major player in the war, soon eclipsing the North Vietnamese Communists in their fight against the Lon Nol forces.

Chew, E., & Chong, A. (2013). Norodom Sihanouk: His Mercurial Art of Preserving a Small State. (RSIS Commentaries, No. 030). RSIS Commentaries. Singapore: Nanyang Technological University. Retrieved 3 july 2024. https://dr.ntu.edu.sg/bitstream/10356/99086/1/RSIS0302013.pdf

CHAPTER 19: WAR BIRDS

From 1969-1973, in an operation known as "Menu bombings," US President Nixon approved a mission of subsequent B-52 strikes inside Cambodia to attack communist sanctuaries there and eventually to assist the United States withdrawal. To keep the secret, as Cambodia was ostensibly neutral, an intricate reporting system was established at the Pentagon to prevent disclosure of the bombing. Although the New York Times broke the story of the secret bombing campaign in May 1969, there was little adverse public reaction in the U.S.. These culminated in a total of 2,756,941 tons of bombs being dropped in Cambodia. The estimates aren't precise, but it's believed that as a result, two million became homeless and somewhere between 100,000 and 600,000 civilian casualties. The United States dropped more bombs on Cambodia than it did during the entire Second World War, which clocked in at just over 2 million bombs dropped. It is believed that Cambodia may be the most heavily bombed country in history. When at last, the United States Congress forced President Nixon to stop the bombing in Cambodia, the U.S. continued to channel millions of dollars in military aid to the Lon Nol government.

Owen, Taylor; Kiernan, Ben (October 2006). "Bombs Over Cambodia" (PDF). The Walrus: 62–69. Archived (PDF) from the original on 24 October 2013. Retrieved 14 May 2024.

CHAPTER 20: THE KILL

In 1973, it was speculated that Norodom Sihanouk returned to the 'liberated zones' in Cambodia. Yet he remained only a figurehead for the Khmer Rouge as he began to lose influence within the leadership. A new leader emerged, influenced by the Marxist ideology of Moa Zedong, who had openly opposed Sihanouk from the beginning. This man was known as Pol Pot, and he spoke openly about his desire to see Cambodia become a socialist egalitarian society —free of class distinction, western imperialism and the imbalance of power that money brings. He would stop at nothing to see his vision come to fruition.

Haing Ngor; Roger Warner Surviving The Killing Fields, New York: Carroll & Graf Publishers 2003. pp. 77-78

CHAPTER 24: ENLIST

After Sihanouk showed his support for the Khmer Rouge by visiting them in the field, their ranks grew from 6,000 to 50,000 soldiers. Many of the new recruits for the Khmer Rouge had no formal political affiliations with communism, of which they had little understanding. Sihanouk's support of Khmer Rouge in rural Cambodia helped them to extend its power and influence to the point that by 1973 it was deeply entrenched, although only a minority of its population. Many people in Cambodia who joined in the fight, believed they were fighting for the restoration of Sihanouk.

Ison, K. and Speidel, D. (2023) Review and Analysis: United States Secret Wars in Cambodia: Long-Term Impacts and Consequences. Open Journal of Soil Science, 13, 295-328. doi: 10.4236/ojss.2023.137013. Retrieved on 3 July 2024.

Chapter 26: Saviors

In April 1975, the Khmer Rouge, who had been waging war against the Lon Nol army for almost five years, returned to Phom Penh. They were the victors, returning to their capital city. It is said that the Khmer Rouge took some things, such as watches and cameras, but they didn't go on a rampage of looting the entire city. They were restrained and acted with discipline, so different from the corrupt Lon Nol with whom they were acquainted. The inhabitants of Phnom Penh rejoiced at first, because the war appeared to be over, the Americans were gone, the Khmer were in charge and order and peace would reign.

Aikman, David. Time Essay: Cambodia: An Experiment in Genocide. Monday, July 31, 1978. Retrieved on 3 July 2024. https://content.time.com /time/subscriber/article/0,33009,946921,00.html.

Chapter 27: The Evacuation

On April 18, 1975, the Khmer Rouge went door to door telling residents they needed to move a short distance outside of their communities but would be allowed to return in a few days when they deemed it was safe to do so. They were told not to worry about anything, including locking their homes, because the Khmer Rouge could be trusted and would take care of everything. These instructions varied and everyone heard something different, but the command remained: leave now because the "Americans are going to bomb the villages." People who refused to evacuate met a violent end. Their homes were burned, and some were shot on the spot. It appeared that the Khmer Rouge were not what they had once appeared to be.

Ross., R. (1987). Cambodian History Part IV. https://phdn.org/archives /www.ess.uwe.ac.uk/genocide/cambhist4.htm#DEMOCRATIC.

CHAPTER 28: YEAR ZERO

The Khmer Rouge takeover started by finding and segregating anyone they considered to be "new people." These were the educated, city dwellers, the foreign property owners and the wealthy. They were seen to be the class of people who had oppressed everyone else and who had not taken part in the struggle of the previous years, like the rural dwellers had. The killings began with the "new people."

Chigas, George, Mosyakov Dmitri (n.d.). Literacy and Education under the Khmer Rouge. https://gsp.yale.edu/literacy-and-education-under-khme r-rouge.

CHAPTER 29: THE COLOR BLACK

The Khmer Rouge renamed Cambodia to "Kampuchea" and believed that they would return it to a "golden age," when the land was cultivated by the "base people," who had been the poor and oppressed for generations. This ideology required society to become flipped on its head, the poor becoming the rich and the rich becoming the poor. By instigating "Year Zero," Pol Pot, with his pet ideologies in tow, aimed to create a state built upon rural dominance that disallowed personal property, religious practice and any form of individual liberty. The ideal of one for all but all for no one was set in perilous motion.

Holocaust Memorial Day Trust: KHMER ROUGE IDEOLOGY. Retrieved on 3 July 2024, from: https://www.hmd.org.uk/learn-about-the-hol ocaust-and-genocides/cambodia/khmer-rouge-ideology/.

CHAPTER 30: HUNGER

By 1975, following the devastating consequences of the Khmer Rouge mismanagement, Cambodia's rice production had dropped by eighty-four percent compared to the 1970 crop, setting in motion one of the deadliest famines in modern history.

DeFalco, Randle C., Justice and Starvation in Cambodia: International Criminal Law and the Khmer Rouge Famine. 2013. Retrieved on 3 July 2024. https://tspace.library.utoronto.ca/bitstream/1807/67245/1/DeFalco_Randle_C_201311_LLM_thesis.pdf.pdf

CHAPTER 31: THE PURGE

Before the Khmer Rouge took over, the largest ethnic minority groups in Cambodia (making up over 15%) were the Chinese, the Vietnamese and a Muslim group known as "Cham." Pol Pot's remedy for this problem was to come up with creative ways to eradicate what he deemed to be ethnic pollution, by systematically singling them out. It is believed that 80% were murdered.

Coomes, Abby; Dean, Jonathan; Perkins, Makinsey; Roberts, Jennifer. Schroeder, Tyler; Simpson, Emily. Racial Ideology and Implementation of the Khmer Rouge Genocide. Morehead State University. Retrieved on 3 July 2024. https://scholarworks.moreheadstate.edu/cgi/viewcontent.cgi?article=1011&context=student_scholarship_posters.

CHAPTER 33: THE SEPERATION

In 1976, the Khmer Rouge sought to break down the family unit to further instill the "collective mentality." Everyone was separated by age and gender into work camps, many of the work units mobile. Everything one did became communalized including eating and sleeping. Designated nurse-maids cared for infants while parents worked; older children lived away from parents with little access or rights to visit. Angkar took over the role of parent for all, demanding unwavering and exclusive loyalty regardless of the cost.

Stiftung, Heinrich Boel (2014). Like Ghost Changes Body (A Study on the Impact of Forced Marriage under the Khmer Rouge Regime). Retrieved on 3 July 2024. https://kh.boell.org/sites/default/files/forced_marriage_study_report_tpo_october_2014.pdf.

CHAPTER 39: MATCHMAKING

"Between 1975 and 1979, thousands of men and women were required to undergo mass commitment ceremonies with spouses assigned by Khmer Rouge agents of the state. Under the surveillance of Khmer Rouge spies, assigned couples were compelled to consummate the marriage through sexual relations in the days following the wedding ceremony. Thereafter, husband and wife were removed into separate work camps, with infrequent visitation. According to the sample for this research, in many cases, the assigned spouses were complete strangers to each other; in most cases, the unions were without choice or the consent of the intended; in all cases, the system was coercively enforced through real or threatened punishment—'re-education,' imprisonment, sexual violence and torture, or death."

Stiftung, Heinrich Boel (2014). Like Ghost Changes Body (A Study on the Impact of Forced Marriage under the Khmer Rouge Regime). Retrieved on 3 July 2024. https://kh.boell.org/sites/default/files/forced_marriage_study_report_tpo_october_2014.pdf.

CHAPTER 43: THE PRISON

"By 1977, the distrust on the part of the leadership had reached paranoiac heights and the purges of suspected traitors increased. Even the ranks of the Khmer Rouge cadres themselves were purged, sending increasingly larger numbers of them and their families to prisons where they were tortured and then murdered. The most notorious of these prisons was S-21, a high school in Phnom Penh that was converted into a prison and torture centre run by Kaing Guek Eav, also known as Duch. Out of an estimated 15,000 prisoners who were sent to S-21, only seven survived. Prisoners housed there were photographed and tortured to produce confessions. When the interrogators were finished, the prisoners' corpses were carried by truck to the 'killing fields' outside of Phnom Penh. There are approximately 20,000 of these mass graves in various locations in the country."

Asia Pacific Education. The Rise and Fall of the Khmer Rouge Regime. Retrieved on 3 July 2024. https://asiapacificcurriculum.ca/learning-modul e/rise-and-fall-khmer-rouge-regime.

CHAPTER 43: THE INVASION

"On December 25, 1978, Vietnam invaded Cambodia. The Vietnamese aimed to affect a 'Blooming Lotus,' first by seizing the capital of Phnom Penh—thereby removing the central command structure of Democratic Kampuchea—then spreading out into the rest of the country. Vietnamese troops, along with Cambodian rebel forces, quickly overpowered Kampuchean forces in Phnom Penh... Four days later, at a meeting of the United Nations Secretary Council, the Vietnamese Ambassador claimed the invasion had been carried out for two reasons. First, Vietnam had intervened to protect its own sovereignty. There had already been a number of border confrontations with Kampuchea from May 1975 onward...Second, Vietnam had intervened on humanitarian grounds to support the Cambodian people in an attempt to overthrow the oppressive regime that had enslaved them."

Carmichael, Cathie. Maguire, Richard C. (2015). The Routledge History of Genocide, Routledge, 2015. P. 122.

It is also believed that the real motive that Vietnam had in invading Cambodia was to bring "fertile new soil under Vietnamese control," and not the chivalrous humanitarian effort that Vietnam's Ambassador suggested. Over the previous years, Vietnams population growth had exploded into sixty million people, which burdened the crop production. This need made the neighboring country of war-torn Cambodia an easy target for seizure. Perhaps the devastated Cambodia could be absorbed into the greater power.

Haing Ngor; Roger Warner Surviving The Killing Fields, New York: Carroll & Graf Publishers 2003. pp. 435.

CHAPTER 48: CHASING RUMORS

"Throughout 1979, tens of thousands of Cambodians fled to the Thai border. Barred by the Thai military from entering the country, a vast number of them—combatants, traders, farmers and many others—accumulated in several makeshift camps along the ill-defined border. Many were starving, had malaria, and were in very poor health. Several of the largest camps, including Nong Chan, Nong Samet, and Mak Mun, grew into vast open-air markets, each controlled by a different faction of Khmer Serei also known as the 'freedom fighters.' Conditions in the border camps were very poor: most of those who settled in the camps lived in squalor with access to no basic services. The Thai military controlled most activity along the border and exerted tremendous power in some of the border camps. Though the Thai military's primary concern was the threat of the Vietnamese army and a potential invasion, they also ensured that the Cambodians did not cross the border. This policy was not consistent though: large groups of Cambodians were periodically allowed into Thailand and given aid by local Thai villagers, while other times the Thai military put up barbed wire along the border crossing points and threatened to shoot anyone who crossed."

Columbia University (2007) Refugee Relief Crisis. Retrieved on 12 January 2021. http://forcedmigration.ccnmtl.columbia.edu/book/export/html/ 26.

CHAPTER 51: SHELLING

On June 23, around 200 Vietnamese soldiers attacked Nong Chan refugee camp and the Thai military retaliated with artillery, in an effort to hold the border. This incursion lasted three days, killing an estimated 400 refugees who were caught in the crossfire while forcing hundreds of others to flee back into Cambodia or resettle in another camp. This garnered international attention, as the First Lady Rosalynn Carter had recently visited the border camps and declared it to be "like nothing she had ever seen."

Kamm Henry, New York Times, 24 June 1980.

Kamm Henry, New York Times, Nov. 10, 1979. https://www.nytimes.com/1979/11/10/archives/mrs-carter-visits-thai-camp-its-like-nothing-ive-seen-buying-from.html

CHAPTER 52: THE BUS

"Throughout most of 1979 the Thai government refused offers of humanitarian assistance from the United Nations for the Cambodians at the border. Thailand was not a signatory to the 1951 Refugee Convention, and it insisted that any Cambodian who entered Thailand was an "illegal migrant" rather than a refugee. As the situation at the border grew more desperate, considerable international pressure and the offer of substantial amounts of money convinced the Thai government to allow UNICEF and ICRC to begin a formal border relief operation as well as a program to assist Thai villages at the border affected by the Cambodian influx. The Thai government reversed its policy of barring the Cambodians from entering Thailand and implemented an "open door" policy. The Thai government informed the United Nations High Commissioner for Refugees (UNHCR) in Thailand that within a few days Thai border authorities would start busing thousands of Cambodians into Thailand to designated holding centers. The Thais requested UNHCR to build and manage these holding centers inside Thailand. International NGOs, such as CARE, CRS and IRC, worked in the holding centers and in the border camps."

Columbia University (2007) Refugee Relief Crisis. Retrieved on 12 January 2021. http://forcedmigration.ccnmtl.columbia.edu/book/export/html/ 26.

CHAPTER 55: SUNDAY

A Christian and Missionary Alliance mission began in Cambodia in 1923, and by 1962 the mission had converted about 2,000 people. American Protestant missionary activity increased in Cambodia, especially among some of the hill tribes and among the Cham after the establishment of the Khmer Republic, but their efforts were mostly unfruitful. Observers reported that in 1980 there were more registered Khmer Christians among the refugees in camps in Thailand than in all of Cambodia before 1970. The destruction and brutalization of a nation gave birth to revival.

PediaPress (2008). Cambodia: Religion in Cambodia- Christianity. pp. 341

Another such organization that poured humanitarian aid as well as Jesus' love and salvation into this ravaged place was YWAM, a global movement of Christians from many cultures, age groups, and Christian traditions, dedicated to serving Jesus throughout the world. One of the leading members being Joe Portale, who pioneered refugee work in Khao-I-Dang refugee camp.

Portale, Joe. Taking On Giants. YWAM Publishing Seattle WA, 2010. pp. 187-210.

CHAPTER 61: BREAKING SILENCE

Author of "What My Bones know: A Memoir of Healing from Complex Trauma," Stephanie Foo, found that working with Cambodian genocide survivors has been a difficult and incredibly delicate matter. Due to the commonly held tradition and cultural entrenchment in Buddhism, it's believed that somehow the evil and destruction that they had experienced under the Khmer Rouge was either from personal, collective, or generational "bad karma."

"They felt like they had probably done something horrific in their past lives and were being punished in this life." Additionally, it's believed that "they can protect us [the hearer] from that trauma by not sharing it." A common Cambodian proverb states, "if you have an open sore on your body, why poke it with a stick to cause more bleeding?"

Essentially, not discussing these traumatic events is a way to redeem that bad karma. Thus, suppressed trauma, verbal and physical abuse and addiction has run rampant in survivors who rarely recount freely what they have endured without healing and safety.

NPR Interview, Therapy Ghostbusters. How a Cambodian Practitioner Helped A Community dealing with PTSD [transcript], 2022. https://www .npr.org/transcripts/1124139592.

CHAPTER 66: AMERICA

In 1997, a Khmer Rouge splinter group captured Pol Pot. They placed him under house arrest, and he was put on trial. He was sentenced to life imprisonment by a "people's tribunal," which critics derided as a show trial. Much of the international community hoped his captors would extradite him to stand trial for his crimes against humanity, but he died in his sleep on April 15, 1998, at age 72 due to heart failure. A United Nations-backed tribunal has convicted only a handful of Khmer Rouge leaders of crimes against humanity. Pol Pot said in an interview shortly before he died that, 'I did not join the resistance movement to kill people, to kill the nation. Look at me now. Am I a savage person? My conscience is clear.'

Mydans, Seth. In an Interview, Pol Pot Declares His Conscience Is Clear, Oct. 23, 1997. Accessed July 2024 https://www.nytimes.com/1997/10/23/world/in-an-interview-pol-pot-declares-his-conscience-is-clear.html

AFTER THE STORY

Many other refugees were sent to the Philippines to be processed, but due to Rindy's connections, they were able to fly directly to the United States. With the help of a local church and refugee aid, they rented a home.

In 1983, Rindy began a job as a janitor for a hospital and then as a translator for the health department. He worked alongside social workers; aiding the medical staff in helping the patients understand and take treatment, many of whom had tuberculosis.

In 1984, Rindy applied for the Southwestern Adventist University in Keene, Texas. He was admitted to pre-college classes before he began his undergraduate courses. Unsure of what to study, he decided to major in history with a minor focus on pre-med.

In 1988, He graduated with a BA in history. In 1990, he completed a second degree in the nursing program, after receiving a scholarship from a hospital in Florida, with which he gained employment after.

In 1992, Rindy attended the University of North Dakota's School of Medicine in Grand Forks, North Dakota. In 1994, he graduated as a Physician's Assistant before moving back to Florida.

While living in Orlando, Florida, Rindy made a four-hour commute each week to a Cambodian Christian church in Jacksonville. Here he met a pastor who told Rindy of his niece, named Chriya (who was still living in Cambodia), who he sought to arrange a marriage for. Rindy agreed to begin correspondence with her. Eventually, Rindy bought a ticket and flew to Cambodia to meet the woman he hoped to marry, accompanied by Chriya's aunt. In 1994, they were indeed married. The visa petition process typically took months to years, but due to Rindy's connection with the U.S. Embassy, Chriya was permitted a visa in a mere three months, reuniting with Rindy in Florida.

In 1997, after a move to Waco, Texas, they had their first child, whom they named Samuel. In 1998, they had a daughter whom they named Maylia. In 2001, they had their third and final child, whom they named Sarrett.

In 2001, they relocated back to Florida to be closer to Chriya's family who were beginning to migrate to the United States. In addition to his work in the medical field, Rindy became involved with church ministry and went back to school to obtain his Master of Divinity, becoming an ordained pastor.

While working in the E.R., Rindy met a fellow Christian and missionary named Dr. Scott Smith, who went with Rindy on his first medical mission trip to Cambodia in 2011 and then again in 2016. In 2023, Rindy returned to Cambodia on a pastoral mission trip and hopes to raise funds to conduct more missions trips in the future.

Dr. Smith introduced Rindy to a family friend named Olivia Talbott, who is the author of the book you are now holding.

Rindy in Khao-I-Dang Refugee Center

THE MISSION

Half of the profits from this book will go to assisting Rindy in his mission work in Cambodia. He has conducted both medical and pastoral missions trips in the past and hopes to raise the funds to do more in the future. To learn more about Rindy or to give to an upcoming mission trip, visit Rindy's facebook page: *The Cost of Calling of Christ Ministry: Rindy's Mission to Cambodia.*

By purchasing this book, you have been a part of sharing Christ's love and redeeming power with the people of Cambodia, many of which have never heard. If this book or mission has resonated with you, please consider leaving a review, sharing it with a friend or giving financially to Rindy's mission work.

Thank you!

Rindy & Cambodian Children

Rindy baptizing new Cambodian Christians

Rindy in Cambodia

Authors Note

In April 2014, I got an unexpected phone call from a man named Dr. Scott Smith. He was a family friend who does mission work in Kenya, Africa and serves as the director of Dreamweaver International.

"I heard through your grandma that you want to be a writer and just came back from Cambodia," he said. "I have a writing opportunity for you."

It was true, I was pursuing a degree in creative writing and English and had just returned from a three-month mission trip to Cambodia. I was a nineteen-year-old with my head full of grandiose plans of the future. I was eager to hear more.

"I have this friend named Rindy who I work with in the E.R., and he has the most incredible story you've ever heard."

Rindy, I thought, *that's a good name. A name that belongs in a book.*

Scott went on to tell me a little bit about Rindy's life and instantly, just like that, I was in love with a story I hadn't even fully heard. I wanted to write about Cambodia, as the culture and its wounds had significantly impacted me, and I felt the Cambodian Genocide was underrepresented. I loved history but I had never heard about *that* part before traveling there. I wanted to write true stories that were real and not sanitized, because truth trumped fiction every day. Books like *Unbroken* by Laura Hillenbrand, *The Hiding Place* by Corrie ten boom, *Chasing the Dragon* by Jackie Pulinger and *Bruchko* by Bruce Olson had formed me. I wanted to write stories that mattered and impacted culture. And deep down, I had the dream of becoming a famous and successful author, and I thought that by writing this book (a book based on an incredible true story), it would be a guaranteed success. I didn't deliberate much over the decision.

At Scott's invitation, my mom and I flew to Florida. With my colossal and ancient laptop in tow, I was brimming with excitement and inexperience, eager to meet Rindy. With legs like noodles, I stepped out of Scott's car and met a man with a welcoming smile.

"I'm Rindy," he said in Khmer-accented English extending his hand. "Scott has told me about you."

After inviting us inside, Rindy and I settled onto his floral couch, and I began with questions I had prepared the night before.

"What is your earliest memory?" I began, fingers poised over my laptop keys.

"I remember...oh going back when I was eight or nine years old that my family and I lived in the jungle in a silt house. We lived there because of a tiger, and every night my dad would take up the ladder, afraid that the tiger might climb it."

Are you kidding me? I thought. *This is too perfect.* I was already writing the beginning of the book, my mind painting vivid pictures of a grassy hut, standing on legs in the middle of the Cambodian jungle. I could see the tiger, hear its purr, and feel its yellow eyes. Sitting on Rindy's couch, the first chapter of "A Boy Named Rindy" was born.

I interviewed Rindy for most of the day, starting with questions and transcribing everything he said as quickly as I could type. I was surprised and thankful for the amount of detail he remembered and how easy he was to talk to. The material was riveting, and I couldn't believe how captivating, yet tragic, the events of his life had been. At one point, he and his wife, Chiyra, demonstrated the meager amount of rice they were typically allotted while in the labor camps, being barely half a cup. I was surprised yet intrigued by the ease—and dare I say it—humor that Rindy exhibited as he talked about his memories. I think this was due to the almost implausibility of his story, but also the miraculous nature of his survival.

This ease lasted until he recalled the memory of the death of his friend whose name he couldn't recall (who I named Chivy in the book). As tears clouded his vision and it became difficult for him to speak, it was clear that this memory was his Achilles' heel, and my heart throbbed for him. Emotion and memories paraded across his countenance as he relayed it all—the good, the evil, the death, the salvation, and then the forgiveness. I couldn't comprehend what he had been through, and I couldn't believe that the man sitting before me with the kind, smiling eyes had been through more pain and suffering than most people had to endure in ten lifetimes.

Upon completing the interview and returning home, I was full of passion and optimism, but I can honestly say I had absolutely no idea what I had just said "yes," so eagerly too. Scott and Rindy gave me few parameters, saying essentially "here are the facts; fill in the rest." Would this be a biography? Fiction? Narrative nonfiction? Something in between?

The week after I returned home, my wonderful boyfriend, Steven, proposed, and I said another cosmic "yes." Wedding planning, college work and waitressing part-time ate up my schedule. I wrote the first few chapters and then it sat, as my quickly changing life swept me into the ocean of newness. I told myself, "Once I complete my BA, I'll have a better idea of what I'm doing, and I'll have more time to write this book." However, in August 2017, the day my classes ended, I went into labor with our first child. I again thought, "I'm a stay-at-home mom now with nothing but time to write."

Now, for any moms reading, you know this is a gross misconception, as if caring for a tiny person who is completely dependent on you for her overall wellbeing is somehow a small task to be fit in on the side.

Despite this vulnerable and tenuous season of my life, I did indeed begin in earnest. I poured over the two sets of interview notes (one from Scott and the other that I had gathered) until I wore holes in the pages, and I could almost recite them forward and backward. I dialogued with Rindy, asking him questions and trying to keep him informed of my progress. I knew this story needed to be told through Rindy's eyes—in first person point of view—so that was one of the few decisions I didn't fall into crippling deliberation over.

As I wrote, I grappled endlessly with how much creative license to take. I came to a point when I knew this book needed to be a work of fiction because I felt like my hands were tied otherwise, and I loved the art of storytelling. After this decision, I was able to write more freely when I created a story around the historical events of Rindy's life. After all, Rindy's story didn't need much added to it to make it exciting.

I deviated as little as possible from the event's of the story as Rindy had relayed them to me, endeavoring to corroborate what he described as well as present it in the way that was congruent with my research. Thus, all the events that transpire in these pages really did happen. My job was merely to give them life and make you, the reader, feel as if you have lived them too. I added dialogue, dramatization of actual events and condensed memories to help with flow and pacing. In the end, I essentially turned a 17-page interview into an over 400-page manuscript, further confirming that this book needed to be categorized as a work of fiction "based on a true story."

During this season, I struggled deeply with the balance of writing a book this heavy and research-dependent while traversing life as a new mom, although I don't think I was fully aware of it at the time. I had little understanding of how difficult and shaping it would be to walk hand in hand with someone else's memories of trauma and survival, while taking on Rindy's voice and skin. I wish I could say I handled it seamlessly, took the right number of breaks, didn't spiral into bouts of depression and anxiety, but that's not entirely the case. Writing the initial draft was costly in more ways than I can even express.

Thus, limping and yet triumphant, I finished the first and second draft of my book in 2019. Before proceeding further, my hope was to gain Rindy's approval, so I emailed my manuscript to him and waited with bated breath. I told myself that if he didn't like it, I would chalk the whole thing up to experience and walk away from the project.

Rindy began to read and got halfway through and then stopped. Months went by. Did he hate it and not know how to tell me? Was he rethinking this whole thing? I tried not to panic and reached out to Rindy.

He responded with, "it's good, but it's just hard for me to relive the memories."

This hit me in the gut, but I was also relieved. *It felt real to him.* I had written it in a way that felt real. I had accomplished my goal.

I quickly reached out to Scott and asked him to check in on Rindy and his mental health. No book was worth it if Rindy wasn't ready for this. Scott responded with a virtual thumbs up and told me Rindy still wanted to proceed. Rindy did eventually finish the book, had some insightful adjustments and inclusions and I continued onward towards publication.

Scott and I had talked briefly of self-publishing at the initial visit, but in keeping congruent with my dream of being a "famous" author, I planned to pursue traditional publishing at all cost. I had a deep and intrinsic fear of failure and an even greater hunger for validation that made the idea of self-publishing a distasteful one. So, I researched, read books on breaking into the traditional publishing world, and complied literary agents.

In October 2019, I sent my first tailored query letter to my dream agent. I've done a few terrifying things in my life, but let me tell you, they call this phase of publishing the "query trenches" for a reason. It's brutal, with days of exhilaration as you find a new potential agent followed by weeks and eventually months of waiting to end in silence or a polite "no thank you." I did receive some interest, several "almost, but..." until eventually I felt like I'd run out of options. I had run out of gas in the middle of a desert.

As months turned into years, I saw my dream dwindling as well as my confidence in my book. I had been convinced that because Rindy's story was incredible I would have no problem landing a book deal. But it turns out that, a book about a boy that is "based on a true story," which takes place in the obscure country of Cambodia, isn't an easy sell. I was discouraged and felt let down, not only by the publishing world but more importantly by God. I had thought that after all the hard work and because it was a worthy cause, my dreams would be instantly granted, and I would experience His favor in its pursuit.

Then, two years later in 2021, as a last-ditch effort, I queried a small press publisher that didn't require agent representation. Much to my delight, I soon received a contract for publication. I was elated. I thought, it all had been worth it, and this book would finally be published traditionally. The book's publication date was set for September 2023, and it couldn't come soon enough for me. In the meantime, I wrote a novella for a Christmas anthology and learned a little bit more about what goes into publishing and marketing a book. The closer I got to September, the more nervous I became. Would they do a good job on the cover? Would the editing be thorough? Would they handle Rindy's story with the care I wrote it? That's when things went downhill and ultimately the publishing company terminated my contract with only four months until my scheduled publication date.

Once again, I found myself deflated and questioning the way forward. I just wanted to be done with this book, and I doubted I would ever write again. After coming out of a distasteful publishing experience, I wanted to just keep my obligation and self-publish it with the hopes of keeping the September release date I had been marketing towards. I felt like a fool and a fraud, but something in me couldn't let this story die. After hiring a cover designer and taking a crash course in self-publishing, I searched for a developmental editor who would help make my manuscript publishable. Much to my delight, I thought I found a perfect fit and eagerly sent my manuscript off to her. More waiting ensued.

If I had thought receiving the terminated publishing contract was painful, the editing feedback I received was debilitating. It sucker punched me in a way that highlighted every secret fear and every insecurity. Instead of giving me direction forward with positives and negatives, it discouraged me so fully I couldn't write for months. It invalidated my research and Rindy's story, it listed few positives, and it felt mocking and condescending. I wanted to give up so desperately and I felt like the most profound failure of all time. But there was something in me that couldn't let this story go. I still believed in it, even if no other person in the world saw its worth. In these ashes, I sat and learned. I learned that confidence can only be built in the face of opposition. That not all criticism is valid, even if you paid for it. That there is a mixed bag: some bones and some truth, and that "digging through" was hard work. That not every voice is to be heeded as truth. That the only way to the other side—is through the ugly.

In October of 2023, after taking several months off to fight back the fear and failure, I underwent the task of rewriting my novel. I knew there was truth amid the destructive criticism I had received, and it took much painful excavating to extract. I knew I did need to make improvements before this novel could be published. I knew I had failed in areas. I knew that I could do better, before it was truly ready to be published. Before I was truly ready. Before it was time.

During the rewrite, I did extensive research into Cambodia and its history, fully immersing myself in the place and time I was describing. Several such books that helped me understand this confusing and intense time in history were *Surviving the Killing Fields,* by Haing Ngor, *Beneath the Banyan*, by Vaddey Ratner, *Cambodia* by Henry Kamm, and *The Pol Pot*

Regime, by Ben Kiernan, to name a few. I included many of the historical snapshots I uncovered throughout the book, in the "historical notes" to connect Rindy's story to the larger historical and cultural context. I am by no means a historical scholar on Cambodian history, although I did my best to portray it accurately. In researching and writing this book, I drew on my experience while spending three months in Cambodia prior to meeting Rindy and beginning the book, as well as visualizing locations and contexts through Google Maps Street view, which traverses a shocking amount of Cambodia's countryside. As any writer can attest, sometimes hours of "visualizing" and "planning" went into a mere three sentences.

During this rewrite, the book required me to pour more of myself into it than I had before, pushing it even further into the fiction space. Previously, it contained all of Rindy's memories, but in the rewrite I had to remove the ones that didn't serve the plot. I sought to weave together and tighten the plot and in some instances excavating it. I capitalized on Rindy's character growth more and his struggle with "survivors guilt," his relationship with Vuthy as well as laid breadcrumbs for his encounter with Christ.

As I rewrote it, I lived it again. The beginning stages were excruciating as I knew what material I would soon have to traverse again. My confidence was in the gutter, but I forced myself to wake up at 5:30 am every morning to write before my young kids would awaken. I don't want to trivialize or downplay the trauma of living through such an event as genocide, but as I wrote the memories Rindy described, at times I felt I put his skin on and lived them too. Coincidently, so many of the struggles Rindy went through were also my struggles.

In the span of writing this book, I completed a degree, became engaged and married, bought a house, sold a house, and became a mom of three. It has taken over a decade. I wish I could say writing this was a walk in the park, but the truth is, it wasn't. However, I have learned that most things worth doing are incredibly difficult and they break you a little in the process. There were times when I thought I would never complete it, but the dream of seeing Rindy's story go out into the world and make an impact in whatever way God saw fit, propelled me onward. The fact that you are holding his book is a miracle.

So, in many ways, the writing of this story has been tied to my own identity, as I've carried it for many years and through many stages. As I reread it, no matter how many times I have edited or revised it, I weep. The utter darkness and destruction are only dimmed in light of the beautiful redemption and new life that Rindy found when he surrendered his pain to the only One who wanted it—the One who died to own it. To me, Rindy's story shouts into the fray the unmatched and unmistakable love of God and how he wants to redeem all which is broken.

My prayer for you, dear reader, is that if you have places of brokenness and defeat in your life, that you will allow Rindy's Savior to be your Savior. I pray that wherever this book finds you, you will experience the same transformation Rindy experienced and the same death to life experience he did. This is not just Rindy's story, it's God's story, and He longs to intersect with the darkest moments of our lives and turn them into something beautiful. I hope the reading of this book not only informs your mind on a little-known portion of history and the struggle of survival, but that it infuses your heart with hope.

"There is no pit so deep, that God's love is not deeper still" – Corrie Ten Boom.

ACKNOWLEDGEMENTS

First off, I'd like to thank Rindy Nong for trusting me with your story. It's been a true honor to tell it. You've shown me such grace and understanding in the various stages towards publication, and I am deeply appreciative of that. Without you, there wouldn't be a book. I pray God uses this to bless you in unexpected ways.

As mentioned above, this book would not be in your hands if Scott Smith hadn't gotten the ball rolling in having the initial vision. Thank you for your confidence in me and your grace in the great length of time that this book has taken.

Thank you, Jamie Ogle, for not being creeped out by a random girl on the internet who "wanted to be friends," and for offering your guidance and support as I worked through editorial feedback. You shined a light into one of the dark places of this journey with such grace and insight that I could never repay you.

Thank you, Naomi Craig, for your kindness to me in navigating the struggles of publishing and for offering your support repeatedly throughout this journey. You've encouraged me, checked on me and offered a shoulder to cry on when I needed it most.

Thank you, Mommy Christian Writers network, for being an unspeakable gift to me in your offering of community, encouragement, and overall goodness. I didn't know how beautiful it would be to have a community of other mothers who were also doing the same thing I was attempting to do. You all blew the lid off what I thought possible for what mothers could accomplish in the intense season of child-rearing. You are incredible!

Thank you for the unexpected gift and creative rehab that I found in the Goodlit writer's retreat. Thank you, Angela Correll, for making this incredible retreat possible. I was honored to attend and glean from your experience, faith, and guidance at a time when I thought I'd never write again. This retreat was a gift at the exact time I needed it. I trust it's been that for many writers and more to come. Thank you to the instructors and creative masterminds of Brett Lot, Beckie Newsbit, Allie Bridge, Russ Ramsey and Jennie Burke (who spoke identity and truth to me when I needed it most). Thank you to my fellow writers/authors: Kristine Neely, Penny McGinnis, Noni Broome, Sammy Beuker, C.I. Aki, Sarah Jane Murray (I still have your note on my desk), Kristin Sanken, Deb Krygiel, CL Monroe, John Heard, Ben Palpant, Beth Ernest and David Somerville. Your feedback and insight into this book gave me the confidence and boost that I needed to see it to the final stage.

Special thank you to those who offered beta feedback: Storm Shultz, CL Monroe, Kristine Neely and Jill Knoll. Your insight, attention to detail and even interest in this story means so much to me.

Angela Allen, thank you for your incredible kindness and lavish gift of your time and energy. I thought I was gaining a writing buddy when I met you, but I gained so much more. You've been a mentor, my website consultant, my beta reader, my copyeditor and most importantly, my friend. Thank you for the support and encouragement you've offered in more ways than I can express.

Thank you, Sarah Everest, for your proofreading expertise and for catching all of the overused "that's," and exclamation points. Your insight, encouragement, promptness and thoroughness is deeply appreciated.

Thank you to my friends and family (you know who you are) who have asked over the years about this book and cheered me to the finish line. Your kindness and support of this marathon has been such a gift to me. Even if you didn't always understand this "crazy writer thing," you always cared and supported me in any way that you could.

Thank you, Grandma Mae, Grandma Nancy and Aunt Jenny for your endless prayers for this book. For years you've told me how often you've prayed for me as I wrote it. Your love and care for this project has not gone unnoticed by me or by heaven. The book is finally here!

Thank you, Mom and Dad for encouraging me in my writing interest and for the (hundreds at this point) times you've asked me, "how is the book going?" Thank you also for your financial investment, which made this book possible. Thank you, Mom, for being one of the first people to read it and for the encouragement and insight that you offered in the early stages. Thank you for helping me weed through the valleys of this journey and always encouraging me not only to rest when needed, but to press on to the finish line. Thank you for the countless times you've watched my kids so I could write. I owe much to your support, tutelage, and sacrifice.

Thank you to my sweet babies Adelaide, Elsie and Alec. You've had do share me with this book over the entirety of your lives and I know it's been a sacrifice. Without the lessons I've learned in motherhood, I know this book wouldn't be half of what it is. I love you more than you'll ever know!

Thank you to my husband Steven, who put up with much in the drafting of this book. You picked up my slack, encouraged me to continue and believed that I could, long before I did. Even when you knew I would likely not make much (if any) money from this very costly endeavor, you constantly said "you've come too far to quit now."

Thank you, God, for teaching me more than I can ever express through this journey and for working into me so many of the truths that Rindy also experienced. You don't care about the "end product," but the process of the becoming. I owe my life to You. And to You, I freely give it.

CONNECT WITH THE AUTHOR

Olivia has shared a behind the scenes look at the drafting of this novel as well as stories from her personal life on her blog. It can be accessed on her website:

oliviatalbott.com

Follow her on:

facebook.com/authoroliviatalbott
book group: facebook/compellingchristianfiction

instagram/olivia_talbott_author

x/oliviatalbott27